WINTER NIGHTS AT THE BAY BOOKSHOP

JESSICA REDLAND

First published in Great Britain in 2025 by Boldwood Books Ltd.

Copyright © Jessica Redland, 2025

Cover Design by Lizzie Gardiner

Cover Images: Adobe Stock

Interior Image and Icons: Boldwood Books and Adobe Stock

The moral right of Jessica Redland to be identified as the author of this work has been asserted in accordance with the Copyright, Designs and Patents Act 1988.

All rights reserved. No part of this book may be reproduced in any form or by any electronic or mechanical means, including information storage and retrieval systems, without written permission from the author, except for the use of brief quotations in a book review. This book is a work of fiction and, except in the case of historical fact, any resemblance to actual persons, living or dead, is purely coincidental.

Every effort has been made to obtain the necessary permissions with reference to copyright material, both illustrative and quoted. We apologise for any omissions in this respect and will be pleased to make the appropriate acknowledgements in any future edition.

A CIP catalogue record for this book is available from the British Library.

Paperback ISBN 978-1-83518-310-6

Large Print ISBN 978-1-83518-311-3

Hardback ISBN 978-1-83518-309-0

Trade Paperback ISBN 978-1-80635-243-2

Ebook ISBN 978-1-83518-312-0

Kindle ISBN 978-1-83518-313-7

Audio CD ISBN 978-1-83518-304-5

MP3 CD ISBN 978-1-83518-305-2

Digital audio download ISBN 978-1-83518-308-3

This book is printed on certified sustainable paper. Boldwood Books is dedicated to putting sustainability at the heart of our business. For more information please visit https://www.boldwoodbooks.com/about-us/sustainability/

Boldwood Books Ltd, 23 Bowerdean Street, London, SW6 3TN

www.boldwoodbooks.com

To librarians and booksellers, book bloggers and BookTokers, Book Fairies, readers, authors and everyone involved in the publishing process. Keep creating, producing and recommending books because they are truly magical x

AUTHOR'S NOTE

I don't think it would be possible to set a novel in a bookshop without mentioning specific books and authors but, with millions of books on Kindle UK alone, choosing books that my readers are all familiar with is a challenge. Therefore I've only mentioned books which are so well known that, even if my readers haven't read them, they're likely to be familiar with them. To serve the purposes of this story, I've also made up some authors and book titles. Please forgive me if this leads to some searching for titles which only exist on the pages of this book and within my imagination. I should also add that, if books or authors with my fictional titles and names materialise after this book is published, that's one of those strange coincidences that sometimes occur.

I don't know what lies around the bend, but I am going to believe that the best does.

—*ANNE OF GREEN GABLES*, L. M. MONTGOMERY

1
LILY

So many people I knew claimed to hate Mondays but I loved them. There was something so exciting about starting a fresh week full of possibilities. Of course, it helped that I loved my job as joint owner of Bay Books on Castle Street in the popular North Yorkshire seaside town of Whitsborough Bay. I knew how lucky I was spending my days surrounded by books – my absolute number one passion – while working in partnership with my amazing dad, whose parents had established the bookshop.

But today my usual start-of-a-fresh-week positivity evaded me. I was awake half an hour before my alarm, feeling sad and listless. Sighing heavily, I reached for the well-thumbed copy of my favourite childhood book – L. M. Montgomery's *Anne of Green Gables* – which I kept by my bed, but even the wit and wisdom of Anne Shirley failed to lift me.

I shuffled through to the kitchen to put the kettle on, hoping a strong coffee would jumpstart some positive vibes. Cassie – my best friend since senior school who worked part-time at Bay Books – had given me a set of four mugs with *Anne of Green Gables* quotes on them one Christmas. I looked at the one which seemed appropriate for today:

If you can't be cheerful, be as cheerful as you can.

I'd smile at our customers and exude positivity as we discussed books and they'd never know what I was masking.

Ready for work a little later, I cupped my hands around my mug and stared at the calendar hanging on the wall, tears pricking my eyes. I'd done my best with the Tipp-Ex to obliterate the large red marker pen heart drawn around today's date but I could still see the shape of it, still feel the heartbreak.

Hearing the beep of Dad's car unlocking outside, I took one last gulp of coffee and left my mug in the sink to wash later. I lived in a cosy one-bedroom annexe next to my parents' house, Everdene. It wasn't where I'd expected to be at the age of thirty-four, but sometimes life didn't go to plan. Six years ago, I'd bought a three-bedroom semi near Hearnshaw Park with the first of my two long-term boyfriends, Ewan. We'd only been able to afford it because it was a wreck and had spent eighteen months gutting it and starting over. It was hard, exhausting, dirty work but worth it to create the beautiful home for the family we both wanted. Except we never quite got to that part. We never even made it as far as moving in together.

When the relationship ended, Mum and Dad offered to help me buy Ewan out but living without him in the home we'd painstakingly refurbished together held no appeal. House sold, I remained in my childhood bedroom at Everdene, but I found it a struggle. Even though I had a fantastic relationship with my parents, I'd been ready for my independence. When they suggested I move into the unused annexe, it seemed like the perfect solution. Decorating the annexe – which I affectionately named Green Gables – and making it feel homely was a welcome distraction from my broken heart, but it was only meant to be a temporary solution. Temporary had stretched into years but I'd had a new plan to move out in the New Year. A plan that fell through exactly six months ago.

I glanced at the calendar again and shook my head, blinking back the tears. 'Cheers for that, Wes. Heartbreaker.'

Outside, Dad was placing his packed lunch and coat on the back seat of his car which prompted me to grab my coat before I locked up. We were just over a week from the end of September but the arrival of autumn had seen the temperature drop so layers were needed for getting some fresh air at lunchtime.

'Morning, Lily!' Dad said as I joined him.

'Morning,' I replied with a brightness I didn't feel. I wondered if he'd register the date. He was usually good with things like that.

We set off into town and I gazed out of the window at the grey sky peppered with dark rainclouds, reflecting my mood.

'Are you all right?' Dad shot me a concerned glance as we stopped at some traffic lights on red.

I shrugged. 'Feeling a bit meh this morning.'

'Your mum and I thought you might be. Wes was due back today, wasn't he?'

The lights changed to green, taking Dad's attention back to the road, so he missed the tears pooling in my eyes. I attempted to discreetly wipe them away as I didn't want my parents worrying about me and I certainly didn't want to cry over Wesley Sawyer again. I'd wasted far too many tears on him over the past six months, although it was perhaps inevitable that another wave of sadness would hit me today. After putting my life on hold for two years while my second long-term boyfriend furthered his career in Dubai, today should have been the day Wes returned for good, meaning we could start searching for a home together and get engaged, as we'd discussed so often. Except he wasn't my boyfriend anymore, he wasn't coming back to the UK for another four years – if at all – and I was still living in my parents' annexe with my hopes and dreams dashed for the second time by a man who'd promised me the world but had chosen to conquer it on his own instead.

'I was determined not to fixate on it, but now that it's here...'

'Completely understandable,' Dad said when I tailed off.

We usually chatted all the way to the shop but I didn't feel like a conversation this morning and loved how Dad recognised that and just let me be for the rest of the journey. We pulled into the private parking space out the back of Bay Books at ten to eight. The shop didn't open until nine but we always arrived at least an hour ahead of opening time to deal with any orders and queries which had come in overnight.

'Any regrets about ending it with Wes?' Dad asked as he pulled on the handbrake.

'No. It was the right thing for both of us. I'd never have moved to Dubai and, if he'd come back here, he'd never have settled and I'd have been permanently on edge, wondering when he'd leave. I'm just a bit fed up about how many years I've wasted, first with Ewan and then with Wes when I could have...'

I broke off, shrugging. I'd been about to say *been with someone who loved me* but I wasn't sure that had actually been the issue for either of them. I think they *had* loved me – just not enough to choose me when push came to shove.

Dad twisted in his seat to face me. 'I liked Wes. I liked Ewan too. But I didn't think either of them were your Gilbert Blythe.'

Despite my melancholy, that drew a smile. Gilbert Blythe was Anne Shirley's perfect match (and also my ideal book boyfriend) although the pair of them didn't actually get together until the third book in the series – *Anne of the Island*.

Dad kept his eyes fixed on mine. 'And, deep down, I don't think you did either. But you'll find him eventually, probably when you least expect to and, of course—'

'*The unexpected things in life are often the best,*' I said at the same time as him, laughing together that we'd both thought of Mum's favourite saying.

'I hope so, Dad.'

'I know so. It's how it happens in our family.' He gave my hand a gentle squeeze, and I knew he was referring to how he and Mum got together. 'Ready to face the day?'

'I am now. Thank you.'

Dad unlocked the back door and deactivated the alarm while I flicked on the lights. My spirits couldn't help but lift as the children's section lit up, revealing the colourful spines on the paperbacks, beautiful illustrations on the picture books and adorable bookish soft toys. I loved this shop so much and experienced such a sense of belonging every time I walked through the doors and breathed in the smell of books. This was my world and had been for as long as I could remember. It was hard to believe that Wes could have thought for even a minute that I'd be willing to walk away from it to move to Dubai with him. I realised that, in isolation, that made me seem selfish but the reality of our relationship was that he'd known that I never wanted to leave Whitsborough Bay and he'd been fine with that because he'd felt exactly the same way. At first.

A wide archway took me through to the front of the shop where we kept the commercial fiction titles and showcased new releases and bestsellers on sturdy wooden tables and display stands. It was also home to a range of beautiful stationery products and book-related merchandise. We kept the classics and poetry on level one and the non-fiction titles on the upper levels. Customers often likened the shop to Doctor Who's TARDIS as it didn't look very big from the outside but step inside and it went back a long way as well as up all of those levels, giving us the space to stock a fabulous range of titles and making us the leading book retailer in town.

I dumped my handbag on the counter and switched on the computer which connected the till, ordering and stock control system.

'Would a treat from The Chocolate Pot take the edge off?' Dad asked.

'I think it might. A hot chocolate and maybe one of Tara's brownies for elevenses.'

The Chocolate Pot was a gorgeous café three doors along from us. It had opened just over twenty years ago and was one of the longer-running businesses on the cobbled street, although Bay Books was by far the oldest, celebrating a whopping forty years next summer. The Chocolate Pot's owner, Tara, made the most incredible brownies with the perfect balance of gooey loveliness inside and a slight crunch on the edges. Actually, all the food she made was divine but the brownies were my personal favourites. The café didn't open for the takeaway trade until half eight but, as Tara was in the kitchen baking way before that, she didn't mind the Castle Street traders messaging her with an order. It was such a lovely, supportive community and I was proud to call many of the traders my good friends.

'I'll take the bags and coats downstairs while you message Tara,' I said.

Dad passed me his belongings and I headed down to the lower ground level – home to our staff room, a kitchenette, staff toilets and a storeroom. Cassie and I were on a mission to keep Dad on the ground floor as much as possible. He'd been really struggling with his knees and, any day now, was expecting confirmation of a date for a double knee replacement operation. He didn't like us making a fuss but there was no point him suffering unnecessarily with the stairs, especially when there were so many of them. Bay Books was a five-storey building with a unique layout inside. My grandparents had taken on a builder who'd restructured the upper three floors to create six levels. The smaller rooms gave the bookshop a cosier feel as well as making it easier to categorise books by genre or subject.

All those stairs provided a daily workout but we didn't need to carry new stock to the upper floors or bring drinks up the stairs thanks to the genius move by my grandparents of installing a dumb waiter behind the till. They'd affectionally called it Jeeves after Bertie Wooster's valet in the P. G. Wodehouse books – an invaluable member of staff.

After his knee operation, Dad would need a fair amount of time off to recover so we'd agreed to advertise a fixed-term contract for a four-month period, allowing for a week's handover and some leeway at the end. The job description and advert were ready to go as soon as the date came through. Dad thought we should also advertise for a part-timer to give some flexibility but I was adamant I'd be fine working seven days a week instead of my usual five. It wasn't like I had a boyfriend who'd feel pushed out if I upped my hours and, in all honesty, the distraction would be welcome.

'Tara says we can pick up the order in five minutes,' Dad said when I returned upstairs.

He was busy working through the overnight orders so it made sense for me to go. I stepped out onto the cobbles, locked the door behind me and breathed in the freshness of the morning. In my opinion, Castle Street was the best street in Whitsborough Bay. All the shops and cafés were independently owned and beautifully maintained. The cobbles and Victorian lampposts gave a quaint olde-worlde feel which made for an inviting shopping experience, especially at Christmas.

Immediately next door to Bay Books was Castle Jewellery but I averted my gaze. The last thing I needed to see this morning was a selection of sparkling engagement rings, taunting me that my own engagement wouldn't be happening. Conveniently positioned next to the jeweller's – and also far from ideal today – was The Wedding Emporium owned by my friend Ginny. I'd have avoided looking at that window too but Ginny was standing outside with her hands on her hips, frowning at the display, so I could hardly dash past ignoring her.

'Morning!' I said. 'You look puzzled.'

'Something's wrong and I can't for the life of me work out what it is.'

I stood beside her for a moment studying the autumnal window display and smiled as I spotted the problem. 'Your bridesmaid's arms are on back to front.'

Ginny clapped her hand to her forehead, laughing. 'How on earth did I not see that? Cheers, Lily.'

'Pleasure. It's a stunning display.'

'Thank you. I like creating my spring and summer displays but there's something about the autumn and winter ones that excites me so much more.'

'I'll leave you to fix your bridesmaid's broken arms,' I said. 'Hot chocolates to collect.'

'I might have to get one for myself before I open. I have a feeling it's going to be one of those days where sugar's the only thing that gets me through.'

'You and me both!'

In The Chocolate Pot, I requested an extra hot chocolate for Ginny and called in at The Wedding Emporium on my way back.

'Aw, Lily, that's so kind of you,' Ginny said, smiling gratefully. 'Thank you.'

'Got one of your favourites too,' I said, handing her a bag containing a millionaire's shortbread. 'Elevenses.'

'You angel! But I don't think it'll last that long. Is there such a thing as half-eightses?'

Outside, I paused by the window to check out the bridesmaid mannequin, who was looking much better with her arms now attached the right way round. Ginny had created a stunning autumnal display with garlands of red, orange and brown leaves draped round the window and loose leaves on the plinth alongside flameless candles. The bride's dress was ivory with long lace sleeves, the bridesmaid's was burnt orange and a child-sized mannequin displayed an ivory dress with an orange sash and cape.

Although Wes had wanted to wait until he returned from Dubai before we got engaged, we'd talked about our wedding on several occasions and had agreed that autumn would be best, sandwiched between the bookshop's peak times of back to school and October half-term but well ahead of Christmas – our busiest time of the year.

The bridal gown in Ginny's window was beautiful but not for me. I wanted something with less lace and a fuller skirt when I married Wes. I closed my eyes for a moment, ejecting that thought. I *wasn't* marrying Wes. That ship had sailed twice and I was through with men, at least for the foreseeable future. I'd trusted Ewan and Wes and they'd both broken my heart. I couldn't face that happening again. And even if I was feeling brave enough to date again, there wasn't time. With Dad out of action soon and Christmas approaching, I had more than enough to keep me occupied at the bookshop. That was my focus for now and exactly the way I liked it.

But Dad's words from earlier crept into my mind: *I liked Wes. I liked Ewan too. But I didn't think either of them were your Gilbert Blythe. And, deep down, I don't think you did either.* Was he right about that?

2

LARS

I opened the front door on Monday morning expecting to see Mick or one of his colleagues from the removals company outside, but instead it was a courier.

'Signed delivery for Lars Jóhannsson,' he said.

'That's me.'

The squiggle I made with my finger on his handheld device bore little resemblance to my real signature, but it didn't matter. It was the signatures on the documents in the thick cardboard envelope he passed to me that counted. I thanked him and closed the door, ripping the tab from the envelope and pulling out the sheaf of papers. I'd already checked my banking app this morning so I knew that the final payment had come through, but it somehow hadn't felt real. It was just a bunch of numbers – albeit a lot of them – and I hoped that the signed paperwork would help it sink in.

When I was at school, I hadn't a clue what I wanted to do with my life. I excelled in all my subjects and didn't have any particular favourites so that didn't help me with career choices. Narrowing down the subjects for sixth form was a massive challenge. I'd received A-stars across the board for my GCSEs and I'd wanted to do four A levels rather than the standard three but they wouldn't let me, so I chose an eclectic mix of business studies, geography and German and enrolled for an A level in English literature online. It was the latter which unexpectedly led me to my career. The distance learning provider was the market leader at the time but, if they were the best, the bar was clearly set very low. The system was clunky to navigate, the materials were uninspiring and the tutor support limited.

'I could set up something a million times better than this,' I'd lamented to Nanna one evening, closing the system down in disgust after three failed attempts to upload an assignment.

'Then why don't you?' she'd asked, a twinkle in her eye.

So I did. I'd always been a computer geek and had developed several websites, so developing a reliable user-friendly online learning platform couldn't be that difficult. My business studies A level had also got me interested in entrepreneurship and I quite liked the idea of working for myself.

I was so proud of My Study Hub. The business had started small, offering distance learning GCSEs only before expanding to include A levels, professional qualifications and tuition in the creative arts. The student experience was at the heart of what we did with simple, intuitive navigation and learning materials available in a range of formats and layouts to cater for all needs from visual impairments to dyslexia to neurodivergence.

Last year, My Study Hub won its latest of many awards and, after the ceremony, I was approached by Calvin Warboys, CEO of the UK's biggest online learning provider who, at a subsequent meeting, offered to buy the business. I genuinely hadn't considered selling but his offer was too good to turn down and, with assurances that he'd keep my team on, I eventually agreed to his proposal. I'd spent the last six months gradually reducing my hours as I handed over my business but now I faced a major problem – what the heck was I going to do with myself?

I placed the paperwork on the stairs to take up to my office on the top floor later. I'd have a proper look through the contents then file it away, bringing a close to the first chapter of my career.

'Was that Mick?' Nanna asked when I returned to the lounge.

I shook my head. 'Delivery for me. It's official. Got the money, got the paperwork and I'm now unemployed.'

Nanna laughed. 'Unemployed? What are you like? I think this calls for a celebratory drink.'

'Nanna! It's only nine o'clock.'

'I was thinking more along the lines of another cup of tea.'

'That I can cope with.'

In the kitchen, I rested my back against the worktop as the kettle boiled and stared at the boxes piled up at one end. The sale of my business wasn't the only chapter coming to an end today. Nanna was moving into Bay View Care Home – the leading facility in Whitsborough Bay for the elderly who either wanted to live independently but with help onsite or who needed some additional support with their health and mobility. I'd taken Nanna out for a meal to celebrate the start of handing over My Study Hub when she startled me with the news.

'I've been thinking about the future too and, while I've been blessed with good health so far...' Nanna had touched the leg of the wooden dining table, '... that might not always be the case. I put my name down for a room at Bay View a while back and—'

'What? Why didn't you say?'

'Because they had a long waiting list so it could have been years before I had the chance of a room,' she responded. 'However, they had their plans approved last year to expand into the hotel next door. The refurbishment's progressing and the show apartment's now ready for viewing. I've made an appointment for tomorrow and I'd love it if you'd come with me.'

'Of course, but...' I shook my head, struggling to take it in. 'Are you sure about this? You love that house.'

Nanna had lived in the same three-storey four-bedroom terraced house just outside Whitsborough Bay town centre since marrying my grandpa, Norman, sixty-three years ago. Sadly, Grandpa had only lived to the age of fifty so I'd never met him, although I felt as though I knew him through Nanna's stories of how happy they'd been together. When my parents separated and my dad – or Pabbi in Icelandic – returned to his native Iceland, they sold our family home and Mum and I moved in with Nanna. I was eleven and I vividly remember Mum saying it would be temporary. Twenty-three years later...

'I *do* love my home but I have to be practical about the future. Geraldine's already looked around and put a deposit down, and Hilary's got a viewing next week.'

Geraldine and Hilary were Nanna's two closest friends and, like her, had been widows for many years. The three of them met up regularly and went on holiday together and I'd been extremely grateful for that friendship because working weekends and evenings had been the norm for me, meaning I wasn't great company for Nanna.

'Oh! I get it now,' I said, faking my indignation. 'You'd rather live with your besties than me.'

'It's not like that. It's—' She broke off, laughing. 'You're teasing me.'

'Obviously. But can I make sure you're exploring this because it's what you really want and not because you think you'd be a burden on me if your health or mobility did take a downturn? Because you could *never* be a burden.'

'You're a good lad, Lars, and I promise that's not the reason. I know you'd move heaven and earth to help me. I'm doing this because it feels like the right thing for me. However, I'm conscious that if I like the apartment and decide to move, you'll need to find somewhere new to live.'

'Why? I could buy you out.'

'You could, but I don't want you to. Even if it was your name on the deeds, you'd see it as *my* house and never your own and I don't want that for you. Besides, selling that business of yours means you'll be able to afford somewhere in a nicer area with a garden instead of a yard and with off-street parking. Imagine not having to drive around the block three times to try and find a parking space near the house.'

'Such a thing exists?' I joked. Parking was a huge issue on Fountain Street and the connecting roads as a ridiculous number of our neighbours had large work vans and sometimes two or even three vehicles to a household vying for limited space.

Nanna had loved Bay View, as had I, so she chose an apartment, handed over a deposit and put Fountain Street on the market. A few months later, Nanna accepted an offer from the Clark family and we were aiming for a completion date of late October so they could move in during the half-term holiday. I'd found a house too, or rather Nanna had found it for me – The Lodge in Hutton Wicklow, a village ten minutes' drive south-west from Whitsborough Bay. It had needed a complete refurbishment and would hopefully be ready by the time the sale of Fountain Street went through.

With so much upheaval at the same time – preparing My Study Hub for handover, helping Nanna downsize her belongings and liaising with the builders at The Lodge – it was no wonder I hadn't had any time to think about my next career move but, as soon as Nanna was settled, I'd have plenty of time. And that scared me. What if I couldn't find anything that appealed? What if I found something but, having only ever worked for myself, I was deemed unemployable? What if it took months and months to find something? There'd be so much time on my own to think and... I shuddered at the prospect. I'd have to find something to keep my mind occupied quickly, even if that meant more volunteering. I already spent one day a week at Hutton Wicklow Library. Nanna's friend Hilary was an avid library-user and visited the main Whitsborough Bay one weekly. She'd spotted a poster on the noticeboard seeking additional volunteers for Hutton Wicklow and I'd thought it would be a good way to get involved in the community before my move, while also indulging my passion for books. What I hadn't expected was that I'd become the tech guru. It was my fault. On my first shift, I'd offered to look at a system issue and now I was the go-to man for anything technical – library-based and personal. Not that I minded. It came easy to me so it was no bother to help others who struggled, but I had hoped to spend more time on the books side. Books were, after all, the reason why volunteering in the library had appealed. Perhaps I could increase my hours there? Anything to fill that dreaded thinking time.

3
LARS

'We're loaded up now,' Mick the removals man told us a couple of hours later. 'Ready when you are.'

I glanced at Nanna, who was standing by the fireplace, gazing into the empty grate. 'Can you give us five minutes, Mick? Maybe ten?'

'No worries. Take your time. It's not like we've got far to go.'

Mick was Hilary's great-nephew. He'd moved Hilary into her apartment a fortnight ago and Geraldine last week so Nanna was the last of the three friends to make the big move.

'How are you feeling, Nanna?' I asked.

She turned round with a sigh. 'It's hard to believe that I've lived here for sixty-three years. I sometimes can't remember what I had for breakfast but I clearly remember the first night Norman and I spent here. We'd massively pushed ourselves to buy this place so we had nothing left for furniture – not even second hand. Everything was borrowed or donated. The electrics didn't work and the only source of heating was this fire. My parents said we should wait until we could at least get the place wired properly before we moved in but we were too excited. We spent that first night together eating cold baked beans out of a can, sitting on a pair of high wooden stools my aunt had liberated from a skip and I was so happy at that moment that I thought I might burst.'

'That's a great memory.'

'One of thousands to cherish forever.' She breathed in deeply and gazed around the room before reaching for her coat, draped over the back of the nearby armchair. 'But it's time for a fresh start. I'll text Geraldine and Hilary from the car and tell them to pop the kettle on.'

While Nanna settled into the front passenger seat, I wandered over to the removals van to tell Mick and his colleague that we were ready to leave. Moving Nanna to Bay View wasn't a big job. She'd decided that most of her furniture wouldn't suit a modern apartment so had splurged on several new items. Having her leave most of her furniture behind helped me when I was staying put for another month.

'Hilary says she's baked a chocolate cake,' Nanna said, looking up from her phone shortly after. 'She knows how to make me happy.'

'Do you think the staff at Bay View are ready for you three getting up to mischief together?'

'It's Geraldine. She's the ringleader.'

'I can well believe it.' Geraldine was a larger-than-life character with purple hair, a tattoo of Ursula the sea witch from the animated version of Disney's *The Little Mermaid* on her arm, and the dirtiest laugh I'd ever heard.

Half an hour later, Nanna and I were in Hilary's apartment with Geraldine while the removals men unloaded her belongings.

'The three of us under one roof is going to be so much fun,' Geraldine declared, helping herself to a second slice of cake.

'How's the refurbishment going, Lars?' Hilary asked.

'Really good. Most of the big things are done – building work, rewiring, new heating and replastering. The kitchen's going in this week and it's the bathrooms after that so it should be mainly cosmetic work left when I move in.' I crossed my fingers. 'Hopefully.'

'Have you decided what you're going to do with all your free time?' Geraldine asked.

I shook my head. 'I still don't know.'

'You could retire,' Hilary said.

'He's only thirty-four,' Nanna protested. 'Far too young for that.'

'And I'd be so bored,' I added. 'The refurb and Nanna's move have kept me busy so far but I'll need something for when my house is finished. I'm at the library again tomorrow but six days off is far too much when I'm used to working seven days a week.'

'But you're enjoying the library?' Hilary asked.

'I love it. Thanks again for the heads up.'

Nanna received a call from Mick to tell her they were nearly finished and that a lorry had just pulled up with her new furniture, so we said goodbye to Geraldine and Hilary and returned to Nanna's apartment.

Within a couple of hours, everyone had gone. The delivery team had assembled Nanna's new bed, positioned her other new items of furniture where she wanted them and had taken all the packaging away. I'd helped unpack the boxes for her kitchen and removed a few heavier items from other boxes, but she was insistent on me not giving up any more of my day for her. I suspected it was more a case of her getting tired and also wanting some time on her own to adjust to the change. I was going to find it a big enough wrench to leave 17 Fountain Street and I hadn't lived there for half the time she had so her emotions had to be all over the place. I helped Nanna make her bed with the new duvet set she'd treated herself to and then I left her to it.

'Don't forget to run the vacuum cleaner round before the Clarks visit,' she said as I hugged her goodbye.

The new owners were coming round this evening to show their children their new home and measure up for curtains. I couldn't imagine they'd be bothered by the dust bunnies loitering in the spaces where boxes or furniture had been, but Nanna had always been house proud and was keen for her former home to be presented properly, so her wish was my command.

* * *

As soon as I stepped into the hall back at home, the silence cloaked me and I released a heavy sigh. Living here without Nanna wouldn't have felt right and I was glad she'd refused to sell it to me.

In the lounge, Nanna's floral perfume lingered in the air from where she'd spritzed her wrists shortly before we left this morning and the colourful scatter cushions on her favourite armchair were still indented from where she'd been sitting. My gaze moved to the fireplace. Even though Nanna had taken it with her, I could still hear the steady tick of her antique clock – a wedding gift from her grandparents. When would I stop hearing it? A lump formed in my throat and I shook my head. *Pull yourself together! She's not dead!* No, thankfully she wasn't, but I still felt her absence keenly.

I raked my fingers through my hair, shaking my head. I couldn't stand here all afternoon moping. Like Nanna, I'd never been one for mess. She often said *clean house, tidy mind* which made complete sense to me. I don't think I could have set up and run a successful business if I'd had paperwork everywhere.

On the middle floor, I paused on the landing, wondering which of the two bedrooms to tackle first and going for Nanna's. The sound of the vacuum cleaner's wheels across the wooden floorboards echoed around the room. One of the wardrobe doors had been left open, revealing a few empty hangers on the clothes rail. It felt strange being in Nanna's room. She believed that a person's bedroom was a private space so I'd spent very little time in there over the years – only going in to change light bulbs, to redecorate and, most recently, to help her pack. I'd spent even less time in the other bedroom on this floor – my mum's room.

Mum was in South America at the moment. I wasn't sure of the exact country as she frequently changed her travel plans and I'd learned that it was less stressful if I just pinned her down to a continent rather than trying to keep up with the specifics. After weeks of chasing, Nanna and I had finally managed to get Mum on a video call a fortnight ago where we'd updated her on our changing living arrangements. I'd expected her to be surprised but she'd barely batted an eyelid.

'What do you want us to do with your belongings?' I'd asked.

'Most stuff probably needs chucking,' she replied, shrugging. 'Can you box it up and shove it in storage for me? I'll sort through it next time I'm in the UK.'

'Any idea when that will be?' Nanna asked.

'Maybe October. Christmas? Spring?' Accompanied by another shrug.

Trying to get Mum to commit to dates was fruitless. Nanna never said anything, but I knew it hurt her that her only child never seemed to want to spend time with her. Video calls were short, emails even shorter, and visits fleeting. Even if Mum was in the UK for several weeks, she only managed a few days at the most in Whitsborough Bay.

Mum was a photographer and I was in awe of her talent and extremely proud of everything she'd achieved in her career to date, but I struggled to comprehend how little her family seemed to mean to her. Nanna wasn't the only one hurt by her limited contact. I could have understood it if there'd been some huge falling out but there'd been nothing like that. Mum just didn't seem to think that physically being around us or even maintaining regular contact was important. Over the years, I'd repeatedly told myself that Mum's choices were about her and not me, but that did little to soothe the hurt or the feeling that, just like Pabbi, she'd abandoned me.

Turning the doorknob, I pushed open the door to Mum's bedroom. The afternoon sun shone through a gap in the voile panels on the window, creating a shaft of light in which dust motes danced. As I entered the room, I felt as though I was stepping back in time. It had been Mum's bedroom growing up and, when she married Pabbi and moved out, she hadn't taken her childhood paraphernalia with her. When she moved back in after the separation she said that, as the move was temporary, there was no point packing everything away so she left it like a shrine to her childhood and it still remained that way to this day.

I didn't relish the task of packing up Mum's room. It felt intrusive and I didn't know what I might find. It would have to be done, but perhaps not today when I was feeling emotional about Nanna moving out. I'd finish the vacuuming then head over to Hutton Wicklow to check on progress with my house. Far better to be surrounded by hammering and drilling than be alone here with my thoughts.

Although there was something else I could do – something I'd woefully neglected across the summer. Smiling to myself, I headed up to my office to organise that instead.

4
LILY

'The Paperback Pixie's back!' Cassie cried, waving her phone in my direction as soon as she arrived for her half ten till half two shift the following day – termtime lunchtime cover which fitted around the school run for her two young children, Hallie and Rocco.

'Really? Let me see.'

Cassie handed me her phone and I read the post from first thing this morning on the Paperback Pixie's Instagram feed.

> It's been a while. Have you missed me? I've missed sharing the book love with you all. I was needed on important pixie business but I'm back now and will be leaving extra books in and around Whitsborough Bay over the next couple of months to make up for the missed summer. As ever, if you find and keep one of my books, please share a photo and tag me in – #paperbackpixie – saying where you found it. Thank you and happy reading!

'*Important pixie business,*' I quoted. 'Loving that.'

'Me too.' Cassie joined me behind the counter as I scrolled through five photos showing books left at different locations around the town.

'I think you'll recognise all the locations this time,' she said.

The first photo showed a picture book about sailing boats placed on a bench beside the boating lake in Hearnshaw Park and the second location was the train station. E. Nesbit's classic, *The Railway Children*, was perched on a stone ledge with a train just visible in the background.

'Are they all themed?' I asked Cassie, surprised because the locations were usually random.

'They are this time.'

I scrolled through the final three photos which were all commercial fiction novels – a crime novel featuring a murder at a lighthouse left by Whitsborough Bay's red-and-white-striped lighthouse, a romcom featuring dancing placed on the bandstand in the outdoor area of The Bay Pavilion and a historical book set during World War II resting against the town's war memorial.

'It's good to see the Pixie back,' I said, 'but it's still killing me that we have no idea who they are.'

The Paperback Pixie had been leaving gifts of brand-new books around Whitsborough Bay for fifteen years, possibly longer. At first, they were somewhat of an urban legend with rumours that there was a book benefactor in town but, with no social media set up, there was no photographic evidence. Across the summer a year after I graduated from university, the Pixie left a book out every week and our local newspaper, *Bay News*, picked up the story. The article included photos of a couple of the books and interviews with recent and previous finders but no insight into who the Paperback Pixie was. It stated that the journalist had never intended to identify them because they personally believed that much of the charm came from the mystery behind it. Dad had laughed at that and said it was more likely the journalist had failed in their attempts to expose the Pixie and was trying to save face.

After the news article, the Paperback Pixie ramped up their activities, setting up on the socials and gifting books more frequently. There were occasionally non-fiction books – usually nature-related or local interest ones – but the majority were fiction and I loved how they embraced all genres and all ages with their book choices. They were beautifully presented too with a piece of colourful ribbon tied in a bow around the book, which was then placed in a clear plastic bag to avoid damage. One of our customers found a novel and brought it in to show us. Inside was a Paperback Pixie-branded bookmark and a postcard congratulating them on finding the book, hoping that reading it brought them *happiness, escapism, adventures to new places and a chance to meet new friends*, along with a request to add a photo and tag the Pixie on the socials.

'I'd better get myself sorted,' Cassie said, taking her phone back and heading towards the stairs. 'Cuppa?'

'Ooh, yes, please.'

'Where's your dad, by the way?'

'With a customer in the children's section. Better make him one too.'

'Will do. I'll send them up in Jeeves.'

I checked behind me and pushed the button to send Jeeves down to the lower ground floor to wait for the drinks. A customer came down the stairs with a guidebook on the Cleveland Way – a 109-mile walking route which passed through Whitsborough Bay – telling me he'd completed the walk in his twenties, a few years after the trail opened, and was about to do it again now in his seventies. We had a lovely chat about some of his favourite parts but I was dying to get back to the Paperback Pixie's latest gifting so, as soon as the customer left, I whipped out my phone. Scrolling through the latest photos once more, I wondered for the umpteenth time who they were. Cassie believed it was a woman, Dad was convinced it was a man, and I thought it might be a group. We'd often wondered whether they were a customer of ours. They were clearly local and we'd have loved them to buy local too but we knew all our regulars well and, other than at Christmas time when they might buy books for gifts, they typically had favourite authors and genres. I couldn't think of a single regular who'd bought even a selection of the eclectic mix of books the Paperback Pixie had distributed. It was possible they ordered from our website but, if they did, the books were sent to different addresses as we hadn't spotted any correlation between orders and the Paperback Pixie's activities. Presumably they ordered online elsewhere. Probably The-Site-Which-Must-Not-Be-Named – our joking literary reference to the world's biggest online retailer – which was a shame when we could have guaranteed absolute discretion and even offered a discount.

The drinks arrived in Jeeves as Dad approached the counter with his customer, a pile of colourful picture books and a couple of accompanying cuddly toys. The woman looked to be about the same age as Dad so I guessed she was buying for grandchildren. I ran her purchases through the till and took payment while they continued their conversation about books they'd loved as children and how enduring certain titles were like Eric Carle's *The Very Hungry Caterpillar*, which had been first published in 1969 but was still a huge hit with kids today as demonstrated by over 50 million worldwide sales.

'Sounds like you've had a lovely conversation,' I said to Dad after the customer left.

'Her daughter's just adopted three-year-old twins so this is the first haul of bedtime reading. She wanted a mix of big names and new authors so I've been in my element helping her choose.'

Although my dad was a big reader across most genres, his passion was children's books, particularly those for early years. His interest in how children learned to read had initially taken him into early-years teaching but he'd joined the family business after his mum, my Granny Blue (short for Bluebell), had shocked everyone by announcing that she'd secured a significant book deal with a major publisher. She'd never shared any desire to write a book, let alone that she'd actually put pen to paper and written several novels. Under the pseudonym of Josephine Forrest she was now a multi-million-copy seller of sagas set on the Yorkshire Coast. We had a large section in the shop devoted to signed copies of her books and always had a big turnout for each book launch.

'I was beginning to think you'd be there all morning,' I said, smiling at Dad.

'Could easily have been. Have I missed anything?'

I retrieved the drinks from Jeeves and filled Dad in on the reappearance of the Paperback Pixie after their absent summer.

'I'm so glad he hasn't stopped doing it.' He laughed as I raised my eyebrows at him. 'Or she, or they. Still no clues as to their identity?'

'None. I don't think they're a customer and I'm going to have to just live with that.'

'Time to take the poster down?'

Dad nodded towards the large noticeboard attached to the storage cupboard beside Jeeves. It displayed useful information such as our opening times, book club details and forthcoming author events. Pinned to it was an A5 poster posing the question *Are YOU the Paperback Pixie?* and urging them to get in touch – anonymously if they wished – to discuss working collaboratively.

I removed the pins and took the slightly dog-eared poster down, shaking my head. 'No. I'm going to do a new one instead, bigger and brighter this time. If the Paperback Pixie *is* a customer, they'll have no chance of missing it.'

'And if they aren't?'

'Then we've lost nothing.'

Dad's phone beeped and he took it out of his trousers pocket, frowning as he studied something on the screen.

'Everything all right?' I asked.

'It's a date for my knee op. November 6.'

'That's brilliant news.' I checked the calendar by the till. 'Six weeks on Thursday. I'd better get that job advertised and...' I frowned at Dad. 'I thought you'd be happy about it.'

'I am, but the timing's awful. I'm going to be out of action over Christmas. I can't leave you to—'

'You can and you will,' I said, cutting him short. 'I can't bear seeing you in so much pain. Seriously, Dad, you *have* to accept that date.'

I fixed my gaze on his, eyebrows raised, until he smiled and nodded. 'Okay. I'll do it. Yes to getting that advert online, although I still think we should look for two people.'

'I can manage. I always do when you're on holiday.'

'For a fortnight. Four months will be completely different.'

'But a chunk of that time will be after Christmas and it's never busy then. I really will be fine.'

Logging onto the computer, I opened the poster advert I'd prepared for the noticeboard and window. I needed to add a closing date but tutted as I studied the calendar again. The week before the week of Dad's operation was half-term. We were always busier during the school holidays and training somebody new felt more like being one person down rather than having somebody extra because everything was so much slower. I showed Dad the calendar and he agreed that his replacement would need to start the week before half-term to get them trained before the schools broke up. That meant we had less than four weeks to find candidates, interview them, and hopefully offer somebody the job. It was tight but we didn't have much choice. I added a closing date of a fortnight on Friday to the poster, printed off two copies and taped one to the inside of the window so anyone passing could see it.

'Fingers crossed,' I said to Dad as I pinned the second copy onto the noticeboard. 'Please let there be a customer-service-focused bookworm out there looking for a short-term contract.'

I glanced at the poster, chewing my lip, telling myself to stay positive. We'd find the right person for the shop, we'd manage to cover Dad's role between us and, more importantly, Dad's operation would go really well and he'd soon be pain-free.

5
LILY

While Dad was out for lunch, a flustered-looking man, probably in his early twenties, burst through the door and uttered a two-word question.

'Pregnancy books?'

'Go up the stairs to level five and you'll find a selection to the right of the window. My colleague Cassie's up there so give her a shout if you need any help or advice.'

He thanked me and took the staircase two steps at a time, returning shortly after with *Your Panic-Free Pregnancy* – the most popular pregnancy book we carried.

'Great choice,' I said, scanning it at the till. 'It's really user-friendly.'

'Your colleague recommended it.'

'I thought she would. She has two young children and she found it exceptionally helpful when she was expecting. There's another one in the series that guides parents through the first five years. Cassie swears by that one too.'

'I'll probably be back for that once the baby arrives. We haven't a clue what we're doing. Bit of a surprise pregnancy.' His cheeks reddened, as though he was embarrassed to have shared that with a stranger. 'But a good surprise,' he added, holding his phone against the terminal to make the payment.

'*The unexpected things in life are often the best,*' I said, handing him the book and his receipt. 'All the best with the baby.'

I smiled to myself after he'd gone. Had I really just quoted my mum for the second time in the space of two days? I'd also been a surprise pregnancy. Mum had been twenty-one and just finishing her degree. She'd felt tired and nauseous throughout her finals and had assumed it was from a combination of exam stress and late nights revising. Several days after her last exam, she wasn't feeling any better so she went to the campus doctor who asked her if she could be pregnant. The possibility had never entered her head but, as soon as the doctor posed the question, she knew the test was going to be positive.

Her boyfriend, Justin, took the news really well, saying *it's earlier than planned, but who likes plans anyway?* They'd been together for two years at that point, both had jobs lined up in Mum's home city of York for after the summer – Mum teaching A level English literature – and had planned to get established in their careers before getting married and starting a family.

It turned out that Justin did like to stick with plans after all because he wasn't happy when Mum suggested cancelling their summer of interrailing around Europe. He couldn't see why pregnancy should be a problem, brushing aside Mum's concerns that lugging a heavy backpack around and sleeping on trains and in hostels might not be ideal in her condition. After several heated arguments, Justin finally came round to her point of view and agreed to change their plans. Mum assumed he'd book a relaxing beach holiday but, instead, he transferred her interrailing tickets into a friend's name. He claimed he needed to get the travel bug out of his system and assured Mum that he'd fully embrace being a father-to-be once he was back. She wasn't sure she believed him but hoped he'd prove her wrong. He didn't. A summer of interrailing turned into a year of travelling. He let down his new employer by giving up his job as well as letting down Mum and me by not being around – something which became a recurring pattern.

Mum didn't think it was right or fair to only teach for a term and a half before going on maternity leave so she withdrew from her job too and felt terrible about it. Fortunately her parents – my Granny Nora and Granddad Maurice – were incredibly supportive and agreed to look after me so Mum could start teaching the following September. There weren't any positions available for an English A level teacher in York or the immediate area but there was one in Whitsborough Bay. Granny Nora and Granddad Maurice had always planned to retire to the coast so they brought that forward, allowing Mum to pursue the career she'd trained for and provide for me – essential given that no financial support ever came from Justin.

After settling in Whitsborough Bay, Mum became a regular visitor to Bay Books and soon befriended Marcus, bonding over their shared love of literature. They became good friends quickly, meeting up on Marcus's days off during the school holidays. When I was two, they went Christmas shopping together, found themselves under some mistletoe and joked they'd better kiss. Neither of them had felt any romantic attraction until that point but that one kiss unexpectedly changed everything. Within a year, they'd married and bought their first home together. Marcus was therefore my stepdad but I'd always called him 'Dad' because that's what he was to me – the best dad I could ever have wished for.

When I was six, Kadence was born and Hendrix came along four years later, at which point we moved to Everdene. One of the many things I loved about my dad was that he'd always treated the three of us equally. As far as he was concerned, I was as much his child as Kadence and Hendrix. Biology didn't matter.

Kadence, now twenty-eight, was a paediatrician at York Teaching Hospital, living in a trendy apartment in central York with her surgeon husband, Cory. Hendrix was twenty-four and an air traffic controller at Leeds Bradford Airport. He lived in Leeds with his long-term girlfriend, Daisy, who was a brilliant chef. I was therefore the only one who'd stayed in Whitsborough Bay. Even though our jobs meant we didn't get to see each other as often as we'd like, Kadence, Hendrix and I had remained really close.

As for Justin, he drifted in and out of my life and I stupidly let him. The last time I'd heard from him was six months ago, the day before the worst birthday ever. Wes had been due back from Dubai for a week's holiday but, as his parents, extended family and some friends were in Manchester, we'd agreed to spend the week there. Justin was working in Manchester at the time so it seemed the perfect opportunity to celebrate my birthday with him for the first time ever while also introducing him to Wes. Except my phone had buzzed with a WhatsApp notification before I left for my train on the Friday afternoon.

FROM JUSTIN
Sorry, kiddo, double-booked tomorrow. Can't meet you now. In touch soon

I hated him calling me 'kiddo'. It might have been cute once when I actually was a kid but it wasn't anymore. I hadn't appreciated the short notice of the cancellation, but what really hurt was that he hadn't even acknowledged my birthday. It shouldn't have got to me because I'd never received a birthday gift from him and the only occasions I'd ever received a card were if he happened to have a girlfriend at the time who took control of things like that.

I clicked into that last message now and sighed. To be fair to him, the absence of a *happy birthday* message had hurt so much more this year because of Wes and I splitting up on my birthday. That had been nothing to do with Justin and I'd perhaps been unfairly holding it against him as I wouldn't normally have let six months pass without making contact. But as I stared at my phone, I realised I had nothing to say to him, so I closed WhatsApp down and put my phone away.

'You look fed up,' Cassie said, joining me at the till.

'I was just thinking about Justin. He hasn't been in touch since he cancelled on me in March and I was wondering why I bother trying with him.'

'Beats me. I know it's harder to cut someone out of your life when they're family, but when that person is never there for you, is it really such a big deal?'

Cassie hadn't had anything to do with her biological father for years. He'd left when she was eight and, just like Justin, had dipped in and out of her life. He only lived a few miles down the coast in Fellingthorpe so it wasn't like he could use Justin's often-made excuse of living and working hours away. When Cassie found out that she and her partner Jared were expecting Hallie, now six years old, she wasn't sure she even wanted to tell her dad but she decided to give him one more chance. His response to the news had been *you needn't think I'm babysitting*, which had told Cassie exactly what she meant to him and she hadn't bothered with him since.

'I know, but...' I tailed off, shrugging.

'Sack him off,' she said. 'You'll feel so much better for it.'

I remembered Cassie telling me that it had felt like a weight was lifted knowing she never had to see her dad again and how thrilled she was that she'd no longer have to feel that slap of rejection every time he cancelled on her. I hated the rejection from Justin too. It made me feel worthless and I'd thought about cutting him out so many times. It wasn't as though he brought anything to my life and I certainly didn't need him to fill any sort of gap for me. I already had two wonderful parents and was blessed with four fantastic grandparents. Until recently, I'd had six wonderful grandparents because, despite their son's uninterest, Justin's parents had been eager to be part of my life. Sadly, they'd passed away within a few days of each other in February two years ago. The double funeral had been the last time I saw Justin and he'd barely spoken to me then, despite plenty of opportunity at the wake to do so. I'd given him the benefit of the doubt because it was an emotional day and also because Mum was with me and she and Justin hadn't spoken in years, but he'd barely been in contact since. It was always me who did the reaching out, which I suppose spoke volumes.

'Go on!' Cassie urged. 'Cut those ties!'

I screwed up my nose at her. 'I want to, but I just can't do it.'

'Why?'

'I wish I knew. My head's telling me the same as you but there's something inside me telling me to keep trying with him.'

'Like a tapeworm?' Cassie quipped. 'Look, Lily, nobody understands more than me cos I've been there too, but you have to ask yourself if your life is better with him in it or out of it. In the twenty-three years we've been besties, I can't recall a single positive interaction you've had with that man but I could reel off dozens of times when he's let you down or upset you. You deserve so much better so have a word with that tapeworm inside of you, ask it to explain why you're clinging on, and deal with it. Promise?'

'I promise.' I smiled at her, forever grateful for her friendship. 'Onto nicer subjects, you said you'd finalised a cake design with Carly…'

Cassie and Jared were getting married in early December and I'd be a bridesmaid alongside our friend Donna. It would be my third time as a bridesmaid but I refused to get superstitious about the saying *three times a bridesmaid, never a bride*. I preferred to focus on what Dad had said yesterday about finding my Gilbert Blythe when I least expected to. Even though I'd sworn off men for now, it was a romantic notion that made my heart flutter. *The unexpected things in life are often the best.* Like Mum having me, like her meeting and falling in love with Dad, like Granny Blue announcing she had a publishing deal and handing over the business to Dad, and like me becoming best friends with Cassie.

* * *

'I've been thinking about what you said yesterday about Wes and Ewan not being my Gilbert Blythe,' I said to Dad as I drove us home after work. 'Can I ask what made you think that?'

'It was the same two things for both of them. Although Anne and Gilbert clashed at first, what made them so perfect for each other was the deep friendship that developed between them. I'm not saying you didn't have a friendship with Wes and Ewan, but...'

Even if I hadn't glanced across at Dad and caught his grimace, I could hear the discomfort in his words and understand why he'd tailed off.

'We weren't the best of friends,' I finished for him. 'I don't know why I never realised that until now.'

'Different relationships work for different reasons. I've no doubt there are successful partnerships where the couple aren't the best of friends, but I'm not convinced that's right for you.'

Mum and Dad attributed their successful marriage to a love forged through a strong friendship. Just like Anne and Gilbert.

'You said there were two things. What's the other one?' I asked.

'Books.'

He didn't need to expand. It was another thing that seemed so obvious now. Ewan had occasionally picked up a non-fiction title but books weren't a passion for him and Wes had hated reading. When he was first seconded to Dubai, I wrote lengthy emails and even sent letters but he admitted his contempt for reading wasn't limited to books so I stopped writing and we only FaceTimed. The time difference was only a few hours but Wes went out so often on an evening that it was hard to catch him at home, meaning our conversations were invariably short and superficial. Even though I'd never realised it at the time, such limited contact had caused serious damage to our relationship.

'It's healthy for a couple to have different interests,' Dad said. 'Your mum has zero interest in cricket and I can't paint but we both love books. It strikes me that, when somebody's as passionate about books as you are, your perfect match is a person who feels the same as opposed to somebody who hates reading.'

'Why didn't you or Mum say anything?'

'You seemed happy and, as I said before, we liked them both so it wasn't our place to plant doubts. I hope I haven't upset you by saying anything now.'

'Definitely not. I'm glad you brought it up. Lots to think about.'

'You know where we are if you want to talk about it.'

'Thanks, Dad.'

As I got ready for bed later that evening, I ran my fingers along the spines of my *Anne of Green Gables* collection on my bookshelves in the lounge, thinking about the second concern Dad had raised. In the series, Anne and Gilbert had both been passionate about reading but for different reasons. Anne loved poetry and romantic novels which sparked her immense imagination and Gilbert had a hunger for learning with books stimulating his intellect and, yes, I did long for that connection and shared passion with my perfect partner. Which meant that both Ewan and Wes had been far from perfect for me.

So why had I been in long-term relationships with each of them? Why had I bought a house with Ewan? Why had I believed that I wanted to marry him and have his children? And why had I thought the same about Wes several years later? Neither of them had been my best friend and neither of them had shown any interest in my greatest passion. *Aren't you bored with reading yet? Why do you have so many copies of that Green Gables book? How can a book make you cry?*

I raised my gaze to the framed Anne Shirley quote on the shelf above my collection; another gift from Cassie. '*I love a book that makes me cry,*' I whispered. And at that moment, I made myself a promise. If I felt ready to let a man back into my life, there'd be no compromise. He had to be my Gilbert Blythe – a best friend with a passion for books – because I wasn't going to waste any more tears over men who didn't compare yet still managed to break my heart. From now on, only books were allowed to reduce me to tears.

The decision felt empowering but, as I settled under my duvet a little later, I realised it didn't give me any answers. If Ewan and Wes had both been far from perfect for me, why had I stayed with them? I was going to have to do some serious soul searching.

6

LARS

I was usually a good sleeper but my first two nights without Nanna had been restless. I'd spent many nights in the house on my own while she went on holiday with Hilary and Geraldine but knowing she wouldn't be back this time hit differently. The house was too quiet and the thoughts swirling round my head were too loud.

So far I'd managed to fill my days, but the evenings had been tough and the rest of the week stretched out ahead of me, woefully empty. I stirred my second coffee of the morning a little too aggressively, angry with myself for not pre-empting this and lining up a job to walk straight into. But what sort of job, and when would I have had time to search for one? As my business responsibilities eased off, any spare time had been swallowed by volunteering at the library, helping Nanna pack and what felt like a million decisions on the refurbishment of The Lodge. And the decisions still weren't at an end as the builders had asked me to drop by after two this afternoon, which meant I had five hours to kill.

I took my drink into the lounge and picked up the latest novel in a Viking series I was loving, but I couldn't focus on the story and gave up after reading the same page several times. I swapped it for a non-fiction book about Norse mythology but that was worse as I kept staring at the pictures, my thoughts drifting. I closed the book with a sigh.

'Mum's room it is,' I muttered.

In the dining room, I opened a pack of cardboard boxes and taped up the base on six of them while I finished my coffee but, standing in the middle of Mum's bedroom a little later, I felt like the walls were closing in on me. Today wasn't the day for packing up Mum's belongings. I needed to get out of the house instead. I'd go for a drive and maybe a walk somewhere.

My car needed fuel so I stopped off at the nearest petrol station. When I stepped out of the pay kiosk I was in a world of my own, trying to decide where to go for a walk, and almost collided with a blonde-haired woman coming in. I looked up to apologise and did a double-take at my ex-girlfriend, Catryn, who I hadn't seen since our three-month relationship ended amicably two months ago.

'Cat? What are you doing here?'

'Why aren't I at work, you mean?' She gave me a mischievous wink. 'I slept in.'

'Danika didn't wake you?'

Cat lived with her older sister and they both worked for their dad's dental practice, Danika as the practice manager and Cat as a dental nurse.

'I stayed at Miles's house last night.'

'No, Cat! Not Miles again.'

Miles had been Cat's ex when I started seeing her. They'd had an on-off relationship for years which had ended, supposedly for good, after she moved in with him and caught him cheating on her. It was at that point she'd temporarily moved into her sister's house.

'You know he's no good for you,' I added.

'I know, but that's the appeal. If nice boys did it for me, you and I would still be together.'

I chose not to correct her on that. 'Still at Danika's?'

'Yes, and still she's nagging me about the mess and demanding to know when I'll be moving out. Honestly, she's such an old woman!' Cat's phone rang from her handbag and she rolled her eyes at me. 'Speak of the devil! That'll be her now, chasing me again. I'd better go. Lovely to see you again, Lars.' She kissed me lightly on the cheek and dashed inside the kiosk.

I returned to my car and headed out of town, reflecting on Cat's comment about us still being together if *nice boys* had been her thing. There was no chance of that. I'd known that Cat wasn't right for me from our very first date, but Nanna's voice was in my head. She'd caught me scrolling through the dating app I'd been on for months without actually going on any dates.

'What's wrong with her?' she'd said, peering over my shoulder as I was reading Cat's profile. 'She's stunning.'

'She is, but we've got nothing in common.'

'How do you know until you go on a date?'

'It lists her interests.'

She glanced at the profile, shaking her head. 'You can't make a decision about compatibility based on a few sentences. Your problem is that you look for perfection and it doesn't exist. Your grandpa wasn't perfect but did that stop me falling in love with him? All humans have imperfections and that's what makes them interesting, exciting, challenging.'

'I know, but...' I shrugged. 'I want perfect. I can't help it.' We weren't talking perfection in looks – I wasn't that shallow. It was the perfection of the match that I wanted – someone I could talk to endlessly but with whom I could also enjoy the silence, someone with the same interests as me and the same outlook on life, someone who told the truth and kept their promises. Surely that wasn't too much to ask.

'Then you're likely to end up alone which will be a crying shame because I think you'd be an amazing husband and father. You have so many wonderful qualities. You, my darling boy, are ridiculously handsome and, when they were dishing brains out, I think you got a double dose. You're thoughtful, generous and funny. But you do overthink things and you're so cautious and considered.'

'What's wrong with being cautious and considered? My Study Hub would never have been the success it was if I hadn't taken my time to get it right.'

'I wholeheartedly agree, but there's a big difference between the approaches needed for a successful business and a successful personal life. Sometimes I think it would help if you were a little more spontaneous. Throw away the plan and see where life takes you.'

'I can be spontaneous. I was when it came to selling the business.'

She shook her head. 'You might have met up with that Calvin Warboys fella quickly but you took *months* to make the actual decision. Remember I saw the pros and cons Post-its list on your office wall.'

So to prove to Nanna that I could be spontaneous, I contacted Cat and was stunned when she agreed to a date with me, and even more stunned when she wanted to see me for a second one. I liked Cat and she made me laugh, but she was obsessed with her appearance and keeping up with the latest fashion trends. On our third date she shared that, when she was maxed out on her credit cards, she kept the tags on dresses, wore them out, then returned them to the shop the next day.

'Everyone does it,' she said when I challenged her on it. 'Stop being such a boring bookworm and live a little.'

At that point, it was clear that there wasn't just a massive difference in our interests but a chasm in our values too so it was time for me to bow out. I instigated the *I don't think this is working* conversation but Cat talked me down.

'I know I'm high maintenance,' she said, 'and I've no intention of changing that for you or anyone else. It's who I am, just like being steady and reliable is who you are. I know I joked that you should let your hair down and live a little, but I was wrong. I don't think you should change being you because you're great the way you are and, someday, you'll meet someone who wants that and who isn't flaky and chaotic like me. Until she comes along, why don't we have a bit of fun together?'

So we did and it was all right for a while because neither of us were in danger of getting hurt. I knew she was using me as a shield to stop her running back to Miles but the thought that I was using her – even though she had no issue with that – niggled away at me. I didn't really miss Cat after we finally agreed to call it a day but I did miss her sister because I'd developed a friendship with Danika. There were only fourteen months between them but the sisters couldn't have been more different. They looked nothing alike, Danika being brown-eyed and brunette like their dad and Cat being blue-eyed and blonde like their mum. Danika was organised and structured, whereas Cat was all over the place and her timekeeping was shocking. Every time I turned up for a date, Cat was at least half an hour off being ready so I sat in the lounge and chatted to Danika, with whom I discovered I had so much more in common.

I'd been driving on autopilot and registered that I was in Hutton Wicklow so I parked by the green which gently sloped down to the slow-flowing river and exited the car, looking up at the pretty whitewashed cottage where Nanna had been raised. My great-nanna had still been around when I was a child so Nanna had often taken me to visit her before going on a long circular walk. I could clearly picture Great-Nanna on the doorstep wearing a floral tabard apron with a large pocket on the front from which she always plucked a packet of sweets for our walk and a couple of crusts of bread for us to feed to the ducks.

Noticing the curtains on the cottage twitch, I turned to face the river. A woman was crouched beside a young boy who was tossing what looked to be rice and peas towards three ducks. Another two ducks appeared from under the road bridge and the boy squealed excitedly. I could understand that as I'd been duck-obsessed when I was little thanks to so much time spent here feeding them. I'd bring my own kids here to feed the ducks and hope they developed the same love I had. Tutting to myself, I set off alongside the river. What kids?

A wooden footbridge joined a lane which ran past a row of six cottages and across a couple of fields towards the ruins of Hutton Wicklow Castle – a fortified family home built by a wealthy landowner in the early fifteenth century. As I got closer, my pace slowed and I took several deep breaths, battling to keep my emotions in check. This place held so many memories for me and, although most of them were happy, there was one overwhelmingly painful one.

A dog walker said, 'Hello,' as he passed with a bouncy black-and-white springer spaniel and tossed a ball for the dog to chase before disappearing from view. There was nobody else in sight so I had the castle to myself, as was often the case. I paused to take in the stunning view from all directions and smiled as I picked out The Lodge before settling down on a boulder.

My younger sister, Pia, had declared Hutton Wicklow Castle her *favourite place in the whole world*. I could clearly picture her standing in front of the crumbling walls, arms outstretched, her knitted white dragon draped over her shoulder as she gazed up towards the top of the ruins. *It's magical here! Can you feel it, Lars? As magical as Christmas!*

Swiping at the tears trailing down my cheeks, I swallowed hard on the lump in my throat. 'I miss you, little pixie.'

I stayed for a while, lost in my memories, but was pulled from them by a yappy Jack Russell demanding my attention. The owner apologised as she clipped on a lead and dragged the dog away, but that was my cue to leave. I continued across another field before dropping down to Hutton Valley where a wooden boardwalk ran alongside the river for just over a mile, flanked on either side by trees. The boardwalk ended at a footbridge across the river and a short track leading to a small car park and picnic site which were deserted today. At the far end of the car park, I joined a woodland trail which rose steadily to join Hutton Valley Lane where a dozen houses, including The Lodge, enjoyed the most stunning views over the woods, river, castle and countryside.

The Lodge had always been my favourite property on Hutton Valley Lane and it still didn't seem real that I owned it. As a kid, I'd called it Duckling Lodge because the owners, like me, clearly loved ducks. On the left side of the barred wooden gate across the drive was a plaque of a male mallard duck (a drake) with a trio of ducklings and on the right side was another plaque of a female (a hen) with five ducklings, looking as though they were on their way to join the rest of the family. There were ornamental ducks and ducklings either side of the front door too and a pair of soft toy ducks in the window of one of the bedrooms. Every time we did our circular walk, we paused to say hello to the ducks and I told Nanna I'd live there one day. I never imagined that I really would.

'I've got something to show you,' Nanna had said, reaching for her iPad a couple of weeks after our visit to Bay View.

'Let me guess. A house?'

Since securing her new apartment, Nanna had become a little obsessed with finding me somewhere to live and had thrust her iPad in front of me most days, showing me properties she thought might be suitable.

'Ah, but this isn't just *any* house,' she said, her eyes twinkling as she passed me her tablet.

I glanced at the photo of the property and gasped. 'No way! It's Duckling Lodge.'

'And it could be yours.'

'It needs a lot of work,' I said, chewing on my lip as I scrolled through the photos of a dated kitchen, pink bathroom suite and floral wallpaper throughout. It appeared to have been adapted for a wheelchair user too with a stairlift, ramps and other aids which I wouldn't need.

'And it's priced to reflect that.'

I clicked into the floorplans. There were six bedrooms but two of them were tiny and would be better knocked into one to make a large en suite for the master bedroom or perhaps repurposed as a smaller en suite and a dressing room.

'You're very quiet,' Nanna observed.

'Just taking it all in,' I said, clicking back into the photos. 'I always wondered what it looked like inside.'

'You can see the castle from it.'

I paused on images of the views from the front of the house and they really were spectacular. Seeing the castle every day would be exceptionally special.

'I wonder if they still have the ducks on the gates,' I said.

'I wondered that too. You can't tell from the photos. What do you think? Could you see yourself living there?'

The work didn't scare me. I actually liked the idea of gutting the place and starting with a blank canvas, but the family home tag did scare me. What did a single man in his mid-thirties need with such a big house and garden?

'I'm not sure. It's a family home and I don't have a family.'

'Semantics,' Nanna said. 'You've heard that phrase *dress for the job you want*? Well, this could be *buy the home for the family you want.*'

It wasn't quite the same thing but I could see her logic.

'And you *could* have a family if you wanted.'

'If you weren't so fussy about your girlfriends,' we both said together, my tone sarcastic.

'Very funny,' Nanna said. 'But you know it's the truth.'

It was, but I couldn't help it. The problem was that I'd already met the perfect woman for me a very long time ago and I'd stupidly pushed her away. Nobody I'd met since had compared to her and I wasn't sure they ever would.

7

LILY

I spent my day off on Thursday exactly how I liked it – relaxing at Green Gables with a book – and returned to work on Friday feeling refreshed and positive.

'You look brighter,' Cassie said when she arrived.

'I feel it. Monday was tough but what Dad said about Wes not being my Gilbert Blythe – Ewan too – was a light bulb moment. The rejection still hurts but I've accepted that the end was for the best.'

'Glad to hear it. Does that mean you're open to dating again? Jared's got a couple of single mates who—'

'Won't be dating me,' I finished for her. 'I wouldn't have time to think about it this side of Christmas with the hours I'll be working and, even if Dad wasn't having his op, I'm not ready. I need to think hard about what I want before rushing into another relationship and getting hurt again.'

'Fair enough, but you just have to say the word and I'll have you fixed up in a whizz.'

***

All week, I'd been meaning to visit Bear With Me, the specialist teddy bear shop on the other side of the street. The owner, Jemma, was a good friend who'd returned to work this week after becoming a mum for the third time and I was keen to find out how she was settling back in. We'd caught up for a coffee on my day off a few weeks ago and I'd enjoyed cuddles with baby Jasmine and her three-year-old brother, Kieran, but had missed seeing their big brother, Freddie, who, now five, was at school. Not wanting to bother Jemma across the busier lunchtime period, I took my break early at half eleven and headed across the cobbles.

Jemma was by the till, pricing up a box of soft toys, and she smiled widely when she saw me.

'Welcome back!' I said. 'How's it going?'

'Like I've never been away. Annie's such a pro at keeping things running without me. I don't think she really needs me here.'

'I'll always need you,' called a voice and I laughed as Jemma's colleague Annie appeared from behind a giant teddy bear. 'Hi, Lily. Jem, I'm going upstairs to see if we've got any more of those owls in the storeroom, but shout if you need me.'

There were a couple of customers in the shop – an elderly man studying the beautiful artist bears Jemma and her mum created and kept in glass cabinets as a sign that they weren't meant for children, and a woman with a couple of young children in a double buggy. She had her back to me and was picking soft toys from the shelves and showing them to the kids.

'Is it a bad time?' I whispered.

'No, you're fine. So, it's going well. The only tears when I dropped Jasmine and Kieran off with our childminder were mine, but I'm fine now and I was ready to come back to work. And with it being part-time for now, I get the best of both worlds.'

The woman with the buggy approached the till so I moved aside.

'I'll take these two, please.'

She placed a lilac rabbit and a cream teddy bear on the counter and, as she looked up, my breath caught.

'Jordan?'

She whipped her head round and glared at me. 'Oh! It's you!'

My stomach lurched. After all these years, did she really still have to be rude to me, especially when she was the one who'd decided she didn't want to be friends with me anymore?

'How are you?' I asked, keeping my tone friendly.

She placed her phone over the terminal to pay for the soft toys then looked up at me, her eyes narrowed. 'As if you don't know.'

'Know what?'

'I suppose you think it's karma.'

I shrugged. 'I honestly have no idea what you're talking about.'

She snatched up the toys. 'Like I believe that.'

As Jordan pushed the buggy towards the door, Jemma rushed over to open it for her. Jordan paused in the doorway.

'Ozzie and Rhianna?' She raised her eyebrows at me.

'I'm sorry. I really don't...' I shrugged once more.

'It's all over town so you might as well get it straight from me. They've been having an affair since before we were married and now he's buggered off with her. That kid of hers? She's his. Pair of them probably thought it was hilarious asking me to be godmother. She's pregnant again so I'm back at my mum's having to explain to my kids why their daddy chose them over us. Fun, eh?'

She'd gone before I even had a chance to respond.

'I didn't realise you knew her,' Jemma said, wincing.

'We were best friends in primary school but she ditched me for Rhianna.'

'Ah! That explains the karma comment.'

I nodded. 'Except I would *never* think something like that, especially when someone's world has just been turned upside down.'

'She comes in here every so often with her kids and usually has a quick chat, but obviously I've been off with Jasmine so I hadn't seen her for ages. I asked her how she was and out it all spilled. She went to her mum's when she found out about the affair and, when she returned to the family home, she discovered he'd already moved this Rhianna and her daughter in. Age six, I think she said the little girl was. How do you pick yourself up after that?'

'It's awful. I wouldn't wish that on my worst enemy, although, funnily enough, Jordan and Rhianna are probably just that. The pair of them were horrible to me at senior school but she doesn't deserve that, especially when there are children involved.'

The man approached the till. 'Apologies for interrupting, my dear, but I can't decide between two bears.'

Jemma smiled at him. 'I'll get them out for you, Mr Simms.'

'I'll see you later,' I said. 'We'll organise a night out with Cassie.'

'Sounds good. Bye, Lily.'

Returning to Bay Books, I was dying to tell Cassie who I'd just seen but there was a small queue so I waved and headed downstairs to the staff room, my encounter with Jordan playing on repeat. But as I settled at the table with a mug of tea and my lunch, it was the end of our friendship which was on my mind.

I'd been excited, if a little apprehensive, about leaving behind the small, cosy world of primary school and starting at Laurendale School with so many more kids, but I'd felt confident I'd settle in quickly because I'd have my best friend by my side. Jordan Hughes and I had been inseparable all the way through primary school. She'd lived just around the corner from me so we'd seen a lot of each other outside of school too.

When Hendrix was born during my penultimate year of primary school and we moved to Everdene in a different part of town, I'd been worried about not seeing my best friend during the school holidays. Our parents had ensured that didn't happen, dropping us off at each other's houses to spend time together. I'd expected the summer between primary and senior school to pan out the same, but every time Mum got in touch with Jordan's mum to make arrangements, there was an excuse. Halfway through the summer break, I was helping my Granny Nora run the tombola at her village's summer fete, my job being to retrieve the prizes. Jordan appeared but obviously hadn't noticed me, considering her shocked expression when she gave me her winning tickets. I'm not normally one for confrontations – never have been – but I was so upset that, as I handed over her prizes, I couldn't stop myself from blurting out, 'Don't you want to see me anymore?'

I'll never forget the coldness in her eyes as she dished out her truth. 'No. Because I'm sick of you yabbering on about books all the time.'

'But I thought you liked books.'

'They're boring, Lily. Just like you. Rhianna's my best friend now.' She curled her lip at me then ran off to join her new bestie.

Granny Nora witnessed it and wrapped me in a bear hug. 'Someone capable of treating you like that isn't worth your friendship, sweetheart, and they're certainly not worth your tears.'

But I couldn't help it. I was distraught at losing my best friend and so hurt by what she'd said about books being boring, about me being boring. I'd never have believed she could turn on me like that. And with Rhianna Black of all people – the girl who'd picked on me from the moment we met in reception class.

Across the rest of that summer, books were my friends and my escape. I devoured the entire *Anne of Green Gables* series which I'd received in a boxset for Christmas, longing to live in Avonlea with a *bosom friend* like Diana Barry and a friend and love interest like Gilbert Blythe. The books helped restore my belief that there were true friends out there who were worthy of my friendship. I just needed to find them.

That first day at Laurendale School, I was terrified and so very alone. My primary school had fallen between two senior school catchment areas and all my other friends were going elsewhere. What if I didn't make any new friends? What if everyone had gone up with their best friends from primary school and, as mine had ditched me, I'd forever be on the outside?

Walking up the school drive, my heart sank when I spotted Jordan and Rhianna huddled together. I dipped my head and tried to slink past them unseen but no such luck.

'Book bore approaching!' Rhianna called. 'Run before she sends you to sleep.'

I glanced towards Jordan, hopeful of an apologetic shrug, but she was laughing. My former best friend was actually laughing at what my bully said. Granny Nora had been right. She wasn't worthy of my friendship, but where did that leave me?

I leaned against a wall, far away from Jordan's and Rhianna's sight, and removed *Anne of Green Gables* from my bag, desperate for some escapism before we were called into assembly to be split into our form classes. I felt sick with relief when I heard that neither Jordan nor Rhianna were to be in my class, but I didn't know a single soul who was and they all seemed to be paired off as we made our way from the hall to the classroom. I was the last to enter and the only space left was a double desk in front of the teacher. I slipped into it and, to this day, I have no idea how I managed to hold in the tears.

Across my five years at Laurendale School, I didn't have much to do with Jordan and Rhianna. We didn't have any classes together or any friends in common. If I did see them around, I'd be subjected to dirty looks or snarky comments, but I never rose to it. I found it quite pathetic that their way of getting their kicks was to bring down others.

I remembered Ozzie from the year above us. He'd been Jordan's boyfriend when she was fourteen but they broke up when he left school. They'd evidently got back together at some point without me realising because I'd been shocked when Dad pointed out their wedding announcement in *Bay News*. It must have been about eight years ago because I remembered discussing it with Ewan and we hadn't been together for long at the time.

I really felt for Jordan. It must be bad enough discovering your husband had been having an affair but for it to be with your best friend of twenty-three years was the ultimate betrayal. I just hoped she had other friends who could help her through it because she was certainly going to need them. I wouldn't be trying to reconnect, though. Some relationships were definitely best kept in the past.

8
LARS

When I'd returned from my walk on Wednesday, I picked up a voicemail asking if I could do another shift at the library so I'd spent yesterday there and actually managed to focus on books rather than IT for most of the day, but today stretched out empty before me and I was going to have to tackle Mum's bedroom.

I placed one of the boxes on her bed and emptied the shelves first, giving each trophy and medal a cursory glance to check the sports represented – swimming, hockey and archery. As far as I knew, Mum was still a keen swimmer. I knew she'd played hockey at school, but I couldn't recall her ever mentioning archery. On the wall beside the shelves were her framed degree certificate and graduation photo. I lifted them from their hooks and added them to the trophies box along with various miscellaneous items.

Two boxes were soon filled and I moved onto a tallboy. The top two drawers contained T-shirts and the third contained shorts but, at the bottom of that drawer, I found an old photo album. Assuming it would contain photos from Mum's childhood, I opened up the first page and gasped at the inscription written in swirly black cursive.

Pia Bryony Jóhannsson
Taken too soon, aged only 7
Rest in peace our little pixie

I sat down on the edge of Mum's bed, slowly turning the pages. Each photograph was carefully mounted with photo corners and my little sister was in every single one, sometimes accompanied by Mum, Pabbi, Nanna or me. Beside each photo was a handwritten note including the date, location and Pia's age as well as comments and observations such as *Pia loved twirling in this dress*, *I love how the light reflects on Pia's hair* and *Such a happy day out*.

The lump in my throat grew with each turn of the page but one photo near the end, taken on Christmas Eve, broke me. Our family had always embraced the Icelandic Christmas Eve tradition of *Jólabókaflóð* – translated as Christmas book flood – where Icelanders give and receive books and spend the evening reading them. In the photo, Pia was sitting on the floor, cross-legged, her eyes shining as she cradled her new books. Mum had written *Looking at that gorgeous smile, it's hard to believe she was so ill and would be gone in less than two months*.

As a tear splashed onto the page, I swore under my breath and quickly blotted it with the bottom of my T-shirt, relieved it had missed Mum's note and the photograph. I wiped my palms across my cheeks before lying the album on the bed beside me, safe from any further tears as I continued to turn the pages.

A family photo taken on Christmas Day – what had turned out to be my sister's final Christmas – was followed by one of her lying on the sofa on New Year's Day with her favourite picture book, *Anna and the Snow Dragon*, open on her lap. The final photo had been produced in black and white. Pia's favourite stuffed animals, including the knitted dragon she never let out of her sight, were lined up on her bed with a single white rose across their tummies. Mum's accompanying note gave the date of my sister's death and three words which set me off again – *I am broken*.

I'd been three weeks away from my fourth birthday when Pia was born and all my early childhood memories revolved around her. Born prematurely at twenty-eight weeks, Pia's lungs didn't get the chance to fully develop, leaving her with various respiratory problems. Severe asthma attacks meant she was a regular patient on the children's ward at Whitsborough Bay Hospital. She missed so much school that making friends was difficult but she said she didn't mind because she had her soft toys, her books and me.

I'd adored my little sister and was constantly amazed by her ability to find a positive spin for everything. She could easily have complained about being ill and the limitations her asthma placed on her but, instead, she focused on the gift of how many books she could devour when spending so much time resting, and all the fantastic places she could visit through the pages. I'd always liked books but it was through Pia that I became passionate about them. I spent as much time as I could with her, listening to her read or reading to her when she was too tired. One day she'd be absorbed by a book aimed at teenagers, the next she'd find joy in a toddler's picture book and she was always eager to talk about the story, often sharing her thoughts on what happened to the characters beyond the final page. I was too young to realise it at the time but looking back on her final months, I'm convinced that the ending-beyond-the-ending was her way of exploring her own mortality and the idea that she could live on even when the final chapter closed on her own story.

I flicked back several pages to a photo taken during Pia's only trip to Iceland. She'd been four when we spent Christmas with Pabbi's family in Húsavík. It was my first time seeing the aurora borealis, known as the northern lights or, in Icelandic, *Norðurljós*. Even though I'd just turned eight, I could remember it as though it was yesterday. Mum and Pabbi had shown us photos but seeing the aurora in real life was something else. The bands of green and aqua were so vibrant as they shimmered and rolled in the sky alongside thinner ribbons of pink and purple. And the stars! I'd never seen so many stars. Pia had been as captivated as me, her mouth open as her eyes darted left and right, as though scarcely able to believe what she was seeing. I'd lifted her up – not easy when she was so bundled up in all her layers and a thick snowsuit – and the image Mum had captured and placed in the album was of the pair of us silhouetted against the lights, both pointing at the sky.

With a heavy sigh, I closed the photo album and gently placed it on top of the tallboy, feeling an overwhelming sense of loss. It would have been our little pixie's thirty-first birthday in November. If she'd been born to term with fully developed lungs, what would our relationship have been like? My guess was exceptionally close but with merciless teasing. What career would she have chosen? Would she have found love by now? Had children? I thought of her often, acknowledging birthdays and the moments when she'd have reached a milestone like leaving school, college and graduating from university, and it hurt like hell that she'd never been able to do those things.

It didn't feel right to confine the photo album to storage. I'd keep it at my new place and ask Mum about it when she came back. I couldn't imagine she'd want to get rid of it, but I barely knew her anymore. She wasn't around enough to let me. And that hurt like hell too.

* * *

'I'm impressed!' I exclaimed, looking round Nanna's apartment at Bay View on Sunday morning. Pictures had been hung on the walls and everything appeared to have been unpacked. 'I thought it'd take you longer than a week to get straight.'

'Me too,' Nanna said, 'but the maintenance team have been so helpful hammering in nails and putting up shelves. I feel settled already.'

I adjusted a couple of cushions and sat down on the sofa. 'Glad you made the move?'

'Very, although I miss you, of course.'

'And I miss you. It's so quiet on my own and very echoey.'

'What have you been doing with yourself this week?' she asked, passing me a mug of tea.

'I did an extra day at the library and completed our old circular walk, which was nice. I've been to the house a few times, made a couple of tip runs and packed up Mum's things.'

'Did you find somewhere to store them?'

'I'm going to keep them in my garage. No point paying for a storage unit when I've got the room.' I reached into the bag I'd bought with me. 'I found this photo album in Mum's drawers. It's devoted to Pia, but I don't remember her making it. Have you seen it before?'

Nanna flicked through the first few pages, shaking her head. 'No, and she's never mentioned it either. She could have done it before you both moved in with me.' She continued working through the pages. 'My goodness, that little girl had the most beautiful smile.'

She closed the album and handed it back to me. 'The photos are no surprise – Jayne does, after all, live and breathe photography – but the comments are unexpected. I've never known her to express anything in writing.'

'Yeah, the comments surprised me too. She's not normally sentimental. I'm going to keep the album in the house and ask her about it when she visits. *If* she visits.'

'Oh, she will. I just wouldn't hold your breath for it being over Christmas or New Year. You know she finds the thirteen days too difficult.'

There were two things I remembered Mum and Pabbi strongly agreeing on which had heavily influenced my childhood. The first was that Pia and I had to be fully bilingual – not just able to speak Icelandic fluently but to read and write it too. The second thing was that, despite living in England and recognising English traditions, we also needed to embrace Icelandic traditions, especially at Christmas. As well as *Jólabókaflóð*, Icelanders recognised the thirteen Yule Lads – *jólasveinar* in Icelandic – instead of one Father Christmas. The first mischievous Yule Lad arrived on 12 December, triggering the start of thirteen days of Christmas running through to Christmas Eve, during which time children left their shoes by the window hoping that the Yule Lad arriving that night would place a gift inside if they'd been good as opposed to a rotten potato for being naughty. Pia and I loved the Yule Lads. What child wouldn't love thirteen days of gifts, plus *Jólabókaflóð*, and then the English tradition of putting our stockings out for Father Christmas to arrive at some point in the early hours of Christmas morning? Embracing the traditions of both cultures absolutely worked for us!

If only Mum and Pabbi had been in agreement on more than that, especially when it came to my sister. What they each considered to be best for Pia was frequently debated. Loudly. As though my sister and I couldn't hear just because we were upstairs in bed. Pabbi wanted us to move to Húsavík, saying the air was cleaner in Iceland. Mum claimed it was too cold for Pia and she was too weak to travel anymore. Neither of them ever asked Pia what she wanted. If they had, they'd have discovered that she longed to live in a hot country, spending her days floating lazily around a pool on an inflatable dragon or unicorn and getting lost in her books.

In the months following my sister's death, Nanna was the one who comforted me. I don't know what I'd have done without her because Mum and Pabbi were too distracted with blaming each other, too busy instigating their divorce, too occupied with dividing up their belongings and putting our family home on the market to notice that they had an eleven-year-old son who was falling apart.

It was the evening before I was due to start at secondary school when Mum finally seemed to remember that she had another child. I was filling my new pencil case with the back-to-school stationery which Nanna had bought me from Bay Books when Mum knocked on my bedroom door and entered without invitation. She wandered over to the window and looked out into the street. I waited for her to speak and, when she didn't, I resumed my task.

'Are you looking forward to going up to big school tomorrow?' she asked eventually without turning to face me.

'Not really.'

'Your nanna said you've got everything you need.'

'She took me shopping,' I said, wondering if she'd even registered my response to her original question.

'I'm going away for a while.'

My stomach dropped to my feet and I felt sick. Pabbi had already left me and now Mum was leaving too. Did neither of them care about me anymore? What was I supposed to do without them?

'When?' I'd had to force the word out over the lump in my throat and it came out so quiet, I wasn't sure she'd even heard it.

'Tomorrow,' she said, just as I was poised to ask again.

Silence as she continued to stare out of the window.

'Where are you going?' I asked when I couldn't stand the silence any longer.

She finally turned to face me. 'Eastern Europe. Photography assignment. I need to...' Her voice caught and she cleared her throat but didn't finish the sentence.

'How long will you be gone?'

'I'm not sure. You'll be okay.'

It felt as though that should be a question but her flat tone of voice made it sound more like a statement so I didn't say anything. Nothing about my life at that moment was okay. The sister I loved more than anyone else in the world was dead, my parents were getting divorced, my pabbi had returned to Iceland and had only spoken to me once across the summer holidays, my mum lived in the same house as me but might as well have been living on the moon given how little she had to do with me, and I was about to start at senior school where I already knew I wasn't going to fit in. But I couldn't share that with her because I didn't believe she was capable of saying or doing anything to make things all right, even if only for one evening. I didn't believe she cared about me and her announcement that she was packing up her camera equipment and leaving confirmed that. My already broken heart took another beating.

'You will come back?' I asked hesitantly, fearful that the answer might be no.

'Of course.'

'And you'll stay then? We'll get our own house?'

She cocked her head to one side, looking puzzled.

'You said moving in with Nanna was only temporary,' I prompted.

'You don't like it here?'

'I do, but...' I wasn't sure how to expand on that without sounding disloyal towards Nanna. I'd always been exceptionally close to her but I hadn't expected her to have to replace Mum. Nanna had become my everything since Pia died and, while I would forever be grateful for that, what I really wanted was my mum. And my pabbi. And I wanted my sister so badly.

Mum's gaze turned towards my wardrobe where my uniform was hanging on the outside.

'You're going to look so smart tomorrow, Lars. A blazer. So grown up. We'll need a photo of you in the morning.' She pulled her long blonde hair back into a ponytail and secured it with a bobble from around her wrist. 'I'd best finish my packing.'

She stood there for a moment, staring at me. Her hands twitched by her side and she took a pace closer to me. I thought she was going to hug me – something she'd always done to Pia but which I couldn't remember her doing to me for so long – but she slipped her hands into the pockets of her combat trousers instead.

'Listen to your teachers and be good for your nanna,' she said, her voice sounding strained. And then she left and closed my bedroom door behind her.

When I rose the following morning, Mum was already gone. Nanna was the one who took the photo of me in my new uniform. Nanna was the one who made me a packed lunch, who welcomed me home, who asked about my first day. She was the one who checked my homework, attended parents' evenings, bought me my first shaving kit, took me to Iceland when Pabbi remarried and a thousand other things that my parents should have done.

Meanwhile Mum received critical acclaim as a street photographer, having shifted her interest from landscapes. I found it strange at first that she'd retained her married name but she'd already had some early recognition as Jay Jóhannsson – the Jay being short for Jayne and giving potential for gender anonymity in a career dominated by men. Another thing I found strange was that she was so fascinated by people in her compositions when she showed no interest in them in real life. Or perhaps it was just strangers who held the appeal because she certainly didn't seem to care about her family, which was what made the discovery that she'd created an album devoted to my sister all the more surprising.

'Did you find any more photo albums in her room?' Nanna asked as I placed the album back in the bag. I translated that as *did you find an album devoted to you?* I wouldn't have expected there to be one, though, as this was clearly about capturing my sister's short life.

'Just this one. There could have been loose photos in the box files I packed but I didn't want to rifle through all her stuff.'

'Did I ever tell you how surprised I was when your mum announced she was getting married and that she and Ragnar wanted children?' Nanna said. 'She always seemed content in her own company – bit of a loner – but she threw herself into the role of wife and mother and she was so happy.'

My expression evidently conveyed my doubts as Nanna rose and reached out her hand towards me. 'I've got something to show you.'

I took her hand and, like a small boy, followed her into her bedroom where we stopped beside a framed collage.

'I've not seen this before,' I said.

'It was one of the organised activities last week. These lovely women came in with assorted frames and helped us showcase our favourite photos. Look at Jayne and Ragnar on their wedding day and with you when you were a baby and a toddler. You can't fake smiles that big.'

I studied the photos and she was right. Those early photos depicted a happy family of which I had no recollection.

'When Pia came along far too early, that happiness was replaced by fear. Would she survive the first twenty-four hours? Forty-eight? A week? A month? Your little sister was a fighter but every milestone she reached was replaced by another and neither of your parents knew how to deal with it. Who would? They couldn't control what was happening to Pia so they both focused on the things they could control. Ragnar became obsessed with returning to Iceland. It even got to the point where he wouldn't...' She gasped as though she'd revealed something she hadn't meant to.

'Go on,' I said gently. 'You might as well tell me or I'll imagine something worse.'

'He refused to speak to Jayne in English. It wound her up because they'd made a promise to each other around conversing in both languages and she felt he'd let her down.'

Nanna wiped a speck of dust from the glass before continuing. 'The thing Jayne could control was photography but that also went to the extreme. She lived her life through a lens rather than facing reality.'

'She told you that?' I asked as we set off back to the lounge.

'No. I could see it happening.'

'Did she ever talk to you about why she pulled away from me?'

'No. She never talked to me about anything of consequence. I always offered but she liked to work things through in her own mind. Or hide from them.'

We settled back on the sofa.

'I do have a theory if you want to hear it,' Nanna said.

'Please.'

'I think she was scared of losing you too so she detached herself.'

I shook my head. 'She pulled away from me way before Pia died.' Taking in Nanna's sad expression, I was hit by the realisation. 'She always knew we were going to lose Pia.'

Nanna sighed heavily and nodded. 'They agreed from the start that they wanted any medical professionals to be honest and realistic so that they could be prepared for the potential worst-case scenario. Truth is, how do you really prepare for something devastating like that? Especially when she didn't just lose Pia. She lost Ragnar and she lost you too.'

'She didn't have to lose me. I was only eleven at the time. It wasn't too late to pull it back.' I'd been so desperate for her attention that all she'd needed to do was give me one hug or say a few kind words and I'd have forgiven her for everything. Instead, she left without saying goodbye at a time when I was already feeling vulnerable from my pabbi's abandonment.

'I've always worried about Jayne,' Nanna said, another sigh escaping from her. 'I was especially worried when she was a child and never seemed interested in making friends. I feared she might be lonely but Norman always pointed out how happy and content our little girl was in her own company, especially when she had a camera in her hands. He said that not everyone was like me, feeling energised when surrounded by others, and he and Jayne were proof of that.

'When Norman died and she took off travelling on her own, I worried again. I had this horrible feeling she might never return. And then she met Ragnar and everything changed. I realised that she wasn't averse to spending time with others – she just hadn't found anyone she wanted to spend time with because, when she did make that connection, it was all-consuming. The problem was that, when it crumbled, she reverted to the loner she'd been before. This time I don't think it was about her preferring her own company – it was more that she couldn't bear to be around people anymore. She travels the world photographing strangers. People dip in and out of her life and she doesn't form attachments to any of them because, if she has no deep connections, she can't get hurt again.'

What Nanna had just said about Mum rang true, but it didn't bring me any comfort. That deep connection Mum had had with Pia had been cut by death, and the one with Pabbi by divorce, but what about me? I was still here, as was her own mother. Weren't we enough? Wasn't I enough?

We talked some more about Nanna's observations of Mum growing up. It was interesting hearing how early she'd demonstrated strong decision-making skills and how she'd always been stubborn and fiercely independent.

'She was a bit like someone else I know,' Nanna said, giving me a knowing look. 'When you were a child – and a teen too – you reminded me so much of Jayne, content in your own company, no need for friends.'

I didn't say anything because the truth would hurt her, but she couldn't have been more wrong about that. I'd learned to be content in my own company because I'd had to be. I'd longed for friends but it had never happened in primary school and senior school was even worse. I never felt like I fitted in thanks to a combination of my academic abilities – bright kids being an easy target for the bullies – and my half-English, half-Icelandic heritage. I occasionally blurted out something in class in Icelandic and, because my grades were excellent, most of the teachers humoured me (although I don't think any of them actually liked me), but the other kids didn't. If I had a pound for every time some idiot had followed me around saying *hurdy-gurdy* in some bizarre sing-song impersonation of the accent I'd had back then, I wouldn't have had to fret about my career as I'd have been loaded. To this day, I don't know who started the *hurdy-gurdy* bollocks. It was so stupid. The words sounded nothing like Icelandic but pointing that out didn't do me any favours either.

Nanna's phone began ringing and she apologised as she answered it. 'Hi, Geraldine... Goodness, is it that time already? Can you give me ten minutes? All right, lovey, see you soon.'

'Lunchtime?' I asked, getting to my feet. Nanna had told me earlier that she and her friends were having Sunday lunch in the care home's restaurant as they'd heard wonderful things about the food.

'Yes. This morning's flown. Will you be all right? I'm conscious our conversation today was heavier than usual.'

'I'm fine, Nanna. It was good to get your take on things. Gives me a lot to think about. Enjoy your lunch and I'll see you soon.'

As I went down the stairs, clutching onto the bag containing the photo album, I wondered if I was doing a disservice to Mum by thinking she didn't care. Was it possible that she cared too much? Deep down, I knew that I'd thrown myself into my business and worked every hour God sent to stop me thinking so much about everything I'd lost and it was why the time spread out before me now scared me so much. But what if it was the same for Mum? What if she'd kept moving to flee from her pain, escape from the memories?

I exited the building and set off across the car park towards the visitors' spaces, Nanna's theory about Mum replaying in my head. It didn't sound as though Mum had been lonely before she went travelling, but I wondered whether she was now. As long as she kept moving, she'd always have unfamiliar places to explore, strangers to meet, new photography objectives and therefore plenty of distractions. But if she stopped...

'Lars?'

I did a double-take at the dark-haired woman who'd stopped beside me. 'Danika?'

'What are you doing here?' she asked.

'My nanna's just moved in. You?'

She lifted up a glasses case. 'Patient left these behind yesterday so I said I'd drop them back, save them the trouble.' She glanced at the case, shaking her head. 'No idea why I felt the need to show you these, as if you weren't going to take my word for it.'

We smiled at each other and I felt the warmth of her friendship.

'Aw, I've missed you, Lars. Are you doing anything now?'

'No specific plans.'

'In that case, how about we grab a coffee? Or maybe even lunch? It'll be good to catch up.'

'Lunch would be great.' After a tough week stirring up a whirlpool of mixed emotions, it was so great to see Danika and an hour or so with her would be a welcome distraction and the perfect pick-me-up.

'Brilliant! Wait here while I do my good deed for the day. Won't be long.'

9

LARS

Danika suggested The Chocolate Pot on Castle Street and we agreed to meet inside as we'd be travelling in separate cars. I managed to get caught at every light on red so Danika beat me to it and had already secured us a table and was perusing the menu when I arrived.

'Cat said she bumped into you at the petrol station,' Danika said after we'd placed our order.

'Yes, and she said she'd stayed over with Miles. They're not back together, are they?'

'I don't think so, but I've given up trying to keep up. Seriously, Lars, I love my sister but keeping track of her love life is exhausting. So, how's the last few months been for you?'

'Busy...'

I updated her on Nanna's move, my refurbishment plans and the completion of my business sale, pausing the conversation briefly when our drinks arrived.

'So, what's been going on with you?' I asked.

She shrugged. 'Same old. Still managing the practice and batting away the staff moans about the preferential treatment a certain someone gets. Still wishing Cat would take her drama and mess and move back in with our parents. Again, love my sister but she's exhausting to live with, especially for someone like me.'

'Someone like you?' I asked, not sure of her meaning and wondering if I'd missed something.

'An introvert. People exhaust me. No, that's not quite right. I'm fine around people as long as it's not constant. My job's ideal for it because, although I do have contact with staff and patients, it's intermittent and I can balance that with being on my own in my office and dealing with the paperwork. By the time we close, my energy's spent and I just want to come home and switch off, which is impossible when Cat's around.'

Our food appeared and, both admitting we'd skipped breakfast, we tucked into several eager mouthfuls before resuming our conversation.

'You always chatted to me when I called for Cat,' I said. 'Was that exhausting for you? Be honest.'

Danika laughed. 'Actually, no. You're easy company and, even if I'd had a tiring day, I still looked forward to seeing you, which is more than can be said for most of Cat's other boyfriends. She's had some who've fired a gazillion questions at me and I half expected them to hook me up to a lie detector kit at any moment. There've been some who've done nothing but talk about themselves, and even some who've flirted with me. What's that all about? But you were just you and it was like having a lovely chinwag with an old friend. And, as I said, I've missed it. I even asked Cat for your number, thinking I'd get in touch and see if you fancied a coffee at some point, but she hadn't kept it. Sorry.'

'Don't be. I didn't keep hers either and I regretted not asking for yours. It's not easy to meet new friends when you work from home.'

'Of course! I've always worked at the practice so I'm used to having colleagues I see every day. Just as well the universe sent us to Bay View at the same time, determined to reunite two lost friends.'

We smiled at each other across the table and I loved how, without making a big issue of it, we'd established that it was friendship we were interested in and not something romantic. It wasn't just because the idea of dating Danika after dating her sister didn't sit comfortably with me. It was more because that spark of attraction wasn't there. It struck me that Danika had never mentioned any romantic relationships and if we were going to start seeing each other as friends, which it seemed we were, it made sense to raise it now.

'Are you seeing anyone?' I asked.

Danika shook her head. 'I'm not really interested in a relationship. I've never met anyone who I've wanted to be with for longer than two or three months and

I'm not convinced I ever will. I like my life the way it is and I'm not sure I want anyone disrupting that. Does that sound selfish?'

'Not at all. When you've settled into a routine that makes you happy, it's a huge thing adjusting that for someone else.' As I said the words, it struck me I could easily have been talking about Mum before she went to Iceland and met Pabbi. But then she had met the right person. Or right for a while. And it further struck me that she could have been talking about me too. I wouldn't say I was set in my ways but my time with Cat had proved to me that I'd rather be single than with someone who I didn't see in my long-term future.

'I've never wanted kids,' Danika added, 'so I've never felt the proverbial clock ticking and I've never felt lonely or like I'm missing out on anything. I've got a small circle of friends, I'm close to my family, I love my job and my house. The only thing that would make my life better is if Cat grew up and found herself a meaningful relationship instead of this childish *I adore bad boys* nonsense. If she could find true love and move out, my life would be bliss.'

'So you do believe in love?'

'Absolutely. And, don't get me wrong, I'm not averse to it happening to me. I'd be as shocked as a badger on an electric fence, mind you, but if that *wow!* moment ever happens, I won't run from it. I'm just not bothered if it doesn't happen. What about you? Searching for the elusive one?'

'Searching would imply actually doing something about it. I *would* like to meet someone who isn't after me for my money or my ravishing good looks.' I grinned at Danika and she laughed. 'I'd like to get married, have kids, get a dog and a cat, but working from home isn't exactly conducive to meeting anyone and a dating app is—'

'How you met Cat,' she finished for me. 'Yeah, I can see why that wouldn't sell it. Nothing to stop you getting pets in the meantime.'

'True, but I need to get settled in my new home before I can think about it, and I need to decide what to do with myself now that the business sale has gone through.'

Danika asked me about my role at My Study Hub and why I'd set up the business in the first place. I told her about volunteering in Hutton Wicklow Library and how I wanted to find something else to keep me occupied but wasn't sure what.

'We've got a receptionist position going. Job's yours if you want it.' She barely got to the end of the sentence before collapsing in giggles. 'Yeah, probably not. Something will come along.'

Our plates were cleared and, as there were a few people queuing by the door, we decided it was time to settle the bill and head off. As we stepped onto the cobbles of Castle Street, Danika said she needed to pick up a few things while she was in town, starting with a visit to Bay Books.

'It's been great to see you,' Danika said, giving me a hug outside the bookshop. 'We'll catch up again soon.'

'Definitely. See you later.'

I'd only taken a few paces when she called me back.

'What did I say about something coming along?' she asked, pointing at a poster in the window. 'A four-month contract in a bookshop. Could that be any more perfect for you, Mr Bookworm, while you make some decisions about what you want to do long-term?'

'Sounds ideal,' I said, hoping my tone sounded as positive as the words.

'Take a photo of the details, then.'

I did as she suggested but I knew I wasn't going to apply. In theory, it would be a dream job but there were two huge problems. The first was that Bay Books held so many memories of my sister. I hadn't stepped inside the bookshop since the summer before I started senior school and I wasn't sure how it would affect me if I did so now. The second was that I knew who owned Bay Books and, after how badly I'd behaved towards her at school, there was no way she'd ever even consider me for an interview. I wouldn't in her position.

10
LILY

'You've got to be kidding me!' I cried.

Cassie looked up from checking off the Friday morning delivery. 'What's up?'

'You'll never guess who's applied for the job. Lars Jóhannsson.'

'Lars the Arse? No way!'

'Well, he's going straight into the rapidly growing rejection pile,' I said, giving an involuntary shudder.

'What's he been up to since school? Let me see.' Cassie joined me behind the till and scanned down Lars's CV. 'Wow! Look at all those awards! Impressive. Doesn't surprise me, though. He always was super bright.'

'But, as you say, an absolute arse.'

Suddenly I was back at Laurendale School on my very first day, feeling lost and lonely without any friends. During the morning break, I went in search of somewhere to hide with my book. Rounding the back of the sports hall, my stomach sank when I spotted somebody had beaten me to it. A young lad with spiky blond hair was leaning against the wall, his head buried in a copy of Lemony Snicket's *The Vile Village*. I took a step closer and my heart leapt as I recognised him as a friend from Bay Books. Although I was too young to officially be on the shop's payroll, I often helped out during the school holidays and the occasional Saturday. Each time I'd seen him, we'd chatted about our favourite books and exchanged recommendations.

'Lars?' I said, excitement flowing through me that I might have a friend at my new school after all.

He looked up and I expected him to smile at me, but his expression was blank. 'I'm reading.'

He looked back down at his book and continued reading. I stared at him, stunned by his uninterest. This wasn't the Lars I knew from the bookshop. He *loved* discussing books with me. And then a thought struck me. The uniform. The plaits. He was used to seeing me in casual clothes with my hair down.

'It's me! Lily from Bay Books.'

He raised his head once more and I expected a smile and an apology for not recognising me, but his expression remained blank. 'I came here to get away from everyone.'

'Me too.' I fished *Anne of Green Gables* out of my bag to show him that we were of the same mind. 'I'm so relieved to see you here.'

'Why?'

'My best friend ditched me for this awful girl who picks on me and I don't know anyone else but at least I've got one friend now.'

Lars closed his book with a sigh. 'We're not friends, Lily.'

'I know we don't know each other very well, but we both love books and I thought—'

'We're *not* friends,' he repeated with emphasis. 'The only friends I need are between the pages of books. Leave me alone.'

And he walked away without looking back. I sank against the wall, clutching my book to my chest, tears pooling in my eyes before they broke free and tracked down my cheeks. What was wrong with me? Why did nobody want to be my friend? Jordan had ditched me because of my love of books but if somebody with that shared passion didn't even want to be friends with me, what hope was there?

'He might have changed,' Cassie suggested, pulling me back to the present day. 'School was a long time ago.'

'I'd like to think he has, but...' I closed my eyes tightly and released a frustrated squeal, that painfully familiar feeling of rejection stabbing at me.

'It was his loss and my gain.' Cassie stroked my arm. 'School-day traumas aside, at least you know he hasn't lied on his CV about his passion for books.'

The number of applicants we'd had over the years who pretended to love books never ceased to amaze me. I opened my eyes and looked at the computer screen once more. On paper, Lars was the perfect candidate. He was volunteering at one of the village libraries, had customer service experience from running his own business and was clearly organised. His technical skills were through the roof so he'd have no problems learning our system and, while being completely over-qualified for the role, he'd explained that it would be the perfect length contract for him while he decided on his next career move.

'Do you have many other choices?' Cassie asked.

'Nobody nearly as strong. But he's over-qualified. He's run his own business for seventeen years. What if he tries to take over and tell me how to run mine?'

'I doubt he'd do that and, if he did, you're the boss and you'd find the words to put him back in his box. You could always discuss it at the interview – nip it in the bud straightaway.'

I rested my elbows on the desk and sank my head into my hands. 'What if he's awful to me again?'

'Then he doesn't get the job and you never have to cross paths with him again,' Cassie said, gently. 'But if you don't interview him, I think you're cutting off your nose to spite your face. He's a strong candidate and you know it.'

I raised my head. 'You're right.'

'And if you think working with him might be bearable and you offer him the job and then discover he's still the twerp he was at school, you sack him off. Failed probation. Gone. Easy peasy.'

'Lemon squeezy.'

'Gherkin scones will make you queasy.'

'Where on earth did that come from?' I asked, smiling at her.

'No idea, but it restored your smile so my work here is done. Now do some work, *Little Miss Perfect*.' She winked at me and I shook my head at her.

'If he calls me that again, it's game over.'

'I dunno. Could finally be your chance to find out what he meant by it.'

'After all these years, I'm not convinced I want to find out.'

'You do. Because it's been bugging you for over two decades. If you do take him on, I guarantee you'll ask him to explain himself one day.'

I smiled again. 'I probably will and it had better be a damn good explanation.'

While Cassie restocked the cookery books upstairs, my thoughts drifted back to that first day at school. When break ended, I'd returned to our classroom with a heavy heart, trying not to let my imagination drift into five lonely years ahead of me.

I looked up, astonished, as a pretty girl with long blonde hair slipped into the seat beside me and smiled. 'We've moved house and I don't know anyone at this school, but I've decided you and I are going to be friends.'

It was such a contrast to the confrontation with Lars that I couldn't help feeling suspicious. Was this a wind-up?

'Why?' I asked.

'Which would you rather be if you had the choice – divinely beautiful or dazzlingly clever or angelically good?'

My heart leapt as I recognised the quote and she opened up her bag, revealing a dog-eared copy of *Anne of Avonlea* – the second book in the series.

'I spotted you with book one earlier,' she said. 'Have you read them all?'

'Several times.'

'Me too. My all-time favourite book is *Alice's Adventures in Wonderland*, but this series is a close second. I'm Cassie and it would be *dazzlingly clever*, I think.'

'Lily, and same here although *divinely beautiful* would be nice and…'

The teacher entered the classroom, drawing the conversation to a close, but Cassie gave me the warmest smile and I felt positive for the first time in weeks.

Anne Shirley said she and Diana Barry were *kindred spirits* and, over the weeks that followed, I realised I'd found my own kindred spirit in Cassie Hynde. Or, rather, she'd found me thanks to her spotting me sitting all alone on a wall reading *Anne of Green Gables* after Lars Jóhannsson so cruelly rejected my offer of friendship.

I wasn't in any classes with Jordan or Rhianna but, if we crossed paths during breaks or lunchtime, the pair of them couldn't resist making snide comments. I'd be lying if I said it didn't hurt, but I was largely able to brush it off, especially with Cassie by my side. What was harder to brush off was Lars's rejection, especially when I had so many classes with him. Even though we'd only ever talked about books together, I'd genuinely believed we were friends and it hurt that not only had he not felt the same but that he no longer wanted anything to do with me.

I had to be a glutton for punishment because I tried on several other occasions to connect with Lars. I refused to accept there hadn't been a bond between us and, having seen him so at ease in Bay Books, I was convinced it was the school environment which was holding him back. I also felt sorry for him. He was half-English, half-Icelandic and sometimes spoke in a mixture of both languages. I never knew whether he did it unconsciously or deliberately but it drew the attention of the bullies and the impatience of several teachers. I couldn't bear to see anyone being bullied, especially as I knew how it felt to be on the receiving end. Towards the end of the first term, I suggested to Cassie that we sit with Lars at lunchtime and offer our friendship. But he threw it back in our faces, barely acknowledged Cassie and had a go at me for thinking I was *perfect*. My appearance at the time was anything but perfect and, while my academic record was good, his was better so I couldn't make sense of what he was on about. Next thing I knew, he'd christened me *Little Miss Perfect*, as though I was a character from a Roger Hargreaves book. Fortunately, he didn't have the friendships or influence for my nonsense nickname to catch on.

After that, I stopped trying to salvage the friendship I thought we'd had and steered clear of him but that wasn't always possible as sometimes teachers partnered us up to work together. I hated the tension between us when that happened and, when I was fifteen, I'd had enough. I demanded he tell me what his problem was with me, especially when I'd never behaved unreasonably towards him and was never going to. I'd expected a retort along the lines of, *of course not because you're Little Miss Perfect*, but he looked shocked and suggested we get on with our assignment in silence instead. We weren't partnered up after that so I never found out whether my outburst had any impact.

At sixth form, Lars and I had no A levels in common and, although I spotted him occasionally, we never spoke again and it made me sad because I missed the young boy I knew from the shop and couldn't help feeling that he was still in there somewhere and perhaps I should have tried harder to find him, but how could I? How does anyone find the courage to keep pushing at a door that's repeatedly slammed in their face? It was a bit of a theme for me. If someone pushed me away, I didn't fight for them. I hadn't done it with Jordan or Lars. I hadn't done it with Ewan or Wes either. But I had fought for Justin. My biological father had repeatedly pushed me away and let me down and I kept going back for more. It made no sense to me, especially when he was the one who, out of all of them, had added the least to my life.

I glanced back at Lars's CV. We needed the staff and he was by far the best applicant for the job. And, in all honesty, I was curious. What sort of man had the boy who'd rejected me grown into?

11

LARS

My stomach was in knots as I walked from the car park towards Castle Street for my interview at Bay Books. With setting up My Study Hub at seventeen and being my own boss ever since, I'd never had a formal job interview in my whole life. I'd been an interviewer, of course, while I carefully selected the right people for my team as the business expanded, but it was going to be strange being on the other side of the table. Opposite Lily.

I'd meant it about not applying for the job at Bay Books but Danika had appointed herself as my careers advisor and messaged me each day asking if I'd submitted my CV or even if I needed help putting a CV together – something else I didn't have because I'd never needed one. After a few days of fobbing her off, she'd FaceTimed me.

'This job is perfect for you and we both know it. What's stopping you applying, because I know there's something you're not telling me?'

So I told her about how much of an idiot I'd been at school and how there was no way Lily Appleton would have forgotten the cruel way in which I cast aside our friendship.

'School was a long time ago, Lars,' she said. 'Are you still that idiot?'
'God, no!'
'Are you sorry for what you did?'
'Very.'

'Then apply for the job. Worst-case scenario is she remembers, she's still hurt and you don't get an interview. What have you lost?'

'My dignity,' I joked.

When Danika raised her eyebrows at me, I shook my head. 'Okay, I'll have lost nothing.'

'So write that CV and get submitting.'

Which is exactly what I did, although admittedly only the evening before the closing date. I'm not sure if I'd have even done that if Danika hadn't driven round to Fountain Street and stood over me. I genuinely didn't expect to get shortlisted and had assumed the email which arrived from Bay Books would be a rejection, a thrill running through me when it wasn't. The email explained that interviews needed to be on an evening after the shop had closed and would be with the co-owners Marcus and Lily.

As soon as he opened the door, I recognised Marcus – tall and slim with a friendly face, the only change being that his dark hair was now greying round the temples – and experienced a momentary flashback to my childhood, handing over the books I'd chosen at the till and having him tell me what great choices I'd made.

'Thanks for meeting us after hours, Lars,' he said as he shook my hand. 'We're through the back in the children's section.'

The lights in the main part of the shop were on low and I glanced around me, a feeling of being home consuming me as it always did whenever I was in a bookshop or library. I hadn't been in here for over twenty years but there was a familiarity about the place which had practically been a second home for me growing up. Until it became a place to avoid because of how I'd treated Lily.

I followed Marcus to the rear of the shop and it was like stepping back in time. The shelves were arranged just as I remembered them and there were still colourful tub chairs dotted around the room. Marcus said something but I didn't catch it, a memory overwhelming me of crouching in front of the shelves beside my four-year-old sister. Pia had loved coming here and I'd loved being here with her, seeing her eyes sparkle as she scanned the shelves, ran her fingers along the colourful spines and carefully eased out a book which called to her.

'Are you okay?' Marcus asked.

Swallowing hard on the lump in my throat, I nodded. 'Sudden childhood memory being back here.'

He smiled and indicated that I should sit down in one of the tub chairs.

There were two folding chairs set up opposite it, each with a clipboard and pen on them, and a low table to one side.

'It's not very formal but we prefer to conduct interviews surrounded by books rather than downstairs in the staffroom,' Marcus said. 'Lily will be along in... Ah! That's her now.'

I heard the door closing.

'Sorry, Dad,' a woman called. 'There was a huge queue.'

'Our candidate's here,' Marcus called back.

Lily appeared holding several bottles of water. My stomach started spinning as she placed them on the table then straightened up and looked at me.

'I believe you already know my daughter, Lily,' Marcus said and my nerves cracked up another notch. So she definitely remembered me and her dad knew who I was too.

'It's been a long time since we were at school together,' Lily said, proffering her hand.

I rose and shook her hand, noting how cold it was from carrying the chilled bottles. Her grip was firm and I wouldn't have blamed her if she'd given my hand a hard squeeze – it would have been no less than I deserved. I searched her face for signs of animosity. She wasn't smiling at me, but she wasn't scowling either. As she'd brought up the subject of school, it was probably best to address that straight off.

'Yes, it is,' I said, settling back into my chair. 'So much has changed since then. I've changed, thankfully.'

If I'd been meeting Lily on her own, it would have been an appropriate moment to spill out a heartfelt apology but I didn't feel I could in front of her dad. I wasn't bothered about making a fool of myself but I didn't know what sort of relationship he and Lily had and how much about her school days she'd shared with him, so I hoped this was enough for now.

'Pleased to hear it,' Lily said. 'So, let's get started. We thought we'd tell you a bit about the bookshop and why we're advertising a short-term contract before we go through the questions. Sound okay?'

'Sounds great. Thank you.'

Between them, Lily and Marcus briefly outlined the history of the bookshop, the range of books, the events they held and their values, concluding that the contract was to cover for Marcus who was about to have a double knee replacement operation. They were both so animated as they spoke, the love they had for the shop and their passion for the written word coming across in spades. They viewed Bay Books as an essential part of the community and I loved the initiatives they'd introduced to try and engage with readers from various ages and backgrounds.

I remembered liking Marcus when I was a kid and that warmth he exuded was still present, but it was Lily who stole my attention. If I was asked to summarise in five words the Lily I remembered from school, I'd probably have said quiet, polite, studious, kind and sensitive which made me want to hang my head in shame. She'd never done anything wrong and I'd been horrible to her. Now I still recognised the young girl from school but the five words which sprang to mind were strong, confident, engaging, passionate and inspirational. I wasn't the only one who'd changed since school.

Lily looked different too. She still had long dark hair but it had some lighter streaks in it which really suited her. I remembered her hair being somewhat frizzy but it was now curly. Her long eyelashes accentuated her soft brown eyes. I'd always thought that Lily had a pretty face but now she was beautiful and I kept having to remind myself to look at Marcus too instead of giving all my attention to my former nemesis. No, that wasn't true. Lily had never been my nemesis. She'd only ever offered friendship and had never been unkind to me, even though I'd given her plenty of cause to be.

'Any questions so far?' Marcus asked, drawing my attention back to him.

'No, it's a great bookshop and everything you've done with it sounds really impressive. I used to come here loads when I was a kid.' My voice caught in my throat as another memory snuck up on me of being here with Pia one Christmas. There'd been a shelving unit in the shape of a Christmas tree and it had a special name – the Bookmas tree. I glanced over to where it had been, picturing Pia slowly circling it, beside herself with excitement at all the festive reads tempting her.

'But you've never been in as an adult?' Lily asked, drawing my gaze back to her. Her tone was light, but the words felt like a challenge.

'I set up my business at seventeen and worked seven days a week for years so I rarely made it into town. I've ordered from you online, though. I like to support local businesses where I can.'

'We really appreciate that,' Marcus said, smiling at me. 'Now that we've told you all about the shop, let's move onto the questions for you. Please will you briefly walk us through your career so far, particularly highlighting the skills and experiences which you think make you a good candidate for this role.'

* * *

'It went well,' I told Danika over the phone as I walked back to the car. 'Or at least I think it did.'

'How was Lily with you?'

'Better than I deserved. I hope how much I've changed since school came across, but we'll just have to see. Even if I don't get the job, I'm glad you talked me into applying.'

'Do you want the job?'

'I *really* want the job,' I admitted.

'Then I'm keeping everything crossed for you. When will you hear?'

'They were interviewing their final candidate after me so they said they should be in touch in the next couple of days.'

'Okay. Let me know when you hear back. Don't be discouraged if it's a no, but I've got a feeling it won't be.'

I'd reached my car so we ended the call and I set off back to Fountain Street. I'd surprised myself by how badly I wanted the job. It wasn't because I loved the shop itself, the pleasure of being surrounded by books every day, the events held at Bay Books or their values, good as all of those things were. It was because of the flood of happy memories. Sitting in the children's section just now, I'd felt so close to my sister and, while it had been emotional, it had brought me an incredible sense of peace.

And there was another reason I wanted to work there – Lily. I pictured how her eyes sparkled as she spoke about the shop, the way her curls framed her heart-shaped face. I could still feel the trace of her cold hand in mine, hear her lilting laughter. Even though I'd noticed changes in her, I'd still recognised the young girl I'd met after Mum and Pabbi declared Pia too ill to visit Bay Books anymore, the young girl who'd filled that void my sister's absence created with her exuberant chatter about the books she'd read, the girl I'd desperately hoped would be helping her dad out every time I visited.

I kicked at a stone on the pavement, frustrated with myself that I'd pushed her away. It had never entered my head that she could be at Laurendale School. We'd always been so engrossed in our bookish conversations that we hadn't spoken about where we lived or went to school so her presence that first day had completely thrown me. How often over the years had I wished I could take back everything I'd said and done? Although, at the time, I'm not sure I'd been capable of reacting differently.

Reaching my car, I sank into the driver's seat, ashamed by my foolish younger self and cursing the present-day me for not apologising to Lily.

I couldn't imagine she'd want to work with me. I felt as though the interview had gone well but was it enough to overcome the past? All I could do was hope because I knew that I'd miss her if I didn't see her again, that I'd feel some kind of emptiness inside, that my life would be incomplete. Because that was how I'd felt since the day I told her I didn't need any friends. The day I rejected her before she could abandon me like everyone else in my life had.

12
LILY

'What did you think?' Dad asked when I returned to the children's section after letting Lars out.

'Better than expected. I'll admit that the grown-up Lars is a lot more palatable than the schoolboy one.'

'But...?'

I sank down into the tub chair Lars had vacated. 'But I'm still not sure.'

'What's holding you back? Is it just about how he was at school or was there something from the interview that concerned you?'

'The interview was great. What he did with his business is seriously impressive and there's no doubting his passion for books. He ticks all the boxes for what we want and a million more so it's not him... or it's not the present-day him.'

'You can't shake off how he was at school.'

'I'm sorry, Dad. I want to, I really do. I know it's me and my issue and that's not fair when he's such a strong candidate.'

'Don't feel guilty,' Dad said, shaking his head. 'If you don't feel comfortable around him, then it's a no.'

I did feel guilty, though, and felt the need to justify my thinking. 'It's just that a good team is so important here. The staff we have must be good with customers and I don't doubt that Lars would be, but they have to fit into the team too and Lars would be starting off on the back foot. Most of the team started out as strangers with a clean slate and a positive impression but Lars doesn't have that. I had to keep reminding myself to smile and be professional when all I wanted to do was tell him off for being a tosser at school.'

Dad laughed. 'Tell me how you really feel about him.'

I took a glug from my bottle. 'I'm not saying it's a categoric no. You know I always need to reflect on big decisions overnight so I'll do that with Lars but, at this precise moment in time, my gut is telling me that we'd be better off with Melissa Gilchrist.'

Melissa had applied early on so we'd interviewed her at the back end of last week. A woman in her mid-fifties, she'd recently been made redundant. She wasn't a voracious reader like we'd have hoped, but she'd told us she enjoyed reading. She hadn't demonstrated any sort of snobbery towards particular genres – something that was very important to us. What she'd lacked in book knowledge she made up for in retail experience and, as she'd never be on her own in the shop, there'd always be somebody around who could fill her knowledge gaps if customers needed advice.

'Lars is my frontrunner by a clear mile,' Dad said, 'but Melissa would be my second choice. Mind you, our next candidate looks good on paper.'

I picked up my clipboard and scanned down the CV from a Philippa Rose who was currently a hotel receptionist, had retail experience before that, was a big reader and an aspiring writer.

And a no-show.

We waited for twenty minutes – more than enough time for her if she was running late – before calling it a day.

'I guess it's between Melissa and Lars then,' Dad said, folding up the chairs while I gathered the bottles together.

'Looks like it. I'll give them both some serious thought tonight.'

'You know I'll support whatever you decide,' Dad said. 'It's you who has to work with them, after all.'

'I know, but we're partners so your opinion counts just as much as mine.'

* * *

Lying on my stomach on my bed in Green Gables later that evening, I stared at Melissa's and Lars's CVs and interview notes side by side in front of me. There was no pressure to make a decision tonight or even tomorrow, but we did want the chosen candidate to start on Monday and it was only fair to give them as much notice as possible.

With a sigh, I picked up Melissa's paperwork and flicked through it. I did the same to Lars's and shook my head. There was only one way to do this. Rolling off the bed, I retrieved a notepad and pen from my desk and started a pros and cons list for each candidate.

Twenty minutes later, I sat back and looked at what I'd written. As anticipated, the pros for both were a long list with very few entries in the cons column. The pros emphasised what I already knew – that they were both strong candidates – but I wasn't sure how I felt about the cons. On Melissa's list, I'd written *Does she really love books?* I scanned down my notes again and it was actually the ones I'd made during Lars's interview which set off alarm bells about Melissa. When we'd asked Lars about his interest in books, he'd immediately broken into a smile and had waxed lyrical about how important books were in Icelandic culture, visits to the library as a child, how much he loved volunteering at Hutton Wicklow Library now, his floor-to-ceiling bookshelves, and the books which had made a lasting impact on him. I'd written down a mixture of the words he'd used and how he'd come across: *passionate, animated, part of his culture, lost without books, loves learning/learns something from everything he reads.* On Melissa's interview script, I'd written: *mostly reads on holiday.*

Holding my hands against my cheeks, I shook my head, a strong niggle in my gut that perhaps Melissa wasn't the right person for the job. Every single member of staff we had lived and breathed books – it was their passion for books that had led them to apply for a job with us in the first place. Recommendations to customers were an important part of what we did and was undoubtedly one of the reasons the business hadn't just survived but thrived for nearly forty years. They didn't need to read across all genres by any means, but they did need to understand the market trends and be able to demonstrate that awareness to customers. Would Melissa be interested enough to do that?

I glanced at the biggest con on Lars's list: *School. Can I get over it?* I closed my eyes tightly and scrunched my hands into my curls, releasing a frustrated, 'Argh!'

If I rejected Lars because of how he'd behaved towards me half a lifetime ago, it seemed spectacularly unfair on him. Melissa's major con was about her but Lars's was about me and the hurt I'd clearly been hanging onto. But was it realistic to try to take *me* out of the equation? As Dad said earlier, I'd be the one who had to work with him. I had to be comfortable with that and the rest of the team would take my lead. If they sensed any latent hostility towards Lars, it would influence how they felt about him and that wasn't fair on anyone. We prided ourselves on having created a wonderful place to work with staff who were passionate and loyal. I couldn't risk jeopardising that.

With another heavy sigh, I checked the time on my phone. I could do with speaking to Cassie. She knew Lars from school and had hated the way he'd treated me, but she'd also encouraged me to interview him, saying he'd likely have changed. It was nearly half ten – time for bed and definitely far too late to ring Cassie – so I'd seek her counsel tomorrow.

Settling down under the duvet a little later, I switched off my bedside lamp and closed my eyes, trying to empty my head of pros and cons lists and focus on going to sleep. But it wasn't the lists I couldn't eject from my thoughts – it was Lars's face.

I'd been nine when I first saw him in the shop, sitting cross-legged on the floor reading the blurb on the back of the latest book in the Harry Potter series – *Harry Potter and the Goblet of Fire*. He'd sported a blond buzz cut which, with his square jawline and high cheekbones, made him look all angular and spiky. I'd just finished reading the same book and had hovered nearby, trying to decide whether he looked friendly or scary. I watched as he opened up the book and turned to the first page ever so gently. He smiled as he scanned down it and entered a world of witches and wizards and I knew at that moment that he loved books as much as me and that he was definitely going to be a friend rather than a foe. Which he had been until that day behind the sports hall.

At the age of thirty-four, Lars had *grown into his face* as my Granny Blue would say. His hair had darkened and was long at the top, stylishly swept back from his forehead, with waves at the back, softening his features and accentuating his grey eyes. Those eyes. I'd noticed a sadness and vulnerability in them at school which I hadn't noticed when we spoke about books in the shop. I had no idea why he was sad but I'd thought that showing him some kindness might help him unburden it, which is why I'd tried on several occasions over the years to befriend him, only to have it thrown back in my face every time.

In bed, I turned onto my side, clutching my duvet to my chest, my heart pounding once more as a buried memory surfaced. That first day at school, I'd wanted Lars's friendship but as the school years progressed, it became more than that. Even though he made it clear he wanted nothing to do with me, I felt drawn to him. Fancied him. My very first crush. And my first broken heart.

13

LILY

'We're all in agreement?' I asked, looking from Dad to Cassie and back to Dad late the following morning.

They confirmed they were so I grabbed the cardboard wallet full of CVs and headed down to the staff room where I flicked the kettle on. Cassie had arrived for her shift an hour ago and, between serving customers, Dad and I had updated her on Lars's interview last night and the pros and cons of Lars and Melissa as the only two suitable candidates.

I'd awoken this morning from an unsettled night in which I'd drifted in and out of jumbled dreams of my school days, seeing Lars again evidently having triggered the release of several previously forgotten memories. As I dressed, I'd still felt torn between the two candidates but talking it over with Dad and Cassie had helped and we now had a plan with which I felt comfortable.

After sending some hot drinks up in Jeeves, I sat down at the table, removed Melissa's CV and dialled her number. We'd all agreed that we needed a better understanding of her passion and knowledge for books before we could consider offering her the job but, if she responded well to a few more questions, it was hers.

Melissa answered on the third ring with a cheerful, 'Melissa Gilchrist speaking.'

'Hi, Melissa, it's Lily Appleton from Bay Books. Is it a good time for a quick chat?'

'Absolutely.'

'We've come to the end of our interviews and have narrowed it down to the final few candidates. I just wanted to check a couple of things with you before we make our decision.'

'Fire away.'

'Great. We talked about your interest in books during the interview and I'd just like to explore that a bit further. Is that all right?'

Silence.

'Melissa? Are you still there?'

'Yes, erm... Can I be honest with you, Lily?'

'That would be appreciated.'

'I don't really enjoy reading that much. I used to when I was a kid but then I discovered boys and, let's face it, how many men are turned on by a book geek?'

I stiffened, the smile slipping from my face. *Plenty of men, actually. Men who also like books, men who like women who like books, men who...* I shook my head to dislodge the train of thought and refocused on what Melissa was saying, although I had a sinking feeling that the niggles I'd had about her last night were about to be proved right.

'It's not that I don't read. I *always* take a book on holiday with me, although the one I took to Malta last summer is still by my bed, gathering dust, and I can't for the life of me remember what's happened so far.'

'So would it be fair to say that books aren't a passion for you?' I asked, fighting hard to sound positive.

'That's right.'

'And, actually, you aren't a reader at all?'

'Not really.'

'So what you said in the interview—'

'I could hardly say I hate books, could I?' She sounded indignant as she cut across me. 'You'd never have given me the job if I had.'

She laughed and I laughed with her, thinking how I'd just dodged a bullet.

'Thanks for that, Melissa. As I say, we're down to our last few candidates so I'll let you know by tomorrow at the latest.'

'That's fine. Oh, while you're on the phone, can I just check the hours? You said it's Monday to Friday but you might need me to work some weekends in December.'

'That's right.'

'The weekdays are fine but I don't want to work weekends and you should probably know that I've got a holiday booked in December. I go on the 13th and get back the day after Boxing Day.'

I clamped my lips together, eyes scrunched tightly closed and counted to three before I responded in a positive-sounding tone, 'I've noted that down. Thanks, Melissa. We'll be in touch very soon. Have a fabulous day.'

'I will. You too.'

If I'd been using a landline, I'd have slammed the phone down into its cradle. If Melissa's evident dislike for books hadn't already been a dealbreaker, her lack of availability in our busiest month would have been. I'd made it very clear in the advert how important it was to be free in December.

Grabbing a red biro, I placed a big cross over Melissa's CV and picked up Lars's with a sigh.

'It's for the business,' I murmured. 'I can put my personal feelings aside for Bay Books. I can be a professional.' Although I had to acknowledge the skip of my heart at the thought of seeing Lars again. If he accepted.

My hands were shaking and my heart was thumping so heavily as I attempted to call Lars that I kept pressing the wrong numbers. Finally getting it right, my stomach churned as I waited for the call to connect and for Lars to answer. It rang and rang and I was convinced I was about to get his voicemail when he picked up, giving his full name just like Melissa had.

'Hi, Lars, it's Lily at Bay Books. How are you?'

'Lily! Hi! I'm good, thanks. Yourself?'

I'd noticed during his interview that he'd lost his accent – something that was even more obvious to me when speaking to him over the phone. I wondered if it had been intentional after the kids picked on him about it at school.

'Yeah, fine. Look, erm, we've finished our interviews now and considered each candidate carefully and, erm…' My throat had gone very dry and I grabbed the mug of tea I'd made and took a quick gulp, immediately regretting it because it was far too hot and scalded my mouth.

'It's a no, isn't it?' Lars said. 'I understand. I knew it was a long shot but it was worth a try. It was good to see you and your dad again. I really appreciate you giving me the interview opportunity. I didn't think you would.'

Although I couldn't see his face, I could hear the sadness in his voice that I'd seen in his eyes back at school.

'What makes you say that?' I asked.

'After the way I treated you at school. You didn't deserve that when all you did was try to be nice to me. I was bang out of order but... No, I'm not going to rattle off any excuses. I was totally in the wrong and I'm sorry for any hurt I caused you back then.'

I clapped my hand to my chest, stunned. The last thing I'd expected was an apology and it had been so heartfelt. The knot in my stomach loosened somewhat and I felt a lot more positive about what I was about to do.

'Thank you for saying that,' I said, my voice sounding small and distant as I battled with my emotions. 'It means a lot.'

'I should have said it yesterday. Sorry.'

'The thing is, Lars, it isn't actually a no. If you're still interested, Dad and I would like to offer you a full-time four-month contract at Bay Books.'

There was a moment's silence, presumably while he let that sink in.

'You're serious?' he asked eventually.

'Deadly serious. We're looking for someone who has good customer service experience, which you have in spades, but what all our staff have in common is a passion for books. None of the other candidates came close to you in that regard so we'd love it if you could join us.'

'Really? Yes, please! You've just made my day! I promise you won't regret this.'

'Welcome to the team. Are you still all right to start at half ten on Monday?' I'd need to spend some one-to-one time with him first thing so I wanted to wait until Cassie had arrived for the start of her shift.

'Yes. I'll be there.'

'Great. I'll send you the contract by email as soon as I can – definitely by this evening – and just drop me an email or ring me if you have any questions.'

'I'll see you on Monday, then. Thanks for giving me a second chance. Bye.'

He disconnected the call before I could say anything else. *Thanks for giving me a second chance.* I hoped I wouldn't regret it but something in my gut told me I wouldn't. And something in my heart stirred too.

14
LARS

On Sunday afternoon, I loaded my vacuum cleaner into the boot of my car along with a caddy of cleaning items. Stepping back inside 17 Fountain Street for the last ever time, I took a deep breath. The sale wasn't scheduled for completion until Thursday but, as I was starting at Bay Books on Monday, it made sense to officially move into The Lodge before then. Mick had moved the contents of my bedroom and office over to Hutton Wicklow on Friday, I'd spent yesterday unpacking the essentials, and today's task had been a last clean of Nanna's house.

I thought it would be emotional checking the rooms for a final time but I felt strangely detached. With all her belongings gone, it didn't feel like Nanna's house anymore. Taking the stairs to the top floor two at a time, I checked my bedroom and office, closed the windows in both and felt that same sense of detachment, that it wasn't my home anymore either.

So many major changes had happened in recent months, I could barely catch my breath. Work-wise, I now had a short-term plan which I was excited about but I still had no idea what the long-term one was and, unusually for me – the person who liked organisation and structure – that felt okay.

'*Þetta reddast,*' I said, smiling to myself. Loosely translated as *it'll work out all right* or *it'll fix itself*, it was more than just an Icelandic phrase. It was a philosophy or a mindset deeply embedded in a culture at the mercy of Mother Nature where volcanic eruptions changed the landscape and destroyed homes, and where dark days made way for round-the-clock light. Pabbi used to say it all the time but, as Pia's health worsened, I heard him say it less and less. Personally, I loved the phrase and adopted that mindset where I could but there were some things that couldn't be fixed and would never be okay. Perhaps *þetta reddast* in those situations was more about a recognition that our feelings would be all right in the end even if the situation itself never could be; that gradual acceptance after something tragic.

I'd arranged to visit Nanna so, after placing the keys in an envelope with a note and dropping them through the letterbox at the estate agent's, I drove to Bay View.

'Thanks for doing that final clean,' Nanna said. 'I know some wouldn't bother but I can't bear the thought of passing on a messy house.'

'I can assure you it's dust free and sparkling.'

Over drinks, we chatted about my progress with unpacking and what Nanna had been up to over the past couple of days.

'Freyja rang yesterday,' she said. 'We had a lovely chat. She mentioned she hadn't spoken to you for a while.'

'I missed a call from her earlier in the week and I haven't had a chance to ring back.'

'I did tell her you were a bit swamped with the move.'

'Thanks. I'd hate for her to think I was ignoring her.'

Pabbi had met Freyja four years after returning to Iceland and they married three years after that. I was eighteen at the time and had just finished my A levels so Nanna and I went to Iceland for the wedding and spent a few extra days there. I had no issue with him meeting someone new and had always got along brilliantly with my stepmum. It was just my pabbi with whom I had the difficult relationship.

Pabbi had initially invited me to live with him in Iceland, but Mum wouldn't hear of it, which was rich considering she disappeared on her travels just a few months later. I visited for a week the following summer but, after eighteen months apart, I felt like a stranger around him. I stayed again the summer after that when I was thirteen and it was worse so, with my teenage hormones raging, I unleashed all my anger and pent-up frustration on him. I told him I hated him for abandoning me, for not loving Mum enough to stay together, for ruining my life.

Contact had been limited since then and I suspect it would have been nonexistent if it wasn't for him meeting Freyja and her acting as mediator. She'd pulled out all the stops to get to know me and, later, to ensure I had a relationship with my half-sister Kára, who was now fourteen, and my half-brother Ari, now twelve.

I was still thinking about Freyja when I arrived back at The Lodge an hour or so later and decided to give her a call.

'*Halló*,' she said, quickly answering the FaceTime call, a big smile on her face. 'Kára, Ari, say *halló* to your brother...'

All three of them spoke English fluently but liked to practise it on me so our conversations were often conducted in English on their side and Icelandic on mine as it was my only chance to speak the language.

Kára took the phone first and told me about a recent school trip to Reykjavík. She'd only just finished when Ari grabbed the phone from her to tell me he'd been picked for the handball team. He returned the phone to Freyja who asked about my new home and what I'd been doing with myself since the business sale completed.

'I've got a job in a bookshop,' I told her. 'I start on Monday.'

'A bookshop? Oh, Lars, that is wonderful.'

Kára and Ari mustn't have gone far as they reappeared behind Freyja, expressing their excitement. A love of literature was deep-rooted in the history and culture of Iceland, with a third of the population reading books daily. My brother and sister fired questions at me such as how big Bay Books was, how many books it had, whether I'd get a staff discount and the title of the first book I planned to buy.

'I wanted to invite you to visit for Christmas,' Freyja said when she had the phone back to herself, 'but I see now that it won't work with your bookshop job.'

'Sorry. Being available throughout December was one of the essentials.'

'Perhaps you will spend next Christmas with us?'

'Yeah, perhaps.'

She raised her eyebrows at me and fixed me with a stern look, both of us knowing full well the reason for my hesitation.

'He misses you,' she said.

'I wish I could believe that.'

'It's difficult for him.' She gave me a weak smile. 'Yes, I hear it. It's difficult for you too. I will fix this one day. I promise.'

I appreciated the sentiment but it wasn't her responsibility to fix things between Pabbi and me. Only we could do that and I wasn't convinced he wanted to. Over the years, I'd tried to apologise for my teenage outburst but he'd told me to stop dwelling on the past and focus on the future. If only he'd taken his own advice. We barely spoke and, if I visited, the atmosphere was strained.

'The conversation has become sad,' Freyja said, 'and I don't want this. We love you, Lars. We are so happy you will be working with books. Call regularly and let us know your favourites so we can read them too.'

'I will. I love you all too. Speak soon.'

I smiled at the goodbye shouts from my siblings and the wave from Freyja. I always ended a conversation with them feeling lifted. Even though we weren't physically close, we were emotionally. Just a shame the same couldn't be said for Pabbi.

I'd loved how supportive they were about my job. I'd been looking forward to starting at Bay Books but the enthusiasm from Freyja, Kára and Ari had me really fired up and I couldn't wait for Monday to come round. Putting my phone back in my jeans pocket, I gazed round the sparse lounge and wondered if my Icelandic family would ever visit. I could picture Freyja, Kára and Ari here, but Pabbi not so much. I couldn't imagine him ever returning to the UK. I tried to imagine what the room would look like with furniture and a Christmas tree but I was shockingly bad at visualising things like that. It wasn't how my mind worked. A vision of a woman sitting on a chair bouncing a baby girl on her knee suddenly appeared in my mind and my breath caught. The dark curls, the heart-shaped face. Lily.

15

LILY

'First day for Lars,' Dad said as we set off towards work. 'How are you feeling about him joining us?'

'Nervous.' From the moment I woke up my stomach had felt like it was on spin cycle.

'Because he's a new starter or because of who he is?'

'Bit of both.' I always felt anxious when we had new starters, hoping not only that we'd made the right decision but that they'd made the right choice about joining us.

'But more of the latter,' I admitted when Dad gave me a sideways glance. 'Like I told you, he's apologised so there's a line in the sand and hopefully it'll be smooth sailing from now on. Anyway, how was your swim this morning?'

Dad had turned sixty at the start of last year and had decided that a landmark birthday year was a great time to try new things. He'd kicked that off with joining a friend on a fishing trip but was soon bored rigid and regretting not having a book with him. He'd tried wild swimming but found no pleasure in the bitterly cold North Sea so only managed a few outings before deciding swimming was for him but in the warmth of the indoor pool. His doctor had encouraged him to keep it going, saying that it was great activity for strengthening the muscles around his knees, which would aid him with his recovery post-op.

'Good. It's amazing how good my knees feel when I'm in the water and then I get out and have a stark reminder as to why I need the operation.'

'Did you manage to get ahead with your assignments?' His final big birthday change had been to enrol on a Master's in English Literature with the Open University. He was loving studying again, joking that it kept him out of mischief on his Fridays and Saturdays off.

'Yes, but not as far as I'd originally planned because it struck me that studying might be a good way of relieving the boredom while I'm recovering. I'm dreading it. All that time off! I'll be crawling up the walls.'

'You're going to be a nightmare patient for Kadence, aren't you?' I said, smiling at him.

'I told her not to take the time off, but she wouldn't hear of it. She's a glutton for punishment, that one.'

As Dad's operation was after half-term and Mum would be back at college, my sister had insisted on taking a week off work to keep him company and make sure he didn't try to do too much too soon. Hendrix had booked a few days off at the start of the following week and I felt bad that I couldn't do my bit but Dad had reminded me that I was already doing more than my fair share at the shop.

* * *

Dad and I were unpacking our book delivery by the till when Lars arrived for his first day. He was ten minutes early, taking me by surprise, which I evidently didn't hide very well.

'I hate being late,' he said, his expression apologetic, 'but I think I might be a bit too early. Would you like me to walk round the block?'

'Erm, no, it's fine,' I said, reminding myself to smile because our school days were in the distant past and he'd already graciously apologised. Fresh start. 'Welcome to your first day.'

'From me too,' Dad added. 'Good to have you here.'

'Why don't you head downstairs?' I suggested. 'The staff room's down there. I'll join you as soon as Cassie comes up.'

'Cassie?'

I could practically see the cogs whirring.

'As in your best friend from school?' he added.

'That's right. I'll run through the team and their shifts as part of your induction. She's making the drinks now so do give her your order.'

'Okay. See you soon.'

I gave him the code to unlock the staff room door and he set off down the stairs.

'Do you think I should have warned him about Cassie before?' I asked Dad in hushed tones. 'She's promised to be on her best behaviour but you know Cassie. Doesn't stand for any nonsense.'

Dad smiled. 'Then he'd better be on his best behaviour too and not cause any nonsense.'

Cassie appeared at the top of the stairs a little later and Dad and I looked up at her expectantly.

'How was the reunion?' I asked. 'Did you play nicely?'

'I told him that, if he upsets you again, I'll kill him and his body will be fish food,' she said, her expression deadpan. 'Was that welcoming enough?'

Thankfully there were no customers within earshot as I'm not sure what they'd have made of that.

'I was very nice to him,' she said, smiling. 'Tell you what, that's an impressive glow-up he's had. If I wasn't getting married...'

'Cassie! Although I will admit he *has* improved with age. I just hope his personality has improved too. Wish me luck.'

With being on the lower ground level, the only natural light into the staff room came from some small, high windows at street level and Lars was peering out of them when I joined him.

'This is an unusual view,' he said, turning round to face me. 'I can't believe I haven't noticed these windows before.'

He'd removed his coat, revealing a sky-blue shirt which made his eyes pop and stirred the butterflies in my stomach.

'Is what I'm wearing okay?' he asked, his voice hesitant.

I kicked myself for staring for too long. We didn't have a uniform but asked staff to dress smartly, avoiding jeans, shorts, T-shirts and trainers.

'It's spot on. You look great.' I kicked myself once more. 'Smart, I mean. Exactly right. Let's get started, shall we?'

Lars's induction began with the boring but essential bits – a safety briefing covering everything from fire alarms to using Jeeves instead of carrying hot drinks or boxes of stock up and down the stairs. After that, I showed him a copy of the staff rota, giving him an overview of the team. Everyone except Dad and me were part-time, scheduled in to cover our days off, lunchtimes and busier times like weekends and school holidays when we needed extra bodies.

University student Alec and college students Flo and Cyndi worked regular hours but we had a few casual students we could call on during the summer holidays.

A tour was next, starting on the top floor and working our way down. I pointed out which books were stocked on each level, the logic behind some of the displays, and the bestsellers.

'I appreciate this is a lot to take in,' I said after we'd covered the top three levels. 'I'm not expecting you to remember even a fraction of what I'm saying. There's no test. I'll give you some time to explore on your own across the week.'

'It's all going in,' he said. 'Always been good at retaining information.'

We continued down to the next level.

'I didn't mean to sound like I was boasting,' he said as we paused in front of the shelves.

'I didn't think you were.'

'Good. Can I just say again how sorry I am about—'

I raised both hands to stop him and gave him a reassuring smile. 'No need. Line in the sand, Lars. We've hopefully both changed a lot since school. Fresh start, okay?'

'Okay. Thanks.'

'But if you have retained everything, maybe I will test you after all.'

For a moment, he clearly believed me, his eyes wide, and then he laughed, making his eyes sparkle, and those butterflies stirred once more. There was no denying that the quirky-looking boy had grown into an incredibly attractive man. Not for me, mind. It'd be a long time before I was ready to let someone in again.

'Do you read much non-fiction?' I asked, eager to take my mind away from his looks.

'I read all sorts. I like the occasional autobiography, I enjoy nature books and history. I've read a stack of books about Icelandic history and culture. Anything with Vikings in it and I'm all over it, whether it's Iceland based or not.'

'It's your dad who's Icelandic?' I asked.

'Yeah. My mum met him there when she was travelling.'

'They still live in Whitsborough Bay?'

Lars's expression darkened and his head dipped and I had a flashback to that sense of vulnerability I'd seen in him at school and the frustration that he kept pushing me away when I couldn't help but think he desperately needed a friend.

'Sorry. I don't mean to be intrusive. You don't have to tell me anything you don't want to.'

'It's okay.' He looked up once more, his eyes sad. 'They split up years back. He lives in Iceland now with his new family and Mum travels with her job. I don't see much of either of them.'

I wasn't sure how to respond to that, but a customer appeared and asked if she was on the right floor for history.

'Two levels up,' Lars said. 'Is there a particular period of history you're interested in?'

'World War I.'

'Let me show you.' Lars glanced at me, as though seeking approval, and I nodded at him.

'Is it for you or someone else?' Lars asked as he headed up the stairs with the customer.

'It's for my dad. It's his birthday soon and I haven't a clue what to get him...'

They moved out of earshot so I didn't catch the rest of their conversation but I was impressed with Lars for offering to take the customer to the section she was interested in. I hadn't yet talked about the way we tended to work but one of my requests was to take the customer to their preferred section if it was feasible to do so.

There was no point me going downstairs so I straightened up a few books and moved a couple which I spotted were out of place. I heard footsteps on the stairs and the customer's voice drifted to me.

'...been a great help. My dad's going to love these.'

'Hope he has a great birthday,' Lars responded. 'See you again soon.'

He joined me moments later, looking uncertain of himself. 'I didn't mean to take over.'

'Will you do me a big favour? Will you stop apologising? It was great to hear you sounding knowledgeable and I love that you didn't just point the customer in the direction of the books but took her there yourself. It's all good.'

'That's a relief. I don't want to mess this up.'

'Believe me, Lars, helping customers is *never* making a mess of it.'

'Can I just say something which might sound daft but I need to say it?' he asked.

'Of course.' I kept my voice positive but braced myself for some criticism.

'It's just that...' He paused and scrunched up his nose. 'I've never actually worked for someone else before – well, not since I was a pot washer in my teens – so I don't actually know how to be an employee.'

His vulnerability was so endearing and his honesty refreshing. I'd expected to dislike Lars but I found myself increasingly drawn to him. History repeating itself.

I gave him a reassuring smile. 'Should I let you into a secret? Neither do I. This is the only place I've ever worked and it's a family business so it's not the same. From what I've seen so far, you're doing great.'

He smiled back at me and I couldn't help noticing the tension leaving his shoulders. Working here was evidently a big deal for him and I liked that he cared.

'Let's finish our tour,' I said, 'and then I think we've earned ourselves another cuppa.'

* * *

It made sense for Lars to take the same lunch break as me while I was training him. I'd encouraged him to get some fresh air and he took my advice, asking if he could get me anything while he was out.

'I've brought a packed lunch,' I said, 'but thanks for the offer.'

'How's it going with our new recruit?' Cassie asked, joining me at the till as Lars left the building.

'Pretty well, I think. He's taking everything in and he seems to be great with customers. Could be a good fit. How's the morning been?'

'Fairly quiet, so we've managed to get all the stock out on the shelves and the orders are ready for the post.'

'Great work. So why are you frowning?'

'It could be nothing but, when we were talking about Lars's interview, you said he'd mentioned being an online customer so I looked him up on the system – interested to see what his reading tastes are – but he's not on there.'

'He isn't?'

'No. I've tried his surname with and without the accent over the "o" but it didn't make any difference.'

'Maybe he ordered them under a different name.'

'Maybe.'

The insinuation sat heavily between us.

'I'm sure it's nothing,' Cassie said. 'People lie in interviews all the time. Take that Melissa, for example. She lied about liking reading to impress you.' She winced, clearly realising that the point she was making in Lars's defence wasn't a positive one.

'He probably buys from The-Site-Which-Must-Not-Be-Named,' I said. 'Might have been embarrassed to admit it.'

I tried to sound breezy about it but it bothered me. I understood if Lars bought books elsewhere, especially as he'd also said he rarely made it into the town because of the long hours he worked, but why lie outright like that? Why say anything at all? He wouldn't have been rejected for not being a customer.

When Cassie disappeared to finish assisting Dad, I couldn't help myself and tapped Lars's name into the system, just in case Cassie had entered it incorrectly – perhaps only using one 'n' or one 's' but after every possible combination of spelling I had to concede that Lars Jóhannsson wasn't a Bay Books customer. I wasn't going to ask him about it – none of my business where he purchased his books – but the earlier positive impression of him was tinged with disappointment. Too many men in my life had lied to me or omitted key information and let me down – Justin, Ewan and Wes – and I didn't need another one on that list. Earlier, I'd found myself warming to Lars and could even imagine us one day finding our way back to friendship, but now I felt wary. Yes, this was a small lie and I could imagine it slipping out in a moment of discomfort, but small lies or cover-ups typically led to bigger ones and I'd had my fill of that.

16
LARS

'How was your first day at the bookstore?' Freyja asked, smiling at me over FaceTime.

It was the third time I'd answered the same question in as many hours, having met up with Danika for a quick drink after work and stopped off to see Nanna on the way home, but I wasn't going to answer it any the less enthusiastically. It was nice that they all cared.

'Really good. It's strange being told what to do rather than being the boss, but it's fine. You should see the place. I'd forgotten how big it is...'

When I'd finished filling in Freyja on all the details of my day, she said my sister wanted to ask me something and handed the phone over to Kára.

'We can't wait until next Christmas to see you,' she said. 'It's too long to wait and we miss you so much.'

It tugged on my heartstrings whenever she said anything like that. 'I miss you too.'

'Will you come to Iceland after your job ends?'

'Maybe. I'll think about it.'

She grinned at me and passed the phone back to Freyja.

'Short but sweet,' I said, laughing.

'I'm not short anymore,' Kára shouted from the background. 'I'm really tall now. But I am still sweet.'

I smiled at her literal take on what I'd said. I sometimes forgot that English idioms didn't always translate.

'What do you think?' Freyja asked.

'I don't know.' It would be fantastic to see her and my half-siblings but it wasn't just about them. My stomach tightened. 'Is Pabbi on board?'

A pause. 'You know you're always welcome here, Lars.'

'That's not what I asked. Does he actually want me to stay?'

She tucked her short blonde hair behind her ears – something she always did when she was uncomfortable. 'Of course.'

'Freyja!'

'Okay, so it was our idea and not his but he had no objections.'

I really appreciated the effort Freyja put into making me feel part of the family, but I didn't want to be the cause of any friction between her and Pabbi. I didn't like it but I'd accepted several years ago that I wasn't going to have a close relationship with either of my parents. I'd had to do that or it would have driven me crazy. Not that making that decision made it any less painful.

'Please,' she begged when I didn't respond. 'It's been too long.'

'Okay, but there's one condition and it's not negotiable.'

'What is it?'

'I won't stay at your house.'

'No! Lars! You have to.'

'I can't. You know how uncomfortable the atmosphere was last time I stayed and it's not fair on any of you.'

Freyja shook her head before sighing heavily. 'I accept, but only because I'd rather see my wonderful stepson staying in a hotel than not see him at all. But I have a request too. You stay for longer this time. Two weeks, a month, two months.'

My smile widened as she kept advancing the offer up to a year before suggesting forever.

'Maybe I'll take a month or two and explore more of Iceland. But I can't commit to anything just yet. I'll need to see how Marcus's operation goes and how quickly he recovers. The four-month contract should allow for plenty of time, but I wouldn't want to leave them stuck if he needs longer.'

'Reliable as always,' Freyja said. 'I wouldn't expect anything less. Anyway, I will say goodbye because we only spoke yesterday, but I wanted to see how work was.'

'I really appreciate it. I'll speak to you soon.'

I sat back on my bed after the call ended, trying not to overthink the conversation about visiting. So Pabbi hadn't made the suggestion – hardly shock news. I'd hated saying I wouldn't stay with them as it felt rude, as though I was dismissing Freyja's hospitality, but I couldn't put myself or them through that again. A hotel would be better for everyone and I'd always said I wanted to explore Iceland fully one day. When would I ever get a better opportunity? Financially, I didn't need to rush into another role so, as long as Nanna remained in good health, I could spend some time in Iceland and decide on my next career move from there. Or I could travel a little further afield. I'd always wanted to explore the other Nordic countries and all I'd managed so far was weekend city breaks in Oslo and Copenhagen – not exactly well travelled.

It was getting late and I hadn't eaten yet so I went down to the kitchen. The takeaway companies wouldn't deliver this far out of town unless it was a big order and a one-person meal definitely wasn't 'big' so I opened up a tin of baked beans and tipped it into a pan. Two slices of wholemeal toast and a couple of poached eggs with the beans should be enough to fill me.

Settling down at the breakfast bar to eat, I reflected on my day, cringing at my multitude of apologies I'd made. Lily had been kind to me and I'd really enjoyed my morning with her but it felt like something had changed when I returned from lunch. She seemed a little cooler with me somehow but I couldn't think of anything I might have said or done that would have caused it, so perhaps it was just my imagination. Maybe she'd had a difficult customer or something had happened behind the scenes which I didn't need to know about but which had put her off her stride. Hopefully everything would be fine tomorrow.

17

LILY

'Oh, wow, Lily! It looks amazing in here,' Dad said as we entered Bay Books through the back door on Saturday morning and he paused to look around at the Halloween decorations Cassie and I had put up the night before. 'How long did it take you?'

'A few hours. We made it to The Bombay Palace for just after eight, so not too bad.'

'I'm impressed, as always.'

It would normally have been Dad's day off today but it was the start of the half-term holiday and the extra pair of hands were usually needed. It wasn't just locals coming in but holidaymakers too. I admired their hardiness, determined to enjoy a holiday by the seaside despite the often cold and wet weather. Several of the local caravan parks, eager to prolong the holiday season, offered good deals in October which attracted families to the Yorkshire Coast.

'I need to check the window before we open,' I told Dad, heading outside. It had been dark when Cassie and I finished decorating last night and I wanted to ensure everything looked okay in the daylight.

Most of the window display carried a witchy theme aimed at children. Held open on a cookbook holder, a book I'd made from stained parchment showed a spell containing well-known characters from children's books. The relevant books and the soft toy characters were piled up ready to go into a large cauldron in which there were already a few items. Fake glittery cobwebs covered colourful bottles of potions, and there were spiders and bats of varying sizes dotted around.

On the far side of the window was a smaller adult section. We'd created a display stand from old fruit boxes on their sides, each carrying a range of titles with loose links to Halloween – the latest horror and crime fiction releases, a selection of romantic fiction titles featuring witches and ghosts, and various non-fiction titles about Victorian grave robbers, serial killers and witch trials. Dispersed among the piles of books were soft orange, purple and black pumpkins and black, white and orange flameless candles. Satisfied with the display, I went back inside.

If I hadn't been aware it was half-term, the increased footfall across the day would have told me. Dad, Alec, Flo and I barely paused for breath all day. I loved days like that. Financially we needed them as they compensated for the quiet ones where we sold very few books – the worst being mid-week, mid-term days with torrential rain which kept the shoppers away. But it wasn't the excitement of running off the end of the day sales report and seeing a healthy figure that did it for me. When the shop was busy, there was a buzz of excitement and it was caused by a united love for the written word. I'd never tire of customers telling me why they'd chosen a particular book. *My friend recommended it. My mum loves this author. I can't resist pink covers. My dad's having an operation and I thought this would take his mind off it. I love the cute panda/tractor/cottage on the cover. I loved this book when I was a kid. I've just watched the film and now I want to read the book. My sister's having a tough time right now so I thought I'd help her with some escapism.*

Escapism. Most days I was reminded of how valuable books, especially fiction ones, were for escapism. The opportunity for a reader to switch off from the challenges in their life and immerse themselves in a new world was so powerful. How many times had I heard a customer say, *I need this right now*, or return to the shop later and tell me, *this book came along at the perfect time*? I'd experienced it myself so many times, escaping to Green Gables when Jordan no longer wanted to be my friend, and returning to that world again and again when life tripped me up.

New friends could be found between the pages of a book – new romances even – and readers could learn so much. Sometimes I'd stand in the shop gazing at the bookshelves, feeling blown away by the multitude of lessons that could be learned from just the books in one section, let alone the whole shop. The learning didn't just come from the non-fiction books. Commercial fiction could be just as valuable for educating readers or making them think.

By half four, trade had eased off a little. I was tidying and restocking the children's section when Cassie arrived with Hallie and Rocco.

'I wasn't expecting to see you two today,' I said as they charged at me for cuddles.

'We've been to a party,' Rocco declared.

'Don't tell me. Think it and see if I can guess.' I pressed my fingers to my temples, scrunched up my forehead and stared at them both intently. 'I'm getting something. Plastic balls? Some tunnels? I know! You've been to the soft play.'

Hallie looked stunned for a moment, then started giggling. 'Mummy told you!'

'Busted!'

'You two go and choose a book each,' Cassie said. 'But what do we do with books?'

'We treat them with love,' Hallie and Rocco chorused together.

'And we put them back on the shelf in the right place carefully,' Hallie added. 'No ramming cos it hurts the corners.'

Cassie clapped her hand to her heart. 'My babies! You make me so proud. Off you go!' She turned to me with a grin. 'Just call me Mother of Books.'

'Okay, Mother of Books, how was soft play?'

'Like Satan's playpen. Although that's surprisingly not the strapline the owners of Squishy Joe's went with. Urgh, I *hate* those places but I love my kids so I begrudgingly accept the intermittent torture of a couple of hours of screeching children and competitive mums. *My daughter's a genius. My son's going to the Olympics. My daughter's found a cure for Alzheimer's. My son's solved world poverty.*'

The smarmy show-off voices Cassie adopted had me laughing. She rolled her eyes at me. 'Knowing I was going to hate it but be far too polite to say anything, I went for a silent protest.'

'No! You didn't...'

She unzipped her coat, revealing her *I'd rather be reading books* T-shirt.

'...wear your T-shirt?' I finished. 'You did. I can't believe you did that!'

'It had to be done. I'd never have forgiven myself if I hadn't.'

'Cassie! And you wonder why nobody speaks to you at the school gates.'

'And my life is all the richer for it.'

It was an in-joke as Cassie was actually really popular among the school gate crowd. She had one of those bubbly personalities people couldn't help being drawn to, smiling and chatting to everyone but never being fake. She couldn't abide fake people and the one-upmanship some parents and carers seemed to subscribe to drove her to distraction. 'They're just children,' she frequently lamented. 'Who cares if one isn't as good at spelling or numbers or sport? If some of those blummin' parents would stop making it into a competition and just let their kids be kids, life would be so much easier. They'll find their way. They'll discover their gifts and that won't necessarily be something academic or sporty.'

I used to laugh along with her school gate tales and wonder if I'd experience the same thing when Wes and I had children but the stories hit differently now. I still laughed, but I did wonder whether children were part of my future anymore and occasionally I questioned whether I'd done the right thing by walking away from Wes, especially when letting him go meant letting go of our future plans to get a house and have a family. The thought popped into my head again now, immediately followed by Dad's declaration that Wes hadn't been my Gilbert Blythe. We weren't right together. I could see that now.

'The Paperback Pixie has been gifting again,' Cassie said, bringing my attention back to the present as she thrust her phone in front of me.

'Today?'

'Yes. No theme this time but five books again. She's definitely making up for the missed summer.'

I took Cassie's phone and scrolled through the photos, recognising the various locations around Whitsborough Bay where the Paperback Pixie had placed the books.

'Who are you?' I murmured, shaking my head. The accompanying message just had the usual spiel about tagging the Pixie in for any finds and wishing the finders an enjoyable read.

'I think that's going to forever remain a mystery,' Cassie said as I returned her phone. 'Oh! You know what we've never tried? Searching the system for an email address with *Paperback Pixie* in it.'

I glanced towards the till where Dad was serving a customer. 'I doubt they'd be that obvious but it's worth a try. I'll look after we close.'

'Too right! Okay, I'll leave you to crack on and I'd best see what my two are up to. We'll get books and then Mummy can go home and drink wine until she's obliterated the trauma of Satan's playpen.'

She headed over to where Hallie and Rocco were looking through our Halloween reads and I finished tidying the shelf I'd been working on, thinking about her email comment. It seemed ridiculous now that we hadn't searched on *paperback pixie* before. The search facility was designed to take a partial email address so I could try *pixie* too and see if that brought up anything. My heart leapt at the possibility but my head told me that, if the Paperback Pixie had kept their identity secret for fifteen or so years, their email address wouldn't give anything away.

The end of the day soon arrived and we said goodbye to our last customer. While Dad finished vacuuming, I ran off the sales report for the day, cashed up, then did an email search on *paperback pixie*, *pixie* and *paperback*. The first two brought up nothing but my heart leapt when *paperback* yielded a couple of results. They were a dead end as I knew the customers attached to both – a regular who devoured historical novels, had been in a few days ago and was now on holiday in Lanzarote, and a former regular who'd moved out of the area a few years ago.

Although I was no further forward with identifying the Paperback Pixie, the email address search had given me an idea. Cassie and I had searched on Lars's name but what if he had an account registered under a different name – perhaps his business? I found the email address Lars had put on his CV and tapped that into the search field, generating a customer account for an Aileen Bridges living at 17 Fountain Street. There was a long history of orders, mainly consisting of romantic fiction, Viking fiction and non-fiction books about Vikings, Iceland and photography.

'That's a serious face,' Dad said, reaching round me to unplug the vacuum cleaner. 'Everything okay?'

'Yes. It's relief, actually.'

When Dad raised his eyebrows questioningly, I felt I had to expand.

'I did a thing. You know how Lars mentioned in his interview that he hadn't been in the shop since he was a kid but he bought from us online? Cassie wanted to check out his reading tastes but couldn't find him on the system.'

Dad nodded his head knowingly when I paused. 'So you assumed he'd lied to us.'

'Exactly. And you know what I'm like with liars. It's been bugging me all week but I've just searched on his email address and found a long order history so now I feel awful.'

'Did you say anything to Lars?'

'Thankfully no, but I might have been a bit off with him after Cassie told me and I don't know what to do about it now. If I apologise and he never noticed anything, I'm going to look daft. But if he did notice and I don't apologise, he might think I'm still holding a grudge from school even though I promised it was all forgotten.'

Dad placed a reassuring hand on my shoulder. 'I haven't picked up on any bad vibes between you so I don't think you've behaved as differently as you might think you have.'

I smiled at him, reassured and relieved because Dad was exceptionally observant and would have picked up anything remiss.

While Dad put the vacuum cleaner away, I glanced once more at Lars's order list before shutting the system down. Discovering that Lars hadn't been lying about being a customer should have made me happy but, instead, I felt disappointed, which made no sense to me.

* * *

Most evenings I ate my tea with Mum and Dad in Everdene but they were dining out with friends so I picked up a takeaway pizza on the way home. Dad had said I was welcome to eat in the main house but, after such a busy day, I fancied slipping into my pyjamas before I ate and I didn't want to get all warm and cosy then have to brave the cold as I darted back across to my annexe.

Sprawled out on my bed munching on my pizza while watching a new episode of a drama series I'd been enjoying, I had to admit to myself the reason why I'd felt disappointed when I found Lars's book orders on the system. Aileen Bridges. The woman with whom Lars lived. Girlfriend? Fiancée? She could even be a wife who'd kept her own name, although Lars wasn't wearing a wedding band. Of course, she might not be romantically connected to him at all. Lars had said his parents were divorced so Aileen might be his mum using her maiden name, although he'd also said he barely saw his parents so perhaps not. Could be a sister who'd changed her name through marriage. I didn't remember him having a sister at school or mentioning one when we used to talk about books, although I had a vague recollection of him sometimes buying picture books so it was possible that he had a younger sister. A big age gap would have made her too young to be at senior school at the same time as us.

I desperately wanted to know who Aileen Bridges was but it was hardly something I could ask Lars without admitting I'd been searching for him on the system because I thought he was a liar. I'd have to hope it came up in casual conversation.

As I settled down to sleep, it was still on my mind. I found myself willing Aileen to be family because the idea of her being someone in a romantic relationship with Lars bothered me way more than it should.

18

LARS

The half-term holiday had been and gone and the Monday when schools returned was the start of my third week at Bay Books as well as the first week without Marcus. Although his operation wasn't until Thursday, Lily had insisted on him having the start of the week off to get organised.

Last week had been really busy, helped by a few mild and sunny days at the start of the week and only a couple of short rain showers at the end. Lily had warned me that it was nothing compared to how it could get in December. I'd been shown how to do most things and I'd quickly grasped the point-of-sale system. I could now process in-person purchases, search for books we didn't have in stock, and order them in.

Lily had been friendly all week, even when she was clearly very busy trying to juggle several tasks at once, so I decided that her coolness towards me that first week had just been my imagination. I'd now met all the staff as well as Lily's mum, Shelby, who'd covered Cassie's shift one day with Cassie not working during the school holidays. Everyone had been so warm and friendly as well as being voracious readers so, in quiet moments, I'd had some amazing bookish conversations.

'It's just the two of us today until Cassie gets in at half ten,' Lily said when I arrived for work at 8 a.m. – my new starting time in line with the hours Marcus usually worked. 'It'll probably be quiet – Mondays often are – so that'll give us some breathing space after last week. The first task is to make yourself a cuppa and then we'll run through the plan for today.'

I asked if she'd like a drink but she pointed to a steaming mug of coffee on the counter, so I headed down to make one for myself and sent it up in Jeeves. When I returned, Lily was on a kick stool in the children's section taking down the Halloween spiders and dropping them into a storage crate.

'We need to clear out Halloween,' she said, 'and make way for autumn with a flavour of Christmas.'

'A flavour?' I asked, taking Lily's lead and removing some of the cobwebs from the shelves.

'Nothing too full-blown at this point. I like to go subtle at first – a few festive titles in the window to prompt customers that Christmas is approaching plus a section in here for festive children's books.'

She unpinned another spider and tossed it into the crate while I continued to work my way along the shelves collecting the cobwebs.

'The autumnal vibes are all about being warm and cosy which kind of introduces Christmas anyway,' she said. 'It also works well for Bonfire Night on Wednesday. We don't tend to do a separate display for that – not enough relevant titles to warrant it.'

She paused to re-position the kick stool.

'On Thursday, it'll be exactly seven weeks till Christmas Day so it won't be long before we go full-on Christmas, but I'll tell you more about our plans for that as the week progresses. If we can get the decorations down in here before we open, that would be amazing. We'll sort the window out a bit later.'

I wanted to ask Lily if they'd ever celebrated *Jólabókaflóð* at Bay Books but I'd wait until we were discussing Christmas. If they didn't – and there was no reason why they would as Lily's family weren't Icelandic and I wasn't aware of anybody else in Whitsborough Bay who was – it would mean a lot to me if we could mark it in some small way, although I wasn't sure how. I didn't even know what happened in bookshops in Iceland to embrace the tradition so I'd have to ask Freyja about that.

We'd almost finished in the children's section when opening time arrived so Lily left me taking down the last of the decorations while she unlocked the door. I heard her welcoming a customer in and taking a payment moments later so they were obviously on a mission and knew exactly what they wanted.

'I love it when a customer makes a purchase as soon as we open,' Lily said, joining me once more as I placed the lid on the crate. 'I have this fear of a zero-sales day so I feel more relaxed when I've made the first sale of the day.'

'Have you ever had a zero-sales day?'

'Not yet.' She reached out to touch the nearest wooden shelving unit. 'But we had a shocker once when we only had two customers all day and took less than a tenner. Dad and I call it Black Monday. One customer bought a picture book and the other bought a bookmark. The profit that day wouldn't have even covered the electricity, never mind the wages. Thankfully days like that are rare.'

'Do you know why it was so dead?'

'I do, yeah. It already had a lot going against it – a Monday in late January so quietest day of the week, quiet time of the year, just before payday – and then the great British weather did its worst with non-stop torrential rain. No wonder nobody bothered.'

'The hours must go by slowly when it's like that.'

'They really drag. It's a good opportunity to get ahead with the admin and crack on with the things we can't do when the shop's busy.' She grinned at me. 'Or we can drink tea, eat biscuits and moan about the weather. So British! Do Icelanders go on about the weather?'

'Definitely. They have a colder, wetter climate than the UK and, oh my God, the wind! They know this about their home, but they do still like to complain about it, just like Brits do about the weather here. Icelanders also have something called sun guilt. A nice sunny day is a rarity so it's a case of dropping everything, if that's possible, to do something outside and make the most of the sun. Those who don't take advantage of that then feel guilty for wasting the day.'

'Sun guilt. I love that.' She narrowed her eyes at me. 'You referred to Icelanders as *they*. You see yourself as a Brit?'

'I was born here and Mum's British so officially I am too. If anyone asks me my nationality, I say half-British, half-Icelandic, but I've never thought of myself as Icelandic. I love the place but I've never spent longer than a week at a time there and I haven't fully explored the island.'

'I couldn't help noticing you've lost your accent.'

I nodded. 'It wasn't an intentional thing. It just disappeared over time.'

Geraldine had been the one who'd pointed it out. She'd visited Nanna the day before my twenty-first birthday and had kindly bought me a card and gift. She'd asked how I planned to spend the big day and I remembered her staring at me, frowning, before asking me what had happened to my accent. Nanna and I were stunned that neither of us had realised it had gone.

Lily looked poised to ask another question and I'd have happily told her whatever she wanted to know. I liked that she was interested. However, the door opened and a couple maybe in their sixties asked if we had any soup or slow cooker recipe books.

'We've got both,' Lily said, smiling at them warmly. 'Lars, would you like to show our customers where they are while I move these crates?'

'They're on level two,' I said, leading the customers towards the stairs. 'Who's the chef in the house?'

'Both of us,' the woman said. 'We've always enjoyed cooking together but we've never made soup before so we thought we'd give it a try.'

'And we always make the same thing in the slow cooker so we want to mix it up a bit,' the man added. 'Our daughter told us to get some recipes online but that's not our thing.'

The woman nodded. 'You can't beat a proper recipe book with mouthwatering pictures in it.'

We reached the section and, as I talked them through the books we stocked, I couldn't help noticing the affectionate looks they exchanged and the brief touches. The woman pointed out a recipe she thought the man would love and he did the same back to her and I wondered what it felt like to be with someone who knew everything about you. I'd never experienced it but it was what I longed for. This epitomised perfection for me. After checking if they needed any further help, I returned downstairs. Lily had told me that there was a fine balance between being helpful and pushy. Hovering over a customer definitely fell into the latter camp.

'I've put the crates inside Jeeves so we're not tripping over them,' Lily told me when I joined her downstairs. 'Don't send them down just yet as we need to add in the decorations from the window first.'

'Okay. Do you want me to clear the window?'

'I do, but not just yet. First I'll show you how we deal with the online orders which have come in overnight as they're normally a morning priority. Do you want to come round to this side?'

I'd just joined Lily when the recipe book couple came down with a soup book and two slow cooker ones so I ran the transaction through for them and wished them lots of fun creating their meals together.

With the shop empty again, Lily guided me through what happened when a customer ordered anything via their website. Standing so close to her, I kept getting whiffs of her perfume – something fresh and zesty like oranges – which I hadn't noticed before but which I really liked. She was a natural as a trainer; clear and precise with her instructions and providing sufficient insight into why things worked the way they did without getting bogged down with detail. With pauses to help or serve customers, it took us until Cassie's arrival to finish going through the system.

'Have you seen it?' Cassie asked Lily after she'd greeted us both. 'It's a pixie haul full house.'

'Really? Aw, that's brilliant. It's been ages since the last one.'

As Cassie headed downstairs, Lily took out her phone and clicked a few buttons, smiling. 'That's made me happy. Good manners cost nothing.'

I looked at her expectantly.

'Have you heard of the Paperback Pixie?' she asked, turning her phone towards me with an Instagram account showing on the screen. 'They buy books and they leave them around the town for people to find and enjoy.'

'Erm... Didn't *Bay News* do a piece about it some years back?'

'That's right. Nobody knows who they are. We're convinced the reporter was hoping to unmask them but the Paperback Pixie's identity remains a mystery to this day. We'd love to know who they are but we haven't a clue.'

'Why would you want to know? Isn't the mystery part of the magic, like not knowing who Batman, Spiderman or Superman really are?'

'Oh, absolutely, and we'd never want to share the secret. We'd just like to be the ones who supply the books. Not for any credit on our part, mind. We think what the Pixie does is brilliant and we've no intention of interfering or asking them to add Bay Books branding to theirs. If we could work with the Pixie, we could give them a discount – our little bit to help ease their financial burden while being a secret part of spreading the joy of reading. We've even got a poster up asking for the Pixie to contact us. Long shot but worth a try.'

I glanced past her at the noticeboard behind the till and smiled at the WANTED poster, surprised I hadn't noticed it before although, when I was by the till, I was usually busy serving customers with my back to the wall so I hadn't even spotted there was a noticeboard there, let alone what was on it.

'How do you know the Paperback Pixie isn't already a customer?' I asked.

'None of our orders have tallied with the books they've gifted. We wondered if they'd sourced some books from us and some from elsewhere to avoid being identified, but that would be impossible to work out. So I suppose it *is* possible they're a customer, but we're doubtful. Shame.'

She released a heavy sigh and shrugged. 'Anyway, if you're wondering what Cassie was on about, the Paperback Pixie leaves a branded postcard with every book asking the finder to tag them in on Insta. Cassie and I like to keep watch for the tags to see who finds the books. Most of the time the messages from the finders are short – just a thank you and where the book was found, which is all the Pixie asks for. The ones for children's books can be really sweet but it's the messages from the people who needed those books which we love the most. Some share that they're going through a tough time and finding the book has lifted them or the book itself has really resonated with them, coming into their life at exactly the right time. Loads of those messages have had Cassie and me in tears. Well, me. Cassie isn't really a sobber.'

The door opened and we both said hello to a man who greeted us back and headed straight for the stairs.

'What's the full house thing?' I asked.

'Cassie and I get a bit frustrated when finders don't tag the Pixie,' she said, smiling at me. 'We try not to be judgy because we know there are people who aren't on the socials, those who have a lot going on in their lives and forget to do it and so on, but it's a thank you, you know? So we get excited when we see all the books claimed and the Pixie thanked – a pixie haul full house.'

'That makes sense now, and I get what you're saying about the tags. If the Paperback Pixie has stayed anonymous all these years, they're obviously not doing it for the glory or adulation, but I could imagine the thank-you tags are appreciated. Probably makes them want to distribute more books.'

'Exactly! And that's why we'd love to work with them and give them a discount. So if you happen to know someone who knows someone who knows the Paperback Pixie, do ask them to get in touch. Discretion guaranteed!'

Lily was clearly passionate about the Paperback Pixie. Her eyes shone as she spoke and I loved how she wanted to be involved without any credit or expectation.

'I hope you find your Pixie soon,' I said.

'Me too and I hope I get to meet them in person because I'd like to give them a huge hug and thank them for spreading the joy of reading. They're a man or woman – or a team of people – after my own heart.'

The customer who'd gone upstairs returned with a travel book. While Lily served him, chatting easily about his plans to visit India, I repeated in my head what she'd just said. *They're a man or woman after my own heart.* It was true. I was. Every day, I felt myself being more and more drawn towards Lily Appleton. I couldn't think of a single thing I disliked about her. Even in that first week when she'd been a little cool towards me, I'd still really liked her, admired her, wanted to be around her and now that she'd thawed again, those desires were even stronger.

I thought about all the superhero films I'd watched over the years and those pivotal moments where Bruce Wayne, Peter Parker and Clark Kent could have revealed their alter egos to the women who'd captured their hearts but something stopped them. Now I truly understood why they didn't admit who they were because I couldn't either. *I'm the Paperback Pixie.* Only four words but I just couldn't say them. Not yet anyway. Especially when nobody else knew – not even Nanna.

19

LILY

'I think that has to be the quietest lunchtime I've ever worked,' Cassie said, zipping up her waterproof coat as she prepared to leave on Wednesday afternoon.

The rain hadn't let up all day. We'd had a couple more customers than on Black Monday but we needed quite a few more to hit triple sales figures.

Cassie's phone beeped and she read the message and tapped in a response before looking up at me. 'That was Jared. The bonfire's been cancelled due to the *adverse weather conditions*. They took their time making that decision.'

Jared was the production manager at Huxleigh Foods. As one of the town's largest and longest-standing employers, they hosted a bonfire and fireworks event every 5 November. It had started off as a thank you for their employees and families but had developed over the years into a bigger community event. Cassie and Jared had been planning to take Hallie and Rocco, and Cassie had been checking her phone throughout her shift, hoping they'd cancel, because standing in the rain and mud was not exactly an appealing way to spend her evening.

'Bet you're relieved,' I said.

'If I had the energy, I'd be doing a happy dance round the shop right now. But, as I've got an unexpected free evening, I know how I'm going to spend it...' She marched over to our fantasy section and grabbed herself a book which she plonked down on the counter with a smile. 'I'm going in!'

I knew what the book was without even looking – *A Game of Thrones*, the first book in George R. R. Martin's 'A Song of Ice and Fire' series. Jared had been hooked on the TV series from the start and had kept telling Cassie she'd love it but she wasn't convinced. She'd accidentally caught an episode of the final season and, as Jared predicted, was gripped so they'd gone back to the start and watched all the seasons together.

Lars joined us from restocking some of our non-fiction books. 'Great choice. Is it for you?' he asked Cassie.

'It is. I've already watched the TV series which is unusual for me as I prefer to read the book first but these things happen. I figured enough years have now passed for the memory of the twists and turns to have faded so I can dive into the series and enjoy it all over again.'

'And when she says *prefer to read the book first*, she really means she's a stickler for that. Gets a bit preachy about it, don't you, Cassie?'

Cassie placed her hands on her hips in mock-indignation. 'What do you expect when there's so much more depth in the books? You must have seen memes on the socials about it, Lars, where there's an iceberg and they say the film or TV adaptation is the bit sticking out the water but the book's that bit plus the mass of berg beneath the surface.'

Lars nodded. 'I know the meme you mean and I agree about the depth in books, but I mix it up myself – sometimes book first, sometimes film. I've enjoyed stories both ways. I'm not particularly visual so I don't conjure up what the characters look like when I'm reading a book. If I've seen it on the screen first, I then visualise the actors as I'm reading and it adds a different dimension.'

'Lily's the same!' Cassie cried, pointing at me as though I was a criminal she'd picked out of a line-up.

'I'm not a visual reader either,' I said, shrugging. 'If it's well described, I can picture the setting brilliantly but I really struggle with picturing characters. I have this vague sense of their build and hair colour but that's where it ends. Doesn't spoil my enjoyment of a book but sometimes I like the visual from seeing the screen version first.'

Cassie shook her head and tutted, pretending to be disgusted with me. 'I have no idea why we're friends. Philistine.'

'I loved the books and the TV series,' Lars said, tapping a long index finger on Cassie's purchase. 'A lot of the series was filmed in Ireland but parts were filmed in Iceland so I've done my geeky tourist bit and visited those settings.'

'I didn't realise they'd filmed in Iceland,' Cassie said. 'Although it does seem appropriate that a series called "A Song of Ice and Fire" would be filmed in the land of ice and fire. Right! Time to brave the weather.'

She wrapped the book in a carrier bag and placed it in her handbag, muttering that it had better stay dry. Grabbing her umbrella from the bucket by the door, she bid us goodbye and headed out into the rain.

'I should never have told you about Black Monday,' I said to Lars, as I stood by the door watching Cassie dashing across the cobbles, dodging the larger puddles. 'I think I've jinxed it.'

'I hate to say it but I've just checked the weather app and it's not expected to let up until midnight.'

'Urgh! That's grim.' I returned to the counter. 'Cassie's kids are going to be so disappointed about the bonfire being cancelled. They were really looking forward to it, but at least it means fewer fireworks going off and distressing pets and wildlife.'

'Have you got any pets?' Lars asked.

'No, not even when we were younger with us all being out at work all day. What about you?'

'Same. Until recently, I was living with my nanna and she got a cat maybe ten years ago. We had it for two years and one day it never came home. It broke Nanna's heart and that was it for her – no more pets.'

My heart lifted at the mention of him living with his nanna as that must surely be the Aileen Bridges registered against his email address.

'You don't live with your nanna anymore?' I asked.

'No. Her two best friends were moving into the new apartments at Bay View and she decided it was time to downsize and do the same. She's been there for about six weeks now and she's loving it. I see her several times a week but it's strange not seeing her every day, although I suppose, at my age, moving out and getting a place of my own was long overdue. My ex-girlfriend called me a saddo for still living at home, which was rich when she was crashing at her sister's.'

I widened my eyes at the rudeness of that, while my heart leapt once more at the revelation that he was single. Or was he? Just because he'd mentioned an ex, it didn't mean he didn't have a newer girlfriend.

'Just as well she's your ex, then,' I said. 'I don't think anyone has any right to judge someone's living situation. Age has nothing to do with it. Sometimes it's just the way life works out. I still live at home.'

'You do?'

'Yeah. I bought a house with an ex years ago, but the relationship ended before we got to live there together. I couldn't have afforded the house on my own and the shine had gone off it anyway so we sold it and I moved into a one-bedroom annexe at my parents' place on a temporary basis and I'm still there. Living at home at my age isn't what I expected but the plans I had didn't pan out so *c'est la vie!*'

I wondered whether Lars was going to ask me to expand, but one of our best customers, a voracious crime-reader called Bernadette, burst through the door breathlessly.

'Wow! It's hideous out there,' she exclaimed, depositing her umbrella in the bucket and wiping her feet on the mat.

'We're not used to seeing you mid-week,' I said. Bernadette typically visited every Friday and left with four or five paperbacks to see her through the week.

'I'm having a tooth out on Friday morning so I'll be spending the afternoon at home drooling and feeling sorry for myself. Thought I'd better come in early to get stocked up.'

'We've got the new K. D. Baines thriller in.'

'Yes! I'll definitely buy that today. Time to explore…'

As Bernadette headed over to the new-releases table, I turned to Lars. 'We're up to date with everything and I doubt we're going to get a flood of customers, excuse the pun, so I'm thinking the best plan is for you to spend some time in here or in the children's section really getting to grips with the backlist titles we have. See which authors have lots of titles in stock, read some of the blurbs and check out any customer reviews we've got displayed. It'll help you for when the Christmas rush starts, especially as we get some customers who come in and thrust a list at us of everything they want, sometimes with the wrong titles or authors.'

Lars glanced across to where Bernadette was reading a blurb on the back of a new psychological thriller. 'I'll head out the back. Shout me if a boatload of customers arrive.'

* * *

Darkness had fallen, not that it had got particularly light all day, and the rain was still coming down heavily. It was approaching five o'clock and we hadn't had a single customer in since Bernadette and she'd left before three. Talk about dead! Bernadette's purchase of five novels had taken us into three figures but the sales report for today would be as dismal as the weather.

I'd kept myself busy preparing December's newsletter. I emailed one out to all our subscribers at the start of the month with details of some of the big releases, special offers and any events coming up. With only being five days into November, it would be some time before December's was sent out but it made sense to get ahead with it while I had the time.

Stepping back from the computer, I yawned and rolled my stiff shoulders. Lars had made us both a mug of tea about an hour ago but I hadn't seen or heard a peep out of him since then so I ventured into the children's section where he was sitting on one of the colourful tub chairs, side on to me, with a picture book open on his knee. I opened my mouth to ask him how he was getting on but stopped when I spotted a tear trailing down his cheek. He tilted his head back and looked upwards for a few moments before wiping his cheeks and returning his gaze to the book. Feeling as though I was intruding on an intensely private moment, I sloped back towards the front of the shop, cursing myself as I stepped on the one creaky floorboard between the sections. Lars's head snapped up and he closed the book.

'Sorry,' I said, wincing. 'I didn't mean to intrude.'

'No, it's, erm… Sorry, I need to apologise for reading at work.'

'No need. It's part of the job. Are you okay?'

He gave me a weak smile as he rose from the chair and held up the book. 'Have you read this one?'

I looked at the title – *Anna and the Snow Dragon* by Sigrid Hansen – but it didn't ring a bell. The cover didn't look familiar either – an adorable friendly looking white dragon flying over a volcano and a little girl with white plaits sitting on its back. That said, the children's section was more Dad's domain than mine so there were definitely books in there which weren't on my radar.

'You know, I'm not sure I have,' I told Lars.

'It was my little sister's favourite.' He lowered the book. 'She was an early reader but she still loved it when she got read to, especially by me because I did the voices.'

He smiled, presumably recalling reading that specific book to his sister. I wouldn't have had him down as someone who did all the voices and the little snippet of information was endearing.

'I didn't realise you had a sister,' I said. 'Would I have met her?'

He shook his head. 'She wasn't with me any of the times I saw you. If she had been, we probably wouldn't have had a chance to chat as she'd have been excitedly dragging me from shelf to shelf.'

'Big book fan?'

'Massive. I loved reading but it was Pia who turned it into a real passion.' He stood up, the book clutched between both hands, a gentle smile on his lips. 'I can't believe you've got a copy. You know, I read this book to her so many times I could probably have recited it word for word without looking at the pages. But when she died—'

'She died?' I asked, my stomach lurching at the unexpected revelation. No wonder he'd been crying. *Anna and the Snow Dragon* evidently held both happy and sad memories for him.

Lars nodded. 'Born prematurely, lungs never fully developed, battle with asthma all her life and a fatal asthma attack when she was seven.'

Seven years old? I couldn't even begin to imagine what Lars and his family must have gone through to lose someone so young.

'Oh, my God! Lars! I'm so sorry.'

'Thanks.' He gave me a weak smile before glancing down at the book once more and running his fingers over the cover image. 'I don't know what happened to her copy. Over the years, I've toyed with buying one for myself but it's out of print and I've never found anywhere that stocks it. But even if I had found a copy somewhere, a pristine one wouldn't be the same as the well-thumbed copy Pia had.'

'You never checked our website?'

'I did, but it's not on there.'

'Isn't it? That's strange. I could have sworn all the books we stock are on there.'

'*Anna and Jónas* – that's the name of the snow dragon – must have slipped through the net. It was such a surprise to find it here and I couldn't resist flicking through it but, well, this is what happens...' He pointed to his face, acknowledging the tears that had dried on his cheeks.

'An emotional moment for you.'

'Caught me unawares. Anyway, I'd better put it back.'

I wanted to tell him he could keep the book but doing so would suggest that I hadn't heard him when he'd said a pristine copy wouldn't be the same. Although he *had* said he'd looked for it... Given that Lars had ended the conversation and turned away from me, I imagined he needed a few moments to compose himself so I retrieved the vacuum cleaner and returned to the front of the shop.

As I vacuumed, I kept picturing his face and the tears tracking down his cheeks. I loved the way he'd owned his emotions, not even making the slightest attempt to disguise his tears. He'd spoken about his sister and her love for books with such warmth and my heart broke for his loss. Should I have gifted him the book? No. It wasn't my place to do that. It had triggered a powerful emotional reaction in him and it was up to him to decide whether he wanted it or not. If he brought it to the till, I'd happily give it to him for free, but it wasn't my place to put any pressure on him to take it home.

* * *

'You're sure you're okay?' I asked Lars as I unlocked the front door for him to leave shortly after closing time.

'It wasn't how I was expecting the afternoon to go, but I'm fine. It happens from time to time – this wave of emotion suddenly hits me and there's nothing I can do to stop it so I just go with it and it's usually cathartic. I'm just glad there weren't any customers around. Mind you, if there had been, I wouldn't have been sitting there reading a book. You're sure you don't mind me doing that?'

'I'm sure. Although if you'd broken the spine and folded over the pages, we'd be having a very different conversation.'

He laughed at my stern teacher tone. 'I'll see you on Friday. Have a good day off tomorrow and I hope your dad's operation goes well.'

I pulled the door wide for him and he opened up his golf umbrella as he stepped out. Locking the door behind him, I wandered through to the children's section, removed *Anna and the Snow Dragon* from the shelf, sat down on the same chair Lars had used earlier, and opened the first page.

When I reached the end, I returned to the beginning and read it through a second time, pausing on each page to study the illustrations more closely. Closing the book for a second time, I blinked back tears. What a gorgeous story about friendship, kindness and celebrating differences. Anna was an Icelandic girl who the other children laughed at because of her pure white hair and she befriended Jónas, a white dragon who the other dragons ostracised because they were all red like the fire in the volcanos, blue like the ocean, or green like the land. Anna helped Jónas see how special he was by pointing out that he was the colour of the snow – snow being as important a part of the island as the earth, fire and water. The revelation was the making of Jónas and he told Anna that, as she also had beautiful white hair, she was obviously part of his family and incredibly special too. The pair of them then flew round Iceland finding children and animals who felt different and helping them to celebrate instead of hiding from their uniqueness. Published twenty-nine years ago, the message was just as relevant today.

The author was unfamiliar to me and I was fairly sure we didn't have any other titles by her. It could be that she'd only written the one book but it was equally possible we simply hadn't stocked other titles. I hadn't yet closed the system down so I took the book to the till and checked whether Lars was right about it being out of print. He was and a quick search revealed there'd been no further titles released by that author.

I was fascinated by how the publishing industry worked and, through conversations with Granny Blue and a host of other authors I'd met through events at Bay Books, had gained considerable insights into the author/publisher relationship. Authors who only ever had one book published particularly intrigued me so I hopped onto the Internet to see if I could find any explanation for Sigrid Hansen stopping after one release.

The first result revealed that Sigrid was an Icelandic author and illustrator who'd moved to the UK when she was twenty-two to study a Master's in Creative Writing, had met her husband shortly after, and had been poised to publish the first of two contracted picture books at the age of thirty-one through leading children's book publisher Whispering Fox Books. Three months before the launch, Sigrid and her husband were tragically killed in a helicopter crash while on holiday celebrating their wedding anniversary, leaving behind a five-year-old son and three-year-old daughter. There'd been a big launch planned for *Anna and the Snow Dragon* including lots of personal appearances so, while Whispering Fox Books still honoured the book's release, it understandably had to be a much softer launch. Book two, for which there'd been chatter about soft toy tie-ins, had only been a work in progress at the time of Sigrid's death and the publisher hadn't seen any pages. Book one therefore didn't get the success it deserved and book two never saw the light of day.

'That's so sad,' I murmured, shaking my head. I was about to close the system down when an entry lower down in the search results caught my eye. Clicking into it took me to a website belonging to Sigrid Hansen's daughter, Eva, and I smiled as I read the latest news post. It seemed that Eva and her brother, Axel, had been raised by their paternal grandparents. After their granddad passed away, their grandma decided to move into sheltered accommodation and, while helping her pack, the siblings found several boxes full of their parents' belongings in the attic, which they'd known nothing about. Among them was a notebook containing the completed manuscript for their mum's second book, notebooks containing a further two partially written stories as well as ideas for two more and a portfolio full of illustrations – some complete and others just rough sketches. They'd approached Whispering Fox Books, hoping they'd posthumously publish the second book while knowing it was a long shot. Several months later, the siblings were invited to the publisher's head office. A new editor had read the full series and believed the messages were strong and relevant for today's children. They wanted to relaunch book one on the thirtieth anniversary of its original publication, follow it up with the other three books Sigrid had written and potentially the additional two ideas if the first four sold well. They'd do the merchandise tie-ins originally planned and, as Eva and Axel were talented artists themselves, Whispering Fox Books wanted them to finish the illustrations their mother had started. The relaunch had been confirmed for September next year.

Bursting with excitement at what I'd found, I composed an email to Lars and added in the website link.

To: Lars Jóhannsson
From: Lily Appleton
Date: 5 November
Subject: Fascinating Discovery

Hi Lars, my curiosity was piqued about *Anna and the Snow Dragon* as the author's name wasn't familiar. Turns out Sigrid Hansen was killed in an accident shortly before the book was released, but I also discovered something fascinating about it. I won't say more. I'll let you read the piece for yourself...
Lily

Frowning as I read through what I'd written, I considered not sending it. Would he find it weird that I'd done a follow-up on the book? But I was a bookseller. It was what we did. Before I could overthink it, I pressed send. If Lars had an emotional reaction to the news, he'd be able to do it in the privacy of his own home and he'd have a day away from me tomorrow if he thought I'd overstepped. Had I? No. I couldn't see how what I'd done would be considered overstepping. If anything, he'd be grateful for the heads up. His little sister's favourite book would reappear in bookshops next year and be receiving a lot of publicity and that was something he needed time to prepare for.

As I drove home, I thought about the Paperback Pixie. Even though Lars would have stopped working for us long before *Anna and the Snow Dragon* was reissued next September, I wanted to do something special for him and the memory of his sister. I'd message Eva via her website to see if Bay Books could be involved in any promotional activities and I'd definitely do a display in the shop. I'd also love to donate several copies to the Paperback Pixie to help spread the word about that beautiful story. Maybe they'd identify themselves to us before then. Doubtful, but I'd keep hoping. I could always drop them a direct message suggesting the idea and promising anonymity.

I pictured Lars's vulnerability as he read the book and wondered what his reaction would have been if I'd hugged him. I'd wanted to and it wasn't just because I'd wanted to comfort him. There was something about Lars that made me want to be near him, just as it had done from the moment I met him, as though there was some mysterious force pulling us together. Perhaps the same mysterious force that had placed a copy of *Anna and the Snow Dragon* on our bookshelves because that seemed to be the only explanation for its appearance. The book was nearly thirty years old. No way would it have been on our shelves for that long without selling, without me seeing it and without it being in our system so some sort of divine intervention had to have placed it there. It was improbable but, as Sherlock Holmes stated in Arthur Conan Doyle's *The Sign of Four*, *When you have eliminated the impossible, whatever remains, however improbable, must be the truth*. And I quite liked the idea that some mysterious force might be bringing Lars and me together. Because I liked the idea of Lars and me *being* together and I certainly hadn't expected to feel that way when I'd glared at his CV in my inbox.

20

LARS

A golf brolly and waterproof had done a great job of keeping my top half dry but nothing could save my feet, despite dodging the biggest puddles between the bookshop and car park. I removed my shoes the moment I arrived back at The Lodge and, cringing, peeled off my wet socks. My trousers had soaked up the water and they slapped against my bare ankles as I ran up the stairs. The house was warm thanks to the underfloor heating but I was chilled through and a hot shower would be the best way to warm up quickly.

Had I really cried at work? Spotting *Anna and the Snow Dragon* on the shelf had thrown me. I'd already felt emotional seeing it and should probably have left it there, but I'd heard Pia's voice in my head reading the first page and felt compelled to open it to see if I'd remembered the words accurately. I had. And before I knew it, I'd turned the next page, and another, and another. I'd lost track of time. I'd lost track of where I was. In my head, I was in Pia's bedroom as she cuddled her knitted dragon. She'd wanted a snow dragon like Jónas and Mum and Pabbi had searched the shops but could only find red or green ones. As the fire dragons and earth dragons bullied Jónas, Pia was adamant she didn't want one of those. Nanna's friend Hilary loved knitting so Nanna had asked her if she could knit a white dragon for Pia. Hilary hadn't been able to find a pattern so she'd made it up as she went along and the result was a bit wonky but Pia loved her dragon all the more for its imperfections, saying that, like in the story, differences were to be celebrated. She slept with her snow dragon every night but, as with the book, I had no idea what had happened to it. Might Nanna know?

After preparing and eating my tea, I had a quick check of my emails and spotted one from Lily. Curious, I clicked on the link and read the article about the reissue of *Anna and the Snow Dragon* next year, touched that Lily had taken the time to find out more about the book and the author. I'd definitely want to gift copies of it around Whitsborough Bay in the hope that the children who found them would fall as much in love with the story as my sister had.

I typed in a quick reply.

To: Lily Appleton
From: Lars Jóhannsson
Date: 5 November
RE: Fascinating Discovery

Really appreciate you researching that and sending the link over. Sad news about the author and her husband but great news that the book's being reissued with sequels. It's a special read. L

I wanted to say more. I wanted to thank her profusely and tell her how much this really meant to me but I was feeling a bit delicate so best to keep my reply short and to the point. After sending it, I rang Nanna.

'Sorry, lovey, but I can only spare a couple of minutes,' she said after we'd greeted each other. 'I'm meeting Hilary and Geraldine in the residents' lounge for a beetle drive and a pie and pea supper.'

'What's a beetle drive?'

'You know! I used to play it with you when you were little. You need to be the first to make a beetle. You roll a die and each number corresponds with a part of a beetle but you can't start until you've rolled a six for the body.'

'And you can't add the antennae until you've got the head,' I said as it came flooding back to me. 'Sounds like a fun evening. I won't keep you long, but I have a random question. Do you remember that book about the dragons which Pia loved – *Anna and the Snow Dragon*?'

'Yes. Hilary knitted the dragon from it. Or at least, she tried to.'

'That's the one. Do you know what happened to the book or the dragon?'

There was a brief pause. 'No, sorry. I don't remember seeing either of them after she passed. Why?'

'I'll tell you next time I see you.'

'I gather they weren't among Jayne's things?'

'No. Have fun at your beetle drive.'

When the call ended, I picked up the remote control and aimlessly flicked through the channels but I wasn't in the mood for watching TV so I switched it off again with a sigh. I felt restless and didn't know why. A beer might relax me so I grabbed one from the fridge and took a long glug.

Wandering from room to room, sipping on my beer, I wondered again if I'd made a mistake moving here. The Lodge was still the house of my dreams but I didn't have the life of my dreams and everything felt out of kilter.

'But how do I get the life of my dreams?' I muttered, pausing in the doorway of one of the spare bedrooms and tutting at the unpacked boxes inside.

As I switched off the light and closed the door, Lily's face drifted into my mind and a feeling of warmth enveloped me. I pictured her empathetic expression when she caught me crying earlier, how she'd discreetly drifted away after making sure I was all right, how she'd checked I was okay again before saying goodbye, and the email she'd sent me.

When I'd applied for the job at Bay Books, I'd been worried about the history between Lily and me but all I could think about now was what a future with her might look like, and it was an incredibly appealing prospect.

21

LILY

Dad's operation on Thursday went well. As it didn't take place until late in the afternoon, he was kept in overnight and Mum left college early on Friday to collect him from the hospital. I'd nipped in after work on Friday and again yesterday but only for fleeting visits as he was woozy on painkillers. Mum had messaged me this afternoon to say he was a lot brighter and looking forward to a Sunday roast at teatime.

Arriving back at Everdene, I'd expected to see my sister's car on the drive ready for her week of looking after Dad, but was surprised to also see her husband's. Cory must have decided to drive across as well. Couldn't say I blamed him as Mum's Sunday roasts were legendary.

Kadence had evidently seen me pulling onto the drive as she dashed out of the house, arms outstretched for a hug. 'I've missed you.'

'Not as much as I've missed you,' I responded. 'And I see Cory's joined us too.'

'He said he's going to miss me this week and wants to cling on to me for as long as he can. But in the next breath, he said he was gagging for one of Mum's infamous roasts and, from the way he was salivating, I think the roasts are the real pull and I'm the afterthought.'

'I'm going to dump my bag and have a quick change,' I said, heading towards Green Gables. 'I'll be ten minutes.'

'Five.'

'Seven,' I said, laughing as I waved a temporary goodbye.

Everyone was in the lounge when I'd changed. Cory hugged me and I was pleased to see some colour back in Dad's cheeks.

'I've got about fifteen minutes before I need to disappear into the kitchen,' Mum said, smiling at Kadence and Cory. 'Plenty of time for you to tell Lily about your house move.'

'You're moving?' I asked, surprised. Their York apartment overlooked the River Ouse and was perfectly positioned for an active social life with only being a short walk to the shops, bars and restaurants.

'We felt it was time for a change,' Kadence said, handing me the sales particulars for an old detached house with a large garden in a village near York.

'As soon as we saw it, we fell in love with it,' Cory said. 'We put our apartment on the market the following day and got an asking price offer the day after.'

'Wow! That was speedy.' I flicked through the details and felt a little pang of envy. The city-centre lifestyle had never appealed to me but a property like this with views across open countryside made my heart sing. It was similar to properties Wes and I had found and admired online.

'It's gorgeous. I'm guessing you won't be in before Christmas.'

Kadence shook her head. 'Just a bit too tight so we're aiming for the end of January.'

'Congratulations. I'll look forward to visiting.' I handed back the sales particulars. 'I can see why you fell in love with it but I'm surprised you were even looking. You love city-centre living.'

'We do,' Kadence agreed, 'but we won't be able to sustain that lifestyle from late spring next year because...'

She passed me something else and I squealed as I looked down at a baby scan photo. 'You're pregnant!'

'Fourteen weeks,' Kadence confirmed.

I launched myself at my sister for another hug and gave Cory one too. 'Congratulations to you both. Fourteen weeks would make it a...' I scrunched up my face, trying to do the maths.

'May baby,' Cory said. 'Seventeenth.'

'That's amazing news. Which explains the house move and also why you're here today, Cory.'

I discovered that they'd told Mum and Dad their news as soon as they arrived and Mum wanted to see my reaction. Hendrix would be the last to know but Kadence and Cory were going to FaceTime him after we'd eaten as he'd be home from work by then and we'd all get the big news on the same day.

When Mum headed into the kitchen, I went to help her. It was lovely seeing her so excited about the news of her first grandchild. She and Dad would be incredible grandparents.

With the vegetables bubbling on the hob, Mum rested her back against the worktop and sipped on a glass of wine. 'Are you okay?' she asked, her voice soft.

'Of course! Why wouldn't I be? It's amazing news.'

'It is, but I know it can't be easy for you.'

She didn't need to explain what she meant. If things had worked out as expected with Ewan, I'd have walked up the aisle before Kadence and we'd have had children first. But it wasn't to be. And if things had worked out with Wes, a pretty village home, marriage and kids would have been imminent but that wasn't to be either and, strangely, it didn't bother me nearly as much as it would have a few weeks ago.

I walked over to the fridge and topped up my glass of wine. 'I really am okay. Being thirty-four, single, childless and living at home aren't what I expected but *the unexpected things in life are often the best.*'

Mum smiled. 'They certainly are. Come here, you!' She pulled me into a hug and kissed the top of my head. 'You mightn't be able to see yet why the hurt those two caused you is for the best, but I'm confident you will do soon.'

'I'm already starting to. Dad told me about you both thinking that neither of them were my Gilbert Blythe and I can see that now. Amazing what a bit of time and space can do.'

'I'm so glad you feel that way. He's out there and I'm sure you'll meet him soon. Maybe you already have.'

Lars immediately came to mind and my heart began racing.

'We'll have to wait and see,' I said, smiling at Mum. 'As Anne Shirley says, *I don't know what lies around the bend, but I am going to believe the best does.*'

Could *the best* be Lars? Everything about him had turned out to be unexpected and I had to admit that offering him the job was the best thing I could possibly have done. He'd already proved himself to be an asset as an employee in a very short space of time. He'd fitted seamlessly into the team and I felt as though the friendship we'd forged when we were nine but lost at school was developing nicely. I'd hoped in my teens for more than friendship and those feelings had returned and intensified with the passing weeks. I had no idea what Lars thought of me but if by some miracle he was attracted to me too, could I even consider going there? For a moment, I really thought I could and it warmed and thrilled me.

But then the what ifs set in and my heart sank. What if it all went horribly wrong? We wouldn't be able to keep working together and, without the cover for Dad, I'd be stuffed. As would my heart. I wasn't strong enough to cope with someone breaking it yet again. I couldn't pick myself up, brush myself off and start over again. I just couldn't. After being rejected by Jordan, Lars, Ewan, Wes and repeatedly by Justin, Lars rejecting me once more would be one rejection too many for me and I'd probably never recover.

The idea of a future with Lars was pretty amazing but it needed to stay just that – an idea, a dream, a fantasy. Because the reality of it going wrong was far too scary.

22

LILY

I'd only got as far as switching on the system at Bay Books the following morning when there was a knock on the front door. I looked up, surprised to see Lars peering through the glass. Last night, I'd resolved not to allow my feelings towards him develop any further, but my heart betrayed me now by racing and setting off the butterflies in my stomach. There was no denying that I'd missed him immensely in the two days we'd been apart.

'You're keen,' I said, ushering him in out of the cold. 'You do realise it's only half seven?'

'I woke up crazily early for some reason and, as you'd mentioned you were coming in half an hour early to ramp up Christmas, I thought I'd be more use here than wandering aimlessly around an unfurnished house.'

He paused and I was about to ask why his house was unfurnished but he spoke again before I had the chance.

'Is it a tea or coffee morning?'

I smiled. 'Always a coffee on a Monday. I need the kickstart.'

'Two strong coffees coming up.'

'Jeeves has already brought up some Christmas decorations,' I said, pointing to a pile of crates in the stationery section. 'I've piled some more up in the staff room. Can you send them up? It'll probably take two trips.'

'Will do.'

Lars slipped his coat off as he walked down the stairs, flexing a bicep as he flung it over his shoulder, which sent my butterflies soaring. He hadn't just *grown into his face*, he'd grown into his body too and in a seriously impressive way. And I needed to stop staring at him. But before I could tear my eyes away, he looked back and held my gaze for a moment and the warm smile he gave me sent the butterflies into chaos. Clearly my resolve was extremely weak!

'Was that everything you wanted?' Lars asked when he joined me a bit later. 'No tree?'

'Not just yet. Last week we did a flavour of Christmas, this week is a bit of bling with lights and garlands but next week will be full-on Christmas, putting the tree up and doing a big window display.' I nodded towards the boxes. 'We should be able to get this lot up today but a key priority is getting some posters done and a newsletter out. We've had an author event confirmed for the end of the month.'

'The end of *this* month?' Lars asked, raising an eyebrow.

I nodded. 'Normally it would be an absolute no at this late stage but she's a regular and she always packs the room out. It's my granny, Josephine Forrest.'

Lars's eyes widened. 'Your grandma is Josephine Forrest?'

'Yes.'

'*The* Josephine Forrest? The one who's sold a gazillion books?'

'The very same, although she's just Granny Blue to me.' Lars looked confused by the name so I expanded. 'Her real name's Bluebell Appleton, Blue for short, but her publisher already had a saga author called Bluebell and another with the surname Appleton so Josephine Forrest is a pseudonym from her middle and maiden names. She has a new book coming out on the 28th and she wasn't going to be able to do a launch because she was having cataracts removed the day before but her op's been put back a week so the launch is on.'

'I can't believe Josephine Forrest is your grandma. My nanna loves her. She's got all her books and has read them several times. I'm pretty sure she's been to all her book launches here too, so she'll definitely want to come to this one.'

'Feel free to call her later and check she's free. Tickets are limited as we don't have much space, but she can have first dibs.'

We strung Christmas garlands across every other bookshelf, keeping the ones in between autumnal, and Lars fired questions at me about how Granny Blue got into writing and what it was like having a famous author in the family. It amused me when anyone got starstruck because I never thought of Granny Blue as famous. Obviously I was aware that, with sales exceeding twenty-five million copies around the world, my granny was a *big* name, but she was also the woman who'd bought me quarters of strawberry bonbons from the corner shop when I was little and always stole one before handing them over, who'd baked fairy cakes with me, pushed me on the swings and read stories to me. Every time I saw her these days, she still produced a paper bag full of strawberry bonbons although she no longer stole one, joking that she valued what teeth she had left.

We added colourful fairy lights across the bookshelves in the children's section before moving into the front and starting on the garlands. I unlocked the door but, with no customers during the first hour, we managed to bling the whole of the downstairs, although the lights in the front were warm white rather than colourful.

Lars offered to repeat the process on each level while I worked on the promotion materials for Granny Blue's launch and, even though that kept me busy, I was very aware of missing him by my side. He was so easy to chat to and I loved our conversations about the books we'd read and loved – exactly how our friendship had started.

When Cassie arrived, she went upstairs to help Lars. Every so often, I heard them laughing and it warmed my heart that they were getting on well, but I also recognised a twinge of envy that it wasn't me making Lars laugh. I had to get over this. I couldn't spend the next three months mooning over one of my employees. Employee. That's what he was. Friend too, I hoped, but it couldn't be anything more.

It was a bitterly cold day but the absence of rain meant there were still folk about. We had a trickle of customers across the morning, the numbers picking up over lunchtime. Lars took the first lunch break, during which I managed to finish the newsletter for Granny Blue's launch, email it out and print posters which I added to the noticeboard and window. When Lars returned, I ate my lunch in the staff room then bundled up in my coat, scarf and hat to meander along Castle Street, curious to see which businesses had fully embraced Christmas.

Castle Jewellery next door had gone simple and classy with white fairy lights and sprigs of holly in their windows but Ginny hadn't yet changed the autumnal dresses in The Wedding Emporium's window. I knew that Tara in The Chocolate Pot always converted to full Christmas on Bonfire Night and, as I passed, I smiled at the Christmas tree near the door. Next to The Chocolate Pot, Carly's Cupcakes had a mixture of Christmas-themed celebration cakes and autumn-themed ones in the window and a sign giving the final dates for Christmas cake and cupcake orders.

Continuing to the end of the street, I crossed over and worked back on myself, pausing by Bear With Me. It had two windows, one either side of the door. In the left one, Jemma had gone traditional with a nativity scene. A wooden straw-lined stable contained a manger, inside of which was one of the miniature artist bears Jemma made. Above the stable was a bright star with another of her designs in the centre. Surrounding the manger were larger teddy bears dressed as Mary, Joseph, the angel Gabriel and the wise men, with a soft toy sheep, donkey and camel looking on. It was a beautiful acknowledgement of the true meaning of Christmas. I moved over to the right window, which was more commercial, with colourful teddy bears and soft toys bursting out of boxes, gift bags and Christmas wrapping as though they couldn't bear to stay hidden for any longer. The words *bringing you hugs on Christmas Day and beyond* were written across the window.

It struck me that I still hadn't arranged a night out with Jemma and Cassie. Peering past the bears, I could see Jemma with a customer so I'd message her later with some dates both Cassie and I were free.

I finished my circuit and returned to Bay Books. When I pushed the door open, Cassie looked up from the computer and smiled. 'Nice walk?'

'Chilly, but good. It's beginning to look a lot like Christmas out there.'

'I had a look on my way in. Some gorgeous displays again. I love what Jemma's done.'

'Me too. The little bear in the centre of the star is the cutest. We need to sort a night out with her so check your diary and let me know when you're free.'

I went down to the staff room to ditch my coat, hat, scarf and bag, thinking about my tour of the street. All the traders made a special effort to create captivating window displays all year round but the Christmas ones always seemed to step up a gear. Lars was restocking some of our stationery items when I returned.

'Lars, while it's quiet and before Cassie finishes, can you help me retrieve something from my car?' I asked.

He followed me outside and helped me ease a wooden display unit from the back seat and carry it into the shop.

'Is this the Bookmas tree?' he asked, his eyes lighting up as we began connecting the pieces together in the children's section. 'Is it the same one from when we were kids?'

I smiled at him, thrilled that he'd not only recognised it but he'd remembered what it was called. 'It is. Granddad George wanted something Christmassy to display the children's books on and he couldn't find anything special so he decided to make his own. It's been here since the very first Bay Books Christmas.'

The display was made up of three panels in the shape of Christmas trees which slotted together to create one big tree. Each panel had a rectangle cut out of it into which shelves had been fitted, making it look as though the books were sitting within the branches of the tree. It had been repainted several times over the years and the edges had been sanded to keep them smooth but it was otherwise exactly as Granddad George had created and it tickled him pink that it had been so enduring.

We'd had a steady increase in the number of festive books being delivered across the past couple of months and, while I'd put some out on the shelves, I'd stored most in the cupboards beneath the shelves ready for the arrival of the Bookmas tree. It could take a considerable number of titles and it always amazed me how often we needed to restock them.

I explained to Lars that we placed books for different ages on each level – picture books around the bottom, chapter books aimed at younger readers on the middle level and young adult fiction on the top. The increasingly smaller shelf spaces worked well for the number of titles we had for each age as well as being at the right height for the children at which the books were typically aimed. There were various hooks at the very top for adding stocking fillers like bookmarks, keyrings and pens.

'What's a typical Christmas like for you?' Lars asked as we carried piles of picture books to the base of the Bookmas tree.

'A welcome relief after a busy December,' I said, laughing. 'We love a big family Christmas at Mum and Dad's. My brother Hendrix lives with his girlfriend but she's not close to her parents so she never wants to spend Christmas with them. My sister Kadence is married but her husband's parents always go abroad for Christmas so neither couple have parent clashes, but they all work shifts so getting time off can be a problem. This year, they've all managed to book Christmas Day off so it's going to be brilliant having everyone together. And when I say everyone, I mean both sets of grandparents too so there'll be eleven of us for Christmas dinner this year.'

'Eleven? Wow! That *is* a big family Christmas.'

We began organising the books and placing them on the shelves.

'It could be the last one. Kadence announced yesterday that she's pregnant so it's possible she and Cory will want to do their own thing next year or maybe they'll invite us all to theirs, so I'm determined to make the most of this year.'

'What sort of things do you do?' Lars asked.

'Eat and drink too much – the usual stuff. We always play Trivial Pursuit or Pictionary or some other sort of quiz game and it gets loud and competitive but I wouldn't have it any other way, especially when I know what a really lousy Christmas looks like.'

'Sounds like a story,' he said, pausing his work to look at me.

I hesitated, unsure as to why I'd blurted that out when I didn't normally talk about Justin to anyone except Cassie. But I felt as though I wanted to share it with Lars. He'd let me in on something deeply personal when he spoke about his sister, and I wanted to let him into my life too.

'It was years ago now,' I said, adjusting to a cross-legged position for comfort. 'Against my better judgement, I arranged to spend Christmas Day with my biological dad, Justin. He has a nasty habit of letting me down so I triple checked it was definitely on and, on Christmas Eve, he messaged me to confirm he was already at the hotel in York, Christmas dinner was booked and he'd see me the following day. So I drove to York on Christmas Day, checked in, went to the bar to wait for him as arranged and, as I was a bit early, I ordered a drink. Because I was on my own, I drank it a bit too quickly so I ordered another one and, even though I took it slower, he still hadn't appeared by the time I was finished. I tried ringing him several times but there was no answer so I decided to knock for him. I asked for his room number at reception and discovered he'd checked out that morning.'

'Without telling you?'

I nodded. 'I checked my texts, emails, everything, but the last message I'd had from him was the one promising me he'd be there.'

Saying the words out loud, they sounded unbelievable. What sort of person did that to their own daughter on Christmas Day? I could still feel that sinking sensation in my gut as time ticked on with no sign of Justin, and the embarrassment as the bar staff shot sympathetic glances in my direction. I could also still feel that flicker of hope burning out as my biological dad rejected me yet again. And I let him.

'That's awful,' Lars said. 'What did you do?'

'Spent the rest of Christmas Day on my own in my hotel room.' Tears rushed to my eyes and I blinked them back.

'I'm so sorry, Lily. Why did he do it?'

'I honestly don't know. Because he could?' I pushed down the lump in my throat, annoyed that the memory could still hurt me years down the line. 'Anyway, I was too upset to even think about eating the meal, especially when I'd have been surrounded by families celebrating. I couldn't drive home as I'd had a couple of large drinks on an empty stomach so I had to stick it out all alone for the worst Christmas ever. Well, until the Christmas a few years later when my boyfriend was given a lose-your-job-or-move-to-Sheffield ultimatum on Christmas Eve and I knew it spelled the end for us. It's a toss-up between the two of them as to which was the absolute worst. Still, two crap ones and thirty-two great ones is something to celebrate.'

I was aware that I sounded flippant, but it was the only way I could deal with the two scenarios which had both left scars on me.

23

LARS

Lily was smiling but I could see the hurt in her eyes and hear the pain in her voice and I longed to reach out and hold her. If we were doing this after hours, I might have done just that but I could hear Cassie talking to someone at the till and, even if there hadn't been any customers in the shop, it probably wasn't appropriate.

'I didn't realise Marcus wasn't your biological dad,' I said.

'Most people don't. Kadence and Hendrix are my half-siblings.'

'Are you still in touch with Justin?'

She scrunched up her nose. 'Yes, if you can call it that. I haven't heard from him in over six months. I was meant to be seeing him on my birthday in March but, in typical Justin style, he cancelled on me the day before. At least it was better than a no-show.'

Once again, I could hear the pain despite the smile and jokey tone. 'I'm so sorry you've been through all that.'

She gave me a weak smile before adding a handful of books to the shelf. This Justin sounded like a waste of space and probably best cut out of her life completely, but I knew from experience how complicated families could be. I also knew how confusing it was to know that their behaviour was unacceptable but somehow to feel conflicted by a sense of loyalty towards them if anyone else pointed that out.

I was stunned to discover that Marcus wasn't Lily's biological father and that her siblings were actually half-siblings. And I was furious with myself because my appalling attitude towards her back in school had been partly triggered by my belief and my envy that she had the 'perfect' family when my parents had seemingly rejected me and my only sibling had died.

The day in late August when Nanna brought me to Bay Books to get my stationery ready for senior school I'd hoped to see Lily. Her dad was behind the till but there was no sign of her. Nanna paid for my stationery and left me to browse the books in the children's section while she visited some other shops. I was reading a blurb when I heard Lily's voice and, still holding the book, I rushed to the archway, excited to see her, but stopped dead when I saw she wasn't alone. The woman with her had dark, curly hair like Lily and had to be her mum. Lily was holding the hand of a young girl and there was a baby asleep in a pushchair. Lily's dad was dishing out hugs and he kissed the baby's forehead then kissed Lily's mum. An older man appeared who I guessed was her granddad and he produced a sweet from behind the little girl's ear, making her giggle, and another from behind Lily's. Peeping round the archway watching them, I felt so incredibly lonely. I wished I had what Lily had and, at that moment, the warmth and friendship I'd felt towards her was replaced by envy and resentment. I slunk back into the children's section and hoped she stayed out the front.

That first day at school, I'd never felt so lost and low. I hated Mum for leaving that morning without saying goodbye and I hated the kids at school who'd already taken the piss out of my accent. I just wanted to be alone with my book and couldn't wait to escape into the world of the Baudelaire orphans, relating hard to their situation of being parentless and hounded by bad fortune. My hackles rose as footsteps approached. Why couldn't the bullies just leave me alone? But it was Lily and she was all smiley and friendly and I should have embraced that but, instead, I released my frustration and anger on her. She didn't deserve any of it but I was in self-destruct mode. What was the point in having any friends when they'd only abandon me sooner or later?

'I think that's about it for the picture books,' Lily said, bringing my focus back to the present. 'If we add any more, they'll get shoved back in and damaged.'

She gathered the spares into a pile and I returned them to the cupboard before removing a pile of chapter books for younger readers and carrying them across to the tree. As Lily looked through the pile, I chewed on my lip, feeling the need to explain the mess in my head all of those years ago and how she'd been unfairly the target of my pain, but was the workplace the right place to do that? She might need some time to process it. She might get angry and want to tell me exactly what she thought of me and I couldn't blame her if she did. I was angry with me. Plus, she had said she wanted to put a line in the sand and forget about it all. What if me bringing it all to the fore opened up some old wounds? The last thing I wanted to do was hurt her again, especially when it sounded like so many men in her life had already caused her pain.

Placing a second pile of paperbacks down next to Lily, I returned to the cupboard for more, still debating what – if anything – to say.

'The Bookmas tree's looking good,' Cassie said, smiling as she joined us. 'Every time I see it, it takes me right back to picking out books when I was this high.' She put her hand out to indicate a toddler's height. 'Did I tell you, Lars, that this shop and particularly the Bookmas tree were responsible for my love of books? If I'd told the six-year-old me that she'd end up working here...'

Cassie's eyes shone as she spoke, just like Lily's did and just like Pia's had whenever books were mentioned.

'Anyway, it's half two so I'm off,' Cassie said. 'There's nobody out the front but there are a few customers upstairs.'

Lily stood up and brushed some dust from the navy-blue tunic top she was wearing. 'I'll go through. Lars, are you okay to finish this off?'

'Yeah, no problem.'

As she returned to the front of the shop with Cassie, I felt disappointed that our conversation was over, although that was maybe a good thing. The confession could wait until another day, if ever.

It didn't take me long to finish filling the Bookmas tree. Lily asked me to string some fairy lights around it and directed me to the cupboard where I'd find the stocking fillers for the hooks.

'You've done a brilliant job,' she said a bit later, her hands clasped round a mug of tea. 'Thank you.'

'I enjoyed it.'

We returned to the front of the shop and Lily went round to the other side of the counter to check the computer for emails.

'Is there anything else you'd like me to do?' I asked.

'I'd like more Christmas books in the window ahead of full Christmas next week. How's your creativity?'

'On a scale of one to ten, I'd say minus figures.'

She laughed. 'You designed your own learning portal so you can't be that bad!'

'That's different. It was driven by logic so I found it easy, but I have zero flair for anything else. My house currently has only white walls and I hate them – far too clinical-looking – but I don't know where to start with colour. I don't know where to start with furniture either so I've barely got any of that. The echoes are so loud, it's like living in a cave, albeit a very bright one because of those white walls.'

'Could you consider an interior designer?'

'I could and I even have a contact but she'll want to know my taste and, embarrassingly, I don't know that either. I've never had to consider it until now.'

'I loved picking out colours and designs for the house I bought with my ex. It needed gutting and we had to save up to have everything done so I had loads of time to design the perfect home. I might have gone a bit over the top with mood boards for every room but I got really into it. We were a couple of months away from the fun part – the decorating and furnishing – when Ewan and I split up.'

The name jolted me. 'You don't mean Ewan Cottler from school?'

'You remember him?'

'Remember him? He was a...' I stopped myself just in time. He'd obviously meant a lot to Lily and I had no right to tell her what I'd thought of him at school, especially when my own record was hardly unblemished.

'A pain in the backside?' she suggested, giving me a gentle smile. 'A show-off, overly confident, annoying... I thought the same too but when he was assigned to me as my lab partner I got to see another side of him. Something shifted between us and we both felt it but we didn't act on it because his parents were moving and he was going with them. When I was twenty-four, he returned to Whitsborough Bay because his employer had set up an office here and that was finally our time. Except they decided the two-office thing wasn't working and they closed it four years later so that was it for us. Ewan hated driving and he hated public transport too so we were a bit stuffed. He went back to Sheffield, we sold the house and I never got to see my beautiful mood boards come to life.'

'That was one of your two crap Christmases,' I said, recalling our earlier conversation.

'That's right.'

'Could you have moved to Sheffield?'

'I considered it. I even spotted a job in a bookshop but I couldn't bring myself to apply. The thought of being an employee in a chain store as opposed to a partner in our family-run indie hurt my heart. And the thought of moving away from my family and friends was unbearable, even to be with Ewan. It would be easy to turn against him and say that he chose his career over me so he'd obviously never cared about me, but the same accusation could be hurled straight back at me because I chose mine and Whitsborough Bay over him.'

'You really love it here?' I said, noticing how her face had lit up.

'So much. *Home is where the heart is* and my heart's right here. Anyway, back to decorating, Mum and Dad said I could do up the annexe however I wanted. It was a tad smaller but it gave me something to sink my teeth into and hopefully one day I'll have my own place and be able to put my interior design head on again and create some fresh mood boards. I've no idea when that'll be, mind. I should have been house-hunting with Wes now – my more recent ex – and I can't seem to muster any energy to do it on my own.'

'How recent an ex?' I asked, curious as to how raw it might be for Lily.

'Seven and a half months now. He was meant to be working in Dubai for two years and he came back to visit after eighteen months and casually announced he'd been offered a further four years. He made out he wanted to discuss it but it was obvious he'd already made the decision so I walked away.'

She'd been looking past me, a wistful expression on her face as though questioning for a moment whether she'd made the right decision.

'Happy birthday to me!'

'It ended on your birthday?' I asked, aghast for her. 'And didn't you say Justin cancelled on you then too?'

She seemed to realise where she was and fixed her eyes on me, her cheeks flushing.

'Apologies, Lars. We were talking about getting creative with the shop window and I somehow turned that into sharing my relationship woes with you. As if you wanted a potted history of my boyfriend disasters. But, yes, Justin cancelled on me and Wes and I split up so this year's birthday is vying for pole position with my two crap Christmases.'

'I'm sure next year will be better.'

'It can't be worse. Thanks for listening.'

'Happy to. And, if it helps, my relationship track record is disastrous. I swear I repel women. Maybe I need to change my body spray. Or my personality.'

Lily placed her hand lightly over mine and, even though her hand was cold, electricity zipped up my arm and throughout my body. 'You don't need to change either of those things, Lars.'

My heart pounded at her words. Was she just being nice or was she telling me something?

24

LILY

You don't need to change either of those things, Lars. What had possessed me to say something like that? And where on earth had the husky voice come from? I didn't know my voice was even capable of that tone.

Lars kept his eyes on mine and I was suddenly aware that my hand was still over his and I didn't want to take it away. Neither of us had spoken for far too long but I couldn't seem to find any words. My heart was racing and those butterflies had taken flight once more. I feared that, if I spoke, I might tell him about the unexpected feelings he'd stirred inside me, how I'd sworn off men but would make an exception for him, and how he was the only person I'd ever told about what really happened with Justin that Christmas Day. Mum and Dad had asked me how it had gone when I returned home on Boxing Day and, too ashamed to admit that my own flesh and blood had let me down so badly, I'd fobbed them off with a stack of true but not-the-full-story comments: *not the best, you know how self-centred Justin can be, found myself counting down the hours till bedtime, won't agree to any future Christmas Days with him.*

The shop door burst open and Hallie and Rocco rushed up to the counter.

'Mummy says the Bookmas tree is back!' Hallie cried, grabbing her brother's hand and running into the children's section.

'Just a quick look,' Cassie called to them. 'We need to get home and ready for swimming.'

She smiled in our direction and, when her eyes widened and her mouth dropped open, I realised I still had my hand over Lars's and snatched it away.

'Have I interrupted something?' Her tone was teasing and I knew I'd never hear the end of this.

'We were just talking about the window display.' It wasn't easy to keep my voice sounding innocent when my thoughts had been far from it.

'Right. Cos I always hold my colleagues' hands when we're discussing the window display.'

Lars pointed to the door. 'I'll just take a look. See if I can shift my creativity quotient into positive figures.'

He'd barely closed the door when Cassie planted her hands on her hips. 'Explain yourself!'

'There's nothing to explain.' My burning cheeks suggested otherwise. 'We were talking, he said something self-deprecating, and I put my hand over his. End of.'

She shook her head. 'Lily Appleton, you're granted a stay of execution today but only because we have to get to the pool. The interrogation will resume tomorrow.'

With a laugh, she disappeared into the back in search of Hallie and Rocco, bundling them out of the shop moments later with a wave. I watched out of the window, hoping she wouldn't say anything to Lars, but she was in too much of a rush. Thank goodness for swimming lessons because I couldn't even begin to explain to Cassie what was going on between Lars and me when I wasn't sure how to explain it to myself.

Lars returned moments later, shivering as he stepped into the warm shop.

'I'm sorry about Cassie,' I said. 'You didn't have to leave.'

'I thought I'd leave you two to it and see if inspiration would hit for the window.'

'Did it?'

He wrinkled his nose. 'Sorry.'

'I'm out of ideas too. I've got plans for next week but I forgot to plan the interim window. Why don't you grab eight festive books – the ones we've got most duplicates of – and I'll get some individual display stands out. We can prop up a few of them and fan the others out.'

While Lars fetched the books, I opened the floor-to-ceiling cupboard behind the till. It had deep shelves which were ideal for storing display stands and props for the window. For now, as creativity was lacking, I lifted out some acrylic stands to keep it simple.

A customer arrived wanting help in finding a book she'd read about in a magazine. It was the sort of query that always made me smile – *I don't know what it's called or the author's name but there was a woman in a red coat/a sunset/a house/a dog on the cover* or, even less specific, *the cover was blue/yellow/grey* – but which also made me determined to track the book down for them. On this occasion, the customer thought it might be set in Greece with a lemon tree on the front. It turned out to be Italy with an orange tree but she purchased the book along with another which caught her eye and left with a big smile on her face. A mystery solved and a satisfied customer made me a happy bookseller.

Lars asked me to check over what he'd done with the window while I'd been serving the customer and I was delighted with it. Not only had he displayed the books beautifully but he'd added a couple of Christmassy soft toys and some of the white flameless candles that I'd ordered for Halloween.

'Looking great,' I said as we stood outside. 'Adding the candles gets you plus figures for creativity.'

The wind whipped my hair and wrapped its icy fingers round my arms. Shivering, I dashed for the door, closely followed by Lars. Winter was definitely coming.

'That wind is biting,' I said, rubbing my arms once we were inside. 'Is it like that in Iceland?'

'Usually colder and stronger.'

I rubbed my icy hands together. 'I'm freezing!'

'My hands are always warm,' Lars said, putting them out towards me. 'Can I?'

When I nodded, he cupped his hands round mine and I marvelled at how warm they were and how long his fingers were, completely encasing my hands. I looked up into his eyes, my heart pounding once more. We were standing so close to each other that I could smell his body spray – definitely *not* women-repellent – and see the lighter flecks and a darker rim around his grey eyes. I really wanted to kiss him and I felt sure that, if I did, he'd respond. *I wonder what Cassie would say if she walked in now* was the thought that dropped into my mind, but I didn't voice it. I didn't want to break the moment.

Unfortunately one of our customers did that for us. I groaned as the landline rang and Lars dipped his head as he released my hands.

I reached for the handset. 'Good afternoon, Bay Books.'

'Lily, it's Mr Bryant. Have my books arrived, my dear?'

Mr Bryant was a long-standing elderly customer who'd recently discovered a love for cosy crime and was interspersing the work of classic writers like Agatha Christie and Dorothy L. Sayers with those of contemporary authors. He'd ordered a couple of Christie's Hercule Poirot books.

'They arrived with this morning's delivery. I left you a message on your landline, but you might not have had a chance to check it yet.'

'Apologies, my dear. I visited a friend this morning and I never remember to check for messages. It must be the third or fourth time I've done that. You must think me such a pest.'

'I think no such thing, Mr Bryant. They're both here and you've got about forty minutes until we close or you can drop by tomorrow.'

'I'm keen to start one tonight, so I'll be with you shortly.'

We said our goodbyes and I replaced the handset. Lars had wandered over to the end of the room and was straightening the piles of books on our new-releases table. I wished Mr Bryant hadn't chosen that moment to call. Or perhaps it was a blessing that he had because I could so easily have kissed Lars and that probably wouldn't have been a good idea.

Lars had his back to me and I couldn't help thinking that, if I didn't speak, there'd be an atmosphere – nothing serious but that sense of awkwardness that came with a moment being interrupted. I fished around for something to say. Anything.

'We didn't get to finish our conversation earlier, Lars.'

I hoped he'd remember what the conversation was because, right now, my mind had gone blank. All I could think about was rushing across the shop floor and kissing him. Bad idea. Very bad idea. Although how much longer I could keep telling myself that, I wasn't sure, because my heart was telling me the opposite.

25

LARS

'We didn't get to finish our conversation earlier, Lars,' Lily said.

I turned around and looked at her expectantly. Which conversation? We'd been talking about the weather and that's when I'd held her hands and felt something shift between us. Heat rushed to my cheeks as I thought about it and I hoped she couldn't see that from across the shop.

'About Christmas,' she said after an inordinately long silence. 'I told you about mine. What were your Christmases like?'

Relaxing, I joined her at the counter once more. 'For years, it's just been Nanna and me and she favours a quiet, traditional Christmas. It's breakfast then gifts and I prepare the dinner while she goes to church. We play Scrabble or cards after we've eaten and watch the monarch's speech followed by a film. Tea's turkey sandwiches and it's usually an early night for Nanna because she treats herself to a couple of sherries and nods off in her armchair. Some would call it boring but I enjoy it. Christmas Day was the only day of the year My Study Hub provided no technical support so, for me, it was a welcome chance to switch off for twenty-four hours.'

'I can imagine. What about when you were a child?'

'Completely different. Well, until we lost Pia, that is.' My voice caught and I hoped Lily hadn't noticed as I didn't want her to feel as though she'd asked a difficult question, so I gave her a warm smile. Childhood Christmases were about the only positive family memories I had. 'We celebrated a blend of the two cultures so we had the British advent calendar, stockings out for Father Christmas on Christmas Eve and a traditional roast turkey dinner on Christmas Day. Icelanders celebrate the season of *Jól* which *is* Christmas but it's more like our yule from the olden days. It starts on 12 December when the first of the thirteen Yule Lads arrives...'

As the shop was quiet once more, I explained to Lily that the Yule Lads were trolls who spent most of the year living in the dark castles in the mountains with a big black cat and their parents – a nasty old troll woman called Grýla and her third husband Leppalúði. For thirteen days in a row the brothers, known as the *jólasveinar*, took turns coming down the mountains to create mischief. Each brother had a name which indicated the type of mischief they liked to get up to – most of it somewhat random like licking spoons or stealing sausages.

I'd only ever talked about the Yule Lads to members of my family so began my explanation a little hesitantly but I was spurred on by Lily's obvious interest and encouraging smiles.

'Children leave a shoe out on the windowsill in the hope of the Yule Lads leaving gifts, just like our tradition of leaving out a stocking on Christmas Eve. And in the same way a naughty child here might get a piece of coal, a naughty child in Iceland might find their shoe contains a potato – perhaps even a rotten one.'

I laughed as Lily wrinkled her nose.

'My pabbi told us that, when they checked their shoes one morning, his younger brother had some sweets but Pabbi had been naughty and there really was a potato in his – a manky one with shoots springing off it. Pabbi was mortified and, of course, his brother dined out on that one for years. I believe it still gets mentioned to this day, and not just at Christmas.'

'My brother and sister would do the same,' Lily said, smiling. 'I'm loving the sound of the Yule Lads. So this happens for thirteen consecutive nights?'

'Yes. It's a different troll each night. The gifts are mainly sweets and small toys but occasionally something bigger gets left. Like all traditions, each family will have a slightly different take on it. And each family will also decide on the version they share with their kids because there's a less family-friendly variation where Grýla also comes down with her big stick, packs misbehaving children into her gigantic sack and cooks them in her favourite stew.'

'Oh, gross!'

'Yep! And apparently she has an insatiable appetite but that's okay because there are plenty of naughty kids around for her to eat. The cat – Jólakötturinn or Christmas Cat – also has a penchant for eating children but, if you've had some new clothes or shoes before Christmas Eve, you're safe from being his dinner.'

'How have I never heard about this before?' Lily's eyes were shining, conveying her excitement. 'It's storytelling genius. So what—'

But she didn't get to finish her question as the door opened and Mr Bryant arrived for his Poirot books. I moved out of their way and adjusted a few book stacks while Lily chatted to him about the most recent cosy crime book he'd read and what he thought of it. As soon as he left, Lily called me back to the till.

'I have to know more. If the trolls put gifts in the shoes but Icelanders don't put stockings out for Santa on Christmas Eve, what happens on Christmas Day? Do children get presents then or not?'

'No. They get them on Christmas Eve instead which is also *Jólabókaflóð* – the Christmas book flood.'

'I've heard of that. We've included it as a fun fact in the Christmas newsletter before. You exchange books, right?'

I nodded. 'It's a big thing, dating back to World War II when Iceland was occupied. Very little got imported so domestic books were pretty much the only Christmas gifts available and, with books and reading being such a strong part of the Icelandic culture, it stuck.'

Lily looked thoughtful. 'We've never done anything to celebrate *Jólabókaflóð* in the shop but, with you being half-Icelandic, it would be lovely to do some sort of promotion or celebration of it this year. Any idea what we could do?'

'That would be amazing. Can I have a think and come back to you?'

'Of course.' She glanced at her watch and grimaced. 'I'd love to hear more about what an Icelandic Christmas Eve and Christmas Day look like but it's almost closing time. Another day?'

'I could chat for ages about it so just shout when you want the next instalment.'

Fifteen minutes later, we were locked up and finished for the day. Lily walked me to the front door and asked whether I'd be spending Christmas with Nanna now that she'd moved into Bay View.

'I don't actually know. She hasn't mentioned Christmas, which isn't like her, and that makes me think she probably wants to spend it with her friends but doesn't like to say because it means I'll be on my own. I'll have to ask her next time I see her.'

'If she does want to be with her friends, don't even think about being on your own. We can always make space for an extra body, assuming you can cope with eleven of us.'

Her tone had been jovial but her smile faded as she added in a softer voice, 'I've never felt so lonely as that Christmas Day when Justin let me down and I wouldn't wish that on anyone.'

We stood by the door, holding eye contact, and I could feel a crackle of something in the air between us. My throat felt very dry as I pushed back the urge to hold her tightly and tell her I'd make sure she never felt lonely again because, if she'd have me, I'd be by her side forever.

Nobody spoke. Nobody moved. I was usually hopeless at spotting signals but even I couldn't miss that Lily felt something too. If only I wasn't so hopeless at all this stuff.

Someone shouting on the street outside made us both jump and Lily turned the key. 'I'd better let you escape.'

I didn't want to *escape*. I wanted to stay with her but, being me, I didn't share that. A cold blast hit me as the door opened.

'I really do want to hear more about Christmas in Iceland,' Lily said. 'It's fascinating.'

'Happy to share everything I know.'

Conscious I'd already lingered in the doorway far too long, I stepped onto the cobbles.

'Don't let Grýla and the Christmas Cat gobble you up,' I said and, for reasons I'll never comprehend, I saluted her. I actually raised my hand to my forehead and saluted. *Kill me now!*

My cheeks burned as I hurried along the cobbles, desperate to get away before I made myself look any more of an idiot. The salute had been embarrassing enough but what had I said to Lily? *Don't let Grýla and the Christmas Cat gobble you up.* Argh! She wasn't a naughty child, we weren't in Iceland and there was still over a month to go until the start of *Jól*.

Today had been filled with special moments that I wanted to remember but I could guarantee that the scene which would forever play on a loop in my head would be that excruciating final minute. I could do with Grýla and the Christmas Cat gobbling me up to end my humiliation.

26

LILY

After tea with my parents, I returned to Green Gables and replayed my day – or at least the parts of it that involved Lars. The expression on his face when he said *Don't let Grýla and the Christmas Cat gobble you up* was absolutely priceless. He looked like he wanted the ground to swallow him up. I don't think I've ever seen anyone walk quite so fast, and that salute? From his grimace, I suspected he'd never done that before. So why had he done it to me? The only explanation I could think of was that he had feelings for me which had got him all tongue-tied and tangled up. I needed to talk to Cassie but there was no point calling her now when she had Hallie and Rocco to sort out after swimming followed by teatime, bathtime and bedtime. I dropped her a message asking her to ring me when the kids were settled as something had happened and I needed her take on it.

'It's Lars, isn't it?' she asked, FaceTiming me shortly after 8 p.m. 'You've kissed!'

'No, we haven't! But I wanted to and I'm certain he did too.'

I ran through everything that had happened across the day, right up to our moment by the door after closing time.

'Why didn't you just ask him out?' she asked.

'Because I've sworn off men after what happened with Wes and Ewan.'

Cassie tutted and shook her head at me. 'Lars isn't Wes or Ewan and you can't take yourself out of the game just because those two twonks broke your heart. I think you should ask Lars out.'

'What if I got it all wrong? I'm his employer. How awkward would that be – me hitting on him and us having to work alongside each other every day? He might leave.'

'Woah there! I don't think there's any chance of that. Yes, it would be as awkward as a cow on roller skates if he wasn't interested in you but remember who walked in on the pair of you holding hands earlier.'

'We weren't holding hands. He'd said something deprecating and I was being sympathetic.'

Cassie raised her eyebrows at me. '*The lady doth protest too much, methinks.* Say what you like but I was there, Lily, and the chemistry between you was palpable.'

Trust Cassie to quote Shakespeare to me, but her point about the chemistry was valid. I'd had it with Ewan and Wes so I recognised it, but it had been way stronger with Lars than anything I'd ever felt with either of them and that both delighted and terrified me.

'Anyway, despite me swearing off men, I think I did ask him out. Sort of.'

'You did or you didn't. What were your exact words?'

'Something like, I really do want to hear more about Christmas in Iceland.'

'Wow! With such clear intentions declared, I have no idea why he didn't immediately confirm a time to pick you up on his fearless steed and whisk you off into the sunset.'

I laughed at Cassie's exasperated facial expression.

'Fair enough. I can see why he didn't run with that one. I think he had a little disaster of his own when he left too.'

I told Cassie about his salute, what he'd said about Grýla and the Christmas Cat, and how mortified he'd looked. 'You know what it reminded me of?'

We burst out laughing as we both gave Baby Houseman's quote from *Dirty Dancing* about carrying a watermelon.

'It was definitely a watermelon moment,' I said. 'But it was kind of adorable.'

'That's because you find Lars Jóhannsson *kind of adorable*.'

I sighed dreamily. 'I think I might. How did that happen?'

'I can't tell you how, but I can tell you when and where. The teen years in the school playground.'

If I denied it, she'd quote *Hamlet* again. I'd been drawn to Lars the moment we met in the bookshop and, while I was far too young back then for those feelings to be labelled as attraction, that's definitely what they'd become when we hit our teens.

'You've known all of this time?'

'Of course! I'm all-seeing, all-knowing. To be fair, I had forgotten. Having kids seriously messes with your brain but, seeing you together earlier, it all came flooding back to me.'

Jared appeared on the screen behind her and called *hello* to me.

'Hi, Jared,' I said, waving.

'That wonderful fiancé of mine has just run a bath for me so I need to go while it's still hot enough to almost scald me.'

'Aw, that's so sweet of him.'

'Sweet, my arse. I asked him to do it.' She laughed. 'No, he *is* sweet and I'm incredibly lucky to have him. He's luckier to have me, mind, but...'

She squealed as a cushion bounced off her head.

'Definitely got to go! Cushion fight! See you tomorrow.'

The phone disconnected before I had a chance to say goodbye. I sat back on the sofa, grinning. If Cassie thought there was chemistry, then there was definitely chemistry as she wasn't the sort to give me false hope. But what a shock to discover she'd known I had feelings for Lars back in school. She'd never said anything. Or had she? Knowing Cassie, she would have done and, knowing me, I'd have denied it. The problem now was what to do about it. Despite my determination not to get involved with anyone, I couldn't stop thinking about Lars and wondering if our time was now.

27

LARS

I arrived at Bay Books on Tuesday morning with a knot in my stomach, feeling more than a little nervous about seeing Lily again after whatever it was that had happened between us yesterday and my cringeworthy words and actions when I left. Until that point, it really had been a great day and I'd felt closer to her than I had to anyone in a very long time. But what if she regretted sharing so much about her personal life with me? What if she regretted touching me and things were awkward between us?

I needn't have fretted because, as soon as Lily opened the door, she gave me her warmest smile and a greeting which made me laugh.

'Good morning, Mr Creative-Plus-Figures, window dresser extraordinaire.'

'Good morning to you too, although I'm not sure I deserve that title.'

'Credit where it's due. You made the Bookmas tree look amazing too so I think you have more of an eye for design than you realise.'

She pulled the door closed behind us and shivered.

'Ooh, it's bitter out there again today. I hope you've brought your warm hands with you because I might need them later.'

It broke the ice and we both laughed about it although, as I made our morning coffees, I wondered whether that had been her way of saying *yesterday was about warming my hands up and nothing more so please don't read anything into it.*

I sent the drinks up in Jeeves and joined Lily moments later. She had her hands cradled round her mug and mine was waiting on the counter.

'My hands are freezing,' she said with an apologetic smile. 'The mug beat you to it.'

That statement seemed to confirm my earlier conclusion until she added, 'I really enjoyed yesterday. You're a good listener, Lars. It meant a lot.'

'Any time. You're a good listener too.'

'We got interrupted. It's not easy to—'

The landline rang at that point and she rolled her eyes at me as she reached for the handset. I sipped my coffee as she responded to what appeared to be a cold call about energy bills.

'I was about to say it's not easy to chat when you work in retail,' Lily said when she hung up. 'As that phone call just proved.'

'We'll have to go out for a drink after work one day instead.' I hadn't meant to say that but I'd blurted it out before I could stop myself. It wasn't exactly asking her to go on a date but it was very close.

She smiled. 'That'd be nice.'

Her enthusiastic response made my heart leap. Maybe she hadn't regretted any part of yesterday after all. Best to strike while the iron was hot and pin down a day. But the phone rang again. Why? In the three weeks I'd been working at Bay Books, there'd been hardly any phone calls and now there'd been three in the space of two days, all badly timed.

'Sorry,' she said, reaching for the receiver. 'Good morning, Bay Books... Ah, yes! Thanks for calling back. Did my email make sense?... I'll open it now...'

Lily tucked the handset under her chin and tapped her password into the computer. It sounded like it might be a long conversation so I took my coffee through to the children's section to give her some space. It was my favourite section of the shop, thanks to the happy childhood memories it evoked, especially from being in here with Pia. Looking at the Bookmas tree, I remembered her sitting cross-legged on the floor shortly after her fifth birthday, her hat, coat and scarf abandoned beside her as she carefully studied the cover illustration on a book she'd chosen before turning it over to read the blurb. Nodding her approval, she reached for another and repeated the exercise until she had a pile of maybe a dozen books. Mum appeared at that point and laughed, reminding Pia that she was only meant to be choosing two books to read over the weekend and that, if she wanted the rest, she'd have to see what the Thirteen Lads,

Jólabókaflóð and Father Christmas brought for her. Mum asked me to help my sister back into her coat and make sure she was wrapped up warmly while she paid for two of the books.

'You look lost in thought,' Lily said, appearing by my side and making me jump. 'Sorry! I didn't mean to creep up on you like that.'

'It was me being miles way. I was looking at the Bookmas tree and had a sudden memory of my sister.' I explained what had happened, adding, 'Mum whipped the rest of the books away while she didn't think we were looking. Pia received a couple of the books for *Jólabókaflóð* and the rest on Christmas Day. That's how I discovered that Father Christmas didn't exist and it was really my parents.'

'Aw, Lars, how old were you?'

'I'd turned nine just before Christmas so it wasn't too bad. And it's not like Mum did it deliberately – I was just too observant for my own good. I never spoiled it for Pia, though. She always believed. She thought Christmas was magical. Any time she was really ill, she'd pretend it was Christmas. She said she could feel the magic in the air and it made her feel better.'

'That's a beautiful memory. It sounds like she was an amazing little girl.'

'She was. The absolute best.' The words came out croaky and I could feel myself getting emotional.

Lily placed her hand on my arm and gave me a reassuring smile. 'When we talk away from the shop and all the interruptions, I'd love to hear more about her if it's not too painful to share your memories with me.'

Gazing into her kind eyes, I realised I wasn't just falling for Lily Appleton all over again. It was a done deal. But we were at work and it wasn't the place to do anything about it. I cleared my throat and smiled at her. 'That would be great. So, what are today's priorities?'

'We've had a brilliant response already to Granny Blue's book launch so, after we've dealt with the delivery, we'll get an attendee list started and I'll tell you more about how it'll run.'

* * *

Although Monday had been quiet, business really picked up across the week and the times when there wasn't a customer in the shop were few and far between. We didn't typically have many customers during the first hour of trading but that – and the hour before it – were always busy dealing with orders placed overnight and sorting out the delivery which usually arrived shortly after nine.

I kept blowing hot and cold as to whether to get it all out on the table with Lily about my crazy obsession with her having the perfect life when clearly she'd had her own challenges with her flaky biological father but, even if I had made my mind up to tell her, there wasn't the opportunity. It wasn't the sort of conversation to have in twenty parts between customers.

That wasn't the only conversation we didn't revisit. Going out for a drink after work never cropped up again. I'd psyched myself up to asking Lily out for a drink on Tuesday but it seemed she and Cassie were going out after work with Jemma who ran the teddy bear shop. I hadn't a clue how to raise it after that because I wasn't sure what Lily wanted – a friendly chat with a colleague or something more – and I didn't want to mess things up. There'd been no further honest conversations, no moments between us, no more touches. I wondered whether I'd imagined the chemistry and my confidence gave me a mocking salute before running off down the cobbles.

Danika and I arranged to meet up in The Purple Lobster after we both finished work on Friday. Christmas had arrived in the pub with a large tree just inside the door, colourful paper garlands strung across the ceiling and bar, and paper decorations in the shape of Christmas trees, bells, baubles and snowmen hanging from the beams.

It was busy but there was no sign of Danika. She favoured fruit ciders so I ordered one of those for her and a pint for me and had only just found a table and sat down with our drinks when she arrived, sounding breathless.

'Sorry I'm late,' she said as she placed her coat over the back of her chair and unwound her scarf.

'I honestly don't mind.'

She poured her drink into a branded glass and took several big gulps. 'I needed that.'

'Dare I ask?'

Danika sighed heavily. 'Cat arranged for her latest conquest to pick her up as she finished work, which would have been fine, except she'd forgotten to tell her previous bloke that they were through and they were both sitting in the waiting room. As soon as she walked in, they both stood up, grinning at her, stepped forward to kiss her and realised what had happened. It turns out they already knew each other because one of them had previously had a fling with the other's now ex-girlfriend, so it all kicked off and we had to call the police to break them up. That was fun.'

I winced. 'You didn't get caught up in it, did you?'

'No. I was the one behind the glass partition making the 999 call. Cat was fine too but one of our cardboard promo stands got a fist through it. The upside is that Dad insisted on Cat going back home with him so he and Mum could have a conversation with her about her *life choices*.' She added air quotes to emphasise the last two words. 'Hopefully they can get through to her because nothing I say ever does and...' She paused and scrunched up her face. 'Please don't judge me but I took advantage of the situation. I took Dad aside and suggested he might want to encourage Cat to move home while she sorts herself out because the drama's getting too much for me and I'm on the verge of asking her to leave. Does that make me an awful person?'

I shook my head. 'I think it makes you human. She was only meant to be staying with you temporarily. It would be different if she had nowhere else to go but you've got to be allowed to have your own space.'

'My own *tidy* space,' she said. 'Thank you. I needed to hear that. Anyway, enough about me, how's your week been?'

'Mixed. I need your advice on something...'

Danika already knew about my parents divorcing and me living with Nanna but I hadn't told her about my sister dying and how that tragic loss had triggered it all, so I shared that and how hard the months that followed had been.

'That first day at school when Mum wasn't there to take my photo, it felt as though a red mist descended on me. I hated Mum for abandoning me, hated Pabbi for returning to Iceland and even hated Pia for leaving me. I hated the whole world and was determined never to let anyone in again because, if I didn't let them get close, they couldn't hurt me when they left. Which they would, because that was what people did to me. Sooner or later, they all abandoned me.'

'Aw, Lars, you must have been in so much pain.'

'I was and I took it out on Lily...' I shared what had gone through my mind when I'd seen Lily with her family in Bay Books and how horrible I was to her that first day at school.

'At first, I had no regrets about pushing Lily away. It felt like the right thing to do for both of us. But when I hit the teenage years, I longed to go back and change that conversation behind the sports hall. I'd sometimes catch her eye across the classroom and I had this sense that one encouraging smile was all it would take to change the course of our relationship, and yet I kept this *I'm not your friend* mask firmly in place right up until the day when I walked into Bay Books hoping for a job.'

'So that was why I had to push you to apply.'

I nodded. 'I really wanted the job but I was embarrassed about seeing her again, mortified by how I behaved. I even called her *Little Miss Perfect* and it was so unfair and so stupid because her life wasn't perfect. Her biological father treated her like crap. Still does. I got it all so spectacularly wrong.'

'Don't beat yourself up about it, Lars. You were a confused kid in a lot of pain and I can see why you'd project that onto someone else. And I can see why you'd push Lily away to protect yourself from being abandoned again. You mentioned wearing a mask and you're not alone. I think most of us wear masks. Some don't wear them very often, some wear them in certain circumstances, and some have them on nearly all the time. Like me. Like you.'

I'd done it for most of my life. I'd worn my *I'm fine with being ignored* mask while my parents battled over what was right for Pia because I didn't want to give them further cause to fight. I'd worn my *I'm okay without my parents* mask in front of Nanna because I didn't want her to feel like she wasn't enough on her own or to give her any reason to abandon me like my parents had. I'd worn my *I know exactly what I'm doing* mask while running My Study Hub when, most of the time, I was freewheeling. And I'd worn my *I don't want or need any friends because I'm happier on my own* mask at school, pushing away the one person whose friendship I absolutely *did* want and need.

I'd always kept it real with Pia. My sister had been wise beyond her years. Any time I'd tried to hide anything from her, she'd called me out on it so I'd shared how much I hated Mum and Pabbi fighting and how terrified I was every time Pia had an asthma attack. She told me to think of the magic of Christmas and let my world sparkle instead, but it was so hard to do that after she was gone, especially when Pabbi left next, and then Mum.

'A mask has been my default mode for so long,' I admitted, 'but I haven't worn it around Lily. I feel like I can show her who I really am.'

Finding *Anna and the Snow Dragon* had made me vulnerable around her and I'd shared things with her that I'd never spoken about to anyone else.

'If you feel that way, you need to tell her everything or it's going to niggle away at you and it'll come out eventually, probably at a bad time. You really like her, don't you? As in you want more than friendship?'

I nodded.

'Then it's best to get everything out on the table before that happens. She's already forgiven you because she can see you're not the same person anymore and I can't imagine she wouldn't be even more forgiving when she understands where the behaviour came from.'

'When you put it like that…'

Danika raised her glass and clinked it against mine. 'To being open and honest and letting the people we care about see behind the mask.'

It was a bit long to repeat so I smiled at her and said, 'To that.'

'Speaking of being open and honest and looking behind the mask,' she said. 'I have a date tomorrow night. She's called Milana, she moved here from Latvia when she was fourteen and she's stunning. She was doing short-term cover as a hygienist at work and, oh my God, she has the most perfect set of teeth I've ever seen.'

I can't say I particularly noticed a person's teeth but I could imagine that, having a dentist dad and working in a dental practice, it would be high on the list of what Danika would notice.

'Do you know what really hooked me?' she asked.

'Can't even begin to guess.'

'Milana put some chocolates in the fridge with a Post-it note on them saying *Hands off, Cat! Get your own!* It was only the start of her second week with us and she'd already sussed my sister out. I thought to myself, *this is a woman I have to get to know!* And that really surprised me because I haven't been interested in anyone for years.'

'Who suggested the date?'

'Me. I'd already done my due diligence – casually discovered she was single and her last partner had been a woman – so I decided to go for it.'

'I'm impressed. I'm crap at reading signals and really struggle with the asking someone out on a date thing.' I thought about the conversation with Lily about catching up outside of work and how, after we'd been interrupted and after I'd discovered she had plans that evening with Cassie and Jemma, I'd been too chicken to go back to it and commit to it happening.

'I reckon you're better at reading the signals than you think. You can tell when someone's interested – you just can. It's little things like them holding eye contact for longer than usual, finding reasons for physical contact, turning round and catching them gazing at you and all that sort of stuff. Can you put ticks in any of those boxes for Lily?'

'All of them.'

'Then she's interested and you should go for it. I know it's scary taking that leap but sometimes you just have to. I could have found a hundred reasons for not asking Milana out – most of them being about the impact of letting someone into my life when I like things how they are – but I wouldn't let myself go there. I find her attractive and I'm determined to just go with the flow and take it one date at a time with Milana instead of panicking about her disrupting my routine. And do you know who helped me come to that conclusion? You.'

'Me? What did I do?'

'Disrupt my life with video calls, career counselling and drinks after work. At the risk of sounding soppy, you've made my life better so I figured not all disruptions to my routine are bad ones.'

'You say the nicest things,' I said, grinning at her. 'And it's reciprocal. I've never had a best mate and I like it.'

'I'm your best mate? Aw, Lars, that's the nicest thing anyone's ever said to me. Happy to accept the position and I think I should get another round in to celebrate our new best friendship.'

As she headed to the bar, I chuckled to myself. I'd been seeking a perfect relationship and I hadn't found it with Cat but I'd found a perfect friendship with her sister instead. Life was surprising sometimes, and it could get even better if I took a leaf out of Danika's book and asked Lily out. The worst thing that could happen was a no but what if she said yes? The thought made me feel all warm inside.

28

LILY

I arrived at Bay Books at half seven on Saturday morning. After a bitterly cold start to the week, the wind had dropped and the temperature had risen. With sunshine forecast for today, I knew we'd be in for a busy one and wanted to get as much admin done as possible before opening.

I hadn't confirmed a date for Lars to start working weekends and wondered if that had been a mistake. If it was as busy today as I suspected it might be, lunchtime in particular would be tight with just Alec, Flo and me in.

The first half an hour was as dead as a Monday morning, which wasn't normal. We hadn't had a single customer and, while that meant Alec and I had been able to unpack and check the delivery – a task which could drag on until mid-afternoon on a Saturday – it unnerved me.

'Makes you wonder what they know that we don't,' Alec said, joining me by the window where I was frowning at how eerily quiet Castle Street was for a Saturday.

'I'm stunned by how dead it is. Nice days like this usually bring them rushing out.'

By the time Flo arrived ready for her ten o'clock start, we'd had three customers but only one of them had bought anything. She expressed surprise at the shop being empty before she went downstairs to drop her bag and coat off and make a round of drinks but, when she returned, we'd been inundated with customers as though a coachload had arrived and dropped them off right outside the door.

'How long was I down there?' she whispered as she joined me at the till.

We didn't have the space for two tills but we had a handheld device connecting to the system on which we could take card payments when there was a big queue like now. Flo took payments on that while Alec remained on the shop floor, responding to customer queries between tidying and restocking.

It took until half eleven for us to clear the queue, at which point a woman I didn't recognise approached the till. She had a face like thunder and I braced myself for a complaint.

'Are you the manager?' she asked, a sharp edge to her tone.

My stomach lurched as I hated confrontations, but I'd never let a customer see my fear, so I smiled and said brightly, 'Yes. I'm Lily. How can I help?'

'You need to see this.' She turned and marched towards the children's section.

I left Flo to cover the till and followed the customer, dreading to know what I was going to find.

'They're *not* mine.' She pointed to a young boy and girl sitting on the floor with a selection of picture books from the Bookmas tree strewn round them. As I got closer, my stomach plummeted to the floor. The children weren't reading the books. They were scribbling all over them. My precious, beautiful books! I glanced round the section but all the adults appeared to be accompanied by other children.

'I've already asked,' the woman said. 'No idea who they're with. I asked the pair of them to stop but they refused in words children their age shouldn't know.'

The girl reached for another book from the tree and I dived towards her.

'Let's just leave this on the tree, shall we?' I said, my voice playful as I eased the book from her hand.

'I want to colour,' she cried, trying to snatch it back from me.

'That's lovely, but we colour in colouring books, not story books.'

The boy glared at me and, in an act of clear defiance, grabbed another book and angrily scribbled across one of the pages. If they'd been toddlers, I could have understood the destruction but they looked about the same age as Cassie's daughter Hallie – six years old – so they really should have known better. Spotting the barcode labels attached to the ends of the pens, I realised they'd liberated them from our stationery section.

'I own this shop and I need you to give me those pens,' I said, my voice firmer as I crouched down beside them.

The girl pouted but she handed hers over. The boy responded by scribbling on yet another page.

'Those books don't belong to you, do they?' My voice was even firmer now. 'Fun's over.' I held my hand out. 'Please give me the pen.'

'No!'

He held the pen out of my reach but relinquished his hold on the book. Spotting my chance, I snatched the book from his lap and swiftly gathered the others off the floor. The customer who'd alerted me to the problem came to my aid, standing in front of the Bookmas tree, blocking the children from grabbing any more books.

The girl stayed on the floor, arms folded, looking down and I sensed that she knew she'd done something very wrong, but the boy leapt to his feet and turned to face me, a look of disgust on his face.

'Give me my books back!' he cried.

'They're not your books,' I responded, keeping my voice low, conscious of the hushed atmosphere and the customers watching the interaction. 'They belong to the shop.'

'I want them!' He hurled the pen at me and it bounced off my arm to goodness knows where. Next moment he launched himself at me, pummelling my stomach. For a small child, he could certainly pack a punch. With a yelp, I leapt back and held the books protectively across my stomach but that didn't deter him as he kicked at my shins too, yelling that he hated me. If it hadn't been for his sister grabbing his arms and yanking him away, still kicking, I don't know what I'd have done next. How do you defend yourself from a child attacking you without hurting them?

Next moment, the boy broke free from the girl and I feared another attack but he ran to a woman in a bright red puffer jacket who'd appeared by my side.

'What's going on?' she demanded, wrapping her arms protectively round the boy as he glared at me.

'Are these your children?' I asked.

'Yes. Why?'

'They've been drawing in the books.'

'And?'

'And they've damaged them.' I opened one out to show her. 'I'm afraid I'll need you to pay for them.'

'They didn't come in with pens. Where did they get them from?'

'They took them from the stationery section.'

'Then it serves you right for having pens next to children's books. What did you expect?'

What did I expect? Not this situation, for sure. Red Jacket terrified me and I wanted to run away and cry but this was my shop and her children were in the wrong so I stood my ground.

'They're not kept in the children's section and what I'd expect is for parents or carers to stay with their children to make sure nothing like this happens.'

'You tell her, love,' called one of the customers.

'Those kids are feral,' another one added.

While I appreciated the support, the second comment was extremely unhelpful in the circumstances. Red Jacket's cheeks blazed the colour of her coat and her eyes flashed as she cast her gaze around the customers. I swear that, if she'd spotted who made the feral comment, she'd have decked them.

'If you'd like to come to the till, I can offer you the books at a discount as a goodwill gesture.'

She turned back to me and looked me up and down, curling her lip.

'I'm the only one making any gestures round here and here's mine.' She stuck her middle finger up at me, to gasps all round. 'And you needn't think I'm buying this from you, you stuck-up little bitch.'

She had a guidebook for Florida in her hand and she ripped the front cover off it before hurling it onto the floor. Grabbing each child by the arm, she stamped on the book before dragging the kids out of the shop.

All eyes were on me, shocked expressions all around, murmurs of disgust at the woman's behaviour. Rude customers were sadly all too common in the retail industry and I'd been shouted at and sworn at before but this was a new low, making me feel angry and humiliated. Tears pricked my eyes, my throat burned and I was trembling from the shock. I desperately wanted to run downstairs, lock myself in the loo and bawl my eyes out but I couldn't leave Flo and Alec on their own to pick up the pieces. I was the owner and I needed to be professional.

'I'm really sorry about the disruption,' I said, unable to stop the shake in my voice. 'Please don't let it spoil your day. We can give you a 20 per cent discount for any books you buy from the children's section today to apologise.'

'There's no need to do that,' someone said, but I didn't catch who or I'd have given them a grateful smile.

'Are you okay?' The woman who'd alerted me to the problem was standing by my side, her eyebrows knitted with concern.

'Not really, but thanks for letting me know when you did.' I glanced down and did a quick count of the books in my arms. 'It could have been more than nine books if you hadn't.'

She crouched down and picked up the Florida guidebook and cover and added it to my collection.

'More than ten,' I whispered.

She placed a reassuring hand on my shoulder. 'I don't know how you managed to keep so calm.'

'Me neither. I didn't feel it. Thanks again.'

A young girl – in her early teens at a guess – passed me the two pens.

'Aw, bless you for picking them up for me,' I said, smiling at her.

'I don't like bullies,' she said. 'I'm sorry they were mean.'

'Thank you. Me too.'

She returned to her family and I took a deep breath before going through to the front section to tell Alec and Flo about the discount and to check whether any of the precious books in my arms had survived the pen attack, fighting hard to keep the tears at bay when it became obvious that they hadn't. I couldn't contemplate selling any of them, even at a heavy discount. The mindless destruction and the waste turned my stomach.

Alec and Flo were amazingly supportive. They must have messaged Tara because an emergency hot chocolate and a salted caramel brownie arrived with one of the staff from The Chocolate Pot. The kind gesture from my team had me all choked up.

'We thought you might need it,' Alec said.

'I do. I'm going to savour this.'

'Why don't you take it downstairs?' Flo suggested.

If I had some alone time in the staff room, I wouldn't be able to stop myself from repeatedly reliving that ugly scene. It would make me cry and I wouldn't be able to hide my upset because my eyes frustratingly remained bloodshot for a couple of hours after crying. I'd need that release at some point but I'd save it for the privacy of Green Gables.

'I'm fine here, thanks. Plus, it's time you took your break.'

It took some persuasion but Flo went down to the staff room while Alec took a customer to the poetry section, leaving me alone at the till. All but one of the customers who'd been in the children's section during the incident had now left and all but one had bought books. They all shared how shocked and disgusted they were about the behaviour and how sorry they felt for me, although only one refused the discount. I felt sorry for me too, but I also felt sorry for Red Jacket's children. While what they'd done was very wrong, had anyone actually taught them that? From their mother's behaviour, I suspected not, which didn't bode well for their future.

The final customer made her way downstairs and placed a pile of books on the counter.

'Everyone's getting a book for Christmas this year,' she declared, as if she felt she needed to explain the random selection of titles.

I smiled at her. 'Best Christmas present ever. Although I will admit to being slightly biased.'

'Don't give me a discount on the children's books, though. I was buying all of these anyway and it's not fair you should lose out because of someone else. Are you okay?'

'Not really, but I've got to get on with it.'

'Have you let the police know?'

'They were just kids.'

'I'm thinking more about the mother. She's responsible for the damage they caused because she left them unsupervised, she refused to pay and she ripped up a book herself. There's no excuse for that. She shouldn't be allowed to get away with it.'

She'd become more passionate and steadily louder as she spoke, which she evidently realised as she lowered her voice. 'Sorry. I used to work in retail too and some of the damage customers caused and the abuse they gave staff broke my heart. It's why I left.'

'It can be tough at times. I'm sorry it got that bad for you. What do you do now?'

'I work behind the bar at the theatre so still with customers but a different type. The occasional glass gets broken but it's never deliberate.'

When I told her I hadn't been to the theatre in years, she whipped out a programme of upcoming events from her bag and suggested I treat myself.

'You're going to tell the police, then?' Alec asked after the woman left.

'I might as well. I'll check the CCTV first and, if we've caught her clearly, I'll give Sergeant Haines a shout. I don't know if they'll be able to identify her and, if they do, I don't know that they'll be able to do anything but it's worth a try. That customer was right. There should be consequences for that sort of behaviour.'

Flo returned from her break and, feeling lifted by all the customer support, I decided to take ten minutes to myself after all and enjoy the rest of my hot chocolate and my brownie in peace and quiet. To make sure I didn't focus on the incident, I'd scroll through the socials and see whether the Paperback Pixie had gifted any books today. They'd been quiet recently.

29

LILY

Settled in the staff room with my first bite of brownie melting in my mouth, I took out my phone and clicked into the Paperback Pixie's Instagram feed. They'd been active this morning and I smiled as I scrolled through the photos showing five novels from different genres left in front of the beach huts in North Bay. The huts were painted in bright colours – red, orange, yellow, sky blue and lime green – and the books propped up against them had covers matching those paint colours. Three finders had tagged the Pixie into their finds and I messaged Cassie alerting her to the post. She replied immediately.

> **FROM CASSIE**
>
> You're not going to believe this but the kids and I have been for a walk along North Bay and we saw the person finding the book by the red beach hut. Special moment! I spoke to her and she was so excited. The kids weren't as enthusiastic as me so we're scoffing ice-cream sundaes now as a treat after my embarrassing giddiness. Yes, I know, it's November! I'll tell you more tomorrow. Bring on Christmas! x

How exciting that Cassie had witnessed someone finding one of the Paperback Pixie's books. She'd have been beside herself and I could imagine Hallie and Rocco being completely bewildered by it all. She'd added several Christmassy emojis to the end of her message. Tomorrow evening after we closed,

Cassie and I would be removing everything autumn-themed and fully converting the shop to Christmas including putting up the tree and creating a festive window display. We usually did it with Dad, breaking off after a couple of hours for takeaway pizza. It would take longer with just the two of us but I was looking forward to a catch-up with Cassie on her own, although I knew what the main subject for discussion would be – Lars. I'd made her promise not to do any matchmaking between us but she'd taken every alone moment to express how exasperated she was with us both for not getting our acts together and how she wished she hadn't made me that promise.

I clicked onto Facebook next. Cassie had shared a photo of herself and the kids with their sundaes, all with blobs of ice cream on their noses, which lifted me further. There was a post from our friend Donna announcing that she and her husband Joey were expecting their first baby, with a scan photo attached. I was delighted for them and responded with love, adding my congratulations to the comments.

I was glad I'd come downstairs as I rarely scrolled through my phone during work hours and asked my team not to look at theirs until they were on a break. My social media distraction just now had given me the boost I needed and I could return to the shop floor with a smile on my face and a spring in my step.

Popping the final piece of brownie into my mouth, I scrolled a little further and immediately regretted it. My smile slipped and I gulped down the brownie, my heart pounding as I stared at the couple on the screen. It had never entered my head to unfriend Wes on Facebook because he never used it. In the time we'd been together, the only entries on his feed were ones I'd tagged him in and an annual barrage of birthday greetings to which he never reacted.

Celebrating seven months with this incredible man and never been happier, the caption read, accompanied by a series of photos of a stunning blonde cuddled up to my ex. Seven months? That hurt. A week tomorrow would be the eight-month anniversary of us splitting up. Wes had stayed in the UK for a week which meant he'd got together with this woman within a fortnight of returning to Dubai. Which probably meant he'd already known her. Was maybe even attracted to her when he'd been with me.

Before I knew it, I'd clicked into her profile. Clodagh Quinn, thirty-two from Limerick in Ireland, working at the same company as Wes. So that confirmed they had known each other before. Her feed was full of photos of Wes and her together and it looked like they had an incredible life, always out for meals, at parties and events.

'Stop scrolling,' I muttered. I was only torturing myself by seeing how easily Wes had moved on and how happy he was without me. As I took a final glance at the anniversary post, I realised something. Wes and I had wanted completely different things from our lifestyles. The busy life of partying which Wes and Clodagh so clearly loved didn't appeal to me at all. If Wes had returned to the UK as planned, I suspected boredom would quickly have set in with our home and with me. I'd never have imagined that we'd grow so far apart but the many posts on Clodagh's feed showed how much we had.

A quote from *Anne of the Island* came to mind, from when Anne and Gilbert finally got together. He still had three years ahead of him at medical school and couldn't offer her a glamorous lifestyle, to which she'd replied, *I don't want sunbursts or marble halls. I just want you.*

I clicked onto Wes's profile and sighed. 'I wish you happiness,' I said, 'but what makes you happy isn't what makes me happy because you're not my Gilbert Blythe.'

I unfriended him and that was it, our connection completely severed. Closure. And it felt so freeing that I wondered why I hadn't done it before.

As I was leaving the staff room, my phone beeped with a WhatsApp notification from Justin of all people. He never reached out to me first unless he wanted something.

> **FROM JUSTIN**
> Haven't heard from you in months, kiddo. Have I done something to piss you off?

Wow! He really hadn't a clue. I wasn't going to dignify it with a response – or at least not yet anyway. I needed to think carefully about how I'd word my reply but I couldn't resist clicking into the message itself so that he knew I'd read it. I knew how his mind worked and it would rankle him knowing that I'd read it and not replied. Justin seemed to expect people to drop everything for him but he never reciprocated it. I switched my phone to silent before leaving the staff room. I wouldn't be surprised if there were a stack of messages from him when I looked at it again after closing time.

* * *

I left work late, having called the police after Alec left. Gavin Haines, who'd recently been promoted to sergeant, was the designated contact for the Castle Street traders and he was in town when I rang so I was told he'd drop in to see me. I showed him the damaged books and the CCTV footage which had caught everything, including the little boy attacking me, the mother destroying the guidebook and her giving me the charming parting gesture. Her face had been caught clearly and she was known to Sergeant Haines so he said he'd pay her a visit.

When I arrived back home, I went straight over to the main house to check on Dad. Mum was dishing up a bubbling lasagne and, over tea, I shared the shocking incident at work. Dad was full of apologies that he hadn't been there, but I assured him there was nothing he could have done. Much as his fatherly instinct was to protect me from the dark side of people, it was impossible to do so.

'Thankfully, we don't get that many nasty customers. With any luck, that's the quota for the year.'

'Except for the ones who moan about the price of books,' Mum said.

'But spend a fiver on a takeaway coffee,' Dad and I said together, laughing.

It never ceased to amaze me how many people were willing to spend so much on a drink that would last twenty minutes but begrudged paying a little more for a book which would entertain them for hours and could be consumed over and over again. Sometimes those customers would stare at me as though expecting me to agree with them and offer to sell the book for half price.

'Are you and Cassie still doing Christmas tomorrow night?' Dad asked once we'd settled into the lounge after clearing the dishes away.

'We are. Looking forward to it as always. It won't be the same without you, of course.'

'I wish I could help. Why don't you ask Lars?'

I'd already thought about it and part of me wanted to, but I wasn't sure about the dynamic of the three of us working together. If something was going to happen between Lars and me, I wanted it to happen naturally and not as a result of some stirring on Cassie's part.

'Cassie and I will be fine, although I might need to ask Lars to do Saturdays from next weekend.'

'Sounds sensible,' Dad said. 'Have you got cover for his day off?'

'Cyndi has a Tuesday morning off college and Flo has a Tuesday afternoon off so it works out well to cover it between them.'

Back in Green Gables, I messaged Lars.

> **TO LARS**
> Hope you've had a great day. You know we spoke about you working Saturdays in December? Today was crazy busy so can you start working Saturdays and take Tuesdays off from now on? Thanks in advance

A reply came back within five minutes.

> **FROM LARS**
> Great day, thanks. Hope you did too. That's all fine. I'll see you on Monday but not Tuesday next week. Enjoy the rest of your evening

> **TO LARS**
> Thank you for doing this. I'm so grateful. You enjoy the rest of your evening too

As I replied, I felt sad at the thought of not seeing him until Monday and then having another day away from him on the Tuesday.

'Get a grip,' I muttered to myself.

I spotted four WhatsApp notifications on my phone and I didn't need two guesses as to who they were from. Sure enough...

> **FROM JUSTIN**
> You've read my message. Why haven't you replied?
>
> Why are you ignoring me? I need to see you. I'm coming to Whitsborough Bay tomorrow. What time do you finish work?
>
> ANSWER YOUR MESSAGES!

I flinched at the use of capitals. How dare he shout at me like that?

> **FROM JUSTIN**
> I've looked it up on your website. I'll be at the shop at 4

Clenching my teeth, I tapped in a reply, all the while asking myself *how would Cassie respond?* I read my message through and, satisfied that my reply had channelled my best friend's intolerance for bullshit, I sent it.

> TO JUSTIN
>
> 1. Yes, I am pissed off with you. We had plans to meet on my birthday. You cancelled the day before then never even wished me a happy birthday
>
> 2. I am not at your beck and call, especially when you message during shop hours. I will respond to messages when I have a free moment and not the second they arrive
>
> 3. Never SHOUT at me. If you do that to me again, you won't get a response
>
> 4. I'm not free tomorrow. I have important plans immediately after work. What's the urgency?
>
> 5. I'm 34 and don't like being called kiddo. Please stop calling me that. Thank you!

I stared at my phone and saw that Justin had read my message. Oh, to be a fly on the wall! I waited for a couple of minutes to see if he'd reply, but nothing came and I couldn't be bothered to waste any more time on him. What I really wanted right now was a long soak in the bath with a mug of tea.

The fresh pine scent of the bubble bath made me feel all Christmassy. I placed the mug from my *Anne of Green Gables* set on a ledge beside the bath and smiled at the quote on it:

Isn't it nice to think that tomorrow is a new day with no mistakes in it yet?

Gratefully sinking beneath the bubbles, I pushed aside the dark moments from the day – the mistakes others had made – and focused only on the positives, of which there were far more. Tomorrow would be a fresh day and I was so looking forward to the night. It was always one of my favourites – the moment we transformed Bay Books for Christmas. Then it would be a new week and I'd see Lars again. My heart leapt and I realised I was more excited about that than I was about the Christmas makeover.

30

LILY

Justin hadn't responded to his dressing-down by the time I went to bed and, when I arrived at work on Sunday morning, I checked my phone to find a grovelling message sent in the early hours.

FROM JUSTIN

I'm really sorry about your birthday, kiddo. I genuinely hadn't registered and I know that makes me a bad dad. I'll make it up to you. I still need to see you. Do you take a lunch break?

I shook my head at the *bad dad* comment. He could claim the *bad* part with bells on but, as far as I was concerned, he wasn't my dad and I objected to him using the term. I decided to let it go – that and the use of *kiddo* once more despite my request not to call me that. I wanted to start the day feeling calm instead of incensed.

TO JUSTIN

Not on a Sunday. If you really need to see me, it'll have to be after work tomorrow. Busy day ahead so I won't be picking up any more messages today

* * *

The bookshop was busy but nothing like it had been yesterday and, thankfully, all the customers were pleasant. During the afternoon a woman I'd place in her late thirties asked if I could help her choose a creative writing book.

'It's for my sister,' she said as I led her up the stairs. 'She's been talking about writing a book for years and she's got this brilliant idea but hasn't written a single word because she says she has no idea where to even start. I thought if I bought her a book about the basics it might incentivise her to crack on with it.'

We stopped in front of the creative writing section on level three. 'As you can see, there's quite a selection and we can get hold of others. The ones on this shelf are about specific aspects of craft so I'd suggest they're more advanced, but the ones here are the overviews and a great starting point for a new writer.'

I recognised the rabbit-in-headlights look so I plucked three different books from the shelf and talked her through the differences. Seeing her look more relaxed, I left her to browse.

On the landing, I took my phone out to check what time it was and was surprised to see five missed calls from Cassie.

'Everything okay?' I asked, calling her immediately.

'Jared's mum collapsed earlier and she's been rushed to hospital.'

'Oh, my God! What happened?'

'We don't know. She was out with a friend, said she felt dizzy and next moment she keeled over and hit her head. I'm not going to be able to do Christmas tonight. Jared's dad's visiting an old friend in Luton and he's getting an earlier train home but it'll be hours before he makes it back so Jared's with Lesley now. I'd have asked my mum to babysit but she's away too. I'm so sorry to let you down.'

'Gosh, Cassie, don't worry about the shop.'

'I thought about bringing the kids with me but it'd probably take longer with them than it would if you're on your own. I could manage one night during the week instead.'

'Honestly, Cassie, you focus on Lesley, Ronnie and your family. I'll sort Christmas. If you need the day off tomorrow, just shout. Send them all my love and keep me posted.'

As we said goodbye, the creative writing customer appeared with two books and smiled at me. 'I'll have these, please.'

'Good choices. Let's hope they give your sister the kickstart she needs.'

When she'd gone, I looked around the shop, trying to decide what to do about Cassie not coming tonight. Putting up and decorating the tree was too big a job for during shop hours as boxes of bookish tree ornaments strewn everywhere were a trip hazard. Creating the Christmas window was too big and messy too so it definitely needed to be an after-hours job. Cassie had enough on with her approaching wedding so I wouldn't want to impose on her one evening during the week and, besides, I was psyched up to do it tonight. I'd updated last year's Christmas playlist with this year's festive releases and I was ready to embrace Christmas. But I'd be here until past midnight if I tried to do it alone. There was really only one person I could ask and the thought of it set off the butterflies in my stomach.

> TO LARS
> Please forgive the intrusion on a Sunday but I was hoping to go full-on Christmas tonight with Cassie's help. She's had a family emergency so it's just me. Is there any chance you're free, even if just for an hour or two, to help me out after we close? I will, of course, pay you overtime

> FROM LARS
> I'll be there at closing time on one condition – that you don't pay me. I'm doing this as a favour to a friend. I won't come otherwise

My heart leapt at his kindness.

> TO LARS
> Can we compromise with me paying you in pizza?

> FROM LARS
> You drive a hard bargain but I accept. See you soon

* * *

Lars arrived half an hour later, stirring the butterflies inside me once more.

'I wasn't doing anything so I thought I'd come down early and see if I could be of any help. Cuppa, perhaps?'

'I'd love one. Thanks, Lars.'

Cyndi joined us from the children's section. Lars offered her a drink but, as she only had thirty minutes left of her shift, she passed.

'He's so fit,' she said when Lars was out of earshot. 'Don't suppose he has a younger brother.'

'No, and I thought you had a boyfriend anyway.'

'I did, but we broke up. He thinks I read too much and I think he watches too much telly.'

'Aw, I'm sorry, Cyndi.'

'Don't be cos I'm not, especially as I can spend the money I'd saved for his Christmas pressies on myself instead. Bonus.'

I liked her thinking. And she was right about Lars being *fit*. But, for me, the attraction to him was about so much more than looks. It was about his eagerness to apologise for his behaviour at school, his passion for books, his love for his sister, his gift for engaging with customers, and the way he made me feel every time I was around him. The thought of being alone with him tonight had every fibre of my being tingling and I found myself willing the working day to be over so I could lock the world away and have Lars all to myself.

31

LARS

'We'll do the tree first and then the window,' Lily told me. 'If it's getting too late by then, we can always do the rest of the lights and garlands in the morning but I'd rather get the big things done tonight.'

'Tree?' I asked, frowning at the boxes piled up in the stationery section. None of them were big enough to hold a Christmas tree.

'It's in the car. It lives in the garage at home as keeping it here's a waste of valuable space. I've got some of the things I need for the window display in the car too but we'll get those after we've done the tree.'

I'd messaged Danika after Lily asked me to help out tonight and she'd replied confirming what I'd been thinking – that this was the perfect opportunity for me to confess everything about school without fear of customers interrupting us. It was probably best not to lead with that conversation, though. I'd build up to it. The pizza break could be the best time.

We carried the box through to the front of the shop and I paused, looking around me, wondering where Lily was going to put it without blocking any shelves.

'It'll go under the stairs,' she said, as though reading my mind.

There was a highbacked brown leather armchair and a standard lamp in the recess beneath the stairs which I'd always thought were a nice feature, but I could see how that was the most logical space for the tree. I carried the chair and

Lily carried the lamp to the back door to put in her car later for temporary storage in her parents' garage.

When we returned to the front, Lily put some Christmas music on. 'I refuse to play Christmas music in the shop until December arrives,' she said, smiling at me, 'but tonight's the exception. I've put it on random play so there might be some odd mood leaps between tracks and a couple of dubious choices thanks to Cassie.'

She switched the main lights off, leaving just the warm white fairy lights draped around the shelves and a couple of lamps which gave a cosy feel to the shop. We removed the three sections of the artificial tree from the box and, while Lily added the stand to the largest section, I took the box through to the back. When I returned, she'd already connected the other pieces and was arranging the branches.

'Do you know what this is called?' she asked me.

'It has a name?'

'It's called fluffing the branches. Isn't that cute?'

'I've *never* heard that term before, but it makes sense.'

I went to the opposite side to Lily and fluffed my branches. At one point, we both reached for the same one.

'You've got cold hands again,' I said.

She rubbed them together. 'I've *always* got cold hands.'

'Let me.' I encased her hands with my warm ones, my heart racing at the contact. 'You know what they say? *Cold hands, warm heart.*'

Her eyes met mine and the air felt charged with electricity once more. Freiheit's 'Keeping the Dream Alive' was playing and, with the soft music and lights, it would be the perfect moment to kiss Lily but it felt wrong to do that before I'd told her everything.

The track changed and we both laughed and stepped apart as the sound of Paul McCartney's Frog Chorus filled the room. I hadn't heard 'We All Stand Together' in years.

'I warned you there might be some dubious ones,' Lily said, pressing her hands to her cheeks. 'Cassie made me add it. She says Christmas isn't Christmas without the Frog Chorus.'

'Was it out at Christmas? I'm sure it was before we were born.'

'It was and yes to Christmas, although it didn't get to number one. I have a sneaky feeling The Wombles might be on there too. Again, blame Cassie.'

The moment had been broken, but probably for the best. We finished fluffing the tree, laughing at each other's attempts to make the frog sounds along to the track.

'I'm so relieved you were free tonight,' Lily said, stepping back from the tree to check it had been fluffed evenly. 'I had a vision of me being here until the early hours.'

'Happy to help. I used to love decorating the tree with Nanna. She always got a real one but, maybe ten years ago, she decided it was an unnecessary expense and a faff to get rid of after Christmas, so she bought a small tabletop one instead. It has built-in lights and is already decorated so there's nothing to do.'

'So you haven't decorated a Christmas tree in a decade?'

'No, and I've really missed it.'

'Then I'm extra glad I called on you tonight. Decorating the tree is such a key part of Christmas. I'm a bit greedy because I get to dress three of them – this one, Mum and Dad's because Mum hates doing it, and I have a narrow one in the annexe too. I assume you'll put one up in your new place.'

'I don't know.'

She widened her eyes at me. 'After a decade of deprivation, you don't know if you're going to put a tree up? Lars Jóhannsson, you can't not have a tree, especially for your first Christmas in your new home.'

'But I barely have any furniture so it seems daft getting a tree.'

'Getting a tree is *never* daft. Do it!' She grinned at me. 'I'm going to pester you until you agree to get one.'

'I'll think about it. I promise.'

She narrowed her eyes at me. 'Hmm. As long as thinking turns to doing. Anyway, let's focus on the shop tree for now. Firstly, you can never have enough fairy lights.'

She handed me a couple of boxes of lights. 'Vintage gold,' I observed.

'They're gorgeous. They're an orangey-cream colour. Sounds hideous but I promise it isn't. I spotted them in a garden centre a couple of years ago and fell in love so I got some for home too.'

She also handed me some red lights and said the two colours looked great together so I wrapped them round the tree, taking care to mix the two types, and had to admit they did look amazing switched on.

'Everything's book-themed,' Lily said, opening up the boxes and removing several examples. 'They're all for sale and, each Christmas, I bring out the surplus from previous years and add new stock to it. Sourcing new decorations is one of my favourite activities. This box contains books in various designs.'

When she opened it up, I picked out a pink book stack and a single sparkly silver book. 'I had no idea there were so many book-related options out there.'

When we'd finished hanging up a couple of each style from the book box, we moved on to one of the character boxes. I picked out a pink-and-purple striped Cheshire Cat, clearly inspired by the Disney interpretation of Lewis Carroll's stories, and hung it on a branch before reaching for an Alice figurine.

'*Alice's Adventures in Wonderland* is Cassie's favourite childhood book,' Lily said, 'so I had to stock those for her.'

'What's your favourite?' I asked, hanging Alice on the tree.

'*Anne of Green Gables.*' She paused and fixed her gaze on mine and I knew why. That was the book she'd had with her behind the sports hall. Should I say something now?

'It stole my heart,' she said, reaching for the Queen of Hearts. 'I don't suppose you've read it?'

'No, but Pia did. She'll have told me about it but all I can remember is an orphan with red hair being adopted by a brother and sister.' I added a White Rabbit to a branch. 'Is that right?'

'Yes. Matthew and Marilla Cuthbert want a boy to help on their farm but, thanks to a misunderstanding, they get Anne and Matthew convinces Marilla to keep her. It's such a lovely story of her finding the family, friends and home she's never had. It's warm and funny and there's this gorgeous romantic thread between Anne Shirley and Gilbert Blythe. They meet at school and Gilbert's eager to get her attention but he goes about it completely the wrong way by calling her *Carrots* because of her hair. She's really sensitive about her hair colour – it's a recurring theme – and smashes her slate over his head. From that point on, Gil's her enemy and everything's a competition between them, but we know he's sweet on her and massively regrets teasing her.'

She paused for a moment, her eyes fixed on mine once more, and I wondered if she knew what I was thinking – how closely I could relate to Gilbert's regret for his childhood behaviour.

'Anne just needs time – till the third book, as it happens – to realise how she feels about him too but it's such a beautiful moment that it's worth the wait.' Her eyes welled with tears and she laughed lightly. 'It gets me every time.'

I pictured her behind the sports hall, holding up the book she was reading and telling me how relieved she was to see me after her best friend had ditched her. It was time for my confession.

'You were reading *Anne of Green Gables* that first day at school,' I said.

'I was! I didn't think you'd noticed. You barely looked at me.'

'Your hair was in two plaits. You had a black bobble in one and a blue one in the other. There was a fluffy duck keyring hanging from your bag and you clung onto that book as though it was your only friend in the world.'

'But...' Tears welled in her eyes once more. 'I didn't think...'

'I saw you that day, Lily. I've always seen you and I should have...' I raked my fingers through my hair, nerves engulfing me, but there'd never be a better moment to do this. 'I know you said to draw a line in the sand about what happened at school and I appreciate you not holding it against me, but I owe you an explanation.'

She studied my face for a moment, a Mad Hatter ornament dangling from one finger.

'Okay, but this sounds like a sitting-down chat. Let's go out the back.'

She hung the ornament on a branch and I followed her through to the children's section. Moving a couple of the tub chairs closer to each other, I breathed in deeply as I sat down.

'I told you that my little sister, Pia, died and I told you my parents were divorced and my pabbi moved back to Iceland. What I didn't tell you was that it all happened at the same time...'

I ran through the events of that difficult year but, when I reached the part where I woke up on my first morning of senior school to discover that Mum had left without saying goodbye, a wave of emotion unexpectedly crashed over me. My voice cracked and tears spilled down my cheeks as I struggled to get any more words out. Next moment, Lily took my hands and eased me to my feet. She wrapped her arms round me and hugged me tightly as the emotion poured from me. I'd thought I was okay with everything that had happened – sad and disappointed but okay. Evidently I'd avoided it rather than dealt with it and now I couldn't stop the hurt caused by being abandoned like that from overpowering me. Lily didn't say anything. She just held me, stroking my back, until I stopped shaking and the tears slowed.

'I wasn't expecting that,' I murmured.

'You obviously needed it. Are you okay?'

'I think so.'

She released her hold and pulled her chair closer to mine as I sat back down. As she sat, she placed her hand gently on my thigh. 'You don't have to continue if it's too hard.'

I smiled weakly. 'Thanks, but I think I'm best getting the rest out now. I don't think that'll happen again.'

'I've got some bottles of water in the fridge. I'll grab you one of those.'

I appreciated her giving me a few minutes to compose myself before returning from the staff room with some water and a box of tissues. I took a tissue and wiped my cheeks.

'You've got some tissue caught on...' Lily leaned forward and brushed her hand across my jawline, her gentle touch sending a pulse of electricity through me. 'All gone.'

After taking a few glugs of water, I picked up where I'd left off. 'I was a mess when I started at school. I was grieving for my sister and also for the loss of my parents from my life, but I didn't know that back then. I was so angry and confused. Sometimes I'd sit on my bed with my hands under my legs, desperately fighting the urge to leap up and trash the room. I wanted to hurl things at the mirror, yank my wardrobe doors off, stamp on things, but there was this little voice in my head saying *if you do that, Nanna won't want to keep you and then you'll have nobody* so I'd bury my head in my pillow and scream into it and pound my fists on the mattress.'

'Oh, Lars, that's awful. You must have been terrified.'

'I was. The crazy thing is that my nanna's amazing. We've always been close so I could have talked to her and she'd have helped me through it, but I kept it all locked inside me most of the time because of this fear of her abandoning me too.'

'That's understandable after what your parents did. What were they thinking?' She bit her lip. 'Sorry. I'm being judgy when I don't know the full story.'

'It's not judgy, it's accurate,' I said, shaking my head. 'I kept thinking they'd come back saying how sorry they were and that we could still be a family despite losing Pia. My birthday's in December so I let myself believe they'd come back for that. Or Christmas. New Year... But it never happened.'

I took another swig of water. This was the crux moment. This was the point I was going to tell her why I'd pushed her away.

'I'd never taken much notice of other people when I was out and about – more likely to notice birds or trees – but across the summer before Mum left, I started noticing people more. Specifically happy families. And this ball of anger built inside me. I wanted that. I wanted a mum, dad and sister. I wanted my family back together and I resented everyone who had what I didn't. And one day Nanna brought me into Bay Books to get some back-to-school stationery...'

I told her how much I'd been looking forward to seeing her, how disappointed I was when she wasn't there and my irrational reaction to seeing her with her family.

'We'd never spoken about our families. You knew nothing about mine and all I knew about yours was that your dad worked here, but I saw you all together that day and the green-eyed monster got to me. You had the perfect family and I was so envious.'

Lily's eyes widened. 'Perfect. Is that why you called me...'

'Little Miss Perfect?' I suggested when she tailed off, wincing at the memory. 'It is and you have no idea how much I've regretted that.'

'I always wondered about the name. I didn't get it because I couldn't see anything perfect about me. I had this bird's nest of crazy hair and braces so I knew it couldn't be anything to do with my looks. It couldn't be about grades either because you did better than me.'

'It was such a stupid thing to say and it was never really about you – it was about me and my issues and making huge assumptions about something I knew nothing about.'

I searched her face for any signs of contempt but all I saw was empathy.

'No kid should have to go through what you did,' she said, her voice gentle. 'If you hadn't seen me with my family, do you think you'd have been different with me on our first day at school?'

'That's a great question.' I pondered on it for a moment before shaking my head. 'You know, I'm not sure I would. Mum leaving that morning without saying goodbye was my breaking point in a horrendous year. Nearly all the people I cared about had let me down and I wanted to be on my own so nobody else could hurt me. And then the only friend I'd ever made appeared with a smile and a book in her hand and the protective walls went up. If I let you in, I thought you'd abandon me too because that's what the people I cared about did.'

Tears pooled in her eyes as she took my hand in hers. 'Oh, Lars, I wish I'd known.'

'I couldn't have told you at the time because I couldn't make sense of it myself but, as time went on, I wondered if somehow you did know because why else would you keep trying to be my friend when I didn't deserve it?'

'Because I couldn't help myself. I had no idea what had happened to you or why you'd turned on me but I knew there was something. I could see this vulnerability in you and I wanted to help. I'd see you around school reading a book and I'd ache for the bookish conversations we used to have in this very room.' She bit her lip and lowered her eyes, shaking her head, then looked up at me with a rueful smile. 'As we're confessing things, I should admit that I read all the same books as you so that we could talk about them if you ever changed your mind about me.'

'You never did!'

'I did and I'm forever grateful for that because you read such an eclectic mix of books and widened my reading massively.' She squeezed my hand. 'I wanted our friendship back and sometimes I'd catch you looking at me across the classroom and get this sense that you wanted that too.'

My heart leapt that she'd noticed and I placed my other hand over hers. 'So much, but I'd convinced myself there was no way you'd want to be friends after how I'd treated you. And there was definitely no way you'd consider being...' I gulped and lowered my eyes, staring at our entwined hands, cursing myself for being too chicken to say it.

'Consider being what?' Lily asked, her voice soft and encouraging. 'Look at me, Lars.'

I raised my eyes to hers. There'd never be a better time to admit it. 'We could have been more than friends. I wanted you to be my girlfriend, but I didn't know what to do with those feelings so I wrapped them up with my confusion and envy, repeatedly pushing you away instead. Truth is I thought you were the prettiest girl I'd ever seen and the nicest one too. I know nothing I said or did would ever have given you the impression I felt that way but, believe me, I did.'

She kept her eyes on mine but didn't speak for a moment, and then she added quietly, 'Did?'

'Still do.' My heart was pounding so loudly, I could barely hear the words and wondered if I'd even spoken them but I evidently had because, next moment, Lily's lips were pressed against mine.

She released my hands and her arms snaked round my neck as she ran her fingers into my hair. I pushed her curls back from her face and, as though of one mind, we rose to our feet, never breaking our kiss. My hands slipped down to her waist and she released a soft moan as my fingers brushed against her skin where her T-shirt had risen. The kiss deepened and I'd never felt anything like it. I had no idea this was how it could feel when you were kissing somebody you cared deeply about. I didn't want to stop but we had to come up for air eventually. We stood there, holding hands once more, breathless.

'Well, that was unexpected,' Lily said, 'but my mum always says *the unexpected things in life are often the best.*'

I ran my thumb softly across her cheek and lightly brushed my lips against hers. 'My nanna says *the best things come to those who wait.* That was definitely worth waiting for.'

'For me too.'

I raised my eyebrows questioningly.

'You weren't the only one who wanted more than friendship,' Lily said, smiling at me. 'There was something about you that drew me in from the moment I saw you. You were standing right over there looking at *Harry Potter and the Goblet of Fire.*' She pointed to the bookshelves on the other side of the room.

'You remember which book it was?'

She nodded. 'I remember everything about that day – just like you remembered my odd-coloured bobbles behind the sports hall. You were so careful not to damage the book and your eyes shone as you read the first page and I just knew you were a kindred spirit. After that, the first thing I did every time I came to the shop was look for you. We were too young back then to be thinking of more than friendship but, by my teens, something had changed and I knew I wanted to be with you so I kept trying and you kept pushing me away but it got harder and harder which was why I snapped when we were fifteen, demanding to know why you were so mean to me.'

I grimaced. 'You really surprised me that day and this voice inside me was yelling *tell her how you feel!* But I just couldn't do it.'

'Protective walls?' she asked.

I nodded. 'You had the power to break my heart.'

'You'd already broken mine.'

I cupped her face and drew her into another gentle kiss.

'I'm so sorry. I didn't know,' I said, keeping my arms around her waist.

'I think we were both pretty clueless and too young to deal with some grown-up emotions and, of course, you had so much more going on.'

'We could have been together all that time if I hadn't been such an idiot. All that wasted time!'

'I need to show you something.' She took her phone out and scrolled through it, stopping on a photo. 'When things ended with Wes, I was really upset, not just about it being over but about feeling like I'd wasted years on him and, even worse, that it was the second time it had happened. Mum spotted this in Yorkshire's Best and thought it was perfect for me.'

Yorkshire's Best was a shop at the other end of Castle Street selling the work of local artist Jed Ferguson and a range of locally made hand-crafted items. The photo showed a small wooden sign with flowers in the background and the handwritten words:

Little by little, day by day, what is meant for you will find a way.

'Mum bought it to give me hope that I was exactly where I was meant to be and things would come right in the end.'

'*Þetta reddast*,' I said and smiled when Lily looked at me quizzically. 'It's a saying but also a philosophy for how Icelanders live. It means it'll all work out in the end or it'll fix itself.' I returned her phone. 'So you think this is what's meant for us?'

'I do. What about you?'

'Definitely.' And to prove it, I kissed her once more.

32

LILY

I was kissing Lars and, oh my word, it was incredible. First kisses could be a little awkward but it was as though Lars and I had been made to fit together. Perhaps it was because I'd been dreaming about it for so long. Our first kiss was electric, passionate, knee-weakening and this one was all those things still but somehow more tender and emotional. I never wanted it to end, but this wasn't getting the tree decorated or the window display arranged and it was with reluctance that I pulled apart.

'We need to...'

'Finish the tree,' Lars said, pressing his forehead against mine. 'I know.'

'But there's nothing to say we can't celebrate emptying each box.'

He kissed me softly and we walked hand in hand back through to the front and resumed our work with the character decorations.

'What made you so eager to tell me everything?' I asked.

'Because I liked you more every day and I was hoping what just happened between us would happen. I wanted you to know everything before it did in case it put you off me. It would have felt wrong to kiss you then tell you.'

'It hasn't put me off you at all. It's made me like you even more. As I said, I used to think there was something vulnerable about you and now I know why. I'm so sorry for everything your parents have put you through. Are you in touch with them at all now?'

'I don't really get on with Pabbi – long story for another time – but I'm close to his new wife. I say *new* but they got married when I was eighteen.' He told me about his stepmum and half-siblings. 'As for my mum, she travels the world doing street photography and barely finds the time to check in with Nanna or me.'

I stared at him, the cogs whirring in my mind. 'Hang on a sec. Your mum's Jay Jóhannsson! I can't believe I didn't make the connection. We stock her books.'

'I noticed.'

'Why didn't you say anything?'

'Because it would have led to questions about her which aren't easily answered. We can talk about my mum another time too and I'm all ears if you want to talk about Justin. To answer your original question about my confession, I wanted to tell you from the start but I was okay with you wanting to draw that line in the sand. Then when you told me about Marcus being your stepdad and Justin always letting you down, I realised that you might have an amazing, caring family but your life hasn't been without its challenges.'

'And the Justin ones continue,' I said, rolling my eyes at Lars. 'He messaged me yesterday, had a go at me for not being in touch for months, and sent a shouty capitals message when I didn't reply quickly enough for him.'

'Wow! How old is he?'

'Exactly. We're talking proper moody teenager strop so I told him what I thought about that and, to be fair to him, he apologised in his next message. He wanted to see me tonight but I told him I had plans and it'd have to be tomorrow so that's something to look forward to.'

'What does he want?'

'No idea. He's never the one who initiates contact so this is uncharted territory.' I sighed. 'I will take you up on that offer to talk about him and I'd love to hear about your parents but how about we talk about something nice tonight instead?'

'You're on! Do you have a favourite restaurant in the area?'

I pondered for a moment. 'Salt & Pepper Lodge, Le Bistro, The White Horse in Little Sandby spring to mind. Why?'

'Because I'd like to take you out for tea this week at one of your favourite restaurants.'

My heart leapt. 'I'd love that. It doesn't have to be one of those if you've got a favourite. My only no-no is those really posh places that serve tiny portions. I like to know my tummy isn't going to be rumbling an hour after I've dined.'

'Completely understand that. I haven't been to The White Horse in ages so I'll see if I can get us a table there. If you're seeing Justin tomorrow night, how about Tuesday?'

'It's a date,' I said, sealing it with a kiss. *At last!*

With our school days no longer a taboo subject, Lars and I reminisced about our time there, discussing school trips and favourite/least favourite teachers as we continued to hang the decorations.

'Obviously you stayed best friends with Cassie,' Lars said, 'but are you still friends with anyone else from school?'

'Do you remember Donna Rowe? She wasn't in our form but I knew her from Brownies and Guides.'

'Is she the one who shaved her head for charity?'

'That's her! Anyway, she's Donna Nelson now, married to a lovely guy called Joey and they've just announced they're expecting their first baby. Other than Cassie and Donna, my friendship group's mainly the other traders on Castle Street. They're all so lovely.'

'Everyone I've met seems really friendly.'

'They're the best.' I opened up the box of stationery-themed decorations. 'Occasionally I get customers who I recognise from school and college. Some are really friendly and chat, some say *hello* and leave it there and others act like strangers. It's possible they don't recognise me but I think some do it deliberately. What about you? I'm guessing you're not in touch with anyone from school.'

'I was the weird kid who randomly spoke in Icelandic,' he said, laughing. 'Not exactly a friendship magnet. And, of course, I pushed away the only person I really wanted to be friends with.'

'But she valued your friendship when she had it.' I drew him into a tender kiss. 'And she values it now, especially now she knows the truth. I saw you too, Lars. I always knew there was something hurting you and I hoped one day you'd tell me what it was.'

He held me tightly and we stood there for several minutes, just holding each other, old friends finally united.

'There were a couple of lads I hung out with at college,' Lars said when we returned to the decorating, 'but we didn't stay in touch afterwards. I was too busy setting up My Study Hub.'

'Did you make friends through work? I'm guessing it'd be harder to do that when you work from home.'

Lars paused with a vintage typewriter ornament in his hands, as though contemplating the best way to answer that.

'I built up a fantastic team and, if you'd asked me the same question a year ago, I'd have said I was friends with them all but it turns out they were just virtual friendships. The business was what connected us and, without that, there was no reason for us to be in touch. Contact dipped off during the handover and I've heard from none of them since.'

'Does that make you sad?'

'It did at first. I was in touch with some of them several times a day by message or phone and, because I knew things about them like their partner's name, whether they had kids, where they were going on holiday, which football team they supported and so on, I mistook that for actual friendship instead of for what it really was – polite small talk.'

He hung the typewriter up and reached for an inkwell. 'I split up with my girlfriend, Cat, around the same time, although we'd only been together for three months. We'd never been right for each other and it was all very amicable but I suddenly realised I had no friends, no girlfriend, no business, and I was about to lose my home too with Nanna moving into Bay View. It hit me pretty hard. The refurb on my house was a good distraction but the last thing the builders needed was me hanging around all day every day just so I could have someone to talk to. Volunteering at the library was a godsend and then getting the job here brought me back into a world I've avoided for a long time – where people exist in real life and most of them are nice to me, which is a first.'

He was smiling as he spoke, but I recognised the vulnerability and I knew it cut deeper than a lack of friends. It was about a feeling I knew all too well. Rejection. From his parents, from the kids at school, and now from his former work colleagues.

'Was it really bad for you at school?' I asked.

'It could have been worse. It was never physical but the verbal stuff was constant and not just from kids in our year. It was like every single kid in school knew who I was and had an opinion about my accent or the way I looked. Hundreds knew me and not a single one wanted to be my friend.' He rolled his eyes at me. 'Except you and I screwed that up spectacularly.'

'But you made up for it spectacularly too,' I said, wrapping my arms around him. 'You can make up for it again if you like.'

'Oh, go on then!'

I melted into another of his dreamy kisses.

'I could do this all night,' I said when the kiss ended. 'Just as well Grýla and the Christmas Cat didn't find me and gobble me up.' I couldn't keep a straight face and barely got the last few words out for giggling.

Lars hung his head, his cheeks flushing. 'No! I was hoping that had been a bad dream or you'd have forgotten it.'

'Oh! I missed a bit.'

'Don't salute me!' He looked up, grimacing. 'You have. You've saluted me. Do you know how much willpower it took not to break into a sprint after I did that?'

'I can guess.'

'Please forgive me. That was... No, I can't even begin to describe what that was. Let's put it down to a moment of temporary insanity and never speak of it again.'

I loved that he could laugh about it. I'd never have pushed it as far as I did if it had touched a nerve. I asked him if he'd ever seen *Dirty Dancing* and shared my thoughts about the scene it conjured up for me, although I didn't admit that I'd been discussing that with Cassie. I'd confess that one later.

'Yeah. Definitely my watermelon moment. But it worked for them. Baby and Johnny got together...'

'And it worked for me,' I said smiling before kissing him again.

* * *

When we'd finished decorating the tree, Lars placed a takeaway pizza order at Mario's and made the five-minute walk to collect it while I added metal hooks to the slatted wall under the stairs. The wall was one of several changes I'd made to the shop, specifically to hang up the Christmas decorations. I'd chosen wood rather than metal so it would blend in and not stand out as an empty shop fitting when it wasn't in use. We sometimes used it for extra back-to-school stationery, special offers or new ranges but most of the time it was partially covered by a gorgeous canvas Jed Ferguson had painted of the bookshop.

I was about a third of the way through hanging the Christmas decorations on the slats when Lars returned with pizza, some serviettes and cans of soft drinks.

The delicious cheesy smell made my stomach rumble. We ate at the counter and Lars told me that I shouldn't feel too sorry for him for being a Billy-No-Mates as he did have one friend. Danika sounded lovely and it seemed she'd already made a big difference to him by insisting he apply for the job here and encouraging him to open up to me about his past. I very much looked forward to meeting her at some point soon.

As we neared the end of the pizza, a loud bang on the door made us both jump. I could see the shape of someone standing outside and it looked like a man, although I couldn't make out who due to the limited lighting.

'Lily,' the man shouted, banging on the door again, and my heart sank.

'It's Justin.' I dropped my part-eaten slice of pizza into the box and wiped my hands on a serviette. I'd had the most amazing evening and I had a feeling the mood was about to take an enormous nosedive.

33

LILY

'You took your time!' Justin practically spat the words the moment I opened the door and I reeled at the smell of alcohol on his breath.

'What do you want?' I asked, ignoring his comment.

'To see my only daughter, of course. Is that a crime?'

'No, but I said I was doing something important tonight and it'd have to be tomorrow.'

I'd made the mistake of moving aside, which gave him enough room to squeeze past me. I closed the door behind him with a sigh.

'You ditched me for pizza with your boyfriend?' He curled his lip in Lars's direction. 'That's more important than seeing me?'

Actually, yes! And how self-centred was he if he thought he was more important than any of my plans? But I swallowed down a retort to that effect and gave the briefest of introductions – names only – before repeating my earlier question in a tone much more calm than I felt. 'What do you want, Justin?'

He glanced at Lars then back at me, frowning as he muttered, 'It's private.'

'I'll give you some space,' Lars said, picking up his drink.

'You don't have to go.' I felt terrible that Justin had made him feel uncomfortable.

Lars took my hand as he passed and his expression clearly asked if I was okay being left on my own.

'You could check out those poetry books we were discussing,' I said.

He squeezed my hand to convey his understanding – that I only wanted him to go up to the first level so he'd be able to hear the conversation and come down if things got heated. I hadn't seen Justin this agitated before or under the influence of alcohol and I didn't like it.

As Lars ascended the stairs, I went round to the other side of the till, closed the pizza box and stopped the music.

'I've got loads to do tonight.' I indicated the boxes by the tree. 'I can only give you five minutes. If you want more, it'll have to be tomorrow.'

'Now's fine.' He shuffled awkwardly and ran his hands across his chin, grimacing. 'I'll make it quick. I've lost my job and I'm in a tight spot. I need to borrow some money to tide me over.'

That was a lot of information to take in at once. 'I'm sorry about work, but you've lost your job before and you've always walked into a new one.'

'Yeah, well, that hasn't happened this time. I've got my bank details here.'

He whipped out a debit card and I reeled back, shocked. Talk about jumping ahead several steps! I'd never loaned Justin money before and I had no intention of starting now. My stomach churned with the realisation that he hadn't been desperate to see me; just desperate for cash. The cheek of him!

'I don't need much. Just ten.'

'Ten pounds?' It would be worth handing over a tenner just to get rid of him.

'Grand.'

My breath caught in my throat and I had to force the words out. 'Ten grand? Are you joking?'

'Do you see me smiling?'

I reeled once more at the gruff tone. His eyes were bloodshot and his hair looked in desperate need of a wash.

'I don't have a spare ten grand lying around.'

'That's bollocks! You've got way more than that squirrelled away. You made a profit on the house you had with that bloke... what's-his-name... the one who buggered off to...' He shook his head, evidently unable to remember Ewan's name or that he'd moved to Sheffield. I didn't fill in the blanks for him.

'And you've been living rent-free for years so that hefty sum'll have grown. How much is it now?'

'None of your business. It's my money for my future home. I'm not touching it and I'm certainly not lending it to anyone.'

'Ah, but I'm not just anyone, am I, kiddo? I'm your dad.'

Was he really playing the *dad* card? I could run off a hundred reasons why he was not and never would be my dad, but I chose to take the upper hand.

'I'm not lending you ten grand.'

'Eight, then? Six? Come on, Lily! Meet me partway.'

I shook my head in disbelief. 'This isn't a negotiation. I'm sorry you've lost your job and I'm sorry finances are tight, but it's not up to me to bail you out.'

The look of hatred he gave me sent a shiver down my spine. 'Bloody hell, Lily! It's only ten grand and I know you've got it.'

I stared at him defiantly, my hand planted on my hips.

'You're a crap daughter!' His voice was loud and unnecessarily aggressive. 'Any decent daughter would help her dad out in his hour of need but, oh no, not you. You're all me, me, me! *It's my money for my future.*' The quote of my earlier words was delivered in a high-pitched voice with exaggerated emphasis on the word *my*.

Could he hear himself? Was he even aware of how hypocritical he was being? I could have shouted back at him but I forced strength and control into my voice.

'You think I'm a crap daughter? How about we talk about being a crap dad instead? Let me see.' I put my fingers out and started counting off. 'You abandoned my mum when she was pregnant, you barely saw me growing up and provided no financial support. And if we're focusing purely on money, the only time I've ever had a birthday or Christmas card from you is when you've had a girlfriend who's bothered to send me one. You've never given me a birthday or Christmas gift. I've never had pocket money or a few quid to congratulate me on passing my exams. You didn't pay for driving lessons, you refused to spend money on me on the rare occasions you saw me when I was a kid – not even an ice cream – and when we've met up as an adult, we've either split the bill or I've paid.'

I'd run out of fingers but I hadn't run out of steam.

'So, with that track record of spending absolutely *nothing* on my upbringing, I'm fascinated to hear how you think I owe it to you to lend you ten grand of my hard-earned money. Or should that be *give* you because I doubt I'd ever see a penny of it back.'

The brief flicker of guilt that crossed his face confirmed that for me. I expected him to storm out in a huff but he surprised me by trying a different tack.

'You're right. I've been rubbish. I wasn't ready to be a dad and, after Shelby met Marcus, I didn't know how to compete with that. Didn't think I could after I'd made such a mess of things. All I wanted was to be a good dad but I figured you were better without me in your life. When I stayed away, I was only doing it for you.'

When I stayed away, I was only doing it for you. Did he really think I was that naïve? Or that I wouldn't notice the way he kept pausing between statements, as though gauging my reaction so he knew how far he'd have to go with his sob story? I wouldn't be surprised if he told me next that he was misunderstood.

'I don't think anyone understands me and how tough it's been for me but I want to get better. If you could just look into your heart and find a way to help me out of my current predicament. Please, Lily.'

'What happened to the money your parents left you?'

'Gone.'

'And the house?'

'Sold and the money gone. It's the apps.'

'What apps?'

'The betting ones. It's too easy. I do all the things they say like setting controls but…' He shrugged. 'Please help me.'

I studied his face for several moments – unshaven, dark circles beneath his eyes, the air of desperation and I couldn't help feeling sorry for him. 'Okay. I will help you but not—'

'Oh, thank God! I knew you'd come through. I knew…' His smile slipped at the vigorous shake of my head.

'But not by giving you money,' I said, finishing the sentence he'd interrupted. 'I'm going to look up the numbers for some gambling addiction helplines and send you them later.'

'Helplines?'

'You need help and that's what they're for.'

'But I need money, not some flamin' do-gooder.'

'Then I can't help you.'

'Can't or won't?' he challenged.

'Both. Your gambling problems are *not* my problem to solve.' I headed towards the door. 'I need to finish preparing for Christmas.'

'So I was right earlier. You *are* a selfish little bi—'

'Don't you dare!' I snapped, grabbing the door handle. I didn't need to take that from him. In fact, I needed nothing from him. Cassie's voice was loud and clear in my head – *sack him off!* I'd said I couldn't but what on earth had I been holding on for? Justin had let me down time and time again and the one and only time he'd asked to see me was because he wanted to fleece me. We were through.

'Seeing as you think so little of me, I'm going to make this easy for you. I've had very little to do with you for most of my life and that's been your decision, not mine, but *my* decision now is that I want nothing to do with you. I don't know why I've been hanging on, giving you chance after chance, but I've had enough. I don't need or want you in my life.'

'You can't mean that. I'm your dad.'

'Are you really? Then you'll know all these simple things about me. When's my birthday?'

He winced. 'April?'

'Wrong. What's my favourite book?'

'How am I supposed to know that? Ask me something easier.'

'My favourite colour? Drink? Food?'

When he just stared at me blankly, I threw out several more questions. 'What car do I drive? What's my dream holiday destination? What's my degree in? What do I like most about working here?'

I paused between each question to give him room to answer but he just looked increasingly bewildered.

'You don't know me, Justin, and you've never been interested in getting to know me. These are things I've told you repeatedly and you haven't listened to me.'

'You don't know that stuff about me either.'

'Really? Your birthday's 8 October, you don't have a favourite book because you can't stand reading but your favourite film's a tie between *The Godfather* and *Goodfellas*. Your favourite colour's dark blue, your favourite food is yuk sung but you get annoyed because it's not on the menu of many Chinese takeaways and the one time you tried to make it yourself, it tasted like cardboard. Favourite soft drink is builder's tea, favourite alcoholic one is a pint of bitter, preferably from a local brewery. I don't know what you're driving at the moment because you change your car that often but you have a strong affection for the Audi TT you owned in the late nineties. Your best holiday ever was interrailing after you graduated with your business studies degree, which is a bit of an insulting choice to share with me considering that was the holiday you were meant to go on with my mum before she found out she was pregnant. As for work, you don't love anything about any of the jobs you've had because you claim you could always do better than your manager, your younger colleagues are *jumped up little tossers* and your older ones are *tech-phobic dinosaurs who need putting out to pasture.* Have I missed anything? No? Didn't think so.'

I yanked the door open.

'I think we've said everything we need to say, don't you?'

'The apple doesn't fall far from the tree,' he snarled, shoving past me.

'Meaning?'

'I can see so much of your mum in you.'

'Thank you.'

'It wasn't a compliment.'

'Oh, but I take it as one. Goodbye, Justin.'

The moment he stepped out onto the cobbles, I closed and locked the door and leaned back against it, eyes closed, exhaling heavily.

'Lily?'

I opened my eyes and my heart melted at the concern on Lars's face as he approached me, weaving around the boxes.

'How much did you hear?'

'All of it. Are you all right?'

I smiled widely at him. When Cassie cut off her loser father, she said she'd felt like a weight had been lifted and I felt the same.

'I thought I'd feel upset but I'm actually elated. That was a long time overdue.'

'You were incredible. I was cheering you on upstairs.'

He put his arms out and I gratefully accepted the hug.

'You're trembling,' he whispered.

'I hate confrontations, but I feel so much better for finally letting go.' I leaned back and looked up at him with a grin. 'I bet Justin doesn't think I'm *Little Miss Perfect* after that.'

'But I do. *Little Miss Perfect-for-me.*' He screwed up his nose. 'Was that too cheesy?'

'Not for me. Not when you say it.'

He tenderly kissed me and I knew that, while I wouldn't forget the exchange with Justin for a long time, my lasting memory from tonight would be the time I let go of the man I didn't want or need and welcomed in the one I did.

34

LARS

My face was already aching from smiling and I'd only been awake for an hour. A message from Lily had been the perfect way to start a new week, although I had a feeling there was something I was never going to live down.

> **FROM LILY**
> Last night was my favourite Christmas prep night ever. Thank you for being my Christmas elf, for being so honest with me, for the best kisses ever and for being you. Can't wait to see you this morning. Not sure whether to sign off with a kiss or a salute x

She'd added a saluting emoji after the kiss, which made me laugh. I reread the message, particularly noting the mention of me being her Christmas elf. How close she was! It was nearly time to change the branding on my socials to the Christmas Paperback Pixie. As for being totally honest with her, when would the time be right to reveal my secret identity?

As I drove into Whitsborough Bay for the start of my shift, I replayed last night over and over. We'd dealt with some seriously heavy issues but I also hadn't laughed so much in ages and I marvelled at how Lily had refused to let that difficult confrontation with Justin put a dampener on our night. I believed her when she said she was relieved to have pushed him out of her life, but I was conscious it might hit her at some point later and I'd be there for her whatever she wanted to do – reminisce, vent, cry or a combination of all those things.

I'd hesitated at the top of the stairs last night, ready to rush down if Lily needed my support. Not that I thought I was a knight in shining armour and she was a damsel in distress. Lily was a strong, determined woman who didn't need my protection but Justin was a big bloke who'd clearly been drinking so I'd been ready to intervene if he'd become aggressive. After the way he'd treated her, nothing would have given me greater pleasure than to physically eject him out onto the street. But Lily had maintained her cool and, as I'd told her, I was cheering her on, in awe of her refusal to be manipulated. When she'd said she was going to help Justin, I thought she might hand him whatever cash she had in her purse and send him packing and I certainly couldn't have blamed her for doing that, but I'd jubilantly punched the air when she'd told him her only assistance would be finding helpline numbers.

As well as deepening my admiration for Lily, overhearing her conversation had done something else for me. It made me reflect on my relationship with my own parents. I'd allowed Mum's flakiness to define our relationship and that needed to stop. It was too late for her to be a mother to me and Nanna had already stepped into those shoes, but there was room in my life for her to play a different kind of role. And if she didn't want that, I'd let go. I wasn't going to keep chasing a ghost.

Pabbi was different. He wasn't flaky but he wasn't present either. I knew I carried some of the blame there but I *had* been a teenager so he needed to cut me some slack for that. I wanted him in my life and it wasn't just because I loved Freyja, Kára and Ari. I loved my Icelandic roots and I didn't want to lose that connection. It was part of who I was.

Emotional conversations weren't my family's forte but they were long overdue. I couldn't mutter *þetta reddast* and leave it to resolve itself. If I wanted to keep my family, I needed to take action. Mum would be harder to pin down but I could commit to spending some time in Iceland with my paternal family. Like I'd told Freyja previously, I wouldn't be able to confirm a date but I could tell her I'd definitely visit instead of leaving it as a possibility.

* * *

Even though I was desperate to see Lily, I couldn't help pausing by the window display. The scene was a winter's night in a miniature version of Bay Books. We'd attached strips of black card to the inside of the window to look like panes and had sprayed snow at the bottom of each. A mixture of festive titles and new releases were displayed on small bookshelves and in piles on the floor. A boy mannequin sat on a little burgundy tub chair absorbed in a book while a girl decorated a Christmas tree hung with bookish ornaments. The boy had blond hair and the girl was brunette and we'd commented last night how they could have been us as children.

The door opened and Lily poked her head out, grinning. 'Admiring your first full window display?' she asked.

'I can't help it. It looks so good. I can't believe I was involved in it.'

'Definitely plus points for creativity. And, as I discovered last night, there's something else you're pretty good at too. Or are you? Hmm. My memory's fading.'

I followed her inside and took her in my arms, kissing her passionately until we both broke apart, panting and laughing.

'Definitely ten out of ten,' Lily said. 'Twelve out of ten. Twenty!'

'Same to you.'

'Cassie rang me first thing, by the way. She'll be back at work today. They kept Lesley in overnight but it was just precautionary with her hitting her head. They don't think there's anything to worry about.'

'That's great news.'

'I didn't tell her about us. Would you mind if we keep the focus on Lesley for now? I'm not trying to hide anything. It's just a timing thing.'

I took her hands in mine, appreciating her honesty. 'I don't mind at all and I agree with you.'

The delivery arrived shortly after we opened so we set about unpacking it.

'Do you still fancy The White Horse for tomorrow night?' I asked Lily when we'd finished. 'I can book a table during my break.'

'How about tonight instead? I won't be seeing Justin anymore.'

'How are you feeling about it?'

'Still surprisingly upbeat, although you might have had something to do with that.'

She smiled at me so tenderly that I couldn't resist leaning across the counter to kiss her, hoping the door wouldn't open at that moment.

'Do you think you'll hear from him again?' I asked.

Lily shook her head. 'He'll have got the message and, because I refuse to give him any money, I'm no use to him. It does make me wonder if he only kept me in his life because he knew that, one day, he'd want something significant from me. That makes me sad, but it also makes it easier to walk away.'

When Cassie arrived a little later, she was all smiles. 'Lesley's fine. She's been discharged.'

Lily rushed up to her and gave her a hug. 'I'm so relieved. What was wrong?'

'Blood tests showed she's slightly anaemic. That's what made her faint so she's got some iron tablets and a list of iron-rich foods to get into her diet. I'm so sorry about letting you down last—'

'You *didn't* let me down,' Lily said before Cassie could finish. 'Family has to come first.'

'Thanks.' Cassie looked around the room. 'It's looking spectacularly Christmassy in here. Did you do it all on your own?'

'No. I had help.' Lily smiled at me. 'It was a good evening.'

'Oh, my God!' Cassie cried. 'You two kissed at last! Don't even try to deny it. The air's fizzing!' She fished an envelope out of her bag and handed it to me. 'An invitation to my wedding, although I could have saved myself the effort with the calligraphy as it looks like you'd have been coming anyway as Lily's plus one.'

I glanced at Lily and she shrugged, laughing.

Cassie held her hands up to her eyes like a pair of binoculars. 'As I told you very recently, I'm the all-seeing, all-knowing. I'm going to make some drinks and when I come back up, I expect details.'

I felt my cheeks flushing as she looked back and forth between Lily and me, grinning.

'*All* the details,' Cassie emphasised as she ran down the stairs.

'Aw, you look so adorable with your cheeks all pink like that,' Lily said, her eyes twinkling. 'So it looks like that plan to keep things quiet lasted all of thirty seconds. I was daft to think she wouldn't notice straightaway.'

She returned to the other side of the counter and I ripped open the envelope, removed the invitation and did a double-take at the contents. 'It's for the full day. I thought it would just be for the evening do.'

'You know what this means?' Lily asked. 'That friends list of yours is getting bigger. And Cassie's not the only one on the team who likes you. They all think you're great.'

'Really?'

'Really. People like you, Lars. People like you for being you.'

In my weeks working at Bay Books, I'd never once worn a mask. I hadn't at the library either and I'd been as welcomed there as I had been here. Why hadn't I realised before that being surrounded by books and people who loved them as much as me would feel like home? It seemed such an obvious connection now.

* * *

The manager at The White Horse in Little Sandby told me she was expecting a few work parties in but could squeeze in a table for two so I booked that and arranged to pick up Lily from home. Her parents' house was an ivy-clad Victorian detached property set on a large walled and gated corner plot, although the metal gates were open for me to drive through onto the block-paved drive. The annexe Lily lived in was tucked behind a row of conifer trees to the left of the main house and I parked beside her car, smiling at a wooden pub-style sign with the name 'Green Gables' on it surrounded by white flowers.

I was ten minutes early so I'd been planning to stay in the car in case she wasn't ready, but the annexe door opened and Lily poked her head out and beckoned me over.

'I might not look anywhere near ready,' she said, indicating her dressing gown, 'but I promise I am. Hair and make-up are done so I just need to put on my dress and shoes, but first I need to do this.'

She placed her hands on my cheeks and gave me the gentlest kiss on my lips.

'I'd better leave it at that,' she said, 'or I'll never get ready.'

'I like your hair.' She'd pinned it up at the back but had loose curls hanging round her face and neck.

She gave me a dazzling smile. 'Grab a seat or have a look around if you like, not that there's much to see.'

The annexe was L-shaped and I'd entered through the bottom of the 'L' with a tidy shoe and coat stand to my left and a bathroom on the right. Ahead of me was a kitchen/dining area with base and wall kitchen units on two sides into the corner, and a square dining table with two chairs. To the right was a lounge area with a two-seater sofa, armchair, a writing bureau and a wall-mounted television, and Lily's bedroom was beyond that. It was small but perfectly formed and beautifully decorated. Lily had said she'd picked out the colours and furniture herself and she clearly had a talent for it. Nothing really matched yet somehow it all looked like it belonged together.

I wandered over to a tall shelving unit packed full of books and smiled at one shelf completely devoted to the 'Anne of Green Gables' series with several paperback and hardback versions of each book. A metal sign was propped up against a boxset and I picked it up to read it:

Dear old world, you are very lovely and I am glad to be alive in you.

'It's from the first book,' Lily said, joining me, 'shortly before Anne admits to Gilbert that she's forgiven him for calling her *Carrots* and they agree to be friends.'

I placed the sign back on the shelf and turned to face Lily, my eyes widening and my heart pounding.

'Wow!'

She was wearing a pair of high heels and a dark red dress. I'd never seen her dressed up before and she took my breath away.

'Is it too much for The White Horse?'

'No, you look incredible!'

She brushed her hands down the skirt. 'I saw it in a shop window a couple of months ago and it was love at first sight but I refused to buy it because I never go anywhere I can get dressed up. Plus, I was determined I didn't want to meet anyone, but the dress kept calling to me and eventually I gave in. It must have known that you were going to walk back into my life and that I'd be willing to take a chance on the first man I loved.'

She gasped and her cheeks turned the colour of her dress. It was the first time since our school days that I'd seen her look uncertain.

I took her hand in mine and brushed my lips against it. 'You didn't mean to say that, did you?'

'No.'

'But you did mean it?'

'Yes. I mean, I was young and...' She shook her head. 'Yes. Even though you didn't even want to be my friend, teenage me kept hoping you'd change your mind.'

I cupped her chin and lightly kissed her. 'Teenage me loved you too and regretted my Gilbert Blythe-style *Carrots* moment every single day.' She smiled at me and the smile widened as I added, 'And I don't think I ever stopped.'

Her eyes searched mine, unshed tears sparkling in them. 'Neither did I.' And next moment she was in my arms, her lips on mine, and being a little bit late for our meal didn't matter.

35

LILY

I was on cloud nine all day Tuesday, floating around in a bubble of happiness, although I wished Lars was with me. It was his day off and it felt strange not having him around. I wouldn't see him tonight either. As planned, Hendrix had arrived early yesterday morning to look after Dad and, although I'd nipped in to say 'hello' when I got home, I'd only managed ten minutes before I needed to get ready for my date with Lars. I'd promised to have a proper catch-up with my brother tonight. I could have arranged to see Lars afterwards but I didn't want to seem like I was rushing Hendrix because I had other plans and, if I'd invited Lars to join us, the evening would have become all about my family getting to know Lars better. I saw my brother so rarely that I wanted to focus just on him for now so I'd have to wait until tomorrow to get my Lars fix.

When my lunch break arrived, I returned from the staff room in my coat and scarf and my heart leapt at the sight of Lars waiting for me. It transpired that he couldn't bear to be away from me for that long either and had messaged Cassie to find out what time I'd be taking my break.

It was a chilly day, although not as bitter as it had been the previous week, and the wind had dropped so we took a right outside the shop and wandered round Castle Street in an anti-clockwise loop, peering in the shop windows. The traders had all now fully embraced Christmas and, with just over five weeks to go until the big day, I could feel the excitement of Christmas in the air.

We sat down in Castle Park – a small park with benches overlooking the sea at the end of Castle Street – and I snuggled up to Lars. Pointing to the Christmas tree, I told him about the special traders' event in the park while the general public gathered around the main tree outside the shopping centre.

'The lights switch-on is always the first Saturday of the month, so it'll be a fortnight on Saturday on the 6th.'

'Is it just for the business owners?' he asked.

'No. It's for staff and their families too. It's one of my favourite events and it feels like the magic of Christmas fully arrives at that point.'

Lars squeezed my shoulder. 'You sounded a bit melancholy then. Everything all right?'

'Did I? I didn't mean to. It's just…' I sighed. 'I told you about my two really crap Christmases but there've been other disappointing ones more recently which have taken their toll and knocked the sparkle out of Christmas for me, which is so frustrating when I love this time of year.'

He adjusted his position on the bench so he could see me better. 'Tell me about the recent disappointments.'

It was a small thing but it really touched me that he cared enough to want to understand my melancholy when he could so easily have said something like, *I'm sure Christmas will be great this year*. Which would have been fine, but it wouldn't have demonstrated the deep connection I'd felt between us since our first kiss.

'Wes and I had four Christmases as a couple and never spent a single one together.'

Lars's eyes widened. 'Four Christmases apart? How come?'

'The year we started dating, he'd already promised to spend Christmas with his family, so that was fair enough. The year after, there was a huge extended family holiday abroad to celebrate his grandma's eightieth birthday. I was invited but I told Wes I couldn't go with it being the busiest time of the year in the shop. That wasn't strictly the truth. As a one-off, we could have covered my shifts, but I chose not to go because I got the impression he'd prefer me not to be there. *You'll probably be bored. There'll be loads of people you don't know. I haven't seen some of them for years so I can't wait to catch up.* In other words, he didn't want to babysit me. The following year he was in Dubai. He'd only been there for a few months and said it didn't make sense to fly back so soon. Then last year he came back to the UK in October for Donna and Joey's wedding so he skipped Christmas with me again, saying it was too soon to fly back for it.'

I shook my head, laughing. 'I'm hearing me say that about Wes and wondering why I thought I was happy with someone who clearly didn't want to spend much time with me.'

'So why were you with him? Do you know?'

I mulled it over. 'I met him when I was out for my thirtieth birthday. He was on a stag do and the groups ended up combining. He asked me out but I was on the rebound from Ewan so I said no. That would probably have been the end of it but Donna and Joey got together so Wes became part of our friendship group and I ran out of reasons to keep saying no. He was fun to be around and he was safe too because he swore that Whitsborough Bay was the only place in the world he'd ever want to settle.'

'So you thought there was no chance of him disappearing on you like Ewan had?'

'Exactly. Also, I'd hit thirty and all my friends seemed to be paired up and getting serious. Cassie and Jared had bought a house together and had two kids, Donna and Joey got engaged after six months or so and I think I got scared of being left behind. I thought I loved Wes but I've realised that what I really loved was the idea of who I wanted him to be. I wanted to believe the fantasy so I ignored all the signs that told me that he was all about the fun and not necessarily settling-down material, no matter how much he made out he was.'

'Fear of being left behind has a lot to answer for. Everyone I worked with seemed to be paired off except me so I signed up to a dating app. The only person I dated was Cat and, like I said before, I knew we were wrong for each other from the start. Nanna talked me into it – told me I was too fussy by always trying to find the perfect match – but the thing is, I knew perfection existed because a high bar had already been set by a nine-year-old girl whose dad owned a bookshop.'

The tender look he gave me made me feel all warm and fuzzy inside and, as we kissed, I sent a thank you up to the universe for helping us find a way back to each other.

Feeling the cold a little later, we set off back up Castle Street, pausing to admire the rest of the window displays. Winter had arrived at The Wedding Emporium with two bridal mannequins – one wearing a slinky ivory lace-covered dress with a fur-lined cape and the other in a midnight-blue gown which was so beautiful that it sent a tingle down my spine. It had a fitted bodice and full skirt under which there appeared to be several layers of net and it was covered in sparkling gold embellishments. I'd never have imagined choosing a colour like that for my wedding day but, just like the red dress I'd worn last night, I felt it calling to me and I couldn't help but release a wistful sigh.

'You like that one?' Lars asked.

'It's the most stunningly perfect dress I've ever seen.'

He slipped his arm around my waist and dropped a kiss on the top of my head.

'You'd look incredible in it,' he said, his voice hoarse, and I wondered if his mind had galloped way ahead in time like mine had. Was it too soon to be thinking that this was the man I was going to marry and that I wanted to say *I do* in this dress?

* * *

I drove straight home after work and nipped into Green Gables for a quick change before joining Mum, Dad and Hendrix in the main house.

'Your dad's on the verge of bankruptcy,' Mum said, giving me a start before I clocked that he and Hendrix were playing Monopoly and Hendrix was thrashing Dad as usual.

I kissed Dad on the cheek and ruffled Hendrix's hair which he pretended he hated, but I knew he really liked it because it was our thing that we'd done for years.

'Okay, I'm out,' Dad said, dropping a feeble quantity of low banknotes onto the board. 'You win, Hendrix. Again.'

Hendrix jumped up and ran a lap of honour round the lounge, his hands in the air.

'You're such a child,' I said, laughing at him. 'Do you do that at work?'

'All the time, but apparently it doesn't help land planes.'

'Is that curry?' I asked, sniffing the air. 'It smells amazing.'

'Hendrix made it,' Mum said.

'Seriously?' My brother's lack of skills in the kitchen was legendary. He was the only person I'd ever met who could burn cereal.

'Seriously,' he said. 'Daisy's been teaching me some simple dishes. There were a few incidents at first but I've found my cooking mojo and am actually enjoying it.'

Hendrix's girlfriend was a commis chef in a Michelin-starred restaurant between Leeds and Bradford and she loved her work there but was just as happy creating simpler dishes at home.

'How did your date with Lars go?' Mum asked.

'I never said it was with Lars. Have you had the spies out?'

Hendrix thrust his hand in the air. 'My fault. I couldn't resist a peek and, when I described who'd picked you up, they both knew who it was.'

I should have known somebody would be watching – a hazard of living at home, not that I minded. Without going into the gushy details, I told them that Lars and I were officially an item. They were all really pleased for me, and Dad, who'd spent the most time in Lars's company, said he thought we were perfectly suited, which meant a lot to me, although he did add jokingly that *if he breaks your heart, I'll have to hunt him down and kill him.*

'You know what? I don't think he'd ever do that to me,' I said.

Mum smiled at me. 'Glad to hear it. Aw, it's lovely to see our three babies all so happy.' She focused on Hendrix and I got the impression I was missing something. I looked at him quizzically.

'I'm going to ask Daisy to marry me,' he said.

'Oh, wow! That's brilliant news.' I launched myself at my brother and hugged him tightly. 'When?'

'We're going out on Thursday night. It'll be five years since our first date so I thought it was about time I popped the question.'

'I'm so pleased for you both.'

'Sounds like it'll be a race up the aisle between you and your brother,' Dad said.

'Lars and I aren't...' But there was no point denying it. They were all looking at me knowingly and they were right. I genuinely believed that, after a couple of false starts with Ewan and Wes, Lars Jóhannsson was the man I was going to marry. That beautiful midnight-blue dress popped into my head and what he'd said earlier about how I'd look in it and my heart raced. With my sister expecting, my brother engaged, my best friend getting married, Justin out of my life and my broken heart healed and being properly cared for, it felt as though my Christmas sparkle might finally return.

36

LARS

As I approached Castle Street on Wednesday morning, my stomach lurched at the sight of a police car parked on the cobbles outside Bay Books and I broke into a sprint. The door was wide open and there was a female police officer talking into the radio on her shoulder. She stopped me as I approached.

'The shop's not open yet.'

'I work here. I'm the owner's boyfriend.'

'You're Lars?' she asked. 'You're fine to go in but mind where you walk.'

Assuming there'd been a break-in, I looked down, expecting to see glass, but all I could see was... I scrunched up my nose as the smell hit me. That surely wasn't...

'It *is* what you think it is.'

Lily appeared from the children's section carrying a cleaning caddy in one hand and a bucket of soapy water in the other, looking and sounding thoroughly fed up.

'It was posted through the letterbox but they must have taken their time to fling it or it'd have landed on the mat instead of being everywhere.' She placed the bucket on the floor and the caddy on the counter. 'As you can see, I stood in some before I'd put the lights on.'

'Who posts dog poo through a shop letterbox?' I asked, giving her a hug.

'Someone who hates me.'

I released her and looked into her eyes. 'You think it was specifically you being targeted?'

'The sign was a bit of a giveaway. Didn't you see it?'

She took my hand, led me outside to behind the police car and told me to look up. The shop had two signs – a pub-style one hanging above the door with the shop name and logo on it and one with just the name across the top of the window. On the latter, somebody had painted over all but the letter 'b' on the word 'books' and added four replacement letters so that the sign now read: BAY BITCH.

'That's horrible.'

'Isn't it? I'm upset, obviously, but I'm mostly angry. Angry that somebody would think to do that in the first place and angry that I've got to clean it up now.'

'I'll help. We'll get it sorted.'

A man called Lily's name and she looked across the street to where a police officer was waving at her from the doorway of Forget-me-not Cards opposite the bookshop.

'That's Sergeant Haines,' she said. 'He must have found something on Anne-Marie's CCTV. Whoever did it covered over mine.'

Lily checked the female officer was okay to mind the shop, after which I followed her over the road and into the card and gift shop. Lily did the introductions and Anne-Marie offered her sympathy for the damage.

'Anne-Marie's camera has captured the perpetrator really clearly,' Sergeant Haines said. 'It's not who we thought it was, although she could have got someone to do it for her.'

'She?' I asked.

'The only person I could think of who might have a grudge against me personally was that woman whose kids trashed the books,' Lily said. 'She called me a bitch when she left and Sergeant Haines had a word with her yesterday so the timing works for a retaliation.'

Anne-Marie had twisted her laptop round so we could see the screen and she set the footage playing. Recorded at 3.48 a.m. it showed a figure wearing a dark hoodie approaching the bookshop, carrying a small stepladder and a bucket.

'It's a man!' Lily exclaimed.

'Do you recognise him?' Sergeant Haines asked.

I felt Lily stiffen beside me and I knew why. I'd recognised him so there was no way she hadn't.

'I don't think so,' she said eventually, her voice sounding a little higher than usual. 'Am I okay to go back and clean up?'

'Yes, no problem. If you think of anything else or you want another look at the footage, just say.'

With a parting whispered thank you, Lily ran across the cobbles.

'I think the shock's just kicked in,' I said to the sergeant and Anne-Marie. 'Thanks for your help.'

I closed the bookshop door behind me moments later and locked it. Lily was standing by the Christmas tree with her back to me, trembling.

'I'm so sorry,' I said.

She whipped round to face me, tears streaking her cheeks. 'Why did he do that to me?'

I had no answer. What sort of man called their daughter something so derogatory and then daubed it across her shop? What sort of person gathered up dog poo especially to throw it through a letterbox? Justin Mayes was one seriously disturbed individual. So I gave the only response I could and wrapped my arms round her, holding her tightly as she sobbed against my chest.

'I needed that,' she said, stepping back and looking up at me with bloodshot eyes. 'Do you think I should have told Sergeant Haines?'

'It has to be your decision, Lily. But do *you* think you should have told him?'

She glanced out of the window to where he and his colleague were talking.

'I don't know.'

I understood why she might feel conflicted, but I really hoped she would tell the police about Justin. There had to be consequences for vandalism like this. If there weren't, he might do it again.

'If this was Cassie's shop and her estranged father had just done that, what would you advise her to do?'

Lily closed her eyes for a moment and took a few deep breaths. When she opened them, she gave me a weak smile, nodded and headed for the door. I reached for the rubber gloves in the cleaning caddy and made a start on the floor, grateful that the bookshop had wooden flooring rather than carpet, which would have been harder to clean. There was a can of air freshener behind the counter so I gave a generous spray before going into the yard to empty the dirty water down the drain. When I returned with a stepladder and a fresh bucket of water for scrubbing the sign, Lily was closing the door behind her.

'I told him it was Justin,' she said, before exhaling slowly. 'That was hard.'

'I can imagine.' I put everything down and hugged her once more. 'Are you okay?'

'Not really, but there's nothing I can do about it. I've got a shop to get open.'

I gave her a gentle squeeze and released her so she could get on. 'The floor's done and I'll clean the sign as soon as the police car moves.'

'Thank you for being here.'

'Nowhere else I'd rather be.'

The police car left so I went outside while Lily logged onto the system. Cleaning the sign took some elbow grease but it would have been a lot worse if Justin had used gloss paint. The white paint he'd used to cover up the original letters was emulsion and he'd used spray paint for his replacement letters which came off as I scrubbed and scraped the emulsion.

Half an hour after opening time, there was no physical evidence left from what Justin had done, all the cleaning products were stored away and the smell had gone. I went down to the staff room and sent up mugs of coffee in Jeeves but, when I returned to the till, one look at Lily's pale cheeks and the unshed tears sparkling in her eyes showed the emotional impact.

'Do you want some time out?' I asked. 'I can keep an eye on things.'

I thought she'd protest but she nodded slowly. 'I still can't believe he did that.'

'Me neither.' I hugged her tightly. 'Take as long as you need. I'll send your coffee back down in Jeeves.'

One of our regular customers came in and Lily welcomed her warmly before disappearing down the stairs. I hated Justin Mayes for what he'd done to Lily. She was kind and friendly to everyone she met and she didn't deserve to have anyone treat her with anything other than love and respect. Even when I'd been unkind to her at school, she'd still kept trying and she'd been so understanding and forgiving when I'd shared my story. But Justin didn't deserve her understanding or forgiveness. The difference between him and me was that I'd been an eleven-year-old kid in a lot of pain and he was a grown adult – her father – who should have known better.

37

LILY

The walk down the stairs to the staff room seemed to take forever. My body felt weary, my eyes burned from the tears already shed as well as the threat of more to come and my legs were shaking so I had to grip tightly to the handrail. Outside the staff room, I cursed under my breath for taking three attempts to punch in the four-digit code to unlock the door before sinking down onto one of the dining-table chairs.

As soon as the door closed behind me, there was no point trying to fight my emotions. I sank my head into my hands as tears rained down my cheeks and splashed onto the wooden table. Justin was a terrible father. He'd never shown me any affection and had repeatedly disappointed me over the years but the fact that he met up with me every so often had led me to believe that I had to mean something to him. Clearly I didn't or he'd have never done something so cruel. What made it worse was that it was premeditated. He'd spent two nights gathering what he needed – including all that dog mess – before unleashing all his anger and hate. I'd told him he didn't know me, but it seemed he knew one thing – how much Bay Books meant to me and how attacking my beloved bookshop would be like attacking me.

I grabbed a tissue from the box in the middle of the table and wiped my cheeks but it was fruitless because the tears kept falling and I might as well let them. I'd never let myself cry about Justin before. Even that awful Christmas Day holed up in a hotel room on my own, I'd refused to do it. I'd always told myself that I knew he was unreliable and that, if I was daft enough to keep him in my life, I shouldn't be surprised each time he let me down so there was no point in getting upset about it. But now all the hurt and frustration came pouring out and I needed to let it.

I'd been right to cut Justin out of my life and, even though I'd hesitated about it at first, telling Sergeant Haines that it was Justin on Anne-Marie's CCTV had also been the right thing to do. I couldn't allow a misguided sense of loyalty for the shared genes sway me towards leniency. Justin needed to know he'd been seen. He needed to know that bad decisions had consequences. And he needed to know that he could never contact me or come near me again.

I was so grateful to Lars for not pushing me into what he thought I should do and encouraging me to reach my own decision, although he'd shared afterwards that he thought I'd made the right choice.

Jeeves pinged, indicating its ascent, and I tutted to myself for not removing my coffee. Shortly afterwards Jeeves returned and, wiping my eyes, I wandered over to retrieve my drink. My mug of coffee was still in there but there was a takeaway cup from The Chocolate Pot and I could smell the hot chocolate inside. A paper bag beside it contained a triple chocolate brownie, still warm, and there was a note written in small, neat cursive:

Didn't think the coffee would cut it!
He's not worth your tears because he's not worthy of you. You deserve to be surrounded by people who appreciate you and how amazing you are. I'm here for you with whatever you need – hugs, kisses, a listening ear, distracting conversations. Rubber gloves, a paint scraper and cringeworthy salutes come as optional extras.
Your plus-points creative in training, Lars xx

I marvelled at how, in one of my darkest moments, Lars could make me laugh. There was a notepad and a selection of pens in the staff room so I scribbled my own note and, after removing the contents from Jeeves, sent it back up.

That was the perfect delivery and exactly what I need right now. I might pass on the rubber gloves and paint scraper but I'll take the rest – including the salutes – as long as they come from a half-Icelandic Christmas elf who stole my teenaged heart. Thanks, Lars. You're my northern lights in the darkest of moments xx

After finishing my hot chocolate and brownie, I sat with damp tissues on my eyes to help alleviate the redness. My phone buzzed and my stomach lurched. What if it was Justin? But it was my brother.

> **FROM HENDRIX**
> I'm driving back to Leeds tonight. Any chance I can meet the man who's put the sparkle back in your eyes before I leave? Need to get one over on Kadence by meeting him first!

He'd accompanied it by several laughing emojis and I couldn't help laughing myself. I needed to tell Mum and Dad about Justin and tonight would be as good a time as any, perhaps after Hendrix left. It would be useful to have Lars there for moral support as I knew how upset they'd be which, in turn, would upset me.

* * *

Lars was welcomed with open arms into the family and it was lovely to see how easily he gelled with my brother, even though I knew I'd get some stick later from Kadence because Hendrix had met Lars first. Hendrix hit the road after we'd eaten and we wished him good luck for his proposal to Daisy. Moving into the lounge for coffee, I told Mum and Dad that I had something difficult to share with them.

'He actually asked you for money?' Mum cried after I'd told them about Justin's visit on Sunday night. 'The cheeky... Argh, that blasted man!'

I'd never seen Mum so angry before. Dad placed a calming hand on her arm and she took a deep breath. 'I'm sorry, Lily, please continue. I'll contain my outbursts.'

'You might not be able to when you hear the rest...'

Mum was in tears by the time I'd brought them completely up to speed, and Dad appeared to be on the verge.

'The air would turn blue if I shared what I'm thinking right now,' Mum said, her voice wobbling.

'Mum doesn't like swearing,' I told Lars while Mum grabbed a tissue and wiped her cheeks. 'Being a professor of English, she believes our language is full of so many wonderful words that you don't need to use profanities.'

'On this occasion, they're the only words I can think of.' Mum shook her head. 'I'm so sorry, Lily. You know I don't have a very high opinion of Justin Mayes but I never thought he was capable of stooping so low. Pat and Gordon must be turning in their graves right now. How those two lovely people produced such a selfish individual... Urgh! I can't even...' She took a deep breath. 'You did the right thing by telling the police.'

'Dad?' I prompted.

'I've no words,' he said, his voice small. 'And all this on top of what that woman and her kids did.'

I moved closer to him and took his hand in mine. 'Please don't punish yourself for not being there for either of those things. None of us could have known this would happen with Justin. And I wasn't alone either. Lars was with me and I was safe.'

Dad gave Lars a weak smile of appreciation before turning back to me. 'You promise me you'll never let him worm his way back into your life?'

'I promise.'

'I mean it, Lily. I've always supported your choices when it comes to Justin because they were your choices to make, no matter how many times he broke your heart, but this has to be the end.'

'Believe me, it is. I've told him I want nothing to do with him, I've blocked him and deleted his number. It took me longer to get there than it should have done but he's out of my life for good.'

'Glad to hear it.'

As I hugged him, a thought struck me. 'You do know that seeing Justin was never about filling some sort of dad-shaped void, don't you?'

'Of course.'

My heart sank. The words were positive but there'd been a hesitation before he spoke them. Brief. But definitely there.

'I've *never* had a dad-shaped void in my life. You're 100 per cent my dad and you're brilliant at it. Justin was...' I shrugged, wondering what the rest of that sentence was. 'Justin was just someone I thought I should have a connection to.' I squeezed his hands. 'I'm sorry if me being in touch with him caused you any pain.'

'You don't need to apologise to me. The only one who has done anything wrong here is Justin. You and your mum deserve so much better than him.'

'And we've got it. We've got you.'

38

LARS

Sergeant Haines stopped by just after lunch on Friday to say that Justin had been charged for vandalism and had been instructed to stay away from Lily and the bookshop.

Lily sagged against me when he left. 'What a week!'

'Is there always this much drama in your life?' I asked.

'No, thankfully. I like a quiet life and I usually get one. The only drama I like is contained within the pages of books.'

'Same here.'

'I'm so glad that's over.' Lily fiddled with her phone on the dock. 'You know I told you my rule about no Christmas songs until December except when dressing the tree? I feel an exception is needed to celebrate.'

I laughed as Paul McCartney and the Frog Chorus began playing and several customers paused browsing and looked in Lily's direction, smiling at her music choice.

'It makes me think of the happy parts of Sunday night,' she said, squeezing my hand as we stood side by side behind the counter. 'And the title says it all – "We All Stand Together". That's how this past week has been with you, Cassie, Mum and Dad supporting me through this.'

It had been the proverbial rollercoaster of a week with the highs being all the amazing moments with Lily and the big dips provided courtesy of Justin and I marvelled at how strong Lily had been, especially when telling her parents.

Hopefully the drama was over now and the run-up to Christmas would be all about the highs.

* * *

The following week, Lily and I spent as many evenings together as we could – a production of Charles Dickens's *A Christmas Carol* at the theatre, a meal with her parents and drinks after work in Minty's followed by a meal at Salt & Pepper Lodge on Thursday evening.

Over our meal I told Lily how touched I'd been when she wrote *you're my northern lights in the darkest of moments* on the note she'd put in Jeeves because the aurora was another of my passions. I talked about the occasions I'd seen the lights including the special visit with Pia which Mum had captured with her camera.

'My northern lights app tells me there might be some solar activity over Whitsborough Bay in the early hours,' I said, 'although it's unlikely to be seen by the naked eye. I don't suppose I can interest you?'

'Seeing the northern lights is a bucket-list dream for me and it's so tempting...'

'But you're shattered,' I finished for her, smiling.

'I'm sorry. It would be different if I was guaranteed to see them but, without that guarantee, I'm going to have to choose my sleep. Don't let me stop you, though.'

I could either go back to The Lodge and spend the night on my own or I could stay at Green Gables with Lily. It wasn't a difficult decision.

The following day was the last Friday of November and the launch event for Josephine Forrest's latest novel. The shop had closed at the usual time and it had been a quick turnaround with the event starting at seven and Lily's grandma expected at half six.

'You look nervous,' Lily said as we put the last few chairs in place.

'I am. I've never met anyone famous before.'

'Your mum's famous!'

'Yeah, but she's my mum. This is different.'

'As I told you earlier, she's wonderfully eccentric and very needy. She responds well to hero-worship so just make sure you flatter her lots and you'll be fine.'

She'd warned me to expect a brightly coloured kaftan, lots of jewellery, a bold hair colour, a posh accent, air kisses and everyone to be referred to as *darling*.

The door opened and I looked up, expecting our guest of honour, but the elderly grey-haired woman who entered, shedding a smart black wool coat and handing it to the man beside her, couldn't be Josephine. Wearing tailored grey trousers and a powder-blue jumper with a simple pearl necklace, she was nothing like Lily had described.

'Granny Blue!' Lily declared. 'Happy publication day!'

She crossed the room and embraced her grandparents and I chuckled to myself. She'd evidently been having great fun winding me up this week and I couldn't believe I'd fallen for it.

Lily called me over and introduced me to them both. George shook my hand and Bluebell hugged me, saying – in a soft Yorkshire accent, no less – that she'd heard great things about me and how delighted she was that Lily had found herself a lovely man. Lily led her away to run through the plans for the evening, leaving me with George, who complimented me on how good the shop was looking.

'It's like stepping back in time every time I come in here,' he said. 'The same but different. Marcus and Lily have done wonderful things with our dream.'

'Do you miss it?'

'I do, but I was ready to step down when I did. It gave me more time to read but, more importantly, it gave me the time and freedom to travel with Bluebell on her promotional tours. I loved being here surrounded by books but I love that wonderful woman even more.'

He gazed affectionately across the room in her direction and, as though sensing his eyes on her, Bluebell turned and smiled lovingly back at him. Lily had told me they'd been together for sixty-five years and married for sixty-three and were still as besotted with each other as they'd ever been. Having spent time with her parents, it was clear they were deeply in love too. It was good to see what that looked like. I barely recalled my own parents being happy together and, while I knew that Nanna and Granddad had enjoyed a strong, loving marriage, I'd never seen it myself with Granddad passing before I was born.

Bluebell opened her handbag and handed Lily a pink candy-striped paper bag. That had to be the strawberry bonbons she always gave Lily. It made me think of the advent calendar Nanna had bought for me at a craft fair when I was little. It had a happy snowman with a robin perched on one of its stick arms and she'd filled the twenty-four pockets with chocolates every single year. When I hit my twenties, I'd told her she didn't have to keep doing that but she'd said, *What difference does age make? You're still my grandson and it's a nanna's prerogative to spoil her grandchild.* I'd visited her on Tuesday afternoon on my way back from my lunchtime walk with Lily and she'd presented me with the same calendar full of chocolates in preparation for the first day of the month.

'How are you enjoying working here?' George asked me.

'Loving it. It's an incredible bookshop you've created and it's a privilege to work here surrounded by books and with someone as amazing as Lily.'

He smiled at me. 'She's a special young lady, isn't she? Bay Books was my dream and Bluebell's and I'm proud of the legacy we created. Marcus added something extra to it but our Lily came along and sprinkled it with magic dust. She's the reason it's still thriving today.'

I was on door duty for the evening, welcoming guests and checking them off on the attendance list, so I excused myself to take my post. Marcus and Shelby arrived with Shelby's parents, Nora and Maurice, and I was introduced to them. George joined them and they all collected welcome drinks from the counter before settling on the back row where we'd laid out a chair with plenty of space for Marcus to stretch his legs out and keep his crutches by his side.

Nanna arrived with Geraldine and Hilary shortly after. As Lily was still running through things with her grandma, I told Nanna I'd do the introductions at the end of the event. She'd met Bluebell at previous signings but, to my amusement, had insisted that I introduce her as the nanna of Bluebell's granddaughter's boyfriend.

Lily had ordered brownies from The Chocolate Pot topped with edible images of Josephine's new book and cupcakes with the book on them from Carly's Cupcakes. Once the guests were settled, Flo and Cyndi circulated with a tray of goodies each.

As seven o'clock approached, it was standing room only. Lily had told me earlier that the space didn't really lend itself to events but they did their best. She'd thought about using The Chocolate Pot instead but had decided that there was something special about launching a book in a bookshop surrounded by books. Looking at the rows of Josephine Forrest fans sitting in front of the bookshelves, I had to agree. It wouldn't be the same elsewhere.

'Good evening, everyone!' Lily declared bang on seven, bringing a hush to the audience. 'Thank you so much to you all for coming out on a cold November evening to join us in celebration of a very special author, Josephine Forrest.'

She paused for a round of applause and Bluebell, sitting beside the Christmas tree looking relaxed, smiled and waved.

Lily held up her grandma's book. '*A Winter of Broken Promises* is Josephine's thirty-fourth novel and is out today. Thank you to those who've already bought the book this evening. We still have plenty of copies available and Josephine will be happy to sign them and have her photo taken with you after our chat. I've already read it and it's completely and utterly wonderful but enough from me. Let's hear from Josephine Forrest.'

More applause as Lily took a chair beside her grandma and asked her various questions about the story, the research she'd undertaken and about her writing career so far. Bluebell had everyone captivated with a reading, after which questions were invited from the audience. I'd seen Lily chatting to customers in the shop and had always been impressed with her interactions but seeing her tonight as host, she shone. I was so proud of how articulate and confident she was and how, despite being naturally humorous, she kept the spotlight clearly focused on her grandma. Every so often, she glanced across at me and smiled, making my heart leap. Nobody had ever looked at me the way she did and I never wanted it to end.

Casting my gaze around the enraptured audience, the packed bookshelves and the Christmas tree, I had the strongest feeling of being home. It was a cold winter's night but, right here, I felt the warmth of belonging. I'd fallen in love with Bay Books as a young boy – a love which had been renewed and strengthened over the past six weeks – and the thought of having to leave when Marcus returned to work made me feel queasy. I'd felt so lost after letting go of My Study Hub with no idea what I wanted to do with my future. But I knew now. My future was with Lily and Bay Books. Marcus would be returning in a couple of months and there weren't any vacancies but I knew how eager Lily was to work with a certain Paperback Pixie. I was sure we'd be able to come to some sort of arrangement when I shared that final secret with her.

* * *

An hour or so later, everyone had gone and Lily and I had folded down the chairs and tables and returned the display tables to their rightful positions.

'You were amazing tonight,' I told Lily.

She smiled at me. 'Granny Blue was amazing, you mean.'

'She was, but I mean you were. Everything about tonight was spot on – how you laid out the room, the books on the cakes, the questions you asked, working the signing queue to write down the names for dedications...'

'Years of experience.'

'You can have years of experience at something and still be rubbish at it. I was chatting to your granddad earlier and he said something that I completely agree with. He said that you're the reason the bookshop is the success it is today – that he and your grandma left a great legacy behind but you took their dream and sprinkled it with magic dust.'

Tears pricked her eyes. 'Granddad George really said that?'

'He did. And you haven't just sprinkled magic dust on the shop. You've sprinkled it on my life too.'

A tear slipped down her cheek.

'I didn't mean to upset you.'

'You didn't. It's the nicest thing anyone's ever said to me.'

I gently tilted her chin upwards. 'I mean it. I love you, Lily.'

'I love you too.'

Her kiss was tender at first but, as I pulled her closer, the kiss became deeper, more passionate. My heart raced as she untucked my shirt and ran her hands inside, up my back. I ran my fingers into her hair as I kissed her neck and across her collarbone.

'We can be seen from outside,' she murmured, tugging my hand as she guided me towards the children's section. She stopped in the entrance, groaning. 'It's children's books. It feels wrong.'

The staff room would have been the logical place to go but we'd just dumped the chairs in there for speed to sort out properly tomorrow. Lily took my hand and we raced up the stairs, stopping to kiss on the first landing. We kept moving up the building, pausing every so often in a passionate clinch, but only made it up to the third level before the electricity sizzling between us was too much. The creativity level felt like an appropriate place for what was about to happen.

* * *

'That was unexpected,' Lily said, as we pulled our clothes back into place a little later.

'But don't you say the unexpected things are usually the best?'

'I do and you absolutely proved the point.' She ran her hands through her dishevelled hair and turned to look at the bookcase behind her. 'I don't think I'm ever going to be able to look at the creative writing section in the same way.'

'We've knocked a couple of books off.'

I bent down to retrieve them and we both burst out laughing at the one on the top: Erin Carlson's *I'll Have What She's Having*, exploring how three of Nora Ephron's films – *When Harry Met Sally*, *Sleepless in Seattle* and *You've Got Mail* – reinvented the romantic comedy genre. Everyone knew the iconic scene in *When Harry Met Sally*. It was the perfect reference for what we'd just done, except it had been real for us. So very real.

39

LARS

A week later, Lily invited me over to Everdene straight from work for tea and to help put the Christmas tree up. As soon we stepped into the lounge, I could smell that rich pine aroma from a real tree.

'We'll be eating in about half an hour,' Shelby told us, so Lily insisted we crack on straightaway with the lights.

'Mum hates tinsel,' Lily said after we'd wrapped some warm white and red lights round the tree.

She passed me a couple of lengths of gold-coloured beads and asked me to drape them in the same way I'd drape tinsel, leaving space between each pass for her to fill with red beads.

'That looks really effective,' I said, stepping back once we'd finished. 'Tidier than tinsel.'

'That's one of the reasons Shelby likes the beads so much,' Marcus said. 'She likes things tidy and she thinks tinsel looks messy. You know that lametta stuff? She can't bear that.'

I'd forgotten about lametta and had a sudden flashback to our childhood Christmas tree being covered in the long narrow shiny strips in varying colours courtesy of Pia.

'My sister loved it. She used to smother the tree with it. I remember Pabbi lifting her up so she could drape it over the highest branches. She loved tinsel too and insisted on it being everywhere – on the tree, around picture frames, wrapped around lamps, even draped across the toilet cistern. We'd be picking up shreds of tinsel and lametta for months after Christmas was over.'

'Then we'll have to get some lametta for the tree this year.' I hadn't noticed Shelby appearing in the doorway, wiping her hands on a towel.

'You don't have to do that for me, especially if you hate the stuff.'

'Hate's a strong word,' she said, laughing. 'And we want to. You're part of the family now, Lars, and we like to do something to celebrate the Christmas traditions and decorations of each new member.'

I caught Lily's eye, unsure as to whether Shelby was just being nice to me but Lily nodded. 'We bought some houses that light up because Hendrix's girlfriend – sorry, fiancée – Daisy said they were one of her fondest Christmas memories. She's not close to her parents but she was really close to her grandma who had a huge Christmas village.'

'What was Cory's thing?' Marcus asked, frowning.

'How could you forget that?' Shelby playfully whacked his arm with the towel. 'It's one of your favourite new traditions.'

'Christmas Eve cookies!' he exclaimed, smiling. 'Of course! Cory gave us his mum's recipe and they're so delicious. We close the shop a little early on Christmas Eve and come home to a big family baking and decorating session.'

'It's a bit childish but we love it,' Lily said.

I nodded in agreement. 'If you can't be a kid at Christmas, when can you? Christmas is huge in Iceland and most Icelanders admit to being *jólabörn* which means *Christmas children*. There's a saying – *Ég er mikið jólabarn* – which translates as *I'm a total Christmas-child*, meaning you still look forward to Christmas in the same way you did as a child. Excitement, magic, loving all the sights and sounds that go into the season.'

'I love that,' Lily said, her eyes sparkling. 'We could do with more Christmas children in the UK.'

'Cookies are a massive part of Christmas in Iceland too. They get baked and eaten throughout December.'

Lily and her family seemed really interested in Icelandic Christmas traditions so the conversation continued over our evening meal. They asked about the cookie flavours and I explained that there were lots of popular choices and a good household would make at least seven or eight varieties across the season, especially if there was a member of the household not working and able to bake, but the most classic of Christmas cookies were *piparkökur* (gingerbread) and *sörur*, also known as Sarah Bernhardt cakes.

'Sarah Bernhardt? Wasn't she a French actress?' Shelby asked, and I nodded. 'Did she have a connection to Iceland?'

'No. The cookies were actually created by a Danish patisserie in honour of her visiting Copenhagen in the early 1910s so nobody's quite sure how they became such an intrinsic part of Icelandic traditions but there you go. The Swedish have their own version too and, I have to say, they're delicious so whatever randomness brought them to Iceland, I'm glad it happened.'

They wanted to know what was in them, which was a real test of my memory. Nanna had kept the cookie-making tradition going for several years but I got too busy with My Study Hub to make them with her so that tradition ceased. I couldn't remember any of the quantities but the base was definitely marzipan, sugar and egg whites. A ganache made from butter, sugar, vanilla and cappuccino powder was added to the flat side and then covered in melted chocolate. My mouth watered as I finished and Shelby said she'd be online tomorrow searching for a recipe. I told her I'd ask Nanna if she still had ours although she'd cleared out a lot of recipe books as part of her move so I wasn't hopeful.

After we'd eaten, we returned to the lounge and it was time to put the decorations on the tree. Every single one was gold, red or wooden and the designs varied massively from elaborately decorated glass baubles to simple wooden stars. I'd loved Pia's technicolour approach but the Appletons' tree was beautiful and classy. It didn't so much shout at me as tease me with its elegance.

I thought we'd finished but Lily handed me an old ice-cream container, a mischievous grin on her face. 'One more box of decorations to put up. These ones are extra special.'

I lifted the lid to examine the contents and started laughing. 'Are these your primary-school decorations? Oh, wow! You weren't exaggerating when you said special.'

I lifted out a set of people made from old-style wooden clothes pegs who, from the clothing, were clearly the cast of the nativity. I held up one dressed in blue. 'Any particular reason for Mary having a beard?'

That tickled Marcus and Shelby and out came a story about how Lily came home from school in floods of tears because she'd spent every art session across the week creating her peg people, carefully dressing them, only to fall at the final hurdle when, after adding beards to the kings, wise men and Joseph, she'd accidentally done the same to Mary.

'She'd been telling us all week how proud she was of them and how much praise the teacher had given her,' Shelby said. 'We couldn't wait to see them and I'll never forget her little face, all crumpled up, tears flowing.'

'She tried to flush Mary down the toilet and managed to block it,' Marcus added. 'That was an expensive near-drowning.'

Lily hung her head but I could see she was smiling.

'Mum managed to convince me that the rest of the peg people loved Mary, beard and all, so she needed to stay.'

'Rummage a bit further,' Shelby said. 'There's another peg person in there.'

I found a woman with long black hair, a purple dress and a beard but it looked more professionally made than the others.

'It's Lettie, the bearded lady from *The Greatest Showman*,' Lily explained. 'When I saw the film, I couldn't resist making a friend for Mary so Lettie's also part of our nativity cast now.'

The tub contained various other decorations only a parent could love including a terrifying three-eyed snowman made by Hendrix and a robin Kadence had made which somehow managed to look more like a blood-soaked bat. I was stunned to discover they all got added to the tree when everything else about it was so perfect.

'Scary as some of them are, they represent the magic of Christmases past so they belong here,' Marcus said.

I hung bearded Mary on the tree and added Lettie by her side, smiling at the handiwork of child Lily and adult Lily.

'Huge plus points for creativity,' I said, 'even from a young age.'

When we finished the tree, Shelby helped us display various other items around the room including the light-up houses they'd mentioned earlier. There was a large house, a small cottage and a bookshop which captured their family perfectly.

'Where's the Paperback Pixie?' Shelby asked.

My stomach lurched at the mention of my alter ego and I looked up from where I'd been plugging in the bookshop, expecting to find them all looking in my direction, my identity somehow rumbled, but they were preoccupied with looking through boxes.

'In this one,' Marcus said, removing something protected by bubble wrap from the box on the sofa beside him.

Lily took the item from him and showed it to me. 'Look what we found a few years ago! Our very own Paperback Pixie. Okay, it's an elf really but, seeing as we have no idea who the real Paperback Pixie is, we've got our own fake version.'

The Christmas elf was about eight inches high with fairy lights around its neck. Santa's list was draped over one arm, partly checked, but the elf was evidently more interested in the open book in his other hand. As Lily gave him pride of place on the mantelpiece, my thoughts turned to the books I was going to leave out this Christmas. I always aimed for one last gifting on 12 December because it was the first day of the Icelandic Advent but also my birthday. Bad weather often meant gifting a day or two either side of the 12th as, even though I put the books in protective bags, there was no point putting any out in the rain – very few people around and too much risk of damage. This year I'd be late. The 12th fell on the Friday of Cassie and Jared's wedding and I'd be working on the Saturday but I'd leave them out on the Sunday, weather permitting. I'd decided that every book would give a clue as to my identity. Although the general public wouldn't have a chance of guessing, the books would mean something to Lily. I was dying to share my secret with her but I wanted the reveal to be exciting and romantic. From everything Lily had told me about Ewan and Wes, they'd never done anything romantic for her and I wanted to show her that she was worth it.

I'd almost finalised the books I was going to gift and the last one would be a massive giveaway – *Anna and the Snow Dragon*, which I'd bought last week while Lily was on a break.

Decorating done, we settled down with a well-earned cuppa and the conversation turned to Christmas Day. Nanna had admitted that Geraldine and Hilary had asked her to join them for Christmas dinner at Bay View, and she hadn't liked to accept for fear of me being on my own. I'd told her to confirm her plans with her friends and I'd see her at some point that day or, if not, we'd definitely get together on Boxing Day. Lily had since officially invited me to spend the day with her family but Marcus and Shelby wanted to tell me themselves how welcome I was.

'But we should also warn you it'll be chaos,' Shelby added. 'We'll understand if you need to retreat to Green Gables to get the ringing out of your ears.'

I was looking forward to it. Bit nervous, perhaps, but it would be good to be part of a big family Christmas for once.

Lily said there was something she wanted to show me in the annexe so we said our goodbyes and headed over there. The first thing she did when we closed the door was kiss me.

'I've been dying to do that all night,' she said, 'but I'm also dying to show you this. Close your eyes.'

She took my hands and led me into the lounge area, eased me down onto the chair, and released my hands when I was settled.

'If you hate it or if I've got it completely wrong, please say so. I won't be offended.'

'Okay. Sounds intriguing.'

I could hear her moving about but that didn't give me any clues. When she declared I could open my eyes, she was standing by the sofa and the throw she'd had draped over the back of it was now opened out and covering something, but there were just a few lumps and bumps so it evidently wasn't very big.

'Until you started working at the shop, I never really thought about Christmas in other countries,' she said. 'Obviously I've picked up some things from books, TV and films but I've never really delved into it. It's been fascinating learning about Christmas in Iceland which got me thinking that other people would probably be interested and what if we devoted a section of our Christmas window display each year to a different country? We would, of course, start with, dah dah dah!'

She pulled back a section of the throw to reveal the Icelandic national flag – a blue field with a white-bordered off-centre red cross.

'That flag looks vaguely familiar,' I said, touched by the gesture.

'Someone told me that thirteen Yule Lads make their annual trip down from the mountains, one at a time, starting with this fella on the 12th...'

She pulled back the throw a little further and I gasped at a fantastic canvas painting of Stekkjarstaur, the 'Sheep-Cote Clod' who liked to creep into the sheep cote and drink milk directly from the ewes' udders.

'You drew him? Lily! I knew you were creative but I didn't realise you were an artist too.'

She grinned. 'Are you saying the bearded Mary didn't give it away earlier?' She lifted off the rest of the throw, revealing the next two Yule Lads. 'I have to say, they're a peculiar bunch.'

'With dubious eating habits,' I agreed, getting up and marvelling at her brilliant drawings.

Giljagaur the 'Gully Gawk' visited on the 13th. Despite being the biggest and strongest, he was shy and preferred not to be seen so he made his descent through deep, dark canyons or gullies covered in thick snow where he knew he wouldn't meet anyone. He also loved milk but chose cows over ewes and preferred to slurp the foam after they were freshly milked. The visitor on the 14th – Stúfur the 'Stubby' – was, by contrast, the smallest (or stubbiest) of the brothers and his preference was for licking the burnt leftovers in the bottom of pans. Pia had found him particularly hilarious because she couldn't imagine why anyone would bother to make the long journey down the mountains just to snack on burnt leftovers.

'These are fantastic,' I said, hugging Lily to my side. 'Thank you.'

'I thought I'd better not draw the rest until I'd checked you were okay with it.'

'I'm more than okay with it. This is the best thing anyone has ever done for me.'

'I thought we could put two easels up in the window each day on top of the mini bookshelves – one with the painting and another with their name and story. I can take photos of the pictures and type up the stories for people in the shop to look through if they miss them in the window and then, of course, we'll build up to *Jólabókaflóð* but I'm going to make that your project. Have a think about how we can celebrate it in the shop.'

I still hadn't asked Freyja what Icelandic bookshops did to celebrate *Jólabókaflóð* so I'd do that on Sunday when I rang her to confirm I'd definitely visit Iceland in the spring.

'I can't thank you enough,' I said, hugging Lily tightly.

'Anything for you. I'm interested in your culture because I'm interested in you. Always have been, always will be.'

I felt like a *jólabarn* for the first time since that final Christmas with Pia and it was all thanks to Lily. Her granddad had definitely been right about her sprinkling magic dust on everything.

40
LILY

The first Saturday in December was my favourite day of Christmas trading as it was the annual switching on of the Christmas lights in Whitsborough Bay. A few weeks ago, a flatbed lorry packed with lighting units had slowly worked its way around the town followed by a pair of cherry pickers. Several workers in high-vis boiler suits unloaded the colourful lights and secured them in place along the main pedestrianised precinct. Castle Street was next, with white lights strung in a tight zigzag pattern between each side of the street and a welcome banner at the far end opposite Castle Park. A couple of days later, the enormous tree outside the shopping centre and the smaller one in Castle Park were erected and strung with lights.

I loved the festive feeling the lights created but I particularly loved the tradition of the Castle Street traders gathering together round the Castle Park tree. Tara and her team at The Chocolate Pot provided drinks, Carly provided cupcakes and there were usually chocolates available from Charlee's Chocolates. Many of the traders would go on a pub crawl afterwards, which was a chance to have a proper catch-up – something we didn't have time for during the working day when we all had businesses to run. This year, the evening plans were slightly different. We were still going on a traders' pub crawl but it was doubling up as Cassie's hen party. With so many friends owning businesses on Castle Street and it being tricky to find another diary date that would suit everyone at such a busy time of year, it made sense to combine the two events.

Jared had been on his stag do last night – also a pub crawl round town, ending up at The Bombay Palace. The family called in just after midday to drop off Cassie's costume for tonight. The theme was *Alice's Adventures in Wonderland* in homage to Cassie's favourite childhood book and, with her long blonde hair, she was ideally suited for dressing up as Alice.

'Is it loud in here today?' Jared asked me, grimacing. He definitely looked a little green around the gills.

'Not really. Just a bit busy.'

'It hurts. I might wait outside.'

'It's hilarious watching him suffer,' Cassie said, as Jared headed for the door, 'but I'm conscious I can't take the mickey too much. Whatever I dish out, he'll give back to me ten-fold tomorrow.'

Lars was out on his lunch break so I left Alec and Flo at the till and wandered through to the children's section with Cassie. Hallie and Rocco excitedly pointed out the newest additions to the Bookmas tree and Cassie told them they could choose one book each for their dad to read after the switch-on.

'Small-world moment this morning,' Cassie said. 'You know how you've been dying to meet Lars's bestie? You'll get your chance on Friday. She's coming to our wedding.'

'Really? How come?'

'Jared went to school with her girlfriend, Milana. She's coming to the evening do and had declined the plus one but messaged this morning asking if she could bring someone after all. As soon as I saw the name Danika, I realised the connection.'

'That's brilliant! Lars'll be so chuffed.'

'And how's it going with Lovely Lars?' she asked, giving me a playful nudge.

'Lovely Lars is it now?'

'I thought I'd better ditch Lars the Arse, although I'll keep the moniker in my back pocket for if he ever messes you about.'

I laughed at her stern expression. 'I don't think you'll need it. He's amazing. It's been less than three weeks but it's already hard to remember life before his return.'

'You've got it bad,' she said, 'but so has he and that makes me very happy. Right! Enough soppiness. Let me gather up my offspring and their books and you get back to work, you slacker! I don't know, always skiving off at every opportunity.'

'I'll see you tonight, Alice,' I said.

'Don't be late,' she joked, referencing my character for tonight – the White Rabbit.

When I returned to the till, Lars was back from lunch and it was time for Alec to go for his so I sent Cassie's costume down in Jeeves and asked Alec to hang it up in the staff room alongside mine. We'd considered wearing our costumes for the lights switch-on but Cassie decided that, as she was hijacking the pub crawl for her hen do, the time in Castle Park should be purely about the Castle Street traders. The plan, therefore, was to return to the shop afterwards for a quick change before joining everyone in The Purple Lobster.

* * *

I loved the Christmas lights switch-on but I was especially excited this year to have Lars with me. He'd already met the traders who were my closest friends and this was a chance to introduce him to their partners.

The staff from The Chocolate Pot and Carly's Cupcakes had set up trestle tables with hot drinks and trays of Carly's delicious Christmas-themed cupcakes. While Lars grabbed us a hot chocolate each, I took a couple of cakes then wandered round the park, introducing him to various people.

Just before half six, the crowd hushed and waited for the cheer from outside the shopping centre to indicate that a local celebrity had flicked the switch, lighting the large Christmas tree first. Moments later, we heard it and turned to look along Castle Street, ready for our Christmas illuminations. The zigzagged lights on Castle Street burst into life a section at a time, followed by the welcome sign across from the park. The traders turned to the tree with 'oooh' sounds as the star at the top lit up, followed by the coloured lights on the branches. As per tradition, we sang 'We Wish You a Merry Christmas', followed by a cheer.

'What did you think?' I asked Lars.

He cuddled me closer to his side. 'Loved it. This has to be number three in my top winter nights in the bay.'

'What are your top two?' I asked.

'They're tied first and they were both in the bookshop – the night we put up the tree and the night of the book launch.'

My innards fizzed at the memory of both as I softly kissed him. 'Mine too.'

Lars helped clear away the tables and it warmed my heart seeing him joking with my friends before I left with Cassie to get changed.

* * *

The pub crawl had to be the best ever, although I missed Dad's presence. He loved the traders' night and was gutted about missing it this year. In theory, he could have hobbled round the pubs but the risk of someone bashing into his still-swollen knees in a busy pub was too great so it made sense to stay at home.

The hens had done an amazing job of dressing up as Wonderland characters. We'd agreed that nobody but Cassie could dress as Alice but it didn't matter if other outfits were duplicated. As it turned out, none of them were. Ginny looked incredible as the Queen of Hearts, Sarah from Seaside Blooms was the White Queen, Tara was the Mad Hatter and Jemma was the Cheshire Cat. Carly and her sister Bethany had come as Tweedledee and Tweedledum with bald caps and big padded stomachs and Charlee and her business partner Jodie had also gone for a pair of costumes – a hedgehog and flamingo from the croquet scene. Our friend Donna was the Caterpillar and a few other non-trader friends had come as the March Hare, Mouse and a playing-card guard.

We got lots of attention in all the pubs on our route and posed for several photos with strangers. It was so good having quality time with the traders and I looked forward to spending more time with them at Cassie's wedding but, for me, the best part of the night was seeing my best friend so happy. She literally was a glowing bride-to-be, although the amount of alcohol she'd consumed might have played a part in that.

'She looks happy,' Lars said, slipping his arm round my waist as Cassie belted out ABBA's 'I Do, I Do, I Do, I Do, I Do' on karaoke four pubs in.

'She really does.'

'You've managed to get out of singing with her?'

'If only! She's dragging me up next.'

Sure enough, the song finished and the DJ announced, 'Our bride-to-be Cassie wants her bridesmaids Lily and Donna to join her for Bruno Mars's "Marry You". Take it away, ladies… or should that be girl, rabbit and caterpillar?'

I wasn't the greatest singer but I could hold a note and I think we managed a pretty good rendition of 'Marry You'. I hadn't dared look at Lars as I said the repeated line about wanting to marry but, as the song approached the end, I couldn't resist looking in his direction and singing the words to him. His smile widened and he saluted as he mouthed the words 'me too', making my heart leap.

Tonight was all about Cassie but I knew that one night, in the not-too-distant future, it would be all about me and that amazing man who'd been through so much in his life but who'd come through the other side strong, caring and passionate. A couple of months ago, I'd felt so low but had been determined to live by Anne Shirley's philosophy of *I don't know what lies around the bend, but I am going to believe that the best does.* The best really had been just around the bend for me.

41

LILY

The morning of Cassie and Jared's wedding and Lars's thirty-fifth birthday arrived. Lars had stayed in Green Gables overnight and it was lovely waking up beside him, wishing him a happy birthday and seeing him open his presents. We were big on birthdays in our family and he looked close to tears when I presented him with gifts from my parents, Kadence, Hendrix and both sets of grandparents.

'I haven't even met your sister yet,' he said, staring at her gift in obvious disbelief. 'And I've only met your brother and grandparents briefly.'

'But you're part of the family,' I said, hugging him. 'It's the way we do things. Hope that's okay with you.'

'It's more than okay. I'm just... It's... I...' He rolled his eyes. 'I'm that stunned, I can't even form a proper sentence. Thank you all so much. Your family are amazing. *You* are amazing.'

'True, but sadly not amazing enough to give you your birthday off work. You'd better get going if you're going to be taxi service to my granddads. See you at the wedding.'

He kissed me goodbye and headed off to collect Granddad George and Granddad Maurice, who were helping out in Bay Books this morning. Granddad Maurice didn't know how to use the till but he knew the shop well so would be a valuable extra pair of hands until they closed at half twelve so everyone could attend Cassie's wedding.

As I placed the discarded wrapping paper in the recycling bin outside, thoughts of my own unhappy birthday in March pushed their way into my mind but I swiftly dismissed them. My world was so different now and I knew that Lars would pull out all the stops to make sure my birthday next year was a special one.

I paused to breathe in the fresh, chilled air before going back inside. A heavy frost but a clear blue sky couldn't have been better weather conditions for the wedding. The photos would look amazing. Cassie had clearly had the same thoughts as, when I returned to my bedroom, I spotted a message from her along with a stack of wedding-related and snowflake emojis.

> **FROM CASSIE**
> I'm getting married today. Squee!!!!!! Any chance of you getting here earlier so we can get photos in the garden before the frost melts?

> **TO CASSIE**
> Happy wedding day! So excited for you. Yes, no probs. Be there in less than an hour x

* * *

I'd already seen Cassie in her wedding dress because I'd been with her when she chose it from The Wedding Emporium, but seeing her wearing it on her wedding day with her hair and make-up done and her face radiating happiness had me welling up.

She'd originally been thinking of an ivory dress for herself with the bridesmaids looking Christmassy in deep red, but was concerned that it was all a bit too traditional. Ginny had suggested flipping the colours and showed us a red bridal gown which she thought would be perfect for Cassie. Lace covered with a tight bodice, capped sleeves and gold and red sparkling embellishments around the waist, it was absolutely stunning and no other dress had a look-in after that. Today, her hair was styled in a series of loose knots and plaits interwoven with realistic-looking ivy, red berries and gold sparkles.

The bridesmaid dresses had lacy white bodices and dusky pink skirts and Hallie's flower girl dress was dusky pink all over with gold embellishments. Jared and the groomsmen would be wearing forest-green three-piece suits with red ties, which I wouldn't see until we arrived at the venue, but I had a pretty good idea of how they'd look as Rocco was wearing an adorable matching outfit minus the blazer. He'd chosen a bow tie instead of a regular one, which he kept twiddling while Hallie pirouetted round the lounge in her dress.

The photographer managed to capture several photos in the frost before the December sun reached Cassie and Jared's back garden and, before long, we were on our way to Sherrington Hall – a beautiful old hotel on the top of the cliff twelve miles south of Whitsborough Bay.

Cassie and Jared's Christmas wedding was everything I'd imagined and more. The attention to detail by the wedding planner was exemplary as even the decorations on the many Christmas trees around the building matched the colour scheme. In addition to the gorgeous floral arrangements Sarah from Seaside Blooms had made, there were hurricane candles on every window ledge with swathes of ivy and shiny baubles. Fairy lights twinkled everywhere and the whole wedding felt magical from start to end.

Lars looked divine in a grey three-piece suit and it touched my heart seeing him seeking out each of my family members to thank them for his birthday gifts. Kadence, delighted to finally meet him, was full of compliments.

'This one's definitely a keeper,' she said, hugging me during the drinks reception.

My family had been friendly around Ewan and Wes but there was something different about the way they interacted with Lars and I couldn't quite put my finger on what it was. I mentioned it to Cassie when I was in the bathroom helping with her dress before the wedding breakfast.

'Head versus heart,' she said. 'They welcomed Ewan and Wes to the family because they're lovely people and it was the polite thing to do when they knew they were important to you – a head thing. With Lars, they genuinely love being around him. He's captured their hearts, just like he's captured yours. You've finally found your Gilbert Blythe.'

My heart leapt because I felt that way too. I'd been thinking a lot lately about the connections between Lars's and my story and my favourite literary couple like falling out as children but having a friendship which developed into love, and how Gil's nickname for Anne of *Carrots* became a term of endearment, just as *Little Miss Perfect (-for-me)* had become ours.

Returning to the bar, I spotted Lars at a table chatting to Kadence, Cory, Hendrix and Daisy. They were laughing together as though they were old friends and I could see exactly what Cassie meant. The Bay Books team acted the same around Lars too and the wonderful part was that it was all down to Lars being himself. The boy who'd had no friends and very little family had become the man with a growing circle of friends and a new family and I couldn't be more proud of him.

When Jared announced in his groom's speech that it was Lars's birthday and led the guests in a chorus of 'Happy Birthday to You', all the warm smiles in Lars's direction brought tears to my eyes. And the enormous smile from Lars when Cassie presented him with a bottle of bubbly was priceless. Knowing how much of an outsider Lars had felt for most of his life, struggling to fit in anywhere, it gave me so much joy to see him find where he belonged.

'Best birthday ever,' he said as we slowly moved around the dance floor to the last song of the evening. 'Earlier, I was thinking about how I'd have spent today if you hadn't offered me the job at the shop.'

'Or if Danika hadn't stood over you, making you submit your CV,' I said, glancing across the dance floor at Danika and Milana, both of whom I'd warmed to instantly. 'What would you have been doing?'

'Lunch or tea with Nanna and a FaceTime call with Freyja at some point, but I'd have spent most of it on my own.'

I tightened my hold on him. 'You'll never need to be on your own again. My family and friends all love you and so do I.'

'They're so great. When I saw you with your family in the bookshop and I desperately wanted what you had, I never imagined I'd be lucky enough to get it.'

'*Þetta reddast*,' I said, hoping my pronunciation wasn't way off.

He looked down at me, his eyes sparkling. 'Thanks to you, everything *has* worked out.'

As he kissed me on the dance floor, I knew that my Christmas sparkle had well and truly returned and this was going to be the most incredible Christmas. The Christmas that banished all the demons of bad Christmases past. Bring it on!

42

LARS

At work the following day, everyone was on a high after the wedding, although Alec was definitely nursing a fuzzy head. I removed Stekkjarstaur from the window first thing and replaced him with Lily's brilliant painting of Giljagaur. Several customers had already commented on the Yule Lads and been eager to look through the folder showing all thirteen. We'd introduce the Christmas Cat next weekend as the schools would have broken up and the town should be busy so he'd have the greatest impact then.

This morning, Lily and I had agreed that we wouldn't spend tonight together as we both needed to catch up on some sleep after such a hectic week. Having spent so much time with her recently, it would be strange not seeing her until Monday morning but one glance in her direction during a quiet moment mid-afternoon confirmed it was necessary. She looked absolutely shattered and I suspected the Christmas break couldn't come soon enough for her. I just hoped she had the energy for the final push. It was less than a fortnight away but I knew how exhausting seven-day weeks could be. On top of that, she'd had a hen do to organise, bridesmaid duties at her best friend's wedding and a stack of props for the window to create. I couldn't help thinking that painting all the Yule Lads had turned out to be a bigger project than she'd envisaged and the late nights painting might have taken their toll. No wonder she was yawning.

'You look like you could do with one of Tara's brownies,' I said, joining her at the till after she'd served a couple of customers.

She winced. 'And here was me thinking I was managing to hide it. Yes, please. I need the energy boost.'

I rang an order through to The Chocolate Pot and nipped out to collect drinks and snacks for Alec and Flo too, which were gratefully accepted. The last hour or so of the day massively slackened off. Lily stayed by the till while the rest of us went round the shop replenishing the shelves, putting abandoned books back in the right places and generally tidying up.

'Are you okay?' I asked Lily as we prepared to leave. She'd been unusually quiet as the afternoon progressed.

'Just tired and I've got a bit of a headache. Some paracetamol and an early night should shift it.'

She unlocked the door to let me out and I moved to kiss her but she turned her head and I caught her cheek instead.

'Sorry. So tired I can't even do that properly,' she said, rolling her eyes at me. 'Have a good evening with your nanna. Give her my love.'

'Will do and I hope the head clears soon.'

I decided against going in for another kiss. Lily looked as though she could fall asleep standing up and I didn't want to waylay her, so I gave her a wink and a salute as I walked away but I'm not sure she even caught them before closing the door.

* * *

I drove to Nanna's straight from work. There'd been a packed calendar of Christmas events at Bay View this month and it seemed Nanna was quite the joiner-in so I'd barely seen her. She'd told me it was wreath-making this evening but, as she'd already made one at an earlier session, she was willing to give it a miss for me. Just as well I didn't take anything Nanna said personally.

'Sorry I'm a bit late with it this year,' I said to Nanna, handing her a vibrant red poinsettia plant in a gold pot which I'd purchased from Seaside Blooms at lunchtime. Nanna loved poinsettias and I bought her one every year, but usually at the start of December. 'Hope you haven't bought one for yourself.'

'I nearly did, but I knew you wouldn't forget. This is beautiful, Lars, and I love the pot. Very festive. I've got the perfect spot for it.'

I followed her into her apartment where she placed the plant on a lamp table before disappearing into the kitchen to make a brew. As I looked around the room, I tutted as my eyes rested on the pre-lit, pre-decorated artificial tree which I'd hoped hadn't survived the move. On the coffee table was a flyer for the Christmas events in Bay View and Nanna's signed copy of Josephine Forrest's *A Winter of Broken Promises*. From the position of the bookmark, she wasn't far from the end.

'Enjoying the book?' I asked when Nanna appeared with the drinks.

'Oh, it's wonderful. I should get it finished at bedtime.'

'I can't believe you're still using that bookmark. You must have so many others.'

'But none as special as this one.' She swapped the flyer for the bookmark and passed me the latter. 'It means you and your sister are with me every time I read.'

I'd made the bookmark at primary school. The whole class had created embroidered bookmarks or coasters using pieces of binca. My lack of creativity meant my attempt hadn't been particularly adventurous – a border of crosses and another of straight lines and *NANNA* in capitals. I'd stitched my name in capitals on a second bookmark and took it home for Pia to embroider her name next to mine, after which my teacher helped me stitch the two pieces together to create one double-sided bookmark.

'Pia wanted to add a snow dragon,' I said, handing it back to Nanna. 'We both had a go but it just looked like a melted snowman so we decided less was more.'

'It's perfect as it is.'

As she placed the bookmark back in her novel, I took a deep breath. The forecast for tomorrow was dry and bright so I'd be distributing the Christmas Paperback Pixie's final gifts of the year and (hopefully) revealing my identity to Lily. It felt right to share my secret with Nanna first.

'There's something I need to tell you...'

'You already know?' I stared at Nanna, stunned, after I'd revealed my secret identity. 'How?'

'Box after box of books arriving was a bit of a clue.'

'But I told you they were for me and for work.' To avoid arousing suspicions at the bookshop, I'd ordered some books under Nanna's name and had set up several PO Boxes for the others, all being delivered to Fountain Street.

'Which I never doubted at first,' Nanna said, 'but your bookshelves didn't expand at the rate of your deliveries so I worked it out. I assumed there was a reason you wanted to keep it secret and that you'd tell me in your own sweet time. Admittedly, I didn't think it'd take quite this long.'

'Didn't have you down as Miss Marple.'

'It's the quiet ones you have to watch.' She winked at me. 'What made you do it?'

'You tell me, super sleuth.'

'The use of *pixie* suggests something to do with your sister.'

'Spot on.' I told her how the idea came to me as a way to celebrate Pia and her love of reading with the anonymity being the best way to keep the focus on the books and the finders rather than me.

'I'm so proud of you,' Nanna said. 'I bet our little Pixie is too.'

'I'd like to think so.'

'Seeing as you've shared a secret with me, I have one to share with you, although I've only been sitting on mine for days rather than years. I had a video call with your mum last week and I read her the riot act. I told her that I understand how devastating it was for her to lose two of the people she loved most in the whole world but she still has two family members left and she needs to stop hiding from them or she'll lose them forever too. The upshot of that is I've pinned her down to coming home in early January. Her flight's booked and she's even emailed me the confirmation to prove it.'

I stared at Nanna, stunned that she'd taken such a hard line and that Mum had responded positively to it.

'Let's hope she doesn't cancel,' I said.

'If she does, she does and we know where we stand, but I want to believe that she won't let us down.'

'So do I,' I assured her. 'Good on you for trying. Ball's in her court now.'

I hoped for Nanna's sake that Mum did get her act together and make a decision to be more present in our lives. That didn't mean she needed to stop travelling; just that she needed to make time for us while she was away and between her projects. I didn't think it was much to ask – but could it be too much for her?

43

LILY

I hadn't been lying to Lars when I said I had a headache but I'd lied about the reason. I *was* shattered, but that hadn't caused the headache. It came from the effort of keeping the tears at bay, at pasting a smile on my face when all I wanted to do was scream. My head pounded all the way home and I'd barely closed the door behind me at Green Gables before a strangled sob burst from my mouth. With no energy to make it any further, I sank onto one of the kitchen table chairs, and let my emotions spill out. There was only me here so it didn't matter how loud and messy it all became. I just had to let it be.

During a lull late this afternoon, the team had spread themselves around the shop to restock and tidy up. Alec was covering the whole of non-fiction – usually the tidiest sections – and, as the children's section was typically the most trashed, Flo and Lars had been tackling it together. I'd been restocking the notebooks by the till when I overheard their conversation. Flo had told Lars that visiting Iceland was on her dream holiday list and asked if he'd seen much of the island. He'd told her what I already knew – that his family came from Húsavík in the north so he was most familiar with that area, and that he'd visited Reykjavík and various *Game of Thrones* film settings. But what he'd said next was news to me.

'I'm going to visit my family when my contract finishes here and I've got big plans to explore Iceland and the other Nordic countries. Viking history and culture fascinates me.'

I'd had to grip onto one of the shelves to steady myself. Lars hadn't said anything to me about visiting his family and he certainly hadn't told me he had *big plans*. I'd inched a little closer, my ears pinned for further details. Flo asked him what the difference was between the Nordic and Scandinavian countries so Lars explained that before telling her the various towns and landmarks he was most excited about visiting. So many places. How long was that going to take?

My throat hurt now from crying. Feeling like I had leaden weights attached to my feet, I made it to the sink and downed a glass of water before pouring another one and shuffling through the lounge and into my bedroom. Placing the glass down on my bedside cabinet, I curled up on top of the duvet and closed my eyes.

It was happening again. I'd trusted him. I'd opened up to him about how much I'd struggled with Ewan and Wes choosing Whitsborough Bay as their home and me as their future, only to drop us both when a better offer came along. What was wrong with me? Why did the men I fell for always leave me? Or was there some deeper psychological issue there and it was me who chose men who I knew were going to leave?

I searched my memory bank for anything Lars might have said or done to reassure me that I was mistaken and he had no intention of leaving Whitsborough Bay. He'd bought a house but he hadn't purchased any furniture for it. I hadn't even been invited to visit. He'd said there was no point when there was only one old chair he'd brought from his nanna's house to tide him over, so we'd either gone out or spent the evening here in Green Gables. And when I mentioned him putting a tree up, he hadn't been at all enthusiastic about it, which didn't match with someone who'd told me how much he loved Christmas trees.

Buying a house should be an indication of his intention to stay, but he'd barely said anything about it other than it had needed lots of work. I remembered him saying he'd needed to find somewhere to live because his nanna was moving into Bay View and didn't want to sell him her house. That smacked of convenience rather than a clear investment in his dream home. With no furniture, no enthusiasm for a tree and no invitation for me to visit, it felt as though his house was merely a stop-gap while he decided what to do next. While he prepared for his travels.

But why not rent a house if that was the case? And why apply for the job in

Bay Books when he could have put stuff in storage and gone travelling as soon as he sold the business?

My head was a mess. I returned to the lounge and retrieved my phone from my bag. Back in the bedroom, I placed it on the bed beside me and stared at it. One call. One question. *Are you leaving me to go travelling in the spring?* That's all that was needed. My fingers twitched towards it several times, but I couldn't seem to pick it up and ring Lars because fear had wrapped its icy fingers around me and was squeezing tightly. Yes, Lars might tell me he had no intention of leaving me and we could laugh about it and live happily ever after. But what if he told me he *was* leaving and not to worry because he'd be back? I'd heard that before. I knew how these things went. One month, two, three, six... it could stretch out into so much longer. Like it had when Justin promised my mum he'd just get the interrailing bug out of his system and be back to accept his impending parental responsibilities.

* * *

I tossed and turned most of the night, dreaming of sprinting along airport runway after runway as planes took off, taking Lars away from me. My headache hadn't shifted when I arrived for work but I smiled and acted as though there was nothing wrong. It helped that the shop was busy so the hours raced by. It also helped that I knew there was no chance of Lars dropping in unexpectedly because he'd told me he was spending the day with Danika.

I had so much to think about but the combination of a hectic social life since getting together with Lars, the crazy hours I'd been working recently and the time needed to paint the Yule Lads, Christmas Cat and write out the explanations – significantly more hours than I'd anticipated – had taken their toll and I couldn't seem to process anything clearly. Lars and I needed to talk but I wasn't in the right frame of mind to do it. Even if he told me I'd got it all wrong and he wasn't going anywhere, I didn't trust myself not to say something that had the ability to destroy what we had. I'd accepted the end of my relationship with Ewan without a fight. I'd done the same with Wes. I'd even done it when Jordan ditched me. I'd walked away quietly instead of sharing how hurt I was, how disappointed, how angry. I now realised I'd kept all of those emotions pent up inside me and they were ready to be released. I didn't want to unleash them on Lars but I was terrified that a combination of fear and fatigue might lead to that.

I needed some more space away from him which meant not working together tomorrow.

Alec had finished university for the year and was keen to work extra hours. He was already scheduled in to cover Cassie's lunchtime shift tomorrow while she was in Switzerland on a mini-moon with Jared so I rang Alec and asked him if he was interested in a full shift tomorrow, which he gratefully accepted. He confirmed he could do Tuesday too if needed and it was fine to let him know last minute as he wouldn't be making other plans. Next I rang Granddad George to ask if he could cover the lunchtime shift tomorrow but Granny Blue answered so I asked her how her eyes were doing.

'Healing nicely, I believe. The blurry vision is long gone and it's quite wonderful to see again without glasses.'

'That's good news. I have a favour to ask. I don't suppose Granddad George could cover lunchtime in the shop tomorrow?'

'He'd love to,' she said after breaking off to check with him, 'but I'll come too. You know how much I love a Christmas shift. You can never have too many staff in at this time of year.'

'Thank you. That's really helpful.'

'Who can't make it?'

'Me. Seven days a week has been too much on top of Christmas and Cassie's wedding. I need a day to recharge my batteries.'

'Sweetheart, you sound exhausted. Leave it with us. We'll be in tomorrow and just shout if you need longer off.'

I thanked her profusely and released a few tears of relief when I hung up. I just hoped Lars would forgive me for not letting him know I wouldn't be in tomorrow. If I contacted him, he'd want to know why and I wouldn't be able to keep fobbing him off. It was better to stay quiet for now until I had my emotions in check.

44

LARS

I'd been out first thing on Sunday morning with my Christmas Paperback Pixie books and I couldn't wait for Lily's reaction but I knew she'd be too busy during the day to notice my Instagram post. By Sunday evening, I was on tenterhooks, waiting for her to ring to say she'd pieced together the clues and ask if I was really the elusive Paperback Pixie.

It was midnight before I finally accepted I wasn't going to hear from her and settled down to sleep. I felt a little disappointed at first but I told myself not to be so daft. She probably hadn't even seen the photos. Even though both Lily and Cassie followed the Paperback Pixie, it was nearly always Cassie who spotted the updates and flagged them to Lily but Cassie was away on her mini-moon just now.

As I approached Bay Books on Monday morning, I felt a mixture of nerves and excitement, wondering whether Lily might have seen the feed this morning. I unlocked the front door and was surprised to find Alec behind the counter.

'Hi, Alec! I thought you were doing the lunchtime shift.'

'Lily asked if I could do a full day instead. Her grandparents are coming in over lunch.'

'So Lily's not in today?'

'No. Didn't she tell you?'

'She didn't, unless I've missed...' I checked my phone but there weren't any messages.

'She's taking a day off. Shattered after working so many hours.'

'Oh, okay. I'm not surprised. She looked drained on Saturday and she had a headache.' I tried to sound unconcerned but I was puzzled. Why hadn't she told me she wasn't coming in today?

Going downstairs to drop off my coat, I rang Lily but it connected straight to her voicemail. I left a message saying I'd heard she was taking a day off, I hoped she was able to rest and I'd hopefully see her tomorrow. What more could I do?

When George and Bluebell arrived, they reiterated what Alec had said that Lily needed to recharge her batteries. It seemed she'd actually spoken to them and also to Alec, so why hadn't she spoken to me? Or even just sent me a message? I tried calling her again during my lunch break but it went to voicemail so I didn't leave a second message.

I rang once more as I walked back to my car at the end of the day but it was still voicemail. This wasn't like Lily so I drove to her house after work but the annexe was in darkness. Marcus must have seen me arrive as he poked his head out of the side door.

'She's not in,' he said. 'She's gone to see Kadence in York. Do you want a coffee?'

Thinking they were going to tell me what was going on, I joined Marcus and Shelby but they told me what everyone else had – that Lily was feeling shattered and wanted a day off. Marcus shared how guilty he was feeling that he hadn't insisted on them taking an extra person on and joked how strong-willed Lily could be when she set her mind on something. They were surprised Lily hadn't told me and thought perhaps she'd sent an undeliverable text and hadn't realised. The pair of them were as warm and friendly towards me as they'd always been and there were no awkward silences or loaded looks between them, which helped reassure me that I hadn't upset Lily. Not that I could think of anything I could have said or done that would have upset her.

'Do you know what time she'll be back from Kadence's?' I asked.

Shelby shrugged. 'She said late. I'm sure she wouldn't mind you waiting, but late could mean any time up to midnight.'

'No, it's fine. If she is back late, she'll want to go straight to bed. It's my day off tomorrow but I'll pop into the shop at some point to say hello.'

Driving back home, I wondered if Lily had put together the clues and discovered that I was the Paperback Pixie but it hadn't delighted her as I'd anticipated. What if she was annoyed with me for keeping such a big secret from her? It would explain why she'd spoken to her grandparents and Alec but was seemingly avoiding me. I tossed that idea around for a while before dismissing it as ridiculous. It didn't fit with the Lily I knew and loved. I remained convinced that she'd love the Pixie reveal. Something else was going on and hopefully she'd tell me what it was tomorrow.

45

LARS

On Tuesday morning I dropped in at Bay Books at half nine, my stomach sinking when I spotted Alec behind the counter again. He told me Lily was staying with her sister for a few days and had called him last night to ask if he could work two more extra days – today and tomorrow.

'Everything all right between you two?' Alec asked, presumably thinking it was odd that I was out of the picture.

'We keep missing each other's calls,' I said, embarrassed to admit I was out in the cold. 'I guess I'll see you for tomorrow's shift, then. Have a good one today.'

I wandered down to the end of the street and stood in Castle Park staring at the angry grey waves pounding onto the distant shore, my thoughts just as turbulent. What the hell was going on? My phone beeped with a notification and I grabbed it from my pocket, hoping it would be Lily, but it was Danika suggesting some dates for a pre-Christmas catch-up. I bit my lip. She was at work, but I could really use her advice right now.

TO DANIKA

Any chance I can meet you at lunchtime? I can come to the practice. Something's going on with Lily and I really need your take on it. I think she's ignoring me

FROM DANIKA

Come to the practice at 12

Danika sat in my car over her lunchtime, me pouring out my concerns while she sipped on a flask of soup. I'd definitely ruled out Lily being angry about the Paperback Pixie reveal so I didn't share that part. It didn't feel right Danika knowing before Lily.

'I don't think you're being paranoid,' she said when I'd brought her up to speed. 'It does sound like she's avoiding you, which means something has to have happened. You said everything was fine when you returned from The Chocolate Pot but she seemed distant at the end of the day and there was the odd non-kiss when you said goodbye. That suggests to me that something happened between the snack run and closing time. It might be nothing you've said or done but, to rule that out, I think you should walk me through that hour or two. We're talking step by step in miniscule detail. I want to know *everything* you said and did, no matter how insignificant it might seem.'

It was lucky I had a good memory and we were, after all, only going over a two-hour period. I walked Danika through the customers I'd served, my interactions with Lily, chatting to Flo while we sorted out the mess in the children's section...

'That!' she cried, grabbing my arm. 'Your conversation with Flo about Iceland. Could Lily have overheard that?'

'It's possible.'

'What exactly did you say?'

'Just that I'll be visiting my family when my contract finishes.'

'You've told Lily this?'

My stomach lurched. 'No. And...' I felt sick as I thought about the rest of that conversation. 'Oh, God! I talked about my plans to explore the Nordic region but the thing is, they're not actual plans. They're travel dreams. I don't even have a confirmed date to go to Húsavík.'

I glanced at Danika, who was wincing. 'Didn't you tell me something about her ex-boyfriends abandoning her?'

'I did and now she thinks I'm about to do the same when it's the exact opposite. I want to take *her* to Iceland. A Nordic adventure would be meaningless without her. But I didn't say any of that to Flo so all Lily would have heard was that history was about to repeat itself.'

Danika squeezed my arm. 'I think we've solved the mystery. I've got to get back to work but good luck and you know where I am if you need to talk.'

***

When I got home, I rang Lily once more, unsurprised when it connected to voicemail. Maybe just as well as this was an in-person conversation and I couldn't do that when she wasn't even in Whitsborough Bay. But I knew where she was. Snatching up my car keys, I left the house and set off to Everdene, intending to ask Marcus for Kadence's address, but, partway there, I pulled over. Turning up at Lily's parents' house was a terrible idea. Marcus would immediately know something was wrong between us and he was hardly going to hand over his other daughter's address without permission from her or Lily. Also, while Lily was exceptionally close to her parents, she didn't always confide in them about her emotional problems. I knew she hadn't told them everything that had happened with her exes or with Justin, so she might not appreciate me dragging her dad into our relationship issues.

Cassie would have returned from Switzerland last night and be on the lunchtime shift in the shop today. She was a far better option for getting a message to Lily. I drove into town and killed some time wandering aimlessly until the end of her shift.

'Lars! What are you doing here?' Cassie asked when she emerged from Bay Books shortly after half two to find me loitering by the door. The tone of voice was surprise rather than annoyance, which made me think Lily hadn't told her what she'd overheard.

'I need to talk to you about Lily. I'm worried about her.'

'I'm on my way to the school pick-up so you're going to need to walk me to my car if you want to talk. Although I'm not sure why you'd be worried. She's just having a few days off cos she's knackered.'

'But I haven't heard from her since the shop closed on Saturday.'

Cassie stopped dead and stared at me, frowning, before picking up her pace again.

'That's weird, but I don't know anything about it. I called her yesterday to let her know I was home and she said she was having a rest at her sister's and would be back at work on Friday. Admittedly, I thought all that time off was a little odd because Lily's usually all over Christmas at the shop – can't get enough of it – but I figured she's had a tough year and it had probably caught up with her.'

Conscious we'd reach Cassie's car soon, I briefly outlined my conversation with Flo.

'Overhearing that would definitely have sent her into a tailspin,' Cassie said.

'But why run to her sister's? Why not just ask me about it?'

She stopped and turned to me with a sigh. 'Lars, Lars, Lars, have you learned nothing about our Lily during your time together? If she overheard that conversation, she'll think you're leaving her – rejecting her just like the others did.'

'I realise that, but it doesn't answer my question.'

'It does.' We set off walking once more. 'Rejection is Lily's worst fear and what do most people do about fears and phobias? They avoid them. Lily's shattered from all the hours she's worked recently and, even though she put on a brave face, the incident with the customer whose kids trashed the books devastated her. That was swiftly followed by the Justin drama and, despite her putting a positive spin on it – being relieved he's out of her life – what he did to her floored her and drained her. I guarantee she wouldn't have had the strength to fight for you and you know what they say. It's fight or—'

'Flight,' I finished for her.

'Exactly. So Lily flew to somewhere she knew she'd have support but far enough away to give her the space she needed to sort her head out.'

We'd reached Cassie's car and she opened the driver's door.

'Everything you've just said makes perfect sense, but I'm out of my depth here. When she won't accept my calls, what can I do to convince her I've forever regretted what I did to her at school and I'd never, ever reject her again?'

Cassie placed her hand on my shoulder and gave it a squeeze. 'Hop in. You're going to have to come on the school run with me if you want my advice.'

46
LILY

'Get that down you.' Kadence placed a steaming bowl of carrot and coriander soup in front of me on Thursday lunchtime and pushed a basket of warm bread buns across the table.

I pushed them back. 'I'm not hungry.'

'It's not optional.' She shoved them towards me again with a little more force this time. 'You've barely eaten a thing since you turned up on Monday and I'm not having you driving an hour back to Whitsborough Bay on an empty stomach. Choose a bun and get it and your soup down your neck because you're not leaving until you do.'

'Do you talk to all your patients like that?' I asked, feeling both intimidated and impressed by my sister's authoritative tone.

'Only the ones who won't do what's good for them.' She pushed the butter dish in my direction too. 'You wouldn't want to do battle with a pregnant woman, would you?'

'Oh, for goodness' sake! If I eat the bread and the soup, will you stop your nagging?'

'Absolutely, because my work here will be done.'

I picked up a bun and buttered it. Admittedly, it did smell delicious and my stomach was feeling empty. I dipped one half in my soup and bit into it, unable to resist an appreciative, 'Mmmm.'

'Good, isn't it? You keep doing that until there's nothing left.'

I took another bite.

'So, what are you going to do about Lars?'

'Kadence! You said you weren't going to nag me.'

'Not about food, but I *am* going to nag you about this. I don't get you.' She shook her head. 'That's unfair. I get why you're here and why you're upset and I even understand your logic around not confronting him about what you heard. What I don't get is this... Even if he does have plans in place for some epic Nordic adventure, why would you even think of jumping ship? I have *never* seen you as happy as you are with Lars. We've all noticed it. You two are made for each other. So what if he wants to explore his roots? Let him go on his travels, get it out of his system or whatever, and then he can settle down and live happily ever after with you.'

'Let him travel? Let him get it out of his system? Just like Mum did with Justin? Cos that worked out well.'

Kadence clapped her hand over her mouth, her eyes wide. 'No, Lily! Is that what this is really about?'

I lowered my eyes, stirring my soup. 'It's not just that but, yes, the travel thing scares me. Justin promised Mum he'd come back and he never did.'

'Which turned out to be the best thing that he could ever have done. Remember what Mum always says – *the unexpected things in life are often the best*. Yes, he broke her heart and he's been an absolute dick towards you, but him abandoning Mum took her to Whitsborough Bay where she met Dad and our family became complete.'

'I hear you and I agree it was ultimately for the best. But what if Lars gets the travel bug too and he never returns?'

'And what if he never goes? What if he just goes for a week? What if he takes you with him and you do Nordia together?'

I couldn't help smiling at that. 'There's no such place as Nordia.'

'Well, excuse me, geography police, but you're missing the point. Lars is *nothing* like Justin and, for the record, he's nothing like Ewan or Wes either. He's on a whole different level.'

I knitted my eyebrows at her. 'I thought you liked them.'

'Liked, yeah. Never loved them, never missed them when they were gone, never believed they were perfect for you.'

'But you think Lars is?'

'I know he is and it's a two-way thing. Talk to him, Lily. Don't walk away without letting him explain because it might be nothing. And if it's something big like three, six, twelve months away, then you have a decision to make but don't make it before you know his intentions. Promise me?'

'I promise.'

'Do you want to know what I think?'

I smiled again. 'Haven't you just told me?'

'Ha, ha! I think that, even if he does want to travel, you'll wait for him because, deep down, you know how deeply he loves you and that he will come back for you. And you also know how deeply you love him too. Deeply enough to let him do whatever he needs to do to reconnect with his family and follow in the footsteps of Vikings. Now stop yakking and get that soup eaten.'

* * *

I did finish my lunch so Kadence gave me permission to finish packing and return home. As she hugged me goodbye, she told me to think about what she'd said and, all the way back to Whitsborough Bay, I'd done nothing but think about it. She might be six years younger than me but my sister had a very wise head on her shoulders.

I felt a bit silly for fleeing now. I stood by my need for time and distance while I wrangled with my emotions, but I could have handled things better with Lars. A *lot* better. I'd been spectacularly unfair to him by ignoring him and he hadn't deserved it. I could have at least sent him a message to say I was dealing with a few things right now and we'd talk soon. As for not keeping him in the loop about the work rota, that was downright unprofessional. What must he have thought, turning up at the bookshop and finding Alec instead of me there? If he chose to ignore me now, I certainly couldn't blame him.

Pulling up on the drive at home a little later, I messaged Dad before I got out the car to say I was back and I'd be over when I'd unpacked. As I unlocked the door, a reply came through.

> FROM DAD
> I've put some post on your dining table. The big box arrived at work but it was marked private so my dad dropped it off for you. See you later x

There was indeed a pile of post on the table – a few envelopes, a couple of small packages and a box with my name, the shop address and *private and confidential* on it. It was long and wide but not very deep and not particularly heavy so I couldn't for the life of me think what it could be. I hadn't ordered anything personal to be delivered to the shop. Grabbing a pair of scissors from the kitchen, I carefully scored along the parcel tape and eased the lid open. Whatever was inside was carefully wrapped in several layers of bubble wrap and I couldn't see through it, but there was a folded handwritten letter lying on top and my breath caught as I saw who'd written it – Eva and Axel Hansen.

Dear Lily

We were so touched to receive your email about your friend, Lars, and how much our mother's book meant to him and his sister. Having experienced our own tragedy, our hearts go out to Lars for his loss.

We're delighted that you stocked Anna and the Snow Dragon *in your bookshop and that you're eager to support the thirtieth-anniversary relaunch. We'll be going on a countrywide tour of bookshops and libraries and would be delighted to include Whitsborough Bay in the schedule. We'll be in touch in the spring when we're ready to confirm plans.*

Going back to Lars, we were sorry to hear that his sister's book went missing. We know it's not quite the same, but we'd be honoured if he'd accept this replacement copy. It seems our mother signed several copies for competition prizes before her untimely death but those competitions never ran. If the relaunch is a success and our mother has success posthumously, as hoped, we'll auction them for charity but we were unanimous in wanting Lars to have a copy. We've also enclosed a couple of pieces of signed artwork – one from Mother which you'll recognise from the first book and the other drawn by us from Mother's rough sketches for book three. We'd ask that you don't share the latter until after that book has been published to avoid spoilers.

With very best wishes to you, Lars and your respective families this Christmastime and we very much look forward to meeting you next year.

Eva & Axel

I couldn't in a million years have predicted that my email to them would have led to such generosity. Carefully peeling back the layers of bubble wrap, I took out the signed book, breathing in its aroma before gently placing it aside. Each piece of art was in a cellophane wrapper with cardboard backing to keep it straight. The first image was one of my favourites of Anna and the snow dragon hugging each other on a snowy mountainside. I remembered the exact moment in the story it depicted. The second one was a night-time image of Anna flying on the snow dragon's back with the northern lights glowing in the sky. It was stunning and, even though I didn't know the story, it moved me to tears. I gazed at the northern lights, thinking about how much Lars loved them and all the places he wanted to visit from which the aurora could often be seen. Kadence was right. I loved Lars more deeply than I ever imagined it was possible to love someone and I knew he felt the same way about me. He should definitely spend time with his Icelandic family and visit the other countries that called to him and I'd wait for him for however long that took because I didn't want to lose him. It had taken us long enough to get to this point. No way was I going to let him go.

After packaging everything back up into the box, I dug my phone out of my bag, wincing at the notifications of missed calls and messages from Lars and also from Cassie. I had some explaining to do to her too.

I found the number for Frank Elliott, the owner of Whitsborough Frames on Castle Street. Last year I'd tracked down an out-of-print copy of a book his wife loved for a milestone birthday and he'd said not to hesitate to ask if ever I needed a framing-related favour. Well, I needed a favour now, although I was hesitating as it was a bit of a liberty.

'I know I'm asking for the impossible,' I said when Frank answered the phone. 'Especially at this time of year.'

'We're snowed under, Lily, but as it's you and as we've just had a customer postpone the collection day for the order we were about to start on, you're in luck. Just get here as soon as you can.'

Despite the urgency, I couldn't leave without checking in on Dad first but he was engrossed in writing his latest Master's assignment and assured me he didn't need anything.

'I'm more concerned about you, Lily. We all are, especially Lars.'

'It's been a tough week but my head's clear now and I'm going to get things sorted, but that's why I need to dash.'

'Don't let me keep you.'

I ran out to the car and set off into town. I just hoped I wasn't too late.

47

LILY

Frank said he'd need two hours to frame the pictures so I decided to pass the time in the library. It was on Mariner's Way which ran parallel to Castle Street, housed in the most beautiful old building which had once been a gentleman's club. Although the glass entrance was modern and functional, I always looked up at the ornate brickwork above and imagined how it used to look in Whitsborough Bay's Victorian heyday.

There was a tall artificial Christmas tree in the lobby and colourful garlands strung around the walls in the main library, interspersed with paper chains made in the children's crafting sessions. As I passed the help desk, I smiled and waved at the two librarians there. I knew them well as I sometimes visited the library during my lunch break to see which books they had in stock and compare notes about what was popular, but they were helping customers so I wasn't going to interrupt.

In the centre of the library on top of one of the display tables was a second Christmas tree but this one was made of old books stacked in ever decreasing circles and strewn with fairy lights. It appeared each year and I always marvelled at the time it must take to get it perfectly balanced.

Heading to the far end to a quiet corner, I plonked myself down on one of the soft chairs and took my phone out. Before I saw Lars, I needed to read and listen to his messages. He'd called eight times but he'd only left a message on two occasions and he hadn't sounded angry in either of them – just worried about me. The written messages reiterated the same. He shouldn't have had to chase me like that. I'd got on my high horse about the importance of honesty, but how honest had I been with him? My stomach churned at the thought of how much anxiety I'd caused him this week.

I listened to a voicemail from Cassie next. She was also worried about me but she was a tad more direct than Lars, finishing her message with, *Stop creating problems that don't exist, get your sorry little arse back to Whitsborough Bay and sort things out with Lars. Or do I have to drive to your sister's and drag you back myself? Love you!*

A WhatsApp message she'd sent late on Tuesday afternoon had me intrigued.

> **FROM CASSIE**
>
> OMG! Have you seen the Paperback Pixie's feed from Sunday? I think I know who it is!

She'd followed it up with another one yesterday.

> **FROM CASSIE**
>
> You need to see the Pixie's feed RIGHT NOW! But look at Sunday's before you look at today's. That's very important or today's won't make sense. And STOP IGNORING ME! Apologies for going Justin on you with the shouty caps but it warrants it. Here for you always. COME HOME! x

I had a lot of making up to do with Cassie. With everyone, really, but Lars needed to be my starting point. I clicked into the Paperback Pixie's Instagram feed and did as Cassie had instructed, bypassing yesterday's post and focusing on Sunday's first.

> It's me! The Christmas Paperback Pixie with my final gifts of the year, sharing and spreading the book love this yuletide. Does that make me a Christmas Elf rather than a Pixie? I'm no superhero but, just like Superman, I hide my identity while walking in plain sight. The time has come to share my secret with my very own Lois Lane. I hope it's a good surprise or I might find a rotten potato in my stocking! Merry Christmas everyone and, as always, please tag me and share a photo if you find one of these books. Happy reading!

I glanced down at the first book – *A Game of Thrones* by George R. R. Martin left outside the public toilets in South Bay. I actually laughed out loud at the placing of that one, drawing a curious look from a woman browsing the shelves nearby.

Next was *Anne of the Island*, the third book in L. M. Montgomery's series resting in the branches of the Castle Park Christmas tree. How lovely to see one of my favourite books being gifted. Something stirred in me and I grasped for the connection but I couldn't quite get there. But, as I scrolled onto the third photo, my heart leapt into my throat. Outside the Lifeboat Station was *Anna and the Snow Dragon* by Sigrid Hansen. No way! That was far too random a choice. It had to mean... I pressed my fingers to my lips. It couldn't be, could it?

Heart pounding, I reread the accompanying message. *The time has come to share my secret with my very own Lois Lane.* The books themselves were the clues and they could only mean one thing – that the Paperback Pixie was Lars. *A Game of Thrones* wasn't about the title but the series name – 'A Song of Ice and Fire' as a nod to Lars's roots in the land of ice and fire. *Anne of the Island* was the book in which Anne Shirley and Gilbert Blythe got together. Lars knew they were my favourite books and I'd told him how Gilbert regretted calling Anne names and destroying any potential for friendship at school. As for *Anna and the Snow Dragon*, who else would know that book and what it meant?

Words jumped out at me like the use of *yuletide* instead of Christmas. Lars had described Christmas in Iceland as being more akin to yule. *Christmas Elf?* I'd called him that on several occasions. The Superman reference itself was one he'd made when we first spoke about the Paperback Pixie and why they might want to remain anonymous and the *rotten potato* instead of coal in the stocking had to relate to what the Yule Lads left in the shoes of naughty children. Lars was the Paperback Pixie. He had to be, and Cassie saying she knew who the Pixie was would support that. I couldn't imagine that seemingly random collection of books meaning anything to anyone else.

My hands were shaking as I clicked into the latest post from yesterday and read the message.

Have you been naughty or nice this year? I'm afraid I've been naughty and upset somebody very important to me. Even though I said Sunday's books were my final gifts of the year, I wanted to leave a few more to get back on Father Christmas's good list. Books can speak volumes and I hope this incredible person hears what my choices for today are saying and gets in touch. Have a Christmas that's Perfect (for you) and don't forget to leave Carrots out for the reindeer.

Praying and heart emojis followed the message and, once again, I noticed the word choice. Lars was probably the only person I knew who used Father Christmas rather than Santa Claus and he'd capitalised *Perfect* and *Carrots* – the nicknames for me and for Anne Shirley.

Tears rushed to my eyes as I scrolled through the five books, each left somewhere I'd been with Lars. On a bench in Castle Park was the beautifully poignant picture book *Tabby McTat* by Julia Donaldson. *Anne of Green Gables* had been left outside The White Horse in Little Sandby where we'd had our first date. Book three, left in the theatre's lobby, was Margaret Mitchell's *Gone with the Wind*, and L. Frank Baum's *The Wonderful Wizard of Oz* had been left in the reception at Sherrington Hall where Cassie and Jared had married. Every single one of those books had a strong theme – the importance of home and family and, to avoid any risk of me misinterpreting that as Iceland, the fifth book was a Whitsborough Bay guidebook left on the windowsill outside Bay Books. Message received loud and clear. There was no place like home and Lars wanted me to know that his home was right here in Whitsborough Bay. With me.

> TO LARS
> Hi you, I'm home and I owe you a huge explanation and so many apologies. Could we meet tonight? Name your time and place and I'll be there x

As soon as the message sent, I couldn't resist adding another one.

> TO LARS
> It's Lois Lane, by the way. Posts seen, loved and understood x

* * *

I'd collected the pictures from Whitsborough Frames, handing over a box of goodies from Charlee's Chocolates to thank Frank for the rush-job, and was on my way back to the car when Lars replied.

FROM LARS

I'd have replied sooner but I was at work and my phone was on silent as I don't want to upset the boss again. I'm so sorry. I know what you overheard and I promise it's not what you think. 6.30pm? My house? It's The Lodge on Hutton Valley Lane x

TO LARS

I'll be there. Thank you x

There were about a dozen houses on Hutton Valley Lane, all with views over the river, fields and Hutton Wicklow Castle, and I wondered which one The Lodge was. When I was six, I'd started piano lessons with a lovely woman called Mrs Mayflower who lived on the lane. She'd had to stop teaching a couple of years later to care for her husband who'd been seriously injured in a car crash. I couldn't remember what her house was called but I'd loved going there. The piano had been upstairs in front of an arched window with a view across to the castle which Mrs Mayflower said inspired her as she played. I'd loved looking at the castle but my favourite thing about that room was a pair of large fluffy soft toy ducks she had on the window ledge. She let me cuddle them at the end of every lesson and I remembered telling her I wanted to live in the house when I was grown up so I could see the ducks every day. She'd laughed and said that her husband had given her a duck when each of their children were born and she was very attached to them so, if she ever moved, they'd go with her but, after my final lesson, she gave me a small fluffy duck keyring which I attached to my school bag – the one Lars had told me he'd noticed on our first day at Laurendale School.

Arriving back at the car, I carefully placed the pictures in the boot and drove home where I checked in on Dad.

'You got your assignment finished?' I asked, noticing his big smile.

'Finished and submitted, and I've had the grade back for my last one. Distinction!'

'That's brilliant, Dad. You're smashing it!'

'I can't get over how much I'm loving studying again. I don't know what I'll do with myself when my Master's ends.'

'A PhD?' I suggested.

'I'm seriously tempted. Anyway, hope it goes well with Lars. Whatever it is that's caused a problem between you, I'm sure you can work it out.'

'I hope so. If I'm back quickly, you'll know it's all gone wrong.'

* * *

I was a bundle of nerves as I drove towards Hutton Wicklow that evening and, turning onto Hutton Valley Lane, my stomach lurched. There were no house numbers – only names – so I crawled along the road, trying to spot the signs under the glow of the streetlights.

I couldn't picture Mrs Mayflower's house anymore so doubted I'd recognise it twenty-six years after my piano lessons had ceased. Unless, of course, it still had the ducks in the window. I hadn't thought about the ducks in years, or the keyring on my school bag until Lars had mentioned it.

Hutton Valley Lane inclined steadily and it was at the peak that I spotted a sign for 'The Lodge'. Recognising Lars's car on the drive, I pulled up beside it and took several steadying breaths before opening the door.

I removed the large paper carrier bag from the boot containing the two pictures, the book and the letter from Eva and Axel. Lars had put a kiss on his message and he'd even made a joke about phones on silent at work which suggested I hadn't blown it but, even so, this wasn't going to be easy. But nothing worth doing was easy.

Heart pounding, I made my way towards the front door. Just before I reached it, I glanced up and gasped. There weren't any ducks there but I'd recognise that arched window anywhere. Lars's new home was the home of my former piano teacher – the home I'd said I wanted to live in when I was all grown up. If this wasn't the universe telling me that Lars and I were meant to be together, I didn't know what was.

48

LARS

I couldn't stop pacing up and down in the lounge. I'd never been this nervous about anything in my whole life and desperately wanted it to go well. Best-case scenario was that we'd had a misunderstanding which we could laugh about and put behind us. Worst-case scenario was... I shuddered, barely able to acknowledge it. I was so annoyed with myself. I knew Lily's insecurities from Ewan and Wes abandoning her and it had never entered my head to reassure her that I'd never do that. Whitsborough Bay was my home and always would be for so many reasons. I wasn't sure whether the *there's no place like home* gifting on my Paperback Pixie feed would be enough to convince her on its own but hopefully what I'd done with the house would.

I paused my pacing and turned in a slow circle around the room, taking in the results of my purchasing frenzy after work last night. Thank goodness the garden centre stayed open until late.

Car headlights momentarily dazzled me. She was here. *Deep breath, stay calm!* The doorbell rang – a proper old-fashioned deep *ding-dong* – and I took another deep breath before opening it.

My heart leapt at the sight of Lily standing on my doorstep, a large paper bag in her hand.

'The Paperback Pixie, I presume?' she said, her smile hesitant as though unsure as to whether a joke was an appropriate ice-breaker. It absolutely was.

'Also answers to Christmas Elf or Lars the Arse.'

Her eyes widened. 'Cassie told you that?'

'It might have come up this week and it's true. I *am* an arse. I'm so sorry for... *Helvítis bjáni*, I haven't even invited you in and it's freezing.'

'I have no idea what those words mean, but thank you.'

I hadn't even registered that I'd spoken in Icelandic, but it figured – something I'd always done when I was nervous.

'Damn fool or idiot,' I explained. 'Me, not you. Come through.'

I led her into the lounge. A good host would have offered a drink but I couldn't prolong it by faffing with the kettle. I needed to know if I was dumped or not.

'You bought a tree!' she exclaimed, crossing the room. 'A real one!'

'I forgot to buy baubles but I did get a lot of lights and someone once told me you can never have enough lights.'

She turned and smiled at me. 'Vintage gold and red. It's beautiful.'

'I, erm... I don't have a sofa but I bought some garden furniture.'

Lily had evidently been so transfixed on the tree that she'd missed the dark grey metal bistro set and she did a double-take. 'You've made a very seasonal purchase, I see.'

'Perfect for winter nights spent inside,' I said, smiling at her. 'There weren't any on display in the garden centre but the manager took pity on me and retrieved me a sale set from storage. The seat pads are surprisingly comfy.'

We sat down and I couldn't wait any longer. 'I know you overheard me talking to Flo about travelling and I'm so sorry I hadn't...' I tailed off as Lily raised her hand to stop me.

'I'm so sorry for interrupting but can I say something first? You don't owe me an apology. I owe you one. I've treated you so badly and you did nothing to deserve it. Yes, I overheard what you said and I had a meltdown...'

What she shared with me was a combination of what I'd worked out with some blanks filled in by Cassie, but neither of us had thought about Justin disappearing on his travels and staying away when Shelby was pregnant. With all of that circling around Lily's head, no wonder she'd needed some space.

'I did think it would have to be the end for us,' she said and my heart sank. 'I couldn't bear the thought of yet another man leaving me and never returning but then I thought about who that man was and I know it would be different this time. This is you. Us. We're meant to be together and I want to support you with your dreams as I know you want to support me with mine, so if you want to spend time in Iceland with your family and if you want to travel round the Nordic region, you absolutely should do that. I *want* you to do that and I'll be right here waiting. If I haven't already screwed things up so badly that you don't want me to be here waiting.'

Sharing all that with me had clearly taken it out of Lily. Tears had pooled in her eyes and she looked in desperate need of a hug. I could help with that as I needed one myself. Taking her hands in mine, I eased her to her feet and into my arms.

'You haven't screwed anything up,' I reassured her.

We stood in silence for a while, just holding each other, but there was more to say and I reluctantly released her to sit down. I pulled my chair closer to hers and took hold of her hands again.

'I never met Ewan and Wes but it's obvious to me they were idiots because they walked away from you. Thing is, they're also my heroes as their loss was my gain and I've no intention of ever letting you go. I'd *never* choose being somewhere else over you. Why would I want the world when you're already my world? Yes, I want to spend some time in Iceland and I do have big plans to explore the Nordic countries but I don't want to do those things on my own. I want to do them with you.'

'You do?'

'Of course! I know you've got the shop and I completely understand how important that is to you because I love it too, so I'm thinking we do our exploring during our holidays – a week here, a week there. It's not all about what I want either. We haven't talked about the places you dream of seeing so we need to include those too. My heritage is part-Icelandic and, yes, I do want to explore that but my roots are firmly in Whitsborough Bay. Why else would I have bought this house?'

'It's a beautiful house. Could do with some indoor furniture and a spot of colour but the tree's a great start.'

'I got it for you.'

'The tree or the house?' She winked at me, indicating that she was joking, but I took my chance.

'Both, although I didn't know that about the house at the time. I nearly didn't buy it because it was a family home and I didn't have a partner or a family, but now I do. I told myself I was dragging my heels on the design because I have zero creativity but I realised this week that it's because I didn't want this to be all about me. I wanted it to be about the person I was always meant to share it with. I'm hoping that person is you.'

Her eyes widened and she tightened her hold on my hands but she didn't speak, so I continued.

'You know I said I'd only put lights on the tree? That was a white lie. There's one decoration on there and it's especially for you.'

I followed her over to the tree where, between the branches, a shiny silver key dangled from a red ribbon.

'Lily Appleton, I'd love you to move in with me. I want this to be our home, but only if and when you feel ready. There's no rush to give me an answer now either but, if you think it's something you'd like to do at some point, I'm willing to buy you as many canvases and paint samples as you want to create those mood boards for our very own *House of Dreams*.'

I wasn't sure whether she'd heard my reference to the fourth book in L. M. Montgomery's series – *Anne's House of Dreams* – as she reached for the key and rested it in her palm, staring at it. My heart pounded. Had it been too much too soon?

49

LILY

I stared at the key in my hand – the key to Lars's house, the house Mrs Mayflower had owned, the house I'd told her I wanted to live in when I grew up. Was this really happening? And had Lars just referenced *Anne's House of Dreams*?

'*I dream of a home with a hearth-fire in it,*' Lars said, his voice soft, '*a cat and dog, the footsteps of friends – and* YOU!'

Another L. M. Montgomery reference! My heart melted. It was something Gilbert Blythe said in *Anne of the Island*, which meant Lars had read it. For me! I raised my eyes to Lars's and that vulnerability was there. Did he think there was a chance I was going to say no? I was about to give my answer but he spoke first.

'But if you don't like the house, I can sell it and we can choose one together.'

'You can't sell this house, Lars. You wouldn't have bought it if you didn't love it so I'd never ask you to give up something you love. And you don't need to anyway because it's already the house of my dreams. I used to have piano lessons here…'

'The Mayflowers were the people I bought the house from,' Lars said when I'd finished telling him about my lessons, the ducks and the conversations with Mrs Mayflower about buying the house from her.

'I'm so glad Mr Mayflower is still around, I wasn't sure whether he'd ever recovered from his accident.'

'He was paralysed from the waist down so he used a wheelchair but, as far as I know, he's in good health. Their children were grown up and had moved out and the house was too big for just the two of them so they were downsizing.' He ran his fingers through his hair. 'I can't believe you knew the ducks. That's why I fell in love with this place...'

We returned to the table and he told me about his walks with his nanna and how they'd called the house Duckling Lodge.

'The universe clearly wanted to match us from the very start,' I said, stunned at his story. 'What are the odds on both of us picking out the same house when we were kids?' I closed my hand around the key and smiled at him tenderly as I added, 'And ending up here together?'

His eyes widened. 'Is that a yes?'

'Of course it's a yes! To the house, the hearth, the cat, the dog and most of all to you. Yes, yes, yes!'

I flung myself into his arms. The hug became a kiss and, oh my goodness, had I missed Lars's kisses? I had nearly a week's worth to catch up on, plus lots of making up ones. This could take a while and I was going to cherish every single moment but first I had something to show him so I reluctantly pulled away.

'I did a thing which I didn't run by you because I didn't imagine anything would come of it, but it has and I'm still a little stunned by what happened.' I laughed at his bewildered expression. 'Yeah, that made no sense, did it?'

I reached into the bag and withdrew the letter. 'You'll suss what the thing I did was when you read this. I hope you're okay with it.'

I kept my eyes on Lars's expression while he read, watching his eyes widen then brim with tears.

'Thank you so much. I can't believe you did that,' he said, his voice catching when he'd finished reading.

I passed him the copy of *Anna and the Snow Dragon*. He ran his fingers over the cover before carefully opening the first page, gulping as he read Sigrid Hansen's signature and the words accompanying it:

May you find your snow dragon and soar high on the wings of dreams.

The tears escaped at that point and he drew in a deep shaky breath.

I slipped my arm around his waist and cuddled against him. 'It's beautiful, isn't it?'

While he finished turning the pages, I lifted the pictures from the bag, removed the bubble wrap and rested one on each garden chair.

'I think we've found the first pictures for the walls of our home,' I said when he looked up from the book.

'That was Pia's favourite illustration!' he whispered, clapping his hand over his mouth as he looked at the first one then moved his gaze to the second. 'The aurora! Oh, wow! These are incredible. If Pia was here today to see them. Just a second.'

He bent down and adjusted the chairs to face the front of the house and something suddenly clicked into place.

'She's here, isn't she?'

Lars nodded. 'Pia loved Hutton Wicklow Castle. When she was well, I sometimes gave her a piggyback there and she'd swoop her snow dragon round the ruins. Mum and Pabbi had a horrendous argument about what to do with her ashes. They talked about having half each and I hated the idea of her being taken to Iceland – somewhere she'd only visited once – so I shouted at them to stop arguing because there was only one place Pia would want to rest. They actually listened to me and we scattered her ashes round the castle grounds. That was one heck of a painful day but I'm glad we did it. So Whitsborough Bay is my forever home because this is where the three women who have my heart are – Pia, Nanna and you.'

I noticed the absence of his mum in that list, although that wasn't surprising after the conversations we'd had about her.

'Did you become the Paperback Pixie because of Pia?' I asked.

'Pia's love of books was what gave me the idea and I wanted to share it with the world. The name came from our nickname for her. We called her Pixie.'

'That's such a beautiful thing to do and so generous of you.'

'It's what she'd have wanted. I'd better tell you more about it.'

'I can't wait to hear more but, before we do, I'd love another kiss.'

He cupped my face in his hands and kissed me slowly and tenderly. I'd found my forever home too and it wasn't just The Lodge. It was Lars.

50
LARS

Christmas Eve arrived which meant it was time to celebrate *Jólabókaflóð*. When Lily gave it to me as a pet project, I'd initially been a little apprehensive as to how it would go down but the reaction to the Yule Lads had been so positive that my anxiety had drifted away.

Freyja had been really helpful with her insights on how bookshops in Iceland celebrated *Jólabókaflóð* so I'd proposed several ideas to Lily, thinking she'd go for one or two, but she'd gone for them all. The final Yule Lad arriving today was Kertasníkir, the 'Candle Stealer', although he didn't just like their glow; he liked to eat them. His image and explanation went in the window first thing and the Christmas Cat came out to make way for the explanation about *Jólabókaflóð*.

We'd had flyers made to hand out to customers and we'd partnered with Charlee's Chocolates, Yorkshire's Best and Bear With Me to create some gift boxes for sale in celebration of the book flood and the cosy feeling it evoked. The adult version included a festive novel, a pair of fluffy socks and a bookish mug supplied by Bay Books, a hot chocolate stirrer and box of chocolates from the chocolaterie and a cranberry- or pine-scented candle with a small jar of matches from Yorkshire's Best. The child's version contained a festive picture book, colouring book and felt tips from us, a bag of festive chocolate treats from Charlee and a small soft toy from Bear With Me. The boxes were available in all the partner shops with guidance that the book could be exchanged at Bay Books if the customer already had it.

In the bookshop, we also had a box covered in Christmas paper containing books offered at a reduced price. Each one was gift-wrapped with a sticker on it outlining the key details – age, genre, brief premise. Lily had said they'd done a *blind date with a book* for Valentine's Day a few years back and it had gone down really well so it was definitely worth repeating the concept for *Jólabókaflóð*. None of the activities were specifically a book exchange but more about providing the materials for others to exchange. We were, after all, running a business so couldn't just give a stack of books away.

The shop was buzzing all morning. Cassie wasn't working with it being the school holidays but Alec, Flo and Cyndi were in and Shelby had dropped Marcus off for a couple of hours to sit behind the till and help us across lunchtime. By the time he left, nearly all the *Jólabókaflóð* boxes had sold and we knew they'd gone down well in our partner businesses too with just two people requesting to swap their books. The wrapped books had been heavily depleted too.

By 3 p.m. there were still people in the shop but the queue had died down and the pressure was off. Cyndi finished her shift and Alec and Flo were restocking and tidying.

'I think we've had our first successful *Jólabókaflóð*,' Lily said, smiling at me as I removed the four remaining mystery books from the box and placed them on the counter instead. 'Are you pleased?'

'I am. It's been an amazing day. An amazing week, actually.'

There was nobody in the front part of the shop so I leaned across the counter for a sneaky kiss.

The Christmas playlist was on and we laughed as 'We All Stand Together' came round.

'I keep thinking I should remove it because we get strange looks from the customers each time it comes on,' Lily said, 'but it'll forever remind me of our first kiss, so I can't.'

'Are you calling me a frog?' I joked.

'If the cap fits… Might as well add it to your range of identities.'

By half three, there were only a couple of customers browsing so Lily told Alec and Flo they could head off early, leaving just the two of us. Castle Street was still busy but it seemed to be people rushing home laden with bags of shopping or on their way to the pub rather than anyone actively trying to buy last-minute gifts.

'That's Christmas done for another year,' Lily said, turning round the sign and locking the door at four o'clock. 'And breathe...'

I flicked some of the lights off to convey that the shop was closed while Lily cashed up. I'd already run the vacuum cleaner round so I went downstairs to retrieve our coats and Lily's bag.

'I know we're officially doing *Jólabókaflóð* at your mum and dad's,' I said when I returned, 'but I have a couple of books that, for different reasons, I'd prefer to give you privately.'

'Great minds, because I want to do the same, although I've only got one to give you now.'

Lily removed a large gift-wrapped book from the store cupboard next to Jeeves and I retrieved the two paperbacks I'd hidden under my coat and we went through to the children's section.

'This one first,' I said, passing her one of the paperbacks, barely able to keep the smile off my face.

She ripped open the wrapping and burst out laughing when she saw what it was – *I'll Have What She's Having*. 'Is this the actual copy we knocked off the shelf in our moment of passion?'

'The very same one.'

'That's hilarious. I can see why you wouldn't want to give me that in front of my parents. Might take a bit of explaining.'

I handed her the other one and she gasped as she opened it. 'This is never a...' She carefully opened the cover of *Anne of Green Gables*. 'Oh, my God, Lars! It's a first edition.'

'I inspected your shelves and noticed you didn't have one.'

She lightly ran her fingers over the cover, shaking her head. 'I've dreamed of owning one but never imagined I would. Thank you so much, Lars. It's amazing.'

She placed it down ever so gently before passing me her parcel. 'I hope you like it but please forgive me if it's misjudged.'

Intrigued, I carefully opened the gift wrap, removed a large hardback book and smiled at the title – *Our Winter Nights with the Northern Lights*.

'I know it's not quite the same as seeing it in real life,' Lily said as I flicked through the pages, admiring the beautiful photographs.

'It's the next best thing. Thank you. I don't think I'll ever tire of seeing photos of the aurora.' I closed the book and smiled at Lily. 'I can't wait for you to see it for real.'

'Me neither.'

I leaned in to kiss Lily but she moved away, laughing. 'You haven't realised.'

'Realised what?'

'Look inside at the list of contributing photographers.'

I opened the book once more and glanced down the list, my eyes widening with surprise as I spotted her name.

'Mum's one of them!' I flicked through to the pages against her name, staring at the stunning images in disbelief. 'I had no idea she'd done this.'

'When we've talked about your mum's work, you've never mentioned it and, given how much you love the aurora, I figured you mustn't know about it.'

'Not a clue! I thought she only did street photography now.'

'There's something else,' Lily said, turning to the back of the book. 'You need to read the acknowledgements. They're the reason I wanted you to have this in private.'

I glanced down and read what Mum had written.

> I was twenty when I saw and photographed my first aurora. Those lights soothed me in a world I found increasingly overwhelming, filled with people I didn't understand and who didn't understand me. I spent several years exploring the northern hemisphere, seeking out the aurora, and one of those trips changed my life. I met somebody who got me and who I understood in return. We were blessed with two wonderful children, Lars and Pia. Tragically Pia, our little pixie, couldn't stay and, for years afterwards, I rejected the landscapes, hid from the aurora, cut myself off from the people I loved because it hurt too much. On what would have been Pia's twentieth birthday, I felt compelled to seek out the aurora for her. She couldn't be with me in person but her favourite book and a knitted dragon kept me company and I watched my beloved girl shine in those lights. My contributions to this book are the photos I took that night and the auroras on her birthday and my son's over the next three years. This is for my little girl but it's also for Lars and my mum. I see you all in the lights, I see you in my dreams and I miss you with all my heart xx

'I can't believe she wrote that,' I said, wiping my cheeks after I'd read it through three times. 'If she misses us that much, why doesn't she come back more often or for longer?'

Lily shrugged. 'I don't know your mum but sometimes things scare us so much that it's easier to flee from them than face them. I'm proof of that and so are you.'

I nodded slowly as I mulled that over. When Nanna and I talked about Mum after I found the photo album devoted to Pia, I'd wondered if there was more to Mum's absence – perhaps being that she cared too much rather than too little. The photographs and those heartfelt words would support that. As a kid, I'd felt the fear of abandonment and pushed Lily away before she could leave me. It seemed that Mum had felt the fear of further loss and, just like me, she'd built protective walls. I'd regretted mine and it sounded to me like she regretted hers.

'And now you know what happened to Pia's book and her knitted dragon,' Lily said, her voice gentle. 'Your mum has them.'

I put my arm round her and gave her a soft kiss. 'This is the best book anyone could ever have gifted me. Thank you for finding this.'

'Right back at you with my first edition. And my other special book.'

We sat there for a while as I studied Mum's photographs and the information accompanying them about where she'd taken them and what she'd been feeling. I felt I knew her better – understood her more – through those written words than any she'd spoken over the past two decades and I was convinced more than ever that she was lonely. But she didn't need to be and I'd make sure she knew that when I saw her next month.

I closed the book with a satisfied sigh, feeling so much more optimistic about seeing her again and about having a positive relationship with her going forwards.

'Now that I've made you cry,' Lily said, 'are you ready to go to the other extreme – a cookie-making frenzy with my crazy family?'

'I am. Let's go.'

'By the way, there are some packets of lametta at Everdene waiting for you to add to the tree. I thought I'd better warn you in case it's a bit emotional.'

'Appreciate the heads up.'

While Lily went through to the front to retrieve our belongings, I gathered the books together and turned my gaze to the Bookmas tree. I often pictured Pia in the children's section, including by the tree, but now I had a vivid image of her sitting on the floor with Mum as they looked through a book together. The child me joined them, a book in each hand, followed by Pabbi. He helped Mum to her feet and kissed her, then lifted Pia up and put his arm around me. Everyone was smiling and, with a jolt, I realised this was a memory rather than something my imagination had conjured up. We *had* been a happy family once and I'd forgotten that. I'd been so hurt that I'd pushed away all the good memories and wallowed in the bad ones. Pia would have hated that. *I'll fix our family, Pia. I'll fix it for you.* I kissed my fingers and blew the kiss towards the tree.

Hearing a sound behind me, I turned to see Lily in tears.

'That kiss was for your sister, wasn't it?' she said, her voice choked with emotion.

I nodded.

'I thought *Jólabókaflóð* was meant to be a flood of books, not a flood of tears.'

I wrapped my arms around her. 'Powerful things, those books. Adventures taken, friends made, secrets shared, lessons learned. Why would anyone ever want to live a life without books?'

'Well said, Paperback Pixie.' She squeezed me tight. 'You looked lost in your memories before you blew the kiss.'

'I was. You know how I've always said I can't remember us ever being a happy family? I had this sudden powerful memory of the four of us in here one Christmas and we were really happy. I'd forgotten that. I think I might have forgotten a lot of things.'

'As well as writing my favourite series, L. M. Montgomery wrote a book called *The Story Girl* and there's a lovely quote from it – *Nothing is ever really lost to us as long as we remember it.* I'm sure those happy memories will keep coming back to you when you're ready for them.'

'That's a great quote and very apt.'

Lily waved goodbye to the books in the children's section. 'Happy *Jólabókaflóð* and Merry Christmas. We'll be back soon.'

'I love that you do that,' I said. 'Don't ever change.'

'Because I'm *Little Miss Perfect* as I am?' she quipped.

'Like I said before, you're *Little Miss Perfect-for-me*. In fact, so perfect that I'm going to have to do this to show my appreciation.'

I saluted Lily, making her laugh.

'Don't you ever change either, Lars the Arse-some,' she said, barely able to get the words out for giggling. 'That's awful! It sounded a lot more like *awesome* in my head.'

'It was close,' I said, laughing with her. 'I see what you were trying to do there but I think that might be your *don't let Grýla and the Christmas Cat gobble you up* moment.'

As we locked up and stepped outside into the cold winter night, still laughing, I thought back to how I felt like I'd lost everything three months ago – my business, my home and my friendships – but now I'd found everything I'd ever dreamed of and the future was shining as brightly as the northern lights because the friend I'd found when I was nine liked me for being me. Mask-free. Real.

51

LILY

One year later

Last Christmas Eve, I'd celebrated *Jólabókaflóð* for the first time ever in Whitsborough Bay and this year I was celebrating it in its birthplace. Gazing at the piles of books and discarded wrapping paper in Ragnar and Freyja's lounge and watching Lars hug his dad as they thanked each other for their carefully chosen books, my heart felt as though it might burst with happiness.

What an incredible year we'd had. Lars's mum, Jayne, had flown back to the UK in early January as planned. She'd originally intended on staying for a week but had extended that to a full month. Aileen, Jayne and Lars had spent a lot of time together getting everything out on the table. Lars had found the early discussions incredibly difficult and upsetting but it had been necessary for them to move forward. As suspected, Jayne had indeed fled from her grief and pain and had kept running, feeling like she'd burned her bridges at home as well as being afraid of her emotional state of mind if she slowed down. The whole experience had been cathartic for them all and now, even though Jayne was still travelling the world with her photography, she stayed in regular contact and spent quality time in Whitsborough Bay between assignments.

Dad returned to the bookshop at the start of the February half-term holidays but only on a part-time basis. It could take his knees up to two years to fully recover so he didn't want to push himself too hard too soon, and he also wanted more time to focus on his studies. It was great news for Lars as it meant he could work the days Dad wasn't in and balance that with upping his volunteering hours at Hutton Wicklow Library.

Having tackled the past and found peace with his mum, Lars was keen to do the same with his dad. Even though my dad had only just returned to work in February, the half-term break was a logical time for Lars to visit Iceland due to Flo and Cyndi being off college and available for extra shifts. I'd been dying to visit Iceland myself but it was more important that Lars had some alone time with his dad first.

Lars had expected the conversations with his dad to be more challenging than those with his mum but they'd actually been easier. Ragnar had turned sixty-five towards the end of last year and had retired from his job as a fisherman. He wanted to make the most of the years – hopefully decades – he had left and that included making peace with his son. He'd admitted to being consumed by guilt for abandoning his responsibilities when Pia died. He felt like a failure and seeing Lars acted as a reminder of his bad decisions and what he'd lost. Unable to find a way to deal with his emotions, especially when Lars was young and angry, he lashed out in return. While Ragnar was still prone to the occasional melancholy mood and most of the video calls Lars had were with Freyja and his half-siblings, father and son had thankfully buried the hatchet and I was so relieved for Lars that he finally had both parents back in his life and a meaningful relationship with them.

Lars promised me a birthday to remember. It fell on a Sunday so he arranged cover in the shop so he could take me to Húsavík for a long weekend. His family were so welcoming and on the Saturday evening we all travelled to Mount Kaldbakur – an extinct volcano seventy-five minutes' drive west of Húsavík – where I saw the northern lights for the first time ever.

Lars had been right about photographs being amazing but how nothing beat seeing it in real life. That aurora was mainly green with flashes of blue and I'd been completely mesmerised and quite tearful at the beauty of it. The *Anne of Green Gables* quote I had on my bookshelves sprang to mind – *Dear old world, you are very lovely and I am glad to be alive in you* – and I turned to share it with Lars but he was down on one knee in the snow holding out a ring which sparkled under the lights of the aurora borealis. It was the easiest yes of my life and the best birthday gift ever. Freyja took a sequence of photos showing our silhouetted proposal and we had three of them in a frame on the wall at home beside the photo of Lars and Pia seeing the northern lights when they were little.

Home was The Lodge, although we'd officially renamed it White Gables as a nod to my favourite book and Pia's. One of Lars's Christmas gifts to me last year had been a stack of canvases and sample pots to create my mood boards for the house design and, across the year, it had steadily transformed from being a stark, echoey house to a colourful, welcoming home. I'd officially moved in once we were engaged although I'd spent little time at Green Gables after our first Christmas together.

Hendrix and Daisy had set a date for their wedding in two years' time. Lars and I didn't want a long engagement so we got married in late September – the autumn wedding I'd dreamed of. I wore that stunning midnight-blue dress with the gold embellishments I'd spotted in the window of The Wedding Emporium and everything from the cake to the place settings to the favours was book-themed. Books had, after all, been what brought us together at the start and reunited us years later.

We'd had major changes at Bay Books too. Hitting our forty-year anniversary at the start of the summer was a huge milestone to be celebrated and we ran a big programme of events including the town's first-ever book festival. Lars had been instrumental in organising the incredibly successful festival which we now planned to host annually.

At the end of the summer, Mum and Dad took Granny Blue, Granddad George, Lars and me – the three generations who'd run the bookshop – out for a celebratory meal and Dad made an unexpected announcement.

'I've loved every moment I've spent at Bay Books,' he said, looking round the table. 'It's the place I met my beautiful wife and our wonderful daughter and it has been a privilege to work there with every single member of my family – including our newest member, Lars. But I've also loved every moment of studying for my Master's and I don't want to stop learning so I'm not going to. Next up is a PhD.'

We'd all congratulated him on his decision, but there was more to come.

'I appreciate that working – even part-time hours – and studying a PhD is a huge commitment and I want to ensure I have time to spend with my wonderful new grandson so I've decided it's time to step back from Bay Books.'

'You're retiring?' I stared at Dad, my heart racing. He'd *never* mentioned the 'r' word before, although I shouldn't be surprised. He and Mum had been besotted with Kadence and Cody's baby, Harvey, since he arrived in May – we all were – and he'd frequently said he wished he could see more of him.

Under the table, Lars placed a reassuring hand on my thigh, making me feel calmer as Dad continued.

'I know it'll be a shock for you, Lily, because I've always joked that I'd never retire but it's time. The truth is, I haven't run Bay Books for years. You've been the one in charge and you and Lars have partnered perfectly from the start to achieve great things together. Look at the anniversary celebrations, the festival and the amazing plans you have in place for the relaunch of *Anna and the Snow Dragon*. That's all you.'

'I know, but this is huge.'

'It is, but it's what I want. So there are some decisions to be made, although there's no rush. One idea is that I'm a silent partner and you run the business, Lily, just as you have done for years, with Lars as your assistant manager. Another is that Lars buys me out and you run Bay Books jointly.'

Beside me, Lars gasped. I reached for his hand and squeezed it as I smiled at him and nodded. It was a no-brainer for us both. So Lars had finally found his new full-time career and we were officially the joint owners of Bay Books with big plans for the New Year. The lease for The Hat Box next door – run by milliner Eleanor – had come up for renewal and she'd decided to move to a larger empty premises on the other side of Castle Street, joining forces with a friend who made and repaired garments. The landlord had agreed to sell us the building, giving us the space to install a lift and a much greater capacity for hosting author events. There were exciting times ahead for our bookshop in the bay.

For now, on our second Christmas Eve together, we had more exciting times coming with another excursion to see the northern lights. There were clear skies in the area and Lars's app showed high solar activity. We'd chosen a different location – Ljósavatn Lake, six miles south of Húsavík – and it would just be the two of us this time, which was ideal as I had a special *Jólabókaflóð* gift which I wanted to give Lars without everyone watching.

The lights were even more spectacular than the last time we'd seen them. The increased solar activity meant a broader range of colours and, while there were still the greens and blues like before, there were also shimmers of red, pink and purple. The added visual of the aurora's reflection on the calm lake blew me away. Lars wrapped his arms round my waist – not easy with all the layers I was wearing – and we snuggled into each other as we watched. I couldn't imagine anything on earth more beautiful than the scene above and before me and I could have stayed there for hours but tiredness was creeping in, as it had done for the past month or so.

'I've got you a special *Jólabókaflóð* book,' I said, temporarily removing my thick gloves so I could unzip my jacket and retrieve the gift from the inside pocket.

'It's a very thin book,' Lars observed, his expression puzzled as I handed him the gift-wrapped item.

'It's not actually the book itself. That's waiting for us at home. It would have been too big and heavy to lug out here so I printed off the cover and another photo.'

Lars removed his gloves so he could peel back the tape and I smiled at the sharp intake of breath as he looked at the cover then at me, his eyes sparkling.

'Does this mean...?'

'Turn the page.'

He did that and, next moment, I was in his arms. The photo of a positive pregnancy test behind the cover of *Your Panic-Free Pregnancy* answered his question. It hadn't been easy keeping the news to myself for the past week or sneaking a copy of the tome out of the shop without anyone noticing, but I'd somehow managed because it felt right to share the news beneath the aurora borealis so that Pia could hear it too.

'I'll book a doctor's appointment when we get home but my guess is that Baby Jóhannsson will be due around mid-to-late August.'

Lars placed his hand on my stomach and I thrust it forward as though a baby had just kicked, making him laugh. He crouched down with his hands on my waist.

'Hello, little one, I'm your pabbi or maybe it's daddy. I'll have a think. Anyway, I can't wait to meet you and I bet you'll be *Little Miss Perfect-for-me*, just like your mummy.'

'What if it's a boy?' I asked.

Lars looked up at me. 'Mr Perfect, then, but I have the strongest feeling it's going to be a girl.'

'Weirdly, so do I.'

He addressed my stomach once more. 'Whether you're a girl or a boy, I promise to love you always and to protect you from Grýla and the Christmas Cat.' And he saluted before standing up.

'That's our thing now, isn't it?' I said, laughing.

'Afraid so, but so's this.' And he took me in his arms and kissed me tenderly as the northern lights rippled above us and Pia looked down on us with a smile. The postcard which the Paperback Pixie left with each book stated, *I hope this book brings you happiness, escapism, adventures to new places and a chance to meet new friends.* If one book could do that, imagine what a shop full of them could do! Our bookshop in the bay had delivered all of that for me through the pages of books and through the people who were passionate about them and I couldn't wait to meet my own little bookworm and show him or her how powerful books could be.

52

THE FOLLOWING YEAR

@ Eva & Axel Hansen - AnnaAndTheSnowDragon.com

Posted Thursday, 2nd September

Exactly one year ago today, the thirtieth anniversary edition of Sigrid Hansen's Anna and the Snow Dragon was reissued and, as we've said before, we've been overwhelmed by the response to the reissue of our mother's beautiful story.

Over the past year, we've brought you stories and photos about what this book has meant to those who've befriended Anna and Jónas through the reissue and those who met them many years ago.

We particularly loved the tale shared by Lars and Lily Jóhannsson – our friends from Bay Books in the beautiful North Yorkshire seaside town of Whitsborough Bay. Anna and the Snow Dragon had been Lars's sister Pia's favourite book and, unable to find a soft white dragon anywhere, a family friend was asked to knit one. Sadly, Pia passed away when she was seven years old but her family kept her beloved soft toy which sits in Lars and Lily's home alongside a Jónas dragon.

Today, we're thrilled to share the news that, on the thirty-first anniversary of the original release of Anna and the Snow Dragon, our friends have welcomed their first baby into the world. Aurora Pia Jóhannsson was born at 11.30 this morning and is already demonstrating great taste in books, as you can see from this beautiful photo Lars sent us of baby Aurora in her crib with our mother's debut. We can't wait to meet her in person when we visit Whitsborough Bay in October for the launch of the third book in the series, Anna and the Snow Dragon's Magical Winter. Sending all our love to Lily, Lars and their precious new daughter.

Eva & Axel Hansen

* * *

MORE FROM JESSICA REDLAND

Jessica Redland's next title is available to pre-order now here: https://mybook.to/Escape5BackAd

ACKNOWLEDGEMENTS

Bay Books on Castle Street is mentioned in *Making Wishes at Bay View* – the first book of many set in Whitsborough Bay – and I always knew that, at some point, I was going to write about the father and daughter team who ran it. It was just a case of brewing the right story for them and I hope you've enjoyed it.

It's been lovely writing a novel set in a bookshop and imagining those colourful shelves and that gorgeous smell. How many times did I pause to sniff the air when I was writing this, expecting my office to smell like a bookshop?

I don't know any writers who aren't also readers. Some are voracious readers devouring several books each week but there are others who struggle to find the time around writing and, sadly, I'm one of those. A bit like the builder who has a million unfinished projects in their own home because the last thing they want after a hard day's work is to do more of the same, I sometimes find it a challenge to focus my tired eyes on a book after a long day of reading my own work. I therefore freely admit that I don't read as widely or as frequently as I'd like but, as a writer, I will never underestimate the power of books for education, healing and escapism and I hope that's what has come across as I've told Lars and Lily's story. I do, of course, want to write *Anna and the Snow Dragon* now! And I've loved delving back into *Anne of Green Gables* – a personal childhood favourite of mine – and watching the wonderful 1980s miniseries starring Megan Follows and Jonathan Crombie (RIP) as Anne Shirley and Gilbert Blythe.

It has, as ever, been a joy to return to Castle Street. I love a spot of hands-on research for my books where possible and had hoped to spend a day or two in a local bookshop but time was a little too tight to pull that off, so I reached out to the Facebook community and am incredibly grateful for all the offers of help.

An enormous thank you goes to Kathryn Baldwin of Tea Leaves & Reads who manages an independent bookshop in Weyhill, Andover, with a strong online presence at www.tealeavesandreads.co.uk. Huge thanks also go to author

Julie Caplin who shared her experience of working at Our Bookshop in Tring, owned by a friend of hers, Ben Moorhouse. You can find their website here: www.ourbookshoptring.co.uk.

Both Kathryn and Julie answered copious questions about all the behind-the-scenes activities and 'typical' days in a bookshop. A lot of the detail didn't make it into the book but I like to fully understand the roles I'm writing about to get accuracy and authenticity and I'm so exceptionally grateful to them for giving up their time to help me do that.

A huge thank you to fellow Boldwood Books author, Lisa Hobman, who jointly owns a wonderful pre-loved bookshop in Berwick-Upon-Tweed called Slightly Foxed. While I was on holiday in Northumberland a couple of months before the release of this book, I visited Slightly Foxed and am so grateful to Lisa and her business partner, Claire, for letting me play shopkeeper and take photos for the socials. If you haven't read any of Lisa's books – or Julie Caplin's – then I highly recommend diving in. You can find Slightly Foxed's website here: www.s-lightlyfoxedberwick.co.uk.

Sometimes I turn to my Facebook group, Redland's Readers, for inspiration. I wanted a name for the dumb waiter in the shop and would like to thank Emily Coltman for suggesting Jeeves. Genius! I also canvassed the group for suggestions of unusual display items for the window and had a great response… but that section came out in edits, as can sometimes happen when something doesn't move the story on and when the word count needs reducing.

I tracked down a fabulous book called *Yummy Iceland at Christmas Time* by Ursula Jaeger and Markus Jaeger which was invaluable for information about Icelandic traditions, particularly around cookies and the Yule Lads. Blog posts, websites and YouTube videos filled in the gaps for me.

As is always the case any time I write about anything health-related like Pia's severe asthma, everyone's experience of health issues is different. I intentionally avoided detail in Pia's case because the story isn't directly about her, but the little I've given might not be reflective of the experience of other children with respiratory problems. Please bear in mind this is researched fiction and not a medical book.

Thank you to my amazing editor, Emily Ruston, for her insightful feedback and her kindness and patience in moving my submission deadline after I fractured my arm in a ridiculous freak collision with a car door. Don't ask! Thank you to Cecily Blench and Susan Sugden for their copy-editing and proofreading skills respectively, Lizzie Gardiner for the gorgeous cover and Claire Fenby for my fabulous marketing. So very appreciative of your support. And thank you to the rest of the amazing team at Boldwood Books, at ISIS Audio and Ulverscroft and to the fantastic talents of Lucy Brownhill and Luke R Francis for bringing the audiobook to life.

You'll see that I've dedicated this book to librarians and booksellers, book bloggers and BookTokers, Book Fairies, readers, authors and everyone involved in the publishing process. It felt like an appropriate dedication for a story set in a bookshop. For my first five years as a published author, I struggled to sell any books so I know firsthand how invaluable recommendations are for spreading the word and I'm eternally grateful to anyone who has spread the word about my books to friends, family, colleagues or virtual connections. I wouldn't have written twenty-seven novels without you. Please keep sharing and celebrating the magic of books.

Big hugs, Jessica xx

ABOUT THE AUTHOR

Jessica Redland is a million-copy bestseller, writing uplifting stories of love, friendship, family and community. Her Escape to the Lakes books transport readers to the stunning Lake District and her Hedgehog Hollow series takes them to the beautiful countryside of the Yorkshire Wolds.

Sign up to Jessica Redland's mailing list here for news, competitions and updates on future books.

Visit Jessica's website: www.jessicaredland.com

Follow Jessica on social media:

- facebook.com/JessicaRedlandAuthor
- x.com/JessicaRedland
- instagram.com/JessicaRedlandAuthor
- bookbub.com/authors/jessica-redland

ALSO BY JESSICA REDLAND

WHITSBOROUGH BAY

Welcome to Whitsborough Bay

Making Wishes at Bay View

New Beginnings at Seaside Blooms

Finding Hope at Lighthouse Cove

Coming Home to Seashell Cottage

Christmas on Castle Street Collection

Christmas Wishes at the Chocolate Shop

Christmas at Carly's Cupcakes

Starry Skies Over The Chocolate Pot Café

Christmas at the Cat Café

Winter Nights at the Bay Bookshop

The Starfish Café

Snowflakes Over the Starfish Café

Spring Tides at the Starfish Café

Summer Nights at the Starfish Café

Standalones

All You Need is Love

The Secret to Happiness

YORKSHIRE WOLDS

Hedgehog Hollow

Finding Love at Hedgehog Hollow

New Arrivals at Hedgehog Hollow

Family Secrets at Hedgehog Hollow
A Wedding at Hedgehog Hollow
Chasing Dreams at Hedgehog Hollow
Christmas Miracles at Hedgehog Hollow

The Bumblebee Barn Collection

Healing Hearts at Bumblebee Barn
A New Dawn at Owl's Lodge
A Forever Home at Honey Bee Croft

THE LAKE DISTRICT

Escape to the Lakes

The Start of Something Wonderful
A Breath of Fresh Air
The Best is Yet to Come
Sunshine After the Rain

Boldwood

Boldwood Books is an award-winning fiction publishing company seeking out the best stories from around the world.

Find out more at www.boldwoodbooks.com

Join our reader community for brilliant books, competitions and offers!

Follow us
@BoldwoodBooks
@TheBoldBookClub

Sign up to our weekly deals newsletter

https://bit.ly/BoldwoodBNewsletter

www.ingramcontent.com/pod-product-compliance
Lightning Source LLC
Chambersburg PA
CBHW011949150426
43194CB00018B/2848